# THE FROG PRINCE

He was her very own discovery. This purple-and-black diamond-covered beauty. His every dark eyelash. Every glorious centimeter of the frog from the tip of his black head to his green-spotted back to the tippy toes of his little webbed feet.

"You're beautiful," she said in a hushed voice, not caring that the mist had turned into a soaking rain. She didn't know how, or even why, but finally, finally, her every dream had come true.

Heart still pounding, cheeks streaming with cold rain intermingled with warm tears, Lucy held the frog to her mouth and kissed him square on his lips.

*Poof!*

She fell to the mucky dirt lane, pinned beneath the weight of at least two hundred pounds of manly muscle—*naked* manly muscle.

"Jesu," the man with inky-dark eyes said in a thick Welsh brogue. "That was a damned intolerable nightmare I'm glad to be rid of."

Other *Love Spell* books by Laura Marie Altom:

**BLUE MOON**

# Kissing Frogs

## LAURA MARIE ALTOM

LOVE SPELL  NEW YORK CITY

LOVE SPELL®

January 2004

Published by

Dorchester Publishing Co., Inc.
200 Madison Avenue
New York, NY 10016

ISBN 0-505-52568-2

The name "Love Spell" and its logo are trademarks of Dorchester Publishing Co., Inc.

Printed in the United States of America.

Visit us on the web at www.dorchesterpub.com.

This dedication was won by a dear friend and fan, the divine Ms. Dixie Miller. The day after my son, Terry, drew her name from the entry basket, I asked Ms. Dixie to tell me who she wanted to dedicate the book to. The following is what she said:

> *Since* Kissing Frogs *is a fairy tale,*
> *I want it dedicated to princesses.*
> *Six in particular—Dixie & Anna,*
> *Betty & Hailey, and Laura & Hannah.*

There you go, Dixie . . . Poof! Your wish has come true!

# Kissing Frogs

*Once upon a time in the not-too-distant future . . . a maiden who believed herself quite plain went in search of her very own species of frog—not to kiss—but to make her father proud. For in this time of increased planetary awareness, man has been forced by past environmental sins to focus on the well-being not of himself, but of frogs. In short, if frogs with their permeable skin are healthy, so are we.*

*In this state of frog consciousness, a new breed of superstar has been born. Biologists now grace the covers of major magazines. As popular as the Academy Awards once were, the World Biological Conference held annually in London is now the hot ticket. For it is here humans receive their annual report card. Is the world better or worse off? And what are we supposed to do about it?*

*Mobs crush the doors of this event, but only a select few are allowed inside. The pinnacle of the weeklong affair is the time when new species of frogs are presented. A very rare thing indeed. Most years, this moment passes with somber respect. But this year—oh, this year, Lucy Gordon, daughter of the most revered biologist of all, plans to set the conference—maybe even the whole world—on fire!*

# Prologue

"So . . . in conclusion," Lucy Gordon said, sipping from the glass of ice water sweating alongside her on the podium, trying not to remember how much was riding on this one such seemingly simple presentation. For as long as she lived, she'd never forget this moment. The heavy scent of gardenias gracing the table. The even heavier scent of the tofu lasagna they'd been served for dinner. The sounds—outside, the chanting crowd. *Lucy! Lucy!* Inside, dignified accents of clearing throats and rustling papers.

This was it.

She'd arrived.

After ten years of thankless trekking through steamy New Guinea jungles, here she was—star speaker of this year's World Biological Conference. Here she was, living proof that dreams really do come true. After taking a final deep breath, she said, "I'm sure you all agree that the specimen I've presented today—the one I've taken the liberty of naming *Helena's Dream* in honor of my deceased mother—is an entirely new species of frog that must be studied further not only to prevent extinction, but to learn of its importance to our world." She cleared her throat before adding, "Um, thank you."

There, she thought, straightening her inch-thick pile of supporting documents. That hadn't been so bad. Now, all she had to do was sit back and wait for the crowd to bust her eardrums with applause. Already, ripples of low conversation rose and fell in animated waves.

Leaning toward the microphone in anticipation of wrapping this up—not to mention gathering all of her congratulations, she added, "Are there, um, any questions?"

Just past the stage lights' glare, she made out her father's imposing form. Was he frowning? Hmm, could the great man be a tad jealous of the fact that for once she was the one hogging all the attention?

For a split second, she closed her eyes—just long enough to catch a mind's-eye glimpse of Slate Gordon's Roman nose, high forehead and piercing grayish-green gaze that'd earned him his name. *Time* had on more than one occasion called him the most brilliant scientific mind of his time. Women loved what *People* dubbed his brainy sex appeal. Men loved him for his kamikaze field tactics that rode the thin line between scientific study and science fiction. Lucy loved him because he was everything she'd ever admired and hoped to be. Slate Gordon was the Indiana Jones of the biological world, having discovered dozens of new species and one entirely new subspecies.

Back when Slate earned his first million, folks still hadn't thought biology was sexy, but then drug companies caught on, and began seeing dollar signs in Slate's studies as opposed to just slimy new creatures. For as long as Lucy could remember, she'd looked up to him, had never dreamt for anything more than to earn his respect, and just think, here, tonight—right now—that dream was finally coming true.

After tonight, she'd be exactly like him.

Well, maybe not *exactly*.

He was not only highly intelligent, but charismatic and good-looking and tall and lean and tan. Ha. What a nasty little genetic joke fate played on her. In place of good old dad's rock-hard bod, she'd gotten curves— which wouldn't have been such a bad thing if only they'd been in proportionately attractive places.

As it was, her boobs, butt and belly were a little too big, her legs a little too short and stubby, and her hair a cruel shade of red corkscrew that at Brennan's Private Academy had earned her the nickname, *Pubic Hair Patty*.

Of course, on more than one occasion, she'd reminded the popular crowd that her name was Lucy— not, Patty—but did they care? Noooo. All they'd cared about were their footballs and basketballs and parties and—

"Miss Gordon?" The moderator beside her tapped her shoulder. "I believe the gentleman at table thirteen has a question."

"Oh—oh, sorry," she said, tucking her hair behind her ears. "Would you mind repeating?"

An impeccably dressed Asian man straightened his tie before standing. "Miss Gordon, while your presentation was intriguing, I feel I'd be remiss in failing to point out the fact that the species you claim to have discovered was actually discovered well over three decades ago by—"

"Excuse me?" Lucy grasped the front of her white blouse, tugging on it in a search for air. Poor guy. He'd probably eaten too much of that tofu for dinner. Must've addled his mind for him to make such a ludicrous suggestion.

A titter of laughter started in the back corner and grew into a tsunami of chuckles and chortles and downright brazen belly laughs. Even her father had gotten in on the act, leaning closer than necessary to the leggy blonde seated beside him and whispering something that made her laugh so hard that her big fake boobs jiggled.

Still, Lucy's poor food-poisoned accuser stood his ground. Honestly, couldn't he take a hint?

The moderator gently urged her away from the mike, then gave it a good hard tap that produced a squeal of feedback. "Ladies and gentleman," he said with a wince, "might I suggest decorum."

"I'll second that," Lucy mumbled under her breath. What was the matter with these people? How could they be so callus as to practically laugh that poor guy right out of the room?

Once the crowd calmed down, Lucy returned to the mike, and said, "I'm sorry, sir, but you're mistaken. I assure you, while there have been similar subspecies documented, this one is entirely new. As I'm sure you're aware, my father is one of the most respected biologists on the planet. Believe me, out of respect for him, I've crossed all my *t*s and dotted my *i*s. My research is impeccable."

The laughter started anew.

Boy, was this a rough crowd. The poor guy would never be able to set foot at another conference.

Her father stood and held up his hands. As if he were a scientific Moses, the audience hushed. Eyebrows furrowed, he strode onto the stage. Covering the mike with his hand, he said, "Luce, I think you'd better go."

"What do you mean, Dad? Shouldn't you be asking him to go?" She pointed toward her accuser.

He shook his head. Releasing the mike, he put his arm about her shoulders. "Loosey Goosey, really, trust me on this. Go back up to your room and wait for me. Let me spin this. You know, formulate some kind of damage control."

"Why?" Lucy shook her head. "I don't understand. *Helena's Dream* is my discovery. I have nothing to be ashamed of."

"Yes, baby, you do." The same way he had back when she'd been a kid on vacation from school and living with him in the field, her father patted her head. "What you don't understand, is that your so-called discovery was mine. Aw, Luce . . ." He sighed, eyeing the terrarium housing her former pride and joy. "How could you not have known I found the first of these thirty years ago?"

While the crowd burst into still more chortles and chuckles, Lucy closed her eyes and swallowed hard.

Too close to the mike, he broadcasted to over five hundred of the most respected scientists in the world, "Face it, sweetie, you just don't have what it takes to become a carbon copy of your old man. Never have. Never will. Now, once and for all, baby, please . . ." He planted a patronizing kiss to her forehead. "Be a good girl. Give up on this scientist fantasy and go make me some pretty grandkids."

# Chapter One

*A few years later . . .*

"I hate him." Lucy tightened her grip on the electric mini's wheel, recalling that afternoon's meeting with the headmaster of the exclusive English school where she taught the equivalent of fifth grade biology. "I hate his stupid tweedy clothes. The way he doesn't laugh, but wheezes. I even hate the way he smells." A cross between cabbage, liverwurst and kidney beans.

Aiming the tiny car down the ivy-draped, stone-walled lane leading to Sinclaire Castle, Lucy took deep breaths, trying awfully hard to talk herself down from the headmaster-induced bad mood and into her normal happy state.

Okay, so maybe she wasn't usually deliriously, happily-ever-after happy. And certainly not soul-deep fulfilled happy. But overall—aside from her run-ins with crusty old Festus Grumsworth who disapproved of everything from her teaching style to her hair to the way she dressed and preferred coffee over tea—she was usually content.

And for a woman who'd learned the hard way to take whatever hand life dealt, plain old contentment was a good thing.

Lucy took her eyes off the deserted lane to fiddle with the radio, but static alerted her to the difficulty of her task. Cotswald County only had one radio station, and that was run by Mrs. Greenstromb high in the fourth-floor attic of the Hoof and Toe Tavern. Lucy found the station and replaced static with yodeling, which led her to a decision to blow her next paycheck on a satellite radio.

She looked up just in time to swerve clear of a bar-reling Smythe's Furniture truck. Judging by the rage with which the driver operated his machine, she guessed Freidman, the duke's butler, had forgotten to tip again.

*"The butler,"* she said along with her best imitation of one of the duke's mellow laughs, following that up with one of her own Alabama giggles. Who'd have thought that Lucy Gordon from Springdale, Alabama, would actually be dating a duke?

Even better, word around the castle was that William might even be on the verge of proposing. And why not? He often enough said he thought her quaint. And her hair, far from offending him, reminded him of that por-trait of the first Queen Elizabeth hanging in Sinclaire Castle's great hall gallery.

Lucy tightened her grip on the wheel.

Would hearing news of his little girl becoming a duchess finally make her father proud?

What the—

She swerved again, only this time for a bouncing green blob.

Pop!

Crash!

Her mini's left front tire blew, which threw the tiny car into an out-of-control slide into the passenger-side rock wall—the American passenger side seeing how she never could keep her lanes straight under pressure.

While she rested her forehead against the steering wheel, another pop sounded under the hood, then came a high-pitched metallic shiver.

Great. Just great.

After a particularly long day of teaching Europe's richest—not to mention most precocious, to put it in polite terms—group of young lords and ladies, to be stranded on the shoulder of this desolate lane was the last thing she needed.

Climbing out of the car to survey the damage, she breathed in the chilly mist capping rolling hills in a depressing shroud. Somewhere in the thickening fog, a sheep bleated, and the air smelled heavy of wet weeds and fecund earth.

Brushing rioting curls back from her face, Lucy figured that once and for all, she had to grow up. She had to stop caring about making her father proud, and stop braking for every frog that hopped across the road. Because face it, just like she was never going to find a new species of frog in Cotswald, she was never, ever going to be the famous scientist she'd once dreamed of. She was never going to find even a new ant species, let alone her own special frog.

Face it, she was a boarding-school biology teacher, destined for a nice, normal life that, if she got really lucky, might even include marriage to a real live duke.

Wasn't that enough?

She even lived rent free in a cottage on Sinclaire Castle's grounds—which was how she'd met the charitable duke who housed several of her fellow teachers on his ample estate.

A flash of bouncing green caught her eye.

How ironic that it had been a frog that initially caused her professional ruin, and now, another one was responsible for her mini's ruin. And if she hadn't been so stubborn in insisting she could do everything on her own, right this minute she'd be humming down the lane in the duke's chauffeur-driven Bentley.

For good measure, she kicked the blown-out front tire that'd caused this whole mess.

Or wait a minute—wouldn't the original cause be that overly jumpy frog?

*Ribbet.* Hop, hop.

Lucy darted to her left, then right, but there was no sign of the annoying creature.

Hop, hop.

There it was again, and this time, she wasn't about to let it get away.

*Ribbet, ribbet,* hop—

"Gotcha!" She pounced on it, cupping both hands around the creature's sleek form. "There, now," she said, leaning against the backside of her car. "Let's take a look at you, you little troublemak—"

Lucy's heart pounded as if she'd just completed a marathon as opposed to chasing down a mischievous country frog. "No, this couldn't be. No way."

Not after all she'd given up.

After all the professional dreams she'd finally abandoned along with the certain knowledge that just like her father said, she didn't have it in her to become a field scientist. She'd finally accepted his words of wisdom stating that those who can't do—teach—and she was happy with that.

Teaching was a noble profession. She had nothing to be even remotely disappointed about.

*Oh yeah? Then how come the mere sight of what you're holding has your legs quivering like a stand of pussy willows in a summer storm?*

Just to make sure, she peeked at the creature again, and sure enough, he was just as unique. Just as spellbindingly, magnificently, downright miraculously scientifically undocumented as he had been before.

Somehow, someway, at a time when she'd least expected it, Lucy Gordon had come across the new species of frog that she'd spent nearly a decade searching for, and she'd done it in the most serendipitous way.

Tears springing to her eyes, she took another peek, this time brushing her thumb along the creature's blazing purple and black ventral. But wait, were the black spots shaped like diamonds? Purple and black diamonds! Who'd ever heard of a diamond-bellied frog?

And his eyes—those beautiful dark-lashed eyes. Frogs don't have eyelashes—at least none of the ones she'd ever seen. Which meant he—he was a he, wasn't he?

She flipped him over. Judging by his scarlet red nuptial pads—yes.

Which meant *he* was her very own discovery.

Every glorious centimeter of him from the tip of his black head to his green-spotted back to the tippy toes of his little webbed black feet.

11

"You're beautiful," she said in a hushed voice, not caring that the mist had turned into a soaking rain. She didn't know how, or even why, but finally, finally, her every dream had come true.

Heart still pounding, cheeks streaming with cold rain intermingled with warm tears, Lucy held the frog to her mouth and kissed him square on his lips.

Poof!

She fell to the mucky dirt lane, pinned beneath the weight of at least two hundred pounds of manly muscle—*naked* manly muscle.

"Jesu," the man with inky-dark eyes said in a thick Welsh brogue. "That was a damned intolerable nightmare I'm glad to be rid of."

Lucy coughed, no easy feat considering the guy had straddled her, pinning her in the mud with his tree-trunk-like arms. Questions spun through her head. Who was he? Why was he naked and on top of her? "Most importantly," she said, voicing this last thought aloud, "what have you done with my frog?! You didn't crush him, did you?"

"Frog?" His laugh was a great booming affair that sounded nothing like the always polite duke. This was the kind of brazen outburst one would expect from a medieval knight while he had his way with a comely serving wench. "Oh," he finally said, scratching his rakishly thick beard. "You must mean me."

Struggling out from under him, eager to be safely locked into her car and away from this mad highwayman, Lucy said, "No. I mean, the one-of-a-kind, brand-new species of amphibian I'd discovered right before you unceremoniously dumped yourself on me."

"Dumped myself on you? And here I thought it'd

been the other way around, with you accosting me with that kiss." His dark eyes gleamed with devilish, dangerous fun, and then he was laughing again, and standing, drawing himself to his full—even awe-inspiring—height that had Lucy leaning her head back just to see the whole of him.

Whew.

Scars. So many jagged scars. And the breadth of his shoulders called to mind great warriors, swashbuckling pirates and gallant knights. He was a breed of man she'd never dreamt existed outside of fairy tales and the bodice-ripping romance novels she devoured on lazy Saturday afternoons.

As she stood, too, he swept his eyes boldly up the length of her, the whole time unaware—or maybe uncaring—of his undressed state.

Just his ravishing stare made her shiver. At first, she'd blamed her tremors on the cold rain, but it couldn't have been, as ever since setting eyes on him, her body had been consumed by the craziest shimmering heat.

She willed her pulse to slow.

This couldn't be happening.

No way could she have actually abandoned what could quite possibly be the most unique species of frog on earth in favor of ogling a naked lunatic.

Well, she hoped the frog hadn't strayed far.

And as for this . . . this . . .

Well, she couldn't think of a label for the man, outside of pure crazy, but that was all right. Just as soon as she found her frog, she'd be on her way. Flat tire or no, she'd drive all the way to the castle on the car's rims if it meant escaping the man's opiate stare.

\*   \*   \*

"Well?" Prince Wolfe of Gwyneddor asked. "Aren't you going to break my curse by declaring your undying love?"

"E-excuse me?"

"Go ahead," he said, settling his hands on her ripe hips, appreciating her cheeks' heightened color as she struggled to keep her gaze from straying lower. "Take a peek. After all, for the moment at least, I am in your debt, and 'tis only natural for you to wish to inspect your goods—I can assure you, there is naught in that region of which I am ashamed."

While she coughed, seemingly more determined than ever to look away, Wolfe released her to indulge in a good, long stretch. Ah, such bliss was this to be in possession of his human form. For the first time in over a thousand years, he once again knew the meaning of life. For being trapped in a frog's body had been no life, but a torturous nightmare from whence he'd feared he might never wake.

And now, after all of those years of searching for the perfect woman who might break his curse, here she was.

Aye, dazed, but her physical state mattered not.

'Twas the condition of her heart garnering his concern. For now that she had kissed him, the terms of his imprisonment were quite clear. Either she and only she declared her true and most heartfelt love, or his curse would last for all of eternity and more. The sorceress had given him but one chance to find a wench willing to devote herself to a loathsome frog, and in this fiery-haired beauty, Wolfe knew he'd finally found the one.

"You must declare your love," he repeated. "After all, that *is* why you saved me, isn't it?"

"Saved you?" She coughed.

"Honestly, woman," he said, giving her a hearty slap on her back. "Why must you answer my every question with further questions?"

Hands on her hips, she spat, "Maybe because I'm not accustomed to running into naked men roaming the lane in broad daylight."

"Ahh, but 'tis nearly dusk," he pointed out, graciously sweeping his hand toward the horizon's growing gloom.

"That's not the point and you know it," she said with a charming stomp of her blue leather-covered foot in the ever-deepening mud.

"Then pray tell, what is?" he asked, crossing his legs at the ankles while bracing himself against the trunk of her carriage.

"Argh!" She tried moving him, but her thrashing was futile. What she thankfully didn't know was just how effective her efforts had been upon his body. For when she'd splayed her fingers upon his chest, he was momentarily lost in the crush of his galloping heart, and sweat on his palms, and an awakening in a field long fallow. Gratitude burned hot at the back of his throat, and for only a second, he indulged himself by closing watery eyes. Oh, how he'd missed the gentle warmth of a woman's touch. Oh, how he must never, under any circumstances, fall victim to that damnedable curse again.

Eyes open, resolve firm, he pulled this womanly treasure into the great circle of his arms. "It seems wenches in your time have not changed as much as I'd presumed. For while your initial kiss was pleasant enough, I now see it was but a clever ruse designed to leave me wanting more." And seeing how in his former life he'd grown quite fond of seizing that which he'd desired, Wolfe figured why not start off this new life in the same spirit.

While the wench seemed a trifle dazed, he cinched her closer still, crushing her lips to his to get her past any notion of further struggle. She didn't disappoint, for aye, there was indeed a brief tussle of wills, but then he softened his kiss, hoping to not only imply his desire for their upcoming bedding, but his most heartfelt thanks to her for having saved him.

He slipped his fingers into her riotous curls, cupping the back of her head, urging her sweet mouth open so they might indulge in a mingling of tongues. They shared that and so much more until she was melting against him, molding her curves to the wall of his chest until it was no longer enough to merely kiss her.

He must have all of her—here.

Now.

One hand still buried in her fiery curls, with the other, he lifted her up the length of him, hand on her ample backside to press her against the swell of his need. When she groaned again, the damp heat of her breath, her longing, spilled into him, threatening to wholly consume what little remained of his once legendary control. What new variety of sorceress was she to have so thoroughly seduced him with a mere kiss?

"Ah, wench . . . What have ye done?" Beyond caring, he deepened the kiss still. "In my time, a hot-blooded vixen such as yourself would have been worth her weight in rubies."

16

"Your time?" As if angered by his words, she pulled back. "Are you still stuck on this whole time-travel thing? And as for me being hot-blooded—remember, big fella, you kissed me."

The wee one launched her struggle anew, until finally, tiring of her pretense to not want him, the prince let her go. Bearing a scowl that would have frightened his most battle-hardened warrior she tugged the hem of her sodden white tunic, crossing her arms over hardened buds. Oh, to be sure, her speech may have been a valiant one, but the reddening of her cheeks told him she was not so naïve as to believe she hadn't enjoyed kissing him back.

"I was innocently minding my own business until you showed up."

"And it's a good thing you did," he said, allowing her to change the subject. "After only recently escaping being flattened by that odorous oversized carriage, I couldn't believe my luck to have finally happened upon you traveling my lane."

"*Your* lane?" She laughed. "I've lived at Sinclaire Castle for years and know quite literally every inhabitant of Cotswald County. If, as you say, this were *your* lane, why wouldn't I have seen you at any of the duke's holiday parties?"

"Simple," he said, dragging her back into his arms. "In my cursed condition, I wasn't exactly a suitable guest. But now, all of that has changed. I will resume my rightful station as prince, and you, my savior, shall be gifted with one night in my bed, and then be on your way."

\*　　\*　　\*

17

Lucy hated herself for even momentarily thinking that after that epic kiss, his plan didn't sound all bad, so it was with only marginal sarcasm she said, "Hmm, sounds fun. Just as soon as I find my frog."

Once again, she found herself wrestling free of his hold, only this time, a little more reluctantly. As strange as it sounded, something about being in his arms felt right. More right than anything she'd done in a long time. Which only added to her current state of confusion.

While the naked man watched her with a mocking smile, Lucy looked under the car and all along the rock wall for her missing frog.

Crossing the lane, she peered along the other wall as well. And beneath a sprawling beech tree. And behind at least five large stones. And only after searching all of those places and more, did she realize that she'd allowed her momentary enjoyment of this naked—and quite off his rocker—stud to interfere with the one thing she'd searched her whole life to find.

Not just a unique frog—but her father's respect.

"No, no, no," she said. "This is all your fault that he's gone."

"Who?"

"Who do you think?!" she shrieked. "My frog!"

He sighed. "Must we carry on like this in the rain? Let me repair your carriage and then we'll return to the castle. Serving wenches will prepare us a hot meal and if you're nice, I'll give you the pleasure of rubbing a thousand years' aches from my shoulders."

"How considerate of you."

"Yes, I thought so. Though I'd much prefer the service of a good horse."

"To rub your shoulders?"

"No, to the dreadful inconvenience of your forever crippled carriages."

Tired of not only the rain, but the stranger's exhausting circular logic, Lucy figured what the heck? Why not give him the pleasure of changing her tire? And right after that, she'd take her own pleasure in driving him straight back to the mental healthcare facility from which he'd obviously escaped!

# Chapter Two

On any other day at this rainy, gloomy bridge into night, the village of Cotswald would have been deserted. The inhabitants would've long since gathered round their hearths or dinner tables or at the bar of the Hoof and Toe Tavern. What they weren't usually doing was milling about as if they had nothing better to do than wait on the side of the road for Lucy Gordon to drive by with a naked man!

"Can't you hunker a little?" she asked him on their way past gaping Eleanor Lolly out for a walk in matching rain slickers with her seventeen-year-old dachshund, Rudy. And then there was ten-year-old Charlie Raney floating a model cigarette boat in John Cleavon's birdbath. Shouldn't a boy his age—Charlie, not John—be inside doing his homework?

On the left, the butcher shop was open curiously late, and on the right, Drymore's Chemist was just closing up. To her mortification, Pete Drymore waved as she passed.

Great. Just super.

"I am the prince," Lucy's naked passenger said. "Men of my station do not hunker."

"Right. I forgot." So Lucy hunkered, managing surprisingly well to drive with just the crown of her head peeking over the wheel.

At least for the next ten feet.

"Get your wits about you, wench! There's a body in the road."

"A body?!" Lucy bolted upright. Great. Just great. A dead person to add to her naked person—but wait, that was no mere *body* crossing the road, but Cotswald's resident gossip diva—Ruth Hagenberry. Of all people to come across, she was the worst. A walking talking tabloid rag with a memory as reliable as a state-of-the-art laptop.

Faces, places, dates, times—Ruth knew it all.

Bottom line, the last thing Lucy needed, with the reputation-conscious duke on the verge of proposing, was to have this old snoop telling him his intended had been seen chauffeuring a naked man!

Because the self-crowned prince needed it for scaring her with that *body* line, Lucy smacked him on his shoulder, only to instantly regret it when a distracting heat licked its way up her fingers. She hazarded a glance his way only to be graced with a wide, wicked smile that made her breath catch and heart tumble.

In the gloom, his unreadable dark eyes shone like wet ink, yet his high cheekbones and strong lips wore the determined mask of a warrior entering battle. A battle not about conquering an inferior civilization, but her!

Lucy shivered before looking away and tightening her grip on the mini's wheel.

"You need not feel shamed for wanting me," he said in a voice slow and sinful as hot buttered rum. "Every wench does."

Yeah, well not this one.

"Let's get one thing straight," she said as they passed at least three couples laughing and strolling hand-in-hand into the Hoof and Toe. "I've never been your— or any other man's—*wench*. I am a highly educated, highly independent woman."

"Right," he said with a royal snort. "Which must be why you needed a man a thousand years departed from this age to reassemble your carriage."

"Correction. I didn't *need* you to change my tire. I *let* you. And in case you forgot, *I* was the one who reassembled all of those popped wires under the hood."

"Is that the title for that thing up front?"

"Yes, as you full well know if you'd once and for all give up this delusion." Ah, sweet heaven, the lights of Cotswald County's small hospital shone straight ahead. "Good. We're nearly there."

"Where?"

"The hospital where surely someone can help you."

"Help me with what? Aside from the chilly lack of respect coming from you, I feel quite extraordinary after having spent the last millennium a scant one hand high."

Making the left turn into the hospital lot, Lucy rolled her eyes.

A few more minutes, and she'd be rid of this nutcase.

And seeing how she was *almost* rid of him, she'd even admit to the fact that even with his clothes on, he'd easily outclass any man she'd ever met—or even seen—in the looks department. But then she'd never really sought her companions for their looks so much as their brains. And obviously, what this guy had in the hot bod department, he lacked upstairs!

"Okie doke," she said, putting the car in park and cutting the electric motor. She slipped off her seatbelt and angled on her seat to face him. "Wait here. I'll find a nurse to wheel you inside. I can't tell with all that hair of yours, but . . ." *glorious thick, long, black exotic hair I'd love to feel on my breasts and belly and*—she swallowed hard. *Get ahold of yourself!* With a deep breath, she started over. "What I was about to say is that I suspect you may have a head wound. Just to be safe, let me get you some help."

He leaned close, bombarding her with his sheer masculinity and heady scents of sweat and the musky, mossy pond that she so loved. For a second, she thought he might kiss her, and his proximity made it an impossibility for her to think beyond that instant, that heartbeat, that perfect moment in time when his lips settled atop hers. But then he pulled back, and she was abandoned with nothing but her surging pulse.

On the heels of a short laugh, he said, "Looks like you're the one needing help, wench."

"Arrrggh." Without so much as a hint of a glance in his direction, Lucy got out of the car and trudged up to the emergency entrance.

The hospital's white, bright sterility came as a welcome change from the hot and steamy mini.

"What's up, Luce?" Dr. Luke Hodges, who dated her friend Bonnie, who taught calculus at Lucy's school, strode toward her dressed in blue surgical scrubs. The familiar—not to mention, sane—grin he cast her way warmed her to her toes. The closer he got, however, the more that grin of his faded. "You're looking a bit dicky. Been drinking, have you?"

She managed to crack a small smile. "When I tell you why I'm here, you'll probably think so, but I promise, every word of what I'm about to tell you is true." Though his expression grew increasingly more dubious, Lucy told him start to finish about her supposed prince. Well—he wasn't *her* prince, but surely Luke knew what she meant.

"Let's go have a look at him, shall we?"

Lucy led the way while Luke followed with a wheelchair.

"That Father Bart?" she asked, eyeing a bedraggled-looking soul huddled beneath a stack of blankets on one of the exam tables. He'd long since retired from the church, but he loved Cotswald so, the congregation had built him a quaint cottage alongside the rectory, and he still helped out with occasional clerical duties.

" 'Fraid so. Seems he was well into his evening meal when he spotted Napoleon charging through his tomato sauce."

"This a regular thing for him?" Lucy asked, relieved that she wasn't the only one having a bizarre night!

"Quite. Last week he found the Queen Mum swimming in his jacket potato."

Lucy eyed the poor man one last time. Compared to him, she had nothing to worry about! At least her visions were life-sized!

Outside, the rain had stopped and ghosts of summer wildflowers and the stand of firs at the far end of the parking area flavored the air with a pungent sweetness that tickled her nose and made her think everything just might be okay. The wheelchair's left tire squeaked and the sharp noise echoed across the otherwise silent lot.

More to ease the tension knotting her gut over wondering what the duke would have to say about all of this than because she was in a mood for chitchat, Lucy asked, "Did Bonnie tell you about the school dance we're going to chaperone?"

"Yep. Also said some rubbish about me having to wear a dinner jacket. A dinner jacket! Like I'm going to find one all the way out here?"

"We've got three weeks. Anyway, the duke has dozens. You two are about the same size. Want me to borrow one for you?"

"That'd be decent." Approaching her mini, he said, "I don't see him. Think he could've passed out?"

"I suppose."

"Here, take this," Luke said, passing off the wheelchair, then jogging the last few feet. He jerked open the passenger door, only to freeze.

"What's the matter?" Lucy asked, embarrassingly out of breath from just the short run.

Luke glanced her way. "That's what I was just going to ask you."

"Wait a minute." To clear the internal fog, Lucy shook her head. "You don't think I made all of this up?"

He shrugged, eyed the length of the parking lot, paying particularly close attention to the dark stand of firs. After a few seconds of awkward silence, he released a long, slow breath. "Look, Lucy, Bonnie told me what happened today. Grumsworth has given you an exceptionally rough time of it. Sometimes when a person's upset . . ." He shrugged. "Well, let's just say that on these desolate country lanes, sometimes it's easy to confuse fact with fantasy."

"You can't be serious? You *do* think I made the whole thing up. Like I've been having king-sized delusions, as opposed to Father Bart's minis?"

"I didn't say that. I was just—"

"Yes, you did. Just like everyone else in this town, oh, you play nice enough to my face, but behind my back you think of me as that *crazy Yank*."

"Come on, Luce," Luke said, cupping his hand to her shoulder. "You know that isn't true. Bonnie thinks of you as a sister, and seeing how I hope to one of these days save up enough to make Bonnie my wife, well, I guess I think of you in the same light. You're a breath of fresh air. A nice change in our otherwise dull existence."

Arms crossed, Lucy said, "He was real, Luke. Just as real as you or me."

"Okay. I believe you." He gestured toward the firs. "You know how much wilderness is out here, Luce, what with the Cambrians not that far away. I'll bet your man was spooked by the hospital and took off. With any luck, you'll never be bothered by him again."

Lucy's friend's tone said what his words didn't. That he was placating her. Granted, her latest round of blows with Grumsworth hadn't been pleasant, but it hadn't been bad enough for her to start hallucinating, had it?

No.

And to prove it, she'd darn well find that stupid prince and bring him right back here to shove in Luke's disgustingly concerned face!

# Chapter Three

Two hours and no luck later, crushed didn't begin to describe Lucy's spirits.

She'd searched everywhere.

Starting at the stand of firs at the far end of the hospital lot and ending with the stand of regulars crowding the Hoof and Toe's bar. She parked at the town rose garden and walked High Street in its entirety, peeking into dark alleys and beneath trash piles and parked cars and Talbot Havard's leaning gazebo. She checked the shed behind the chemist's and another shed behind Mr. Dooley's. She checked the church and the spooky graveyard and even the duck pond, but the ducks were all asleep on their island, and surely if they'd had a recent scare by a naked, self-crowned prince, they wouldn't have been quite so settled in for the night.

In short, she'd looked *everywhere* and the prince was nowhere.

Now, she was right back where she'd started, driving her mini down the deserted lane leading toward Sinclaire Castle, and in particular, toward that small portion of the castle grounds that was hers—Rose Cottage.

Who knew, maybe Luke was right?

Maybe she had dreamt the whole thing?

She'd always loved immersing herself in the medieval history of her home, but maybe it was high time she traded history for those spicy Hollywood reads her friend Mary Jane sent along with regular shipments of MoonPies.

Exhausted, Lucy finally pulled up alongside her sweet, vine-covered home.

Acres away across vast formal gardens and rolling lawns, the castle lights glowed, twinkling like a soothing bedtime fairytale against the heavy black sky.

This view reminded her of where her attention should be.

The castle, and the life that with any luck she'd soon be living with William inside of it. She needed him now. His kind heart and gentle laugh. The quiet ease and grace with which he handled every conceivable crisis— not that her imagining herself with a naked prince was a crisis, because it wasn't.

The whole episode had been nothing more than a sign that, as the duke had so many times teasingly pointed out, she needed to spend less time on lesson plans and more time on him!

Shoulders aching, she climbed out of her mini, leaving her school bag on the backseat in favor of just grabbing her purse. It was already after eight and no way did she feel up to doing anything other than making a quick meal of soup and a sandwich, then soaking in a steaming tub.

Inside, the mudroom was dark save for the faint yellow glow from the night light she kept on in the kitchen. The cuckoo clock she'd bought on a holiday to Switzerland merrily tick-tocked, and the faint smell of her morning coffee still flavored the air, along with the ever-present scents of centuries-old plaster and wood.

Tilting her head back and closing her eyes, she sighed.

This place was real. These comforting, familiar scents and sounds wrapped around her each evening like a cozy quilt. Here, where she belonged, her day of pure frustration was finally ending on a mellow note of pure bliss.

Everything was going to be okay.

She was going to be okay.

Happy.

Happy in her marriage to the duke.

Happy in her teaching.

Happy, happy, happy.

Eyes opened, shoulders squared, Lucy kicked off her filthy pumps and wound her way into the kitchen, stopping off at the fridge to see if the Dinner Fairy might've left her a plate of steaming pot roast and mashed potatoes.

No such luck.

There was a small care package from her two-nights-earlier spaghetti dinner with the duke, though, so while that was heating in the microwave, she unbuttoned her mud-encrusted blouse and headed for the stairs.

Rose Cottage had been extensively remodeled a few years back, but the designer had been quite the history buff and instead of opening up the space up like so many people did with their old homes—preserving the exterior while gutting the interior—he'd kept the original boxy plan which made just walking to the living room, let alone heading for the two upstairs bedrooms, a lot like walking the castle hedge maze.

She entered the dining room to see an orange glow dancing on the library's ceiling.

How odd. And how wonderful!

Knowing that she was hopeless at lighting her own fires, the duke must've lit one for her in the living room hearth. Mmm, and with any luck, he'd soon be popping out to surprise her.

"Come out, come out wherever you are," she sang on her way into the coffered-ceiling room, eager to share with him an edited version of the night's events. Meaning, she'd have to come up with a reason for why she was muddy and hours late getting home that didn't involve a naked prince!

After all, a man in the duke's position did have his reputation to consider, and if she were to become his wife, she'd have to embrace his necessity for propriety. "William? William, honey, where are you?"

"Ah, 'tis *honey* you've taken to calling me then, eh?"

Clutching the open halves of her blouse, Lucy screamed.

The prince vaulted over the back of the sofa that faced the hearth, then calmly, confidently—*nakedly*—strode her way.

Lucy gulped.

He looked much different in her cluttered, floral-chintz-and-toile-beruffled home than he had on the lane or in her car. If possible, he'd grown even taller. His dark hair longer, his wide smile even more disarmingly handsome.

"What's the matter?" he asked, coming ever closer.

"H-how, how did you get in here? The door was locked."

He rolled his eyes. "You think a prince doesn't have ways? You forget, I own not only this place, but every other for as far—and farther—than the eye can see."

"Why did you run away from the hospital?"

"I didn't run. I walked."

"But why? I was trying to get you some help."

"But like I tried telling you in that cramped carriage, I need no help."

At that, she laughed. "Oh, so you don't even have any clothes, yet you need no help?"

"I grow weary of your incessant questions, wench." After a regal dismissive wave, he said, "Getting to the heart of the matter, you have earned a royal bedding, which I see by your unbuttoned state of affairs that you must be ready to claim. And after that, I shall storm my castle, and finally get on with the business of ruling."

Lucy could only stare.

The man was certifiable.

*Not to mention gorgeous!*

All those rippling muscles on his chest and abs and those shoulders. *Dear lord, had any man ever had broader shoulders? And his arms looked strong enough to sweep even her off of her feet.*

Lucy licked her lips and dropped her gaze from his spellbinding features to the floor, but on the way down, she accidentally caught another peek at his package.

Dear lord!

*Honestly, Luce, kindly remember this is a crisis you're facing, not a potential date!*

31

"Like what you see?" He laughed, and the rich, bawdy sound filled the room, managing if only for a moment to mask her galloping pulse.

Flames way hotter than those in the hearth crept up her cheeks. "I-I can't imagine what you mean."

"Ah, which must be why your cheeks blush like the rose." His lips curved into a slow smile as his gaze dropped to her breasts. "Also like the rose, your buds are reaching out to me. Begging to be taken into my mouth?"

Dear lord!

Lucy crossed her arms in the hopes that maybe if she covered her *buds*, the prince would stop talking about them.

Wrong!

All that made him do was take a step closer. Even worse, that conquering look was back in his eyes. The one that said she was about to become his, and he knew full well her resistance was weak.

"Most of the fairer sex come to me without coaxing," he said. "But the ones I must woo . . . Ah, now those are the wenches I most enjoy."

What to do, what to do?

She could call the hospital for an ambulance.

She could call the police.

Or she could go with it. With him. With his dark eyes promising the kinds of pleasures of which she'd never dared dream.

No! What was she thinking?

She couldn't, *wouldn't* have sex with a stranger.

Besides which, she loved William. Granted, ten whole minutes of kissing her *almost* fiancé didn't leave her this flushed, but that was because William was civilized and this nut . . . well, suffice to say, he wasn't!

While Lucy had been deep in conference with herself, the prince had taken still another step toward her, and now he was close enough to wreath her in his distinctly masculine, distinctly heady scents. The sweat. The musky, mossy pond. The spirit and ego as big as the whole outdoors.

"Well?" he said, hands on his slim hips. "Are you going to lead me to your slumber chamber? Or shall we proceed with storming the castle and have our tryst in my rightful bed?"

Lucy licked her lips.

He sighed. "Your pretense of not wanting me grows as tiresome as your questions. If it's your reputation or conscience gnawing you, trust me, no man or woman would dare think less of you for bedding a prince."

"Thanks," Lucy said, taking his latest unbelievable self-aggrandizing statement about as well as a bucket of cold water to her face. "That truly does make me feel much more comfortable about the whole thing. So comfortable in fact, that I feel the sudden urge to slip into something more comfortable. Do you mind waiting here, while I run upstairs?"

"Yes, as a matter of fact, I do mind. But since at the moment I am rather indebted to you, I suppose just this once I could put my needs beneath yours."

"Really? Just this once? How kind of you, dear prince." After blowing him a mocking kiss, she made a mad dash for the stairs.

The police *and* an ambulance. That's who she'd call the instant she entered her room.

She'd just picked up the phone from her bedside table, when from outside her window—the same window she'd left cracked open that morning—came the sound of a determined knock on the mudroom door.

"Lucy?" bellowed the duke. "Hurry up and let me in. This damnable rain has started up again."

Heart racing, she looked from the bedroom door to the window.

What had she been thinking?

If she called the police, they'd be out in a flash, sirens blaring. Talk about a stunner to the duke's sterling reputation. She was already in trouble with the school headmaster. Could she really afford any additional scandal now that William was on the verge of proposing? If only she could convince the prince to quietly be on his way, then no one but Luke would ever be the wiser—and he thought she'd made the whole thing up!

Decision made, she opened the bedroom window wider and called down, "Hi, sweetie. I'll be right there."

Palms sweating, pulse surging, Lucy stripped, made a few half-hearted swipes with a hot rag at her back and chest, then dressed in jeans and a burnt orange sweater, finishing by pulling on thick orange socks and shoving her feet into her favorite pair of red rubber mules.

In under three minutes, she dashed down the stairs to thankfully find the prince back on the sofa, aiming a bemused grin at her.

He said, "I take it the nobleman caterwauling at your door is the justification for your need to be discreet where the matter of you and I are concerned?"

"Hide!" she said in a fervent whisper.

"A man of my station does not hide," he said with a less-than-amused snort. "Besides which, if your nobleman harbors any desire to better himself, surely he will see the benefits of having his woman bed the prince?"

Another knock sounded at the mudroom door. This one harder than the first. Then came a muffled, "Lucy! Hurry along, will you? I'm getting rather soaked."

*Rather soaked.*

She did so love William's unassuming manner of speech—as opposed to the brash ways of the crazed naked highwayman lounging on her sofa!

To the prince, she said, "Please. If you have an honorable bone in your body, just this once hide. William already puts up with a lot from me. This—you—he just wouldn't understand."

The prince eyed her, making her feel as if she were under his appraisal, as if he were gauging her worth. After what felt like an eternity, he notched his chin a fraction higher, and said, "The fire's warmth has put me in a charitable mood. I shall recline, but I shall not lower myself to *hide.*" The spin he put on the word made it akin to burning at the stake.

Geesh, who did this guy think he was?

Shoulders sagging with temporary relief, Lucy ran for the front door, but then came a knock from the back.

"Determined chap, isn't he?" The prince said dryly from the sofa.

"Shut up," Lucy said on her way to the back door.

"What was that?" William asked above the rain that now fell in drumming sheets.

"Go around to the front," she hollered, animatedly jiggling the handle. "This, um, lock is stuck."

"What?" Through the small window, she saw him cup his right hand to his ear.

She resorted to pointing toward the front.

He nodded, and by the time she opened the mud-room door, he was there, pushing his way inside.

"Frightfully nasty night," he said with a shiver. "Got any scotch?"

"Um, no." She glanced toward the kitchen, half expecting the naked prince to stroll in. "Um, all I have is milk—and, um . . . it's sour."

He made a face. "No rum? Bourbon? Hell's bells, on a night like this I believe I'd even be content with a spot of tequila."

She shook her head.

"Least you've finally discovered how to get a good fire going," he said, already unbuttoning yellow foul-weather gear. "Guess I'll have to settle for that." Smiling, he leaned forward to give her a kiss. "And a little more of that."

She returned his smile, then inwardly screamed.

William couldn't go anywhere near that fire!

What if he thought she'd actually invited the naked prince into her home? What if he thought she were carrying on some outrageous affair? What if he not only thought all of that, but then broke up with her? Demanded she find alternate accommodations? He was on the board of her school. What if the headmaster told him about her latest transgression? She'd be fired for sure. It'd be like living through the World Biological Conference debacle all over again.

William cocked his head. "You're acting rather peculiar, Luce, and I think I know the reason why."

*You do?!*

"Oh?" She drew her lower lip into her mouth and nibbled.

"Cotswald County has a relatively small population,

my dear." He gave her hand a squeeze. "Surely, you didn't think that by now I wouldn't have heard?"

"Well . . ." Biting hard on her lip, she hazarded another glance toward the kitchen.

"The part that sincerely troubles me, though, is why you think I'd even care that you had another spat with the headmaster." Placing his still rain-chilled fingers beneath her chin, he tilted her head back, forcing her to meet his gaze. "I find myself growing more than merely fond of you, Lucy Gordon. Every crazy, minx-filled inch of you. You can trust me. All I ask in return is the same respect. The same kind of honesty. Can you give me those things?"

*Tell him,* her conscience screamed. *You'll never get a better chance to come clean about the prince.*

She wanted to tell him.

Truly, she did, but her mouth went dry, making it a technical impossibility for her to even squeak, let alone, speak, so she settled for a nod.

"All right, then. Lead me to the fire, fair maiden."

"No!"

"No?"

"I mean, wouldn't you rather head back to your place? I mean, I have nothing to eat or drink, and anyway, my fire's about to go out."

"Funny. It looked rather healthy through the back windows."

"Yeah, well, you know how that thick old glass distorts things."

He scrunched his nose.

"Besides, everything's a mess. I've, um, been so busy with school that I haven't had a chance to tidy."

"Oh. Well, seeing how I fancy myself a bit of a neatnik, I suppose I can see where that sort of thing may matter. But I promise a small mess won't have me thinking less of you."

*Small mess?* She nearly choked.

Nothing about the naked giant camped in her living room could be called small!

"Thank you, William, but I'd really rather keep my messy side a secret." She winked. *At least until our fiftieth wedding anniversary.*

"Ahh, I must say, I'm finding this show of intrigue most becoming, while at the same time maddening."

Smiling—dying—she shrugged.

He pulled her into his arms for another kiss. A safe kiss. A kiss that warmed her to her toes and made her feel secure. Not in danger of drowning in a most pleasurable abyss of wickedly dark-eyed medieval sin!

Shoulders sagging with relief that she was on the verge of making a clean escape, Lucy reached for her red rain slicker while William opened the door.

Outside, still more rain fell in undulating, silvery sheets, pounding the earth and drumming up a moist mossy smell that much to Lucy's dismay reminded her of the wholly masculine scent of the prince's chest.

Cheeks glowing, she ushered the duke outside.

Still beneath the sheltering roof of her small porch, he said, "Are you quite certain you wouldn't rather stay here?"

She shook her head. "Really, let's go."

"All right, then. If you insist, give me your hand."

She'd done just that, congratulating herself on a mission well done, when . . .

"Oh, wench!?" the prince boomed from the living

room. "Before you go, could I trouble you for a spot of ale?"

Nose scrunched, eyebrows furrowed, William stepped back inside, dragging her along with him. Glancing first at her, then at the fire's orange glow dancing on the dining room walls, he said, "Might there be something you'd like to tell me?"

# Chapter Four

"Um . . ." Lucy nibbled her lower lip.

"Wench! This reclining has brought on a most infuriating thirst!"

The duke frowned, looking to Lucy, then the kitchen, before heading in the direction of the booming voice.

"No!" Lucy said, blocking the kitchen pass-thru with arms and legs spread wide. "Don't go!"

"Mind telling me why?"

*Think, Luce, think!*

"Um . . ." Lower lip between her teeth, furiously twirling a curl with her right pinkie, legs still apart, she said, "I'm, ah, taping a movie in there on the telly, and um, my ancient VCR is so sensitive that any little movement throws off the tape."

He made a face. "That's preposterous. No one uses tape technology anymore. Let me pass."

"No—really." She lunged for him, pressing her palms to his smooth cotton sweater. The navy blue pullover was still damp from the rain, and he smelled faintly of his cook's beef stew, and of the cedar closet he stored all of his sweaters in. After they married, her sweaters would smell the same, and she'd have beef stew every night until she grew big as a house, and William wouldn't care because he loved her for her—not her waistline. She was so lucky to have found him, and no way was that stupid naked prince in her living room going to ruin a whole life of cozy woolen hugs and beef stew she'd never even have to chop onions for! "Trust me, William," she said. "It's a *super* old VCR. Made in Bulglammabhad. Really sad workmanship, but you can't blame the people—they're starving and the working conditions are deplorable. Maybe you should bring the subject up next time you see the king?"

At that he laughed, drawing her into a hug. "First off, there is no such place, and second, you know full well there's nothing the king could do. He's only a figurehead in our country, darling. Now, Parliament, they're the ones with the power to affect change."

"You're so smart," Lucy said with a wide grin. "Parliament—yes, that's exactly what I was thinking. Let's form some sort of relief effort over steaming bowls of Cook's stew."

"How did you know she made stew?"

"I smell it on you, silly." She crushed him in another hug. "Mmm, you smell all warm and cuddly—like a teddy bear."

"A teddy bear, eh?" He preened. "I rather like the sound of that."

"Wench! My ale!"

Pulse racing, Lucy rolled her eyes, hoping to achieve a properly bored demeanor. "Honestly, I don't know why I'm even bothering to record this program. Entirely too repetitive, and not a lick of educational quality. Maybe you should take that up with the king as well?"

"Ah, Luce," he said, ruffling her hair while guiding her back toward the door. "How dull my life would be without you."

"Wench!"

"I say," the duke said, peering over his shoulder as Lucy ushered him out the door. "That is a rather redundant program. Wouldn't you rather turn it off altogether?"

"Nah," Lucy said, pulling the door firmly closed behind her. "Why waste time on that bore, when I could be focusing on you?"

When she beamed up at him, he kissed her forehead, then reached for her hand, jolting her out of her cozy cottage, and into cold, driving rain. "Last one to the castle is a rotten bundt cake!"

Thoroughly befuddled euphemisms aside, Lucy had never felt warmer—or more relieved—in her life!

"Now, that was a bloody good spot of stew," the duke said an hour later from his burgundy leather wing chair in front of the study's crackling fire. Lucy sat beside him on an overstuffed peacock-blue velveteen abomination of a chair that, while horribly undignified, held her butt like a skilled lover—not that she'd particularly had one of those to know what such a thing would even feel like, but . . .

*If he's still in your cottage, you could know soon enough.*

Lucy cupped her hands to flaming cheeks.

"Care for another spot of brandy?"

"No, thank you," she said, grateful for the distraction. "If I have anymore, I'll end up seeing spots."

"Ah, we mustn't have that," he said, rubbing the sole of her left foot with the toes of his right. Between their chairs sat a plump paisley suede ottoman upon which both of them rested their sock-covered feet. "After all, one must keep up appearances and such." He winked.

Lucy's lukewarm pink cheeks flamed soiled-lady red!

Did he know about the prince, and all this time, he'd been waiting for her to broach the topic? No. No way, could he possibly, unless . . .

*Ruth Hagenberry.*

But surely even she wasn't that efficient?

The duke cleared his throat, swirled his brandy before taking a leisurely sip. Outside, driving rain pelted ancient windows. Inside, the merry fire danced to the soothing strains of highbrow classical music.

Outside, cold.

Inside, hot.

So why was she fending off a horrific case of shivers?

*Gee, could it be because if this wonderful man knows about the prince, you know you're toast?*

"Cold, darling?" He set his brandy on a mahogany side table, and put his feet on the floor before leaning forward to massage her arches.

"Not at all."

"Why the shivers?"

"What shivers?"

He laughed. "Darling, Luce, are you ever going to feel you can trust me?"

She gulped. "Trust you with what?" *The knowledge that there's a two-hundred-pound naked prince back in my cottage wanting to jump my bones?*

"Darling, please." Fingers curled over the elongated ice cubes that used to be her toes, he said, "You've been jumpy as a stable kitten all evening long, and for no reason. Everyone knows Ruth Hagenberry's one biscuit shy of a whole tin. Do you honestly think for one second I'd believe her latest yarn about you?"

"Well . . ." she nibbled her lower lip. "There was that time with the baby lamb and my student Rebecca's birthday."

"And I told you," he said, giving her toes a gentle squeeze. "As long as you brought the baby back—sans its nappy and dress, everything would be fine. And it was, wasn't it?"

Nibbling her lower lip, she nodded.

"Granted, the poor thing would still rather live in your cottage than the fields, but—"

"William, I told you I was—"

"Shh . . ." Leaning closer still, he ever-so-softly pressed his index finger to her lips. "I've already told you. It doesn't matter. Just as Ruth's ridiculous story about you traipsing through town with a naked giant doesn't matter—how could it, when I fear even if such a tale were true, I'd still hold a fierce longing for you?"

"You do?"

"Of course, I do. You must be daft if over these past few months you haven't realized it." As if admitting such a thing might be the death of him, he picked up his brandy for a chug that would've done any American frat house proud—that is, assuming he'd have traded in his brandy for a beer. When he'd consumed enough liquid courage to once again look her way, he lifted the corners of his lips into a gentle smile that turned his normally intense gaze to a welcoming sea of blue.

"Oh, William," Lucy said, using the backs of her hands to swipe at silly tears.

The brandy went back to the side table, then he was once again warming her toes. "Might I be so bold as to assume your tender smile means you feel the same?"

For some reason unable to speak, she nodded before piling herself onto his lap. "I d-don't deserve you," she said, sobbing messy tears all over the smooth cotton of his vee-necked sweater.

"What's this?" he said, easing her head back, then notching her gaze to his with his fingers beneath her chin. "You don't deserve me?" He laughed. "That's quite amusing considering the fact I feel much the same about you."

"You do?"

"Of course. Why else do you think night after night I instruct Cook to prepare such delicacies as beef stew and meat loaf and spaghetti?"

She shrugged. "I thought you just had great taste in food?"

"I do, but it runs more along the lines of foie gras and beef Wellington."

"So all of these dinners have been specially prepared for me?"

He nodded, and Lucy's heart swelled. Had there ever been a kinder, more generous man?

The prince might have looks going for him, but if he'd taken a few lessons from a true nobleman like William about a thousand years earlier, he wouldn't be in the bind he now claimed to be in!

*Listen to me, as if I believe for one second any of that nutcase's story is for real.*

The heat of the fire, the duke's gentle foot massage

45

and a happy bellyful of stew culminated in a sleepy yawn. "Mmm," Lucy said, closing her eyes. "I could get used to this."

"Good," he said, "That's exactly the effect I've been hoping for."

An hour later, standing outside Rose Cottage beneath the light of a shy moon forever scurrying behind high clouds, William wished for more rain—not because Cotswald County needed it, but because it would give him an excuse to once again take Luce into his arms.

After another hour of fireside chatting, he'd walked her home, holding her small hand tucked safely into his. If only he could keep her in his life forever and ever, all the meaningless drivel his station forced him to contend with might suddenly make him whole.

No—it wasn't the work that would make him whole—it was Lucy with her bright blue eyes, ever alight with passions he could only begin to imagine. Lucy, and all of her minxish charm that to his mother's way of thinking was the very embodiment of all things he ought steer clear of.

A fortnight ago, his mum had lectured him at length—a solid two hours on the virtues of Mother knowing best and an assorted pot of additional rubbish. But here, now, gazing upon his Lucy's freckled complexion, dancing eyes and naughty strawberry blond curls, William, the sixteenth Duke of Cotswald, thought his mother, the great Dowager Duchess, positively daft. For if she couldn't see Lucy's many obvious and assorted charms, then she must be long overdue for a visit to her optometrist.

"You look lovely," he finally said, taking the liberty

of tucking a runaway curl behind her left ear.

"As you would say—rubbish. I look a mess." Though a grin lit her eyes, she wrinkled her button nose before planting a warm kiss to his cheek. Her hands still on his chest, her barely there lily-of-the-valley perfume wreathing him in temptation, she added, "But thank you for being such a gentleman as to make me feel just the opposite."

"You're most welcome." When she once again smiled, William felt ready to burst. What the woman did to him with merely a smile! Despite her fault of not even remotely fitting into his world, they shared a laugh, then granted the few hardy crickets still about entrée into their conversation.

The night had fallen so silent, that from clear across the valley came the howl of Moony Richardson's basset hound demanding to be let in for the night. "Well, then," William finally said. "Do you, ah, mind if I come in?"

"Inside?"

William frowned. In the past, such a question had never prompted a coughing spell.

"Are you quite all right?" he asked, landing a series of hearty pats to her back.

"Sure," she finally said after catching her breath. "I just—wow, must've swallowed a bug."

"Well?" he asked again.

"I, um, so then you're still wanting to come inside?"

"Just for a short while. You know, maybe to properly say goodnight in a more private setting."

Again, came the coughs. "You know, I think I might be better off going straight to bed. Maybe I'm coming down with something."

47

"You were fine a few minutes ago."

"True, but you know how these damp nights can, um, affect the lungs."

Lungs? Of any woman he'd ever known, Lucy had an exceptionally healthy—not to mention, loud—set!

"Okay, then, guess I'll settle for this." Before she could refuse, he settled his hands about her waist, drawing her close for a lingering kiss.

"Mmm," she said when he drew back. "Now I can go to sleep happy."

"Are you happy, Luce?"

"What do you mean?"

"I mean, happy here in your cottage? At the school . . . Perhaps most importantly—with me?"

"Oh, William," she said, cupping his cheek. "Of course. If I've done or said anything tonight to have given you a different impression, please forgive me. I— well, it's been a downright nasty day, and I'm tired. Worried about how to best deal with Grumsworth in the morning. You know how it is when you have a lot on your mind."

He nodded. Did he know. Endless legal matters, and contracts, and distant relatives claiming all that was rightfully his was theirs. At least now he knew his tender spot for Lucy was one issue over which he needn't worry.

"Thank you for understanding," she said, pressing her lips to his. "I hope I'm not being slutty in admitting this, but—"

Now he was coughing. "Honestly, Luce, where do you come up with these unseemly terms?"

"Sorry. Guess I should've said something more along the lines of *forward*. But as melodramatic as this may sound, sometimes I think you're quite possibly the only appealing thing in my life."

If that were indeed the case, then why all of the sudden did her eyes well with tears and lips faintly tremble? "Judging by your expression," he said, "I'm not entirely sure this is a good thing."

Through her misty, unfathomable expression, she smiled, easing his doubt-filled heart. "Trust me, my lord," she said in a butchered Old English accent. " 'Tis a good thing. A very good thing indeed."

# Chapter Five

After William set off whistling across the moonlit lawn, Lucy closed the door to her cottage, then leaned against it, kicking first one red rubber mule, then the other, across the cramped mudroom before rubbing her face with her hands.

What a disaster this night had been!

And yet on the other hand, what a delight!

In spite of her close call with the prince, William had all but admitted he loved her.

Even better, she thought, creeping her way through the silent house and into the living room, the fire had faded to glowing embers, and thankfully, so had the prince—not that he was dead and glowing, but . . .

Exhausted, Lucy collapsed onto the sofa.

Even if no one else in their right mind would understand what she was trying to get at, she did. Bottom line, William still loved her and the prince seemed to be well and truly gone, and to that she mumbled, "Good riddance."

The man was a menace—not just to her body, but her soul.

In him, she sensed all things wild and forbidden.

Her most secret wishes.

Wholly wicked hopes and desires.

But the part of her life wherein she'd allowed herself such fantasies of all-consuming loves and career successes was over. Her dreams of becoming a world-renowned biologist, or of ever earning her father's professional respect had long since faded.

Now, she had different dreams.

Simpler.

Dreams of home, hearth and family that weren't wrong—just unfamiliar in the wake of dreams long since past. She no longer sought thrilling passion, but easy contentment. And she was fine with that.

Now was the time for her to buckle down.

To marry a good and true man like William who wasn't handsome in a rugged, intoxicating way, but in a gentle, family-man way. William was the kind of man who'd stick by her in times of crisis. Who'd always ensure she never went to bed hungry or wanting for warmth or shelter.

The prince on the other hand, was the kind of man who'd make love til they both ran on little but pure desire. He'd see no need for secure havens when he lived on the exposed planes of carnal peaks.

Leaning her head against the downy sofa back, she sighed, and on her next breath, inhaled him. The prince. His musky, bold, utterly intoxicating flavor that in the breadth of a single raging heartbeat turned Lucy into a liar.

He was gone.

And that upset her more than if she'd returned home to find him still there. Which was wrong! She loved William. He was good and decent and everything she was looking for in not just a man, but a husband. A best friend. A lifelong partner with whom she planned to share babies and christenings and weddings and funerals.

Ha! The only thing she'd shared with the prince was frustration. So far the man had brought her nothing but angst and embarrassment so keen it was akin to pain.

Still, she crept her fingers to the rose-colored satin throw pillow the prince had so unwillingly rested his head upon.

Though her fingertips smoothed cool satin, her mind recalled his chest. Hot. Coarse with thick black hairs that reminded her she was all tender woman and he was all virile man.

Swallowing hard, fingers slightly trembling, she eased the pillow to her face, breathing him in. The pond. Damp, musky earth. Hundreds upon hundreds of years worth of primal instinct, shattering her with crying need.

No.

The prince was gone.

She loved William. She would always love William. He understood her. Accepted her in ways no one before him ever had. And lord, how she appreciated that. She appreciated that, and she'd return the favor with heartfelt loyalty.

All of this nonsense about the prince was just that—nonsense. Not only because he'd probably been nothing more than a vagabond vagrant, but because he was gone.

After fluffing the satin pillow, she nestled it just so in the corner of the sofa where it belonged, then pushed herself to her feet, locking up and turning out lights.

When she'd dowsed all illumination but the lamp at the bottom of the stairs, Lucy trudged to the cottage's second floor. All she needed was a good night's rest, and all of this unpleasantness would fade like a bad dream.

She'd feel fresh as a daisy.

Sunshine fresh.

Great. She sounded like a douche commercial!

Rounding the corner to her bedroom, she flicked on the overhead light, drinking in the peaceful garden of her room.

White-washed walls made way for a wildflower-strewn down comforter. Cornflower blue asters and yellow daisies lived happily amongst the faint blue stripes and gingham of ruffled curtains and hand-painted, two-drawer nightstands on either side of her bed.

One thing Lucy loved about being single was that she could decorate all of her rooms as girly-girl as she pleased. When she and the duke one day married, she supposed she'd have to tone down her penchant for floral chintz, but until then, she saw no need to bend to anyone's decorating tastes other than her own.

The duke ran in pretty lofty social circles. Wonder if he knew any offspring of the late, great, Laura Ashley? And if so, would they give him a wedding discount?

Lucy wound her way to the bathroom, flicking on that light only to gasp.

Sprawled in her oversized tub, dead to the world, was the great big prince—still naked.

And still packing—not that she looked!

Her first instinct was to not just wake him, but hurl a shampoo bottle at him, screaming at him to once and for all vanish from her life. But then she paused to look at him—really look at him, and saw that in his sleep, he'd traded his commanding presence for an air of surprising vulnerability.

His lidded eyes were shadowed and ringed from, she presumed, lack of sleep. He'd settled his strong lips into a grim line, causing his crudely shaved features to read exhaustion laced with physical pain. His shoulders were so broad, they almost filled the whole width of the tub, and his long, lean legs hung over the opposite end. Even more disturbing, were the scars—almost too many to count, and each one more savagely healed than the next.

She'd noticed them earlier, but maybe the rain, the dark, or the mental effort it'd taken to keep up with his barrage of sexual banter had kept her from realizing the full extent of his previous injuries.

Whatever the case, if the man ever suffered from cash flow issues, he really ought to sue whoever'd stitched him up.

Across his chest, he wore three long slashes—each a good twelve inches in length or more. The top two were the worst. They formed a crude, elongated X centering near his right nipple. The third crossed his abdomen with such cruelty that tears caught at the back of Lucy's throat.

In this day and age, what could have caused such a

mark? Gang warfare? A motorcycle wreck? Horrific abuse as a child?

She swiped at a few renegade tears, sweeping her gaze politely past the dark thatch between his legs to incredibly muscular thighs. But even as splendid as they were, they, too, weren't without marks. Crosshatches of angry red tattooed them, and still more marred his shins. Even his feet bore witness to past pain both with scars and the fact that he was missing the tip of his right little toe.

A wave of nausea crashed through her just imagining the kind of pain he'd suffered through. No wonder he had such an indefatigable spirit. He'd had to have it just to survive.

Once again sweeping her gaze upward, she saw that his arms, too, were not without scars. And now that he'd shaved and was in brighter light, she could even make out a few etched onto his angular face. One ran beneath his right eye, another slashed across the foot of his chin, and yet another across his right cheek.

His lips twitched.

Touching her own still sensitive lips, Lucy willed them to stop tingling from the all too recent memory of their kiss. A savage kiss that'd been nothing like the honeyed sweetness of William's.

Pulse surging, Lucy fell to her knees on the thick white rug in front of the tub.

Fingertips burning with a crazy yearning to comfort and soothe, she reached for the prince's chest, tracing one bumpy red half of the scarred X, then the other. Initially, his skin felt cool, but then beneath her palm grew warm, so warm.

On an altogether different level, his spirit had warmed, too. In sleep, he was different than he'd been before. His vulnerability made him approachable.

If she were truly a good girl, she should've given him his privacy. She should've been put off by his continued lack of cover. But either she'd grown used to it, or she no longer cared. Maybe in the moment, she wasn't a good girl, but a curious girl.

A hungry girl.

A girl who no longer wanted to be a girl, but a full-fledged woman being ridden hard by a full-fledged man.

*No, no, no!*

Lucy's hands flew to her flaming cheeks. What had gotten into her? This was lunacy!

Right this very second she should be on the phone with the police. She should be running for William, and the safety found within the circle of his arms.

Yes, that's what she *should* be doing, but then she looked at the prince again, only to be hypnotized by his sheer masculine beauty.

His angles and planes, and inky dark hair gleaming with tepid water. Suddenly, she no longer wanted safety, but to be back in the New Guinea jungle—only not by herself, but with a thrilling enigma like him. Living life fully. On the edge. Anticipating that just around the next campnosperma tree awaited her next miracle in the form of her very own frog.

Today, she thought she'd had that, but turns out that castle lane frog must've only been a dream.

And if that were true, what did that say about the prince? Was he a dream, too? His chest rose and fell with a mortal enough pace, but then so had the frog's, and he was long gone.

Heart pounding, Lucy licked her lips before easing her trembling hand toward the prince's forehead. A lock of his hair had spilled over his right eye, and she wanted it gone. She wanted to see all of him. Feel all of him.

Know him as only a lover would.

*No!*

*Oh, yes . . .*

Slowly, slowly, almost there, she crept her hand still closer, fearing her heart's hammer would surely alert him to her presence. But on he slept, his chest rose and fell, rose and fell, and she was almost there. Close enough for his radiant heat to vibrate and hum beneath her sweating palm. Almost there, close enough for her conscience to cry, *turn back now,* while her heart cried equally loud to forge full speed ahead.

Following her heart, she slipped one yearning, burning fingertip beneath his inky black—

"Arrrrrgh!" the prince yelled, fierce as any battle cry. "Ye'll not be killin' me!" Merciless hands gripping her wrists, in one incredibly strong, fluid motion, he vaulted her over the side of the tub, landing her with a great splash—and even greater scream—atop him.

# Chapter Six

Wolfe might have been trapped in a frog's body for a millennium, but one thing he'd never forget was how many men would stop at nothing—even murder—to keep him from one day wearing the kingdom of Gwyneddor's crown. For a damned intolerable row of minutes, he'd lain in the wench's bathing pool awake, aware, awaiting her to declare her intentions. But finally, when she'd gone for his head, he'd had enough of her explorations.

"Well?" he said, finding her ripe curves infinitely more appealing wet and crushed to the length of him. "Is this the truth of it then? You keep refusing to bed me because your true intent is to off me?"

"*Off* you?" she asked, sky blue eyes perilously wide, and not looking the least bit murderous. "As in finally be rid of? Wouldn't that be a relief!"

He tightened his hold, in the process, molding her full breasts to his chest. Even through the heavy wool of her sweater, her swollen peaks of desire were only too obvious to a lover as experienced as he.

"Ahh . . ." Bearing his broadest plunderer's grin, ignoring the rising pressure in his groin, he said, "Now I've come to the true crux of the matter. You've not been wanting to off me, but to bed me."

"I have not!"

"Don't even try denying it, wee one. I know of which I speak." His booming laugh splashed water onto the hard white floor.

"You obviously know nothing," she said, putting renewed vigor into her squirm. "Or else you'd know the extent to which I despise you!"

"Aye," he said, exerting only a fraction of energy to hold her firmly to his chest. "Which explains why your buds are once again calling. Begging to be taken into my mouth."

"Has anyone ever told you what a despicable rogue you are?"

"More often than not, I've heard it from the women of those I've conquered." Skimming his fingers through her sopping red curls, he added, "They tell me at the moment they cry out their womanly pleasure—with my manhood deep within. They tell me with tears in their eyes—not tears of pain, but joy, at having finally learned what it is like to be loved not by pathetic infidels such as the husbands they'd been forced to marry, but by a true and noble warrior like myself. A man as at home on the battlefield as in a bed."

At that, the fiery wench spat at his right eye, but her aim was off, and the warm spittle landed on his cheek. Holding her firm with one arm, he calmly wiped her juices away with his other hand. "Wish to exchange bodily fluids, do you?"

"No! I wish you to set me free." This time when she pushed against him, he released his hold, and the thrust of her own momentum sent her sailing to the rear of the tub, settling with a splash between his spread legs.

"As you wish," he said, once again struck with mirth. "Or perhaps this is what you've truly wished from the start—for you to be the aggressor."

"I thought I was attracted to you," she said from between ground teeth, nostrils flared. "But after this show of brute force, I see I was wrong." Pushing herself from the tub with a great whoosh of water, she continued on with, "You're, you're—"

"Come on," he taunted, sitting upright. "Dazzle me with your worst. I can take it. Lord knows I've dealt with far more dangerous women than you."

Dripping bathwater across the room on her way to get a drying cloth, the wench said, "Is that supposed to frighten me? Make me cower? Because I'll tell you right now, I'm not afraid of you."

"You should be." He rose, too, and in the elevated height of the tub, he stood two heads taller than her.

"Why?" she said, not even glancing his direction while patting her hair. "Because you're bigger than me? Because you're quite obviously off your rocker?"

He stepped over the edge of the tub, slowly walking her way, uncaring of the rivers streaming down his chest and thighs, only caring about making this woman understand the type of man she was dealing with. For over a millennium, he'd been trapped in that wretched bugger's green body, and now that he was free, he damned well intended to stay free—no matter the cost.

No matter who stood in his way.

First, last, and always, he was the Prince of Gwyneddor. Future King. He owed his family a millennium of debts for not being there at their time of need, and he'd damn well see those repaid as well.

Standing before the brave wee wench, he tucked his hand beneath her chin, raising her gaze to lock with his own. "You should be afraid of me," he said, voice lethally low, "for one very simple reason."

"And that would be?" she asked, tone mocking.

"Because as my now long-dead enemies would have you know, I'm dangerous when crossed."

"Who said I was crossing you? I merely want you out of my cottage."

"And as soon as you declare your eternal love, you shall have your wish."

"My love?" She made a quite disrespectful, not to mention unseemly, snort, before wrenching herself free of his hold. "Believe you me, mister, that's one thing you'll never get."

"You, believe me, wench—all women are helpless to my appeal, which is why I was sentenced to such a fate."

"Oh, and what fate was that?" she asked with another laughing snort. "For all eternity acting like a royal jackass?"

He scrunched his face. "While I am familiar with many of your modern terms, that one, I am not."

She rolled her eyes. "It means you're a jerk. A cad. A scoundrel—no . . ." Nibbling her lower lip, she added, "Scoundrel implies a redeeming appeal. You, sir, are just a plain, old garden-variety thug."

"I don't know that one, either."

"Trust me," she said, turning her back on him and sloshing out of the room, "It's not a good thing."

He followed her, finding her clutching the front of a squat dresser for balance while tugging off very wet, very orange socks. "Do you need assistance in removing your wet garments?"

"No, thank you." Ah, she'd reverted to once again speaking from between clenched teeth.

" 'Tis customary for a true gentleman to assist a lady in disrobing before climbing into their bed."

"But I'm not getting into *my* bed—just taking off these freakin' wet socks."

"Freakin'. Another new word. This evening is turning out to be remarkably educational."

Her grin oozed malice. "So glad my misery could entertain you. Do you mind?" she asked, eyeing the pool of dripping water he stood in.

"Mind what?"

"Drying off?"

"I nearly am."

"Well, as a special favor to me, your landlady—please, finish the job."

"Forgive me, fair maiden," he said with a deep bow. "In over a thousand years spent wet and unclothed, I'm afraid I've grown quite accustomed to my current state."

"Wet and naked?" She lifted delicately arched eyebrows he hadn't before noticed to be the most unique shade of russet blond. Nicely done. The wench had grown twin arches of gold above her eyes purely for his amusement.

"Ah, precisely," he said, forcing himself to look away.

"What?" She glanced down at her own dripping mess.

Had she noticed the cloth's seductive cling? How the drape of pumpkin-colored wool clung to her ample breasts with the skill of a lover's hands? And how the blue leggings so many women of her time were fond of wearing hugged her buttocks, thighs and calves with such practiced skill that a tightening stirred his groin, threatening to reveal his innermost thoughts in a most inconvenient way?

Taking deep breaths, he willed his member down.

Weakness was not an option. And at the moment, losing control of the very center of his power was not an advisable course.

"Haven't you ever seen a drowned rat?" she asked.

He clenched his fists, envisioning a most unpleasant stinking and bloated rat he'd encountered two days earlier at his pond. There, now he was back in control. After consuming an obscene quantity of air, he said, "I assure you, madam, you look anything but the part of a deceased rodent."

Her cheeks blushed charming pale pink that highlighted her freckles. When he bedded her, right then and there he vowed to kiss every one of those lovely marks. But until then, he was back to envisioning his rat!

"Um, thanks," she said, looking down, then up, then finally tucking swirling damp curls behind her ears. "I think."

"You doubt my sincerity?"

"Among other things." She brought the drying cloth to her face, dabbing at a rivulet of water cascading down her cheek.

"Please, allow me," he said, crossing the short distance between them to take the drying cloth from her slim hand. Their fingers brushed, flushing her cheeks. Much as he'd seen teenaged lovers do at the pond, he pressed the cloth to her damp hair.

She arched her head back and the simple motion highlighted the lyrical arch of her neck. Wolfe's breath caught in his throat.

How did the wench manage to be a spitfire one moment and a temptress the next?

"Th-thanks," she said, placing her hand atop his. "But I can manage."

Her warm touch railed through him. What had the wench done? Never had he felt such a keen lack of control. Gently sliding her hand off of his, then resuming his entirely-too-pleasant task, he said, "I don't recall thinking you couldn't manage, only that I wished to sample the texture of your hair."

"Oh."

He skimmed the cloth down her spiraling tresses, stopping at the ends to transfer the excess water from her hair into the amazingly absorbent fabric. One fair day maybe twenty or thirty years' past, Wolfe had seen a lad doing this for his lady love and she'd closed her eyes from the simple pleasure. Was his wench doing that now?

Standing behind her as he was, he saw her face naught but in his head, and thus imagined her eyes closed, full lips softy parted, revealing the mere tip of her tongue.

Having done all he could with her hair, he moved the cloth to her back, pressing it against her pleasingly plump behind in firm, yet gentle strokes. Her breath hitched, and she once again placed her hands on him, only this time, spun around to face him.

Lucy closed her eyes for an instant while dragging in a breath.

Dear lord!

The man might turn out to be nothing more than an escapee from a London loony bin, but he sure had some potent moves! "I, um, think I should take it from here."

"Why? Have I done a poor job?"

She swallowed hard. "No, it's just that . . ."

"You need to further remove your sodden things?"

"Yes."

"Fine. I shall assist in that process, as well." He reached for the hem of her sweater, and she wrapped her fingers round his wrist, gasping when the backside of his hand hotly grazed her belly's chilled skin.

"Really," she said, "I can do it." And to prove it, knowing full well the comfy sports bra she wore covered more than many of her friends' skimpy bikinis, she took one safe step back, and then another, then gripped the sweater's hem and gave it a good tug. Only with it wet and sucking her skin as if the damned thing had lips, it barely budged! "Um . . ." stuck with it half off, half on, she mumbled, "Do you think you might, ah . . ."

In a heartbeat he was there, sweeping it over her head, the backs of his hands hotly grazing the sides of her full breasts, shocking her even through the Lycra/cotton blend of her bra.

"Whew," he said, finally tugging it over her head, "I was afraid you might be stricken dead from lack of air, and then where would I be?"

*Back at the asylum?*

An apologetic wave washed through her. Even if she hadn't spoken her thoughts aloud, they had still been cruel, especially in light of the fact that she very well could have suffocated in that sweater! Or at the very least suffered a nasty sprain! Maybe the lesson in this was that she should try a different course. Maybe help him instead of ridiculing him. "Where do you live?"

"Live?" His eyebrows rose. "Why, here, of course. Not as in this house, but I've never ventured far from the Kingdom of Gwyneddor my whole life long."

Wrinkling her nose, unbuttoning her jeans, she said, "I meant before you came here."

"Are you daft?" he said, eyeing her now unzipped jeans, and, she presumed, the hot pink vee of cotton panties she'd just revealed.

"No," she said, eyeing him eyeing her, then marching into the bathroom and closing the door. "Just concerned that your family may be worried about you. You know, wondering where you are."

Just on the other side of the door, he said, "The time for them to wonder has long since passed."

"Meaning you've called them?" Shimmying her jeans and panties off, she left them in a joined ball on the bathroom floor, then reached for the rear clasp on her bra. The ceremonial freeing of her breasts was always a high point in her day, but now, especially so, after having been damp—or downright soaked—for most of the night.

"That also would be hard to do."

Knowing he stood naked just on the other side of the door, and she stood naked a mere twelve inches and strip of wood away from him, put a brave new spin on the word *awkward*. Searching, searching for something to put on, she grabbed a towel, but as luck would have it, it was the one in fifteen sizes too small to wrap all the way around her perkies.

She flung the stupid rogue towel, vowing to later trash it, then began her search anew, thankfully sighting her terry cloth robe with its cottony cloud motif and half-moons, and jumping cows, goats and sheep, forlornly hanging half-in/half-out of the hamper.

Jerking it free, she slipped it on, knotted the matching belt at her waist, then noticed the ugly splotch of brown dribbles. Dried cocoa from when she'd scalded her tongue, then jumped and then dumped practically the whole cup over a cow jumping over the moon. Her scalded left boob hurt just thinking of the incident!

She frowned.

Good grief. It wasn't that she particularly wanted to look cute for the guy, but on the other hand, who wanted to come off like a cocoa-drizzling frump?

"Are you all right in there? If you find yourself in need of additional assistance, I'd be only too pleased to help."

*I'm sure you would!*

"I'm fine. Just, um, freshening up." After giving herself a good conk on the head for yet again sounding like a cornball douche commercial, Lucy tucked her still damp hair behind her ears, licked her lips, took a nice, deep, fortifying breath, then opened the bathroom door. "There," she said. "That feels much better."

The prince all but snarled. "You look akin to a raw pile of fibers having yet to be spun." Shaking his head, while gripping her shoulders and spinning her about, he gave her a light shove back toward the bathroom. "No. This new ensemble simply will not do. Put the other back on. At least it had shape enough that I could tell your gender."

"Now, look," Lucy said, spinning right back around. "I've had just about enough of what you will and will not do, and what you like and don't like. Lest you've forgotten, might I remind you, mister, that you're a guest in this house? A guest I wouldn't mind tossing out on his egotistical ass!"

"Ass. Finally, a downput I understand." Appearing bored by her speech, he crossed his arms and quite blandly said, "When you've finished your tirade, kindly bring me refreshment before we bed. It's been quite some time since I've taken nourishment, and while I am renowned for my stamina, a man does need occasional sustenance to be at the peak of his performance."

"Certainly, Your Majesty." Grasping the sides of her robe, she lifted them as she curtsied. "Anything else you'll be needin' sir, before I toss you out on your royal behind?"

"There is one thing," he said, lips curving into a wickedly handsome grin.

Lucy gulped, vowing no matter how handsome he *looked* to never forget his obnoxious *acts*! "And that would be?"

"This." Before she could even guess what his cryptic declaration might mean, he was showing her. Pulling her none too gently into his arms, settling his meaty hands about her waist, he lowered his mouth, at first crushing, then softly, pliably, deliciously molding his lips to hers.

While she knew it was madness to stand here in her bedroom kissing not only a stranger, but an out-of-his-mind naked stranger, Lucy melted in his arms.

Much as she hated the thought of him being right about his magnetism, he was! She could no more resist him than a pound of Godiva chocolate—speaking of which, was Mr. Godiva English, and if so, did the duke get a discount from him? And see? How could she think of the duke at a time like this? And she hadn't even really thought of him, just in terms of wondering who he knew, so she could get ahold of some purely medicinal chocolate!

Aw, hell, who was she kidding?

With this guy kissing her, who needed chocolate?

But then he was slipping his strong, massaging fingers under the fall of her damp hair, and she fell powerless to think about anything other than the bold strokes of his tongue, and how he tasted faintly, sweetly of tomatoes, and how the cad must've eaten her leftover spaghetti, and she didn't really care because it tasted much better on him than it ever had on her.

"Ready, wee one?"

Wee? He thought her wee?

Dear lord, he was a great kisser *and* didn't think she could stand to lose twenty pounds?

Ding, ding, ding! We have a winner!

"Mmm-hmm," she said on a moan.

As if she weighed no more than one of her beloved MoonPies, with excruciating gentleness, he lifted her into his arms, then kissed her again.

This time, his kiss, given through the merest hint of a smile, was teasing, and all at once soft, yet hard, thrilling, yet enchanting. How did he do it? Make her feel like she was the only woman in the world he'd ever taken into his arms?

He deepened their union yet again, plundering her

soft mouth with his bold tongue, stroking her with rhythm old as time. "Jesu, woman, I've waited so long."

"Mmm-hmm . . ." she whispered, his lips still hovering above hers, his unfathomably dark gaze holding her captive.

Never releasing her stare, he backed a short ways, placed her on the dreamy cloud of her down comforter and then he lowered himself atop her. Then he was kissing her again, kissing her hard-soft-dizzy, nuzzling the upper vee of her robe open, raining still more kisses all along her collarbone and the base of her throat.

She arched her neck to him, inviting him closer while at the same time instinctively lifting her hips to meet the rod of steel bearing down.

With his knee, he parted her robe's lower slit, and then the soft, smooth heat of her legs met with the coarse, cool muscle of his. Calf to calf. Thigh to thigh. Just the tip of him grazing the humming heat between her open legs, he slid partially off of her, easing one of his rough, strong hands low. Gripping the hot, sweating flesh of her upper thigh, then sliding it down.

Out of her mind with thrilling, forbidden heat, she tossed her head to and fro on the pillow when he urged her legs spread wider, and stroked his finger through her dewy need. And then with his other hand cradling her head, he was once again kissing her, mimicking his actions down low, sweetly urging her mouth open with his tongue, then stroking her into a frenzied need.

Lower, much lower, past her swollen, aching breasts, past the tight knot of anticipation in her belly, past still the neatly manicured thatch of red hair between her legs, he stroked her wet, until she was opening herself wider still. Wanting more, needing more, demanding more, and he was obliging, sliding in one finger, then two, priming her, promising her with each masterful stroke that there was something more, so much more yet to come.

"I want all of you," he said, his breath steaming her upper lip.

"Mmm-hmm . . ." she said with a dazed nod.

He fiddled with the knot at her waist, but couldn't work it free. "Argh!" he said with a frustrated roar. "Help me, wench!"

*Wench?*

Wench!

Dear lord, what was she doing? As if dragging herself from a deep dream of insanity, Lucy shook her head, then, elbows braced on the mattress, scooted herself up in the bed. The prince was still hard at work on her robe, but she gently pushed him away.

Still breathing hard, she summoned the courage to say, "No."

Glancing up, he tumbled her heart with the smile of a plundering rogue. "You're right. I'll use a dagger instead of my hands. 'Twill ruin your garment, but that's good, as it doesn't suit you anyway."

Grinning at the kind of logic only he would dream up, Lucy rested her hand on his shoulder. "No, I meant no, as in this isn't going to work."

"I know, are ye daft? I just said that. Wait here, while I scour your scullery for a knife."

"No," she said with another shake of her head, crossing her legs, then tucking the now joined halves of her robe firmly between them. She clutched the upper half of the oversized garment discreetly closed as

71

well, then said, "I can't—*won't*—have sex with you. While your performance just now was everything you'd promised and more, I don't normally—hell, *ever*—do those kinds of things unless I'm with a man I love. A man like the duke."

"I thought we'd been over this?" High, proud forehead furrowed, the prince said, "You, bedding me, is a good thing for all parties. If it pleases the duke, from behind discreet cover, he may even watch to insure himself no acts beyond the realm of normalcy are performed."

Covering her face with her hands, Lucy sat even straighter and drew her knees to her chest.

He drew her hands down. " 'Tis obvious by your manner of speech, that you are not from these parts. Therefore, it is my duty to inform you yet again, that as I am a prince, it is customary for you not to cover your gaze while I am speaking—even that damned sorceress who cursed me knew better than that."

"Cursed you?"

For a moment, he looked at her with pure incredulity, then broke into another of his great, booming laughs.

Staring at him, eyes wide with amazement at his acting ability, Lucy slowly shook her head. "Who are you?"

"Forgive me, milady, for this inexcusable social faux pas." Pinning her to her pillows with nothing more than his dark-eyed stare, he gently lifted her hand to his lips, gracing it with a simple kiss. "I am the prince. Prince Wolfe Graye of the undefeatable Kingdom of Gwyneddor."

# Chapter Seven

*Gwyneddor . . . Gwyneddor . . .*

Why did that name sound familiar?

Possibly because Gwynedd had been one of the earliest kingdoms of Wales. But then that was easily enough discovered in any good tourist shop.

As the prince scooted her legs over, then eased onto the bed beside her, she said, "Tell me more about this supposed curse business." Not that she wanted to know, but maybe if he opened up a little she'd at least figure out how to contact his family.

"Certainly," he said with a formal bow of his head. "First, however, I must preface your request by explaining that for quite some time, I've watched you on your occasional visits to my pond."

She gulped.

Oh boy. Here we go, straight to stalker city!

"Wipe that stricken look from your comely face, wench. Believe me, when I'm courting a woman—she damned well knows! But it's rather difficult to court someone lovely as you while in the body of a loathsome frog."

"A-a frog?"

He sighed. "Sometime during what I presume you would call the mid-ninth century—" Hand to his forehead he grimaced. "Forgive me for not knowing a more precise time, but after having spent the past thousand years and more as an amphibian, I no longer have a head for dates."

"You're quite forgiven," Lucy said. Should she grab a pen and paper? This guy was really something. He'd make a fortune as a novelist!

"As I was saying, over the years, I'd pretty much accepted that I was to forever be trapped in a wretched little bugger's body—until, a number of years back, I saw you." Gaze focused on something so far off she knew it couldn't be found within the room, he said, "You had a certain quality about you. A determined sadness as you stared into the water. I saw you handle one of my green compatriots with the most exquisitely gentle touch, and wondered what it might feel like to have you examine me in such a way."

She leaned forward. "You mean, you saw me handling frogs?"

"Yes. That's exactly what I mean. Are you deaf?"

Scowling, she said, "You don't have to get snippy."

"Snippy. Hmm, yet one more word for my ever-growing vocabulary. Back to my tale, I used to see you wearing the most unflattering black boots made from a peculiar substance I had no prior experience with. And you'd carry a notebook, and sometimes sketch insects and flowers, or larger scenes of the changing seasons."

Lucy's heart skipped a beat.

How could he know that? How could he possibly know all of that unless he had been stalking her not for days, but years? Clutching the collar of her robe even tighter, she leaned into her pillows, farther away from him.

"I'd hear you softly singing. Ghastly songs. Nothing at all like the lyrical clochetes I prefer. Anyway, suffice to say, in you, I sensed a kind soul. One who could quite possibly be my savior. I took to following you, but your long legs were no match for mine—even if I do admit to being quite the jumper."

A hot queasy rush seized Lucy's stomach, and her pulse surged. She had to escape, but how? The man truly was certifiable.

"It took me half the day to hop to the castle lane just to watch for your conveyance. I'd always meant to meet you at the pond, but you haven't been in a long while. With the moon new, I—"

"I-I've been busy. You know, work." *Besides, obviously it's high time I forget my work with frogs. I'm on the verge of becoming a real live duchess, and duchesses do not kiss frogs!*

"Of course," he said, gracing her with another formal bow of his head. "Back to my woeful tale—back at the true start, I'd just been handed false news of my having planted another of my seeds within a fertile womb when the sorceress struck. I still have no concept of her quarrel with me. While I may not have married my babes' mums, I always gave all parties concerned ample coin. No child of mine ever went hungry or unclothed! But by God, a fact any man of my station knows is that

75

he does not marry for ample bosom and hips, but ample quantities of land and jewels."

"Oh—of course," Lucy said, searching frantically for a weapon. Could she bludgeon the man to death with a paperback?

"Well, having grown up in a fine castle full of men who raised me from the time I was but a lad to this high standard of beliefs, you can understand my surprise when the sorceress consulted by my father, the king, as to the timing of his battles turned out not to like my views. 'Course, at the time, I'd just refused to marry her lovely daughter—a comely, fiery-tempered wench who'd stirred my loins like no other until meeting you."

*A box of tissues!*

Yeah, that'd stop him cold. Those sharp corners would definitely draw blood!

"Well, even though I was immensely taken with Desdemona, I knew I couldn't marry her. She had naught to offer my kingdom but a tempting smile and petal-soft skin." He snorted. "Fine lot of good those'd do me when next we needed funds for battle!"

"Fine lot of good, indeed."

*Fingernail clippers!*

Nah, the little pointy thing that slides out of the middle had long since broken off.

"That sorceress didn't much ken to my views, and she warned that if I didn't marry Desdemona, she'd cast powerful spells of famine and poverty upon the land. Well, I knew her to have visions of battle outcomes, but never did I think her that powerful a witch, so I mocked her. Telling her that if she was prepared to go that far, why not go one step further by transforming me into the loathsome pond creature she obviously believed me to be."

"And?"

*The alarm clock!*

Mickey Mouse's plastic ears were nothing to mess with. Shoot, Mickey was as fierce as it got—tantamount to calling out the Marines!

"And the next day I woke to find that I had indeed become just that. A loathsome frog so hideous in complexion that the other frogs wouldn't pay me the time of day. And that's it. For the past thousand and more years, I've hopped up and down the lane forever searching for a woman who'd declare her eternal love."

Leaning forward, Lucy saw an opportunity to catch him in his own convoluted story. "So, you're saying you've been right here, right on the duke's land for over a thousand years?"

"I just said it was so, did I not?"

"Sure, but I mean, if you've been hanging out all that time, then you must've seen some pretty amazing things."

"Aye. That I have."

"Okay, then, how do you explain the fact that for the most part, you speak like a modern-day man?"

Shrugging, he said, "I suppose because I've long been in the company of modern-day men—and women." He grinned. "I've picked up much of your language, and a passing knowledge of how most things in your time are done." Appraising the open vee of her robe she'd unintentionally let fall open during her search for weapons, he added, "And then there are some things— matters between a man and woman—that even in a thousand years more will never change."

Clutching her robe beneath her chin, she answered his bold statement with a forced giggle.

Skimming his hand beneath the hem of her robe and up her calf, he said, "You disagree?"

"No, not at all," she said, snatching her leg away from him, mortified to find her body reacting to his simple touch. "It's just that . . ." *I'd like to get back to kissing you! No, no, no!* "I mean, I'd like to get back to asking you more about your time. For instance, from what I've read, the first castles weren't built until 1050. So if you've been around as long as you say, you couldn't possibly have lived in a castle—let alone this one, which is supposed to have been built around 1240."

Eyes narrowed, he said, "Were you there to see it built?"

"No, but—"

"Then I suggest you drop the matter. Trust me. I was there."

"O-okay, then . . ." Looked like someone hadn't done his homework, and he was more than a little cranky at having been caught! "Tell me what Gwyneddor was like."

Arching his head back, he sighed, and an indescribable sadness darkened his proud features. "Ahh, my fair Gwyneddor. Where to begin . . ."

"You did well today, wee brother," Prince Rufus patted Wolfe's head as they mounted the five stone steps leading to the castle keep. Wolfe knew there were five because each morning Rufus made him mount them in a grueling series of trials he claimed would make legs strong and mind agile. More than anything, Wolfe wanted to be like his brother Rufus, who, during times like these when their father had been called to battle, ruled all within their kingdom with what villagers called an unyielding hand joined with unparalleled justice. Just as his father was thought kind for allowing so many wenches work within the castle, Rufus was thought remarkable for his good humor toward all—save his enemies who feared him like pox. "Keep up this level of training," he said, "and before you reach your tenth year, you'll be riding alongside father's strongest warriors in battle."

"You think?" Wolfe said, skipping ahead of his brother, then whirling about to face him. "And will I get my own armor and broadsword, and get turns at the springald?"

"Aye," Rufus said with an affectionate rub to his back. "But first," he said, snatching an apple from a wooden bowl, "we must get nourishment into that scrawny belly of yours and learning into your head."

Wolfe's lips fell to a pout. "I don't like learning. At the monastery they said I have the concentration of a trout." Gazing up at his adored older brother, Wolfe asked, "Is that a bad thing?"

"Nay." Rufus grinned, giving Wolfe another affectionate rub. " 'Tis a most splendid thing indeed, for fish are swift, fearsome creatures."

"Fish are not fearsome."

"Ahh, then you've never seen a razor-toothed giant of a fish washed upon the shore."

"There's no such thing!"

"What? A razor-toothed fish, or shore?" Rufus winked before offering Wolfe a bite of his apple, which he happily accepted, opening his mouth wide as it could possibly go, which much to his great disappointment didn't come near the size of his brother's.

Determined to equal Rufus in something far greater than his bite, Wolfe trailed after him into the castle kitchen.

"Ahh," Rufus said with a teasing smile. "I've wondered where all the fairest wenches had slipped off to." After lobbing his apple core to Honey, Wolfe's hound that presently lounged in a strip of golden afternoon sun, Rufus slipped his arm around Cook's ample waist, kissing her boldly on her weathered cheek. She shrieked and made a great show of smacking him on his behind with a wooden spoon, but Wolfe hadn't missed the sparkle in her eyes or ill-concealed mirth in her scolding.

"If'n you plan on keeping those handsome lips of yourn, young Prince, you'd best be keepin' them to yourself, or else I'll be tossen' them into my pot for supper."

"And thus deprive yourself of my many pleasures?" Rufus teased, all the while deftly snatching a strip of dried venison right out from under her, then kissing the hands of her two blushing helpers before moving on to the big-bosomed serving wench Wolfe had oftentimes seen his brother making grunting sounds over in the knoll behind the pond. At the time, Wolfe had thought the pair looked an awful lot like rutting hounds, but after the act, when Rufus had lain beside her, stroking her prettily flushed cheeks with a dandelion, Wolfe decided that this, as with all things his brother the prince did, must be good, for at least in Wolfe's eyes, Rufus was incapable of doing wrong.

"Shame," the girl said with a laughing shriek as Rufus nuzzled her neck.

"What?" Hands cinched about her waist, he leaned back and grinned. "How can there be shame in kissing beauty rare as yours?"

She tried slapping his roving hand with a cabbage leaf, but on her hand's downward path, Rufus caught her wrist, snagging a bite of cabbage, along with a nip of her finger.

"Off with you," Cook said while the serving wench giggled. "You, too," Cook said to Wolfe, slipping him a sugared piece of pastry.

Rufus clutched his hand to his chest, making a great show of being hurt.

When Wolfe laughed at his brother's antics, Rufus said, "You find me amusing, wee brother?" After winking to his wench, he lunged for Wolfe, sweeping him high, before tickling him low on his belly and ribs.

"Off! Off!" Cook shrieked over the merriment of all assembled. " 'Tis unseemly for the masters of this castle to carry on so."

"All right, then," Rufus said, setting Wolfe to his feet before easing his great arm about the boy's shoulders. "If Cook says we must behave, my brother, then it seems we have no choice but to await the delivery of our meal."

Rufus blew the ladies a final kiss before leading Wolfe to the great hall. Once they'd taken their seats, Rufus occupying their father's chair, while Wolfe sat beside him on a wood bench, Rufus said, "There are many kinds of education, little brother. And what you just witnessed was your first lesson on the fine art of diddling." Leaning closer, in a merry whisper, he added, "To be true, winning battles is a most satisfying pastime, but if you nay have warm breasts to rest your head upon after the battle has been won, 'tis no reason for you to fight in the first place."

Pretending he knew what his brother meant, Wolfe sagely nodded.

Outside, day faded to night, and inside, the great hall sprang to life. Tables were assembled along the walls, and a light meal of meat pie, eel and cheese was served. After which, a traveling acrobat amazed all present with his skill.

Rufus's mother, the king's first wife, had long since died. Sabina, Wolfe's mother, claimed herself afflicted with headache, and as such, hadn't left her solar to partake in the evening meal. A good thing in Wolfe's eyes! Not that he wanted his mother ill, but that meant he got to shift from his bench to her big chair beside his brother.

After the meal had been cleared, and tables and benches stored away, couples wandered into isolated corners where naught disturbed them but the fire's dancing orange glow. Aside from the occasional feminine giggles, manly grunts, or baying of a hound, the great hall had fallen silent.

This was Wolfe's favorite time of day, for it was then, sated by the weight of a good meal and drink, that his father and brother expounded on all nature of things, such as how to most efficiently spear a blade through one's enemy for a quick kill. Or how to best train a mighty horse for battle. Or scale an enemy's castle walls.

Just as Rufus launched into an exciting tale of conquering a particularly bloodthirsty lot of Scots, his favorite serving wench stepped behind him to refill his silver cup with wine—though many times in private Rufus had told Wolfe he preferred ale.

"Much thanks to thee," Rufus said with a bold wink, cupping his hand to her ample behind.

Giggling, clutching the jug to the deep valley between her breasts, she reddened before curtsying out of the room.

Wolfe practiced his brother's dashing wink, but found that the manipulation of his cheeks made his eyes hurt.

"Ah, wee Wolfe," Rufus said, easing back in his chair, stretching his long legs beneath the table. "She's a good girl. The best I've had in quite some time. 'Tis a good thing I've already been promised to Estrilda, for without that contract binding me, every wench I bed would be wanting to wed."

"Like Father and Mother?" Wolfe asked.

"Aye." Turning serious, Rufus said, "Don't ever forget, wee brother, that one of the most valuable weapons any man—or woman, for that matter—has, is choosing wisely when it comes to marriage. Your wife must be obedient, yet possess enough spirit to properly keep one's castle. She must be faithful, for if she is not, one can never truly know if any babes she carries within her womb are yours, or the woodward's."

Wolfe's eyes grew huge.

"A bad marriage can be very bad. I've heard tales of Viking kings being slaughtered in their sleep by wives not akin to their way of thinking. Or even trying to capture their husband's crown as their own. A good marriage, however—the kind that all kings and princes of Gwyneddor have had—gains more land and riches and respect than a hundred conquests. This is why gently courting the fairer sex is especially important."

After swigging more wine, Rufus said, "Take your mother, for instance. True, Father arranged his marriage to her, and in doing so, gained a fortune through her dowry. But to keep her, Father has had to gently woo her. And this goes beyond the giving of jewels and such. Just as one listens to one's partners in battle, one must also listen to his wife. Many do not prescribe to this theory, for they feel it opens them to potentially fatal wounds of forming emotional attachments, but I believe, as does our father, that emotional attachments make for the best of marriages, because a content woman makes for a content lot in life."

Thoroughly confused, Wolfe asked, "Do I have to kiss a girl to make a good marriage?"

"Nay," Rufus said, roaring with laughter. "But it sure helps pass cold nights."

"How? Wouldn't a pile of furs and fire in the hearth work better at keeping a body warm?"

"You're a bright boy, but still have much to learn on the ways of women. Come," he said, pushing himself to his feet, then gulping the remainder of his wine. "I should have long since sent you to bed, then joined my wench for a roll in the grass."

"To scratch your arse, like Honey, my hound?"

Rufus roared once more. "Bedding isn't about satisfying an itchy arse, but an itchy—" Ruffling Wolfe's hair, he said, "Ah, I'm well into my cups and no doubt sharing more than a lad of your tender age need know. Come," he said, holding out his large, calloused hand. "I'll see you to your bed, then it's off to the grasses for me."

They'd just reached the castle's upper level, when

Rufus paused beside Wolfe's mother's chamber.

"What's that noise she's making?" Wolfe asked. "Is she terribly ill?"

"Shh!"

Wolfe clamped his lips tight. When Rufus took that tone, he meant whatever order he'd commanded to be obeyed. Biting his lower lip, Wolfe prayed as his tutor had taught him that his mother would be all right—such was the frightening urgency behind her groans, and the rhythmic thumping going on behind the door.

Wolfe glanced at his brother. A thunderous scowl forced Rufus's eyebrows into the kind of glare he'd only seen the likes of the time Father had told him he couldn't ride with him into his latest battle.

"What's the matter with her?" Wolfe dared ask.

Instead of ruffling the hair on his head, Rufus gave it a sharp tug. "When I order you to hush, I full well expect you to obey."

Rufus had never spoken to him in such a manner. Fearing his mother must be gravely ill indeed, Wolfe cowered against the cold stone wall.

His brother tried the door, only to find it blocked. "Sabina! Unlatch this door at once."

His mother's moans, as did the thumping, stopped.

"Now!" Rufus thundered.

Seconds later, the door slowly creaked open, and Wolfe sneaked a peak at his mother who indeed appeared most ill. Her cheeks were flushed and normally smooth blond hair hung wild. Clutching her dark robe beneath her chin, she said, "What do you want? As you can plainly see, I'm not feeling my normal self."

"Do you think me daft?" he said, sweeping her aside to march into the chamber.

"Mother?" Wolfe said, clasping her right hand. "Shall I fetch Cook to make you one of her potions?"

Worrying her lower lip, she shook her head. Free hand cupping his cheek, she said, "Be a dear boy and run along to bed. Your brother knows better than to keep you up so late."

Rufus had paused before the massive oak-timbered bed, eyeing the crumpled linens with a deadly stare. Gaze narrowed, he sniffed the muggy air. "It smells of rutting in here. Where is he?"

Her gaze darted wildly. "I-I know not what you mean."

"Lying whore!"

Rufus's harsh tone made Wolfe and his mother jump. Why was he being so cruel? Couldn't he see she felt unwell?

"I'll ask once more. Where . . . is . . . he?"

Wolfe's mother shook her head. "Stop this. Not in front of the boy."

"And why not in front of the boy? You seemed to have no compulsions about committing acts treasonous to his father under the nose of your so-called boy. Pray tell it's time Wolfe learned the kind of unfaithful bitch you really are." Dagger in hand, Rufus knelt to peer under the bed. "He's not here," he said, once again to his feet. "Oh, but in so many subtle ways, Father assured me he would be."

"He knew?"

"Of course, he knew. Why else would he not send me into battle when his rightful place should have been dealing with matters of Gwyneddor? How else could he have learned the truth of your depravity?"

"I-I am not depraved. I have needs. Needs that your father could not answer."

"Whore!" Rufus yet again spat, flinging aside a bed curtain with the tip of his dagger's blade.

He next turned toward tall window tapestries—the only other hiding spot in the room. Wolfe had hidden there himself while playing on rainy days.

"I know your location," Rufus said. " 'Tis only a matter of time before I feel the beat of your traitorous heart against my palm." Rufus took another step closer, and another, and Wolfe looked from him to his wide-eyed mother.

When Rufus stood but a mere foot away, then jerked the curtain open, things happened too fast.

His mother screamed, "Leofwan! Watch out!"

Leofwan? Before Wolfe could comprehend the meaning of a man hiding in his mother's room, a tall, naked blond man roared out from the curtain's shield, wielding a mean dagger of his own, which he plunged into Rufus's heart, but not before Rufus plunged his knife as well.

In less than an eye blink, both men fell in a wordless tangle to the floor, each gripping the other's weapon.

Covering her gaping mouth with her hand, Wolfe's mother began to tremble, then screamed, "Nooooo! Nooooo!"

While Wolfe stood transfixed, barely registering the footfalls of a dozen or more servants scurrying up the stairs, he wondered why his mother wasn't seeing to Rufus. He was their family. He was the one they all loved.

The back of his throat felt tight, and though he was mightily afraid, Wolfe took one brave step, then another toward his brother, knowing if Rufus was to be saved, tonight—nay, this instant—he'd have to quit being a boy, and start being a man. Now running, heedless to the hot tears streaming from his eyes, he said, "I'll save you, Rufus. I'll save you."

"Hush!" his mother said, gripping his shoulders and giving him a violent shake. "You can't save him because he's dead. Dead! Do you hear me? Dead!" Turning once more to the blond man, she wept over him, trailing strands of her long blond hair into the fount of red, red blood bubbling from the man's wound.

"What in the—" Cook stopped at the solar's door, making the sign of the cross on her chest.

Rufus's favorite serving wench screamed.

And then came his father's men, Hamon, Godwin and Peter, all standing in the open door, mouths agape, watching Wolfe's mother weep over the body of a stranger.

But then she did an even stranger thing when she jerked Rufus's dagger from his chest, then slowly, regally, stood, facing all who had assembled.

"Ye'll be burnt for this," Cook said, crossing herself once more.

"Nay, the king'll have her head."

"Aye, her head."

Wolfe's mother shook her pale hair, untying the belt at her robe's waist. She opened it, and the crowd gasped. Holding her chin high, she slipped the robe over her shoulders, standing before them naked and proud. "Nay, your king will never have my life again," she spat. "He's stolen me once, but never again."

Cook dashed across the room to take Wolfe into her ample arms, covering his eyes with her hands.

But he saw. Oh, yes, he saw his mother stab the dagger into her own heart, then crumble atop the blond stranger.

Cook turned him away from the gruesome scene, pressing his face into her soft belly. "There, there," she said, stroking the back of his head. "We'll send Peter for your father and everything'll be okay."

But Wolfe already knew what had happened here in this chamber wasn't okay. It would never be okay. For his very best friend and mother were never coming back. And til the day he died, he'd sorely miss both.

# Chapter Eight

"Um, wow." Lucy forced back tears. "I don't know what to say."

"There's nothing to say. You asked of Gwyneddor, and I told you of one day in tens upon thousands that stands above all others." The look he cast her, far from being that of the wounded little boy from his tale, was that of a hardened warrior with neither the time nor energy to worry himself over matters of the heart. But if that were truly the case, then why had he chosen to share that story, when if even a fraction of what he'd said about the curse was true, he must have witnessed countless more historically significant events that would have been far less painful to recall?

"Just supposing what you said about that curse is true—and I'm just supposing here—then tell me who your father lost his crown to?"

"Rhodri Mawr—a good man, but never the equal of my father."

"Wait here," Lucy said, off to dig for her favorite

book on medieval Wales. Back, book in hand and finding his answer correct, she asked, "Who ruled after him? No, wait that's too easy. Who came two rulers later?"

He rolled his eyes. "Hywel Dda."

"What'd you think of Empress Matilda?"

"Not that I personally knew her, but I heard from the wenches bathing in the pond that the woman had a fearsome temper. Only ruled but a year, did she not?"

Lucy nodded. This was too much.

He could've easily learned every bit of this the same way she had—through books. The notion of his actually having been there was too fabulous to even comprehend.

Plus, he'd gotten his castle dates all wrong.

"What's sapping?"

"Dredging under a castle wall in the hopes of weakening it enough to force a topple."

"What kinds of fish did you commonly eat?"

"From our pond we took trout and pike."

"Did you use a fork?"

"Nay."

Frowning, she flipped a few pages back. "What's an anghenfil?"

"It's a terrific beast—and you're saying it wrong. Say it like this," he said, the word exotic and foreign-sounding when rolling off his practiced tongue.

"What did—"

"Enough!" the prince roared, pushing himself up from the bed to pace. "Believe me or don't, but don't sit there questioning me like I'm some half-wit child shipped off to the nearest monastery."

"I-I'm sorry," she said, taken aback by his flash of anger.

"As well you should be. I've been through quite an ordeal, yet all you dwell upon is your attempt to prove me a hurtyn."

Now it was Lucy's turn to stare blankly at him.

"What?" he said, in her face with an angry expression. "Have I stumbled upon a word not on your pages?"

She returned his hateful glare, then consulted her book, only to find that the word was there. And it meant idiot. Raising her chin, she said, "For all I know, you could very well be just that."

"Then you tell me," he said, "how I know which afternoons you're most likely to be at the pond, and what times I'm most likely to happen upon your carriage on the lane?"

Refusing to be intimidated by either his size or the intensity of his stare, she said, "All of that's easily enough explained. You've obviously been stalking me."

"Stalking?" He scratched his head. "Another of your damnedable new words."

"Oh, come on! Like you've never heard of stalking prey?" Clutching her robe around her neck, she stood, too, only she didn't just pace, but left the room.

"Where are you going?" he demanded, following her.

"To the kitchen. I have to stress-eat."

"What's that?"

"When a person eats and eats and eats because they don't know what else to do."

Powerful hand gripping her shoulder, he stopped her at the top of the stairs, spinning her to face him. "In other words, you wish to medicate your spirit?"

"Yep. That about sums it up." Wrenching free of his hold, she stormed down the stairs. The sound of his barreling footsteps told her he was still hot on her trail—like she'd thought for a second he'd leave her to eat in peace?

"Damnation!" he bellowed.

"What?" She paused on the bottom step, watching him rub his forehead. Must've nipped it on the low beam.

Too bad it hadn't knocked him out!

In the kitchen, she found little in the way of comfort food, and wound up settling for peanut butter and jam—not too bad considering peanut butter was one of those forbidden foods she normally tried steering clear of. But obviously everything about this situation was about as far from normal as life could get, which meant calories didn't count!

"Want a PB&J?" She'd turned to ask only to come face to face with the prince's rock-hard chest. Mouth dry, strangely out of breath, she added, "They're, um, really good."

"I know not of which you speak, but to insure you have no wish to poison me, I will only dine from the same plate as you."

"O-okay."

Under the prince's heavy stare, Lucy made a triple decker, figuring since she was having to share, that *really* voided the calorie count!

"Milk?" she asked, standing at the open fridge.

He blanched. "I'm accustomed to either wine or ale at mealtime."

"Tough. Round here, you get what you get and you don't pitch a fit."

Setting the carton on the table, she reached to a nearby open shelf for two glasses, but the prince circled the wrist of her right hand. "One mug will suffice. Again, if your goal is to off me, at least we'll both go together."

Plate and glass in hand on her way to the dining room, she asked, "At the asylum from whence you escaped, has your therapist worked with you on paranoia issues?"

"Para-noy-ya? I know not that word."

"Gee, why doesn't that surprise me?"

Seated on opposite sides of her small dining room table, Lucy thought she was safe, then she stretched out her bare feet and legs, only to collide with Wolfe's. Wolfe. His name even fit his story. Just as her cold left foot fit perfectly into the warm arch of his right foot.

Swallowing hard, tucking both of her feet beneath her on the support brace of her chair, she said, "Well, guess one benefit of your not trusting me is that I get the first bite."

"Aye." His gaze followed her every move from the time her fingertips sank into the soft white bread to her sinking her teeth into the crust, then allowing the ooey, gooey peanuty goodness and sweet tang of the strawberry jam to melt on her tongue.

Wolfe eyed the wench. While chewing, she held her eyes half-closed, as if the sensation of the flavors washing her tongue were akin to—he snatched the creation she'd called a pee, bee and jay from her hands, and took a bite.

"Hey!" she complained. "That's mine. This half is yours." She pointed to the as yet untouched portion of the meal still sitting on the shining round white trencher.

"Ah hah! So you *are* trying to poison me, or why else would you be so insistent upon my eating that portion?"

Rolling her eyes, she reached for the remaining half and took a big bite. "There," she said after she'd chewed and swallowed. "Now, are you satisfied?"

"This is quite glorious," he said, holding the creation back for a better look. "What do you call it?"

"PB&J, which is short for peanut butter and jelly— or in this case, jam. It's really popular in America—the country I'm from."

After taking three more ravenous bites, he nodded. "Ah, yes, at my pond, I've heard villagers who are fishing talk of your kind. They say you are a brute, garish lot. Loud, and always with a need to be in control. If, as you say, you are one of these thoroughly disagreeable people, then I'm not surprised by your lack of integrity in following through on your vow."

"What vow?" she asked, slamming down the milk. "And Americans are cool—especially me!"

"While I admire your kinship with your people, 'tis your vow to love me for all eternity with which I am most concerned. For 'tis only that which will break my curse." Taking the clear, handleless mug from her hand, he drank after her, closing his eyes in appreciation of the flavor of this most unmilklike chilled drink. "Mmm. Quite good. Are you sure this is milk?" He held the mug to the light.

"Quite, sure. And thanks a lot for gulping it all."

"You're most welcome," he said while she fetched

more. Upon her return, he asked, "Now, what say you about your vow?"

"How about that not only do I not love you, but most of the time, I don't even like you. You're egotistical, crass, bad-mannered, foul—"

"Handsome. Rich." He grinned.

"Did I mention egotistical?"

"Did I mention I was the best swordsman in all the land?"

Now she was grinning too, and the sight of her smile warmed him heartily. So much so, that he pushed back his uncomfortable chair and circled to her side of the table to hold out his hand. "Milady, would you care for a sampling of my thrusting finesse?"

Reddening, she spluttered her latest sip of milk. "Um, I think I've seen quite enough of that particular skill."

Tossing his head back, howling with mirth-filled pride upon her natural assumption, Wolfe said, "I'm not talking about my legendary bedchamber prowess, wench, but my talent for—"

"Whoa," she said, allowing him to pull her to her feet, but then shocking him by placing her fingertips against his lips. "Your talent for kissing has already been established as well."

"But that isn't it, either," he said, holding her by her wrists to draw two of those dainty fingers into his mouth for a good hard suck.

A faint tremor shimmered through her and her sky blue stare became drowsy and dazed. Licking her lips, she said, "Look, I, um, more than anyone, fully appreciate all of your skills, but whether you're a frog prince or not, there are some things about me you have to know."

"Such as?" he said nipping the fleshy pad of each finger on her left hand, then right.

"Well," she said with still one more fetching lick of her lips. "First of all, if that was you this afternoon—in the frog suit—I didn't kiss you for you, the prince, but for you the frog. You see, I'm a biology teacher, but I used to dream of becoming this world famous biologist/explorer. You know, traveling the globe in search of exciting new species of animals. And well, frogs were kind of my specialty."

Not understanding half of what she was saying, Wolfe continued with his sampling of her fingers.

"So you see, when I kissed you, I was kissing the frog—and only the frog. I already have a man in my life. The Duke of Cotswald. He's a wonderful man who—"

"Fails to stir you the way I do just by breathing against your skin?" Wolfe knew his claim to be true by the catch in the wench's breath and eyes. For much as sun and shadow affected the blues of the sea, his touch affected the passion of her stare.

She jerked her hands free, and because he also knew her to be frightened by the passions he evoked, he allowed her this small taste of freedom.

"Now see?" she said, tucking her hands into the pockets of her most unflattering robe. "This is just the kind of thing I'm talking about. I'm practically engaged to the duke and he wouldn't understand about you. Not at all."

"Then he's obviously a fool."

The wench turned her back on him and now it was

Wolfe whose breath was catching. In his brief life, no woman had ever turned away from him. Not unless it'd been part of an elaborate ruse designed for him to roughly tug her back within the circle of his arms.

In his experience, women had found just being with him tantamount to riding into battle. They expounded at length about his scars, and the pain he'd endured. They'd wanted a piece of him as if in lying with him they'd receive a token of his most fiercely won battles. But this woman, she was an enigma. She seemed to want nothing from him other than for him to leave her alone—which was the one thing that if he hoped to keep his current human form, he could never do.

Stepping behind her, Wolfe settled his hands atop her shoulders, gently spinning her around.

"What?" she said, tears brimming in her big blue eyes. "Please, I'm so confused. Can't you just go?"

For all of his supposed bravery in battle, Wolfe had always hated seeing a woman cry, and with the rough pads of his thumbs, he brushed away her tears. Clearing his throat he said, "You have been truthful with me, and now I shall show you the same courtesy."

On a ragged breath, she nodded.

"No matter how much I wish to honor your request for me to leave, I cannot."

"Why?"

"Because you, and you alone hold the key to my future. Whether you believe my tale or not, if, by the next full moon, you have not declared your eternal love, then I shall be transformed back into the frog you first kissed—only this time I won't be trapped in that most cumbersome body for a millennium, but for all eternity."

98

"Really?" she asked with a tiny sniffle.

"Aye. I would not lie about a matter as grave as this, any more than I would lie about my desire to carry you up to bed and keep you there, pendulous breasts bared, nipples ripening in my mouth, legs spread, beckoning my seed."

"You are really something." Laughing, Lucy shook her head. "You almost had me feeling sorry for you, then you had to start in again with your egotistical bedroom B.S." Turning away from him, she headed for the living room where she'd have more space to think.

If what the frog prince had just admitted were true, then by the next full moon, she'd have her very own species of frog back!

Granted, she should be committed for even considering his story to be true, but so much of what he said, she knew from her obsession with local history to be historical fact, right down to the fascinating tidbit of the King of Gwyneddor's first son having been murdered by his stepmother's lover and the king's second son tragically disappearing. At the time, his disappearance had been blamed on bloodthirsty Vikings, but what if what Wolfe had told her could be true?

Then her every hope and dream could be achieved in one month's time. Not only her professional dreams, but her dreams for once and for all earning not just her father's love, but respect.

One month.

Lucy sat down hard on the sofa, and reached for a needlepoint pillow. The stupid thing had taken six months to create, and during each of the intricate stitches of the bucolic castle scene, she'd wondered what it must have been like for women living in that time. Women who didn't just needlepoint for fun, but to upholster chairs and make tapestries to help keep out drafts.

*What have you made lately, Luce?*

The question hurt.

She wanted to believe her teaching made a difference in her students' lives, but they weren't kids like she'd been. These were a sophisticated lot who for the most part couldn't give a flip about science—and why should they when they spent weekends in the south of France, dining with presidents and kings?

*What've you made lately, Luce?*

This time, the question burned.

It'd be so easy—keeping this man. Keeping the frog he might again become.

Seductively easy.

Everything she'd fought for in her life had been ridiculously hard. Launching her career, fighting for her father's love. Was it that far out of the realm of possibility to think that maybe, just maybe, Lady Fate had sent the prince to her as a belated consolation prize for all the other assorted crap She'd put Lucy through?

And even if the frog prince turned out to be the fruitcake she still halfway suspected him to be, she was no longer afraid of him. The fact that he'd allowed her to call things off back in her bedroom told her that whatever else he may be, he was at heart a gentleman. Maybe a horny gentleman. Maybe a deranged gentleman. But a gentleman all the same—a gentleman from whom she sensed she had nothing more than her own attraction to him to fear.

"Have you decided my fate?"

Hand to her chest, she jumped before glancing his way. "Geez, give me a heart attack."

"Sorry. 'Twas not my intent—whatever this affliction of your heart may be."

"Yeah, well . . ." As when she'd seen him in the tub, if only for an instant, his expression seemed vulnerable. Somehow soft. Why? Fear of the unknown? Uncertainty where she was concerned?

Breath catching at the sheer tortured beauty of his face, for the first time since her heart raced with excitement over the possibility of getting back her frog, it occurred to Lucy that in making her every dream come true, she'd be destroying not just Wolfe's dreams, but his very life.

Toying with the pillow's fringed trim, she said, "I, um, need you to clarify something for me."

"If I can."

"Tell me more about this sorceress. You said you refused to marry her pregnant daughter, but that doesn't seem like enough to inspire such a hatred, that she wouldn't just take your life, but destroy it for all time."

He looked down. "It happened so long ago. I'm not sure I remember."

"Try."

Crossing to the sofa, he sat beside her, at which point, she politely placed her pillow on his still very naked lap.

He smiled. "Afraid the mere sight of it'll inspire lustful needs?"

*Yes!*

"No." She licked her lips. "It's just that we're talking, and while I can't speak for your times, in my time, it's not considered polite to sit around gabbing without clothes."

" 'Tis a shame," he said, fingering strands of her hair. "For if more women of your time were to go about their days in the altogether, more of you would be contentedly home with your babes, and not off working in faraway fields."

Lucy snorted. "Of all the—voicing thoughts like that, no wonder you got zapped! And I don't work in a field, I'll have you know, but a school! A very highly respected school. A school in which I'm quite happy to spend my days."

*Liar. Weren't you just the other day wishing for a more exciting life?*

*Shut up!* she said to her nosy conscience who obviously didn't know a thing!

"Then I'm happy for you." Head bowed, he added, "All I meant was that you might enjoy a softer life. For if your duke truly loved you, he'd forbid you to work."

"Because my William does love me, he wouldn't dream of forbidding me to work."

*"Monchyn!"* The prince spit into the fireplace. "A man who has lost control of his own woman is not a man at all."

Lucy took a deep, not in the least bit calming breath. She'd look up whatever the prince had just called her beloved later, but until then, "Okay, before you say something so outrageous I'm forced to call the police, get on with telling me about the sorceress, and that last night."

He cleared his throat, staring into the long-dead fire. "Desdemona was beautiful . . . her long, pale hair calling to mind honey warming in the sun." His gaze as far off as the thousand-year-old story he presumably shared, he said, "I was not the only man who lusted for her. I was, however, the only man she lusted for in return . . ."

# Chapter Nine

"Aye, you think you're a looker, don't ye, fine prince?" Desdemona danced around Wolfe where he lay beside the pond, her green eyes sparking in the sun, her hair long and lustrous, playing hiding games with her lush hips and breasts.

Wolfe, reclining on the grassy hillside, arched his head back, roaring with mirth. The wench wasna afraid of him, he'd give her that. "Come here," he said, sitting up to snag her about her slim waist. "Let me taste that which you've teased me with all afternoon."

"Not so fast," she said, breaking free only to skip through the tall grass, streaming her hair like a glorious banner behind her. From his vantage, the blue of her dress met with the sky, making the two appear as one. Breath caught in his throat, he couldn't help but stare. Was she real? Or but a figment of his dreams?

Laughing inside, he figured she'd been real enough in weeks past when he'd buried himself deep within her slick womanly folds.

"Before I let you kiss me," she sang, "first, I must have your most solemn oath."

"Argh!" No longer in the mood for her dancing games, but for her body, he grasped her about her ankle, pulling her down, then dragging her to lie beside him, her head cradled in the crook of his mighty arm.

"You beast!" she squealed on a breathy laugh, pummeling him when he rolled atop her, lowering his mouth to hers.

"You'll soon enough think me a beast when we rut right here in this field." Catching her mid-laugh, he crushed his mouth to hers, stroking her tongue with his own. She tasted sweet, of the apple they'd only just shared. He'd always been inordinately fond of the fruit, and to taste it on his woman was a most heady pleasure indeed.

"Wolfe," she said, when he'd kissed her till her lips swelled from his pleasure. "I-I have something I need to tell you."

Shaking his head, he moved his kisses further down the fair-skinned column of her throat, "I've no desire to speak."

"Then what would you do?" she asked, coyly smiling to present the dimples he so admired on her cheeks.

"Mmm," he said, sweeping aside great locks of her hair, to feast on the sun-salty skin of her chest. "I wish to bury myself within you. I wish to drink of you till I've had my fill, then take you again until the moon rises high, and again until the first rays of dawn. Then, and only then, will I allow you to speak."

"Allow me?" Her dimple faded to frown, and anger made her warm eyes cold. "Unless you are willing to make me your princess, and the seed already planted within me next in line for your throne, then you have no say in when I wish to speak."

He paid little heed to her speech. She had snipped at him thus before, and always after he had taken her teats into his mouth, her wrath gave way to passion. She'd soon enough confess to not being in possession of his growing seed, but of a dream. For lest there be confusion, Wolfe had made it plain during the summer of their first attraction that their dalliance would never lead to more.

He was prince first.

Warrior second.

Lover third.

And even whilst playing the last role, he did not partake in the fickle games of many of his fellow noblemen by planting the empty promise that were a wench to but fall into his bed, she would be Gwyneddor's future queen.

"Be gone with your ire," he said, smoothing her hair back to admire its glint in the sun. "I battle enough with my enemies, must I do battle with those I hold affection for as well?"

Ah, that brought the grassy green back to her concentrated stare. "Do you mean that?"

"What?" he asked, slipping his hand down the front of her gown.

"That you hold affection for me."

When his fingers reached her right breast, he caught the teat with his thumb, rubbing til it rolled hot between his fingers like an unripe berry warmed in the sun. He normally took great pride in watching her gaze darken with need, but today, he found no pleasure where there only lived pain. Her lower lip trembled just as tears began to fall.

Removing his hand from her breast, swiping the offensive, glistening drops from the soft blush of her cheeks, he said, "Tell me? What have I done to hurt you?"

She shook her head and looked away, but he was the prince, and as such, no one looked away from him when he asked a direct question. *No one*. Not even his most favored wench.

"Tell me," he insisted a final time.

"I'm with child, Wolfe. Your child."

He laughed. "You've said so before, and each time you've been wrong."

"This time, 'tis true. My mother saw the babe in my future."

"But not in mine?" he asked, mirth crinkling the corners of his eyes. While his father, the king, placed great store in the sorceress's visions, he did not. Instead, he preferred the certainty of his own might and sheer will to any foolish magic.

"Oh, Wolfe . . ." Tears flowing once more, she violently shook her head before looking away. "My mother says you will not make me your future queen. That you are too filled with lust for power and riches." Turning back to him, she pressed her palms to his chest. "I told her she was wrong. That this was one time in which her vision would not come true."

"And you know that how?" Wolfe asked, eyes narrowed.

"Because above even myself, I know you. I know that while you've fathered other sons in the past, this one, because he is growing inside of *me,* will be different.

For it is foreseen in this wee one's future that he is to one day be king."

"On this, fair maiden, you are wrong." Abruptly releasing her, then storming to his feet, Wolfe said, "Hear me and hear me well. Tis true, I enjoy burying myself within you, but I regretfully cannot offer you more. As much as it pains me, there will be no marriage between us for the fact that you have naught but your fair hair and pretty smile to give to my father's kingdom."

"What of your son?" she shrieked. "Do you claim him to be of no value?"

Grasping Wolfe's hand, molding his fingers to her belly's swell, she said, "Here, deep within me, he already grows. Aye, I, and all the other fair wenches you've rutted know of your base greed. A greed that denies the fact that even your own father who you hold in such high regard couldn't hold onto the woman he did not love. He bartered for his wife in the fettered and bloodied grasses of a battlefield. She was but chattel, and look what his actions gained him. A dead son— and another who is dead in here."

She moved his hand from her womb to between her breasts where her heart thundered beneath him. Had he wanted, he could have snatched her very life from her, such was the depth of his fury.

Snatching his hand free, through clenched teeth he said, "Ye will not give voice to my mother's despicable act again."

"Why? Because she's the one woman in your life who never loved you?"

Wolfe turned from the raving woman, but she flung herself at him, hair wild as she clawed his face and chest. "You will marry me! You will!"

"Calm yourself," he said, clasping her wrists. "Or you'll harm yourself and the babe."

Her laugh was that of a madwoman. "What do you care of my babe?" she said, tearing at her womb. "I would just as soon kill it now as wed you even if you were to insist."

"Enough!" he roared. "Such talk is lunacy."

"And you should know, seeing how your own mother didn't even want you! And truth be known, I don't want your babe! My mother cast a spell upon me to be fertile, just as she cast a spell upon you to find me irresistible enough to one day make me your queen!"

Her ranting startled blackbirds into noisy flight, and in a far-off field, farmers stopped the harvest of their wheat to stare.

Desdemona openly wept, crumpling to the tall grasses, her pale blue gown symbolizing the falling of Wolfe's sky and spirit.

Despite her harsh words, his very palms itched to go to her, but his feet refused to move.

For wasn't this always the way? Wasn't every woman he'd ever bedded in wanting? In heat? Only they wanted not just to sample his prowess, but they wanted a piece of him. A piece of his father's kingdom in the form of a babe.

There were ways for a woman to keep barren her womb, yet more times than not, he'd been tricked.

This time was no different.

Desdemona, as countless others, wanted infinite power and riches, but those were not things one could simply wish for and they would appear. They were hard fought and won over the blood of countless noble warriors seizing the incalculable riches found only in truth and righteousness and honor. And they seized all of those good things not with wiles, but with mighty blows of their axes and swords.

This woman, lying before him, just like so many before, knew not what it meant to be a ruler. She knew not of the responsibility to unfold. For he had no choice in the matter of whom he'd one day wed. It would be divined by fate. For only fate knew of the riches to be found far afield. Riches that would one day soon make his father's kingdom—nay, his own kingdom, the strongest in all the land.

"You are not human," she said on sobs heaved between torn breaths. On hands and knees, moving toward him in jerking fits like those of a rabid dog, she spat, "You are a demon! Thrust up through the underbelly of this world."

"And you are not the woman I thought, for the woman I once held in such high regard would never condone casting spells for affection, let alone of bringing harm to an innocent babe."

"Arrgghhh!" Rising up, she slapped him, and cold fury replaced whatever affection for her he might have once had.

Slinging her over his shoulder, he stormed across hills and fields, far from the idyllic pond and into the village with her kicking and shouting the whole of the way.

"I hate you!" she railed, pounding his back with her fists, her further condemnations only broken by more tears.

And still Wolfe marched on, past the chuckles of men and scornful eyes of women. And on, past wee ones hiding behind their mums, some of them his wee ones. Children which he had been ever diligent in patting their heads, and insuring they had no need for coin. Was that not enough? Would that not be enough for the babe of the wench he now carried?

On he walked and further on, beyond the castle wall to the great cave beside the sea where the sorceress brewed her worthless spells.

"Here," he said, placing Desdemona on the circular stone table in the center of the soaring, smoke-filled room. Exhaustion had finally claimed her, and she lay limp before her mother's condemning eyes.

"What have you done to her?" the sorceress asked, malevolent green gaze piercing his.

Head bowed, he said, "I tried calming her, but failed. Yet the blame for her exhaustion, as well as her grief, can be put upon no one but yourself."

"Yet 'tis your seed that has placed her in this condition."

"A condition I will support by my coin and presence, but not my vow."

Desdemona's mother, Castanea, was as bewitching as her daughter, yet the undiluted hatred flashing from her eyes failed to stir Wolfe's loins. Stroking Desdemona's pale hair, humming a joyless tune, the sorceress said to this younger version of herself, "I will make him pay, dear one. He will not rape us as his father raped our land."

"Raped your land?" Wolfe asked with a disgust-filled snort. "My father and his warriors *saved* your land—not to mention your daughter and you."

"What do you know of our plight? You were but a boy!"

"A boy of twenty and two who not only witnessed

that bloody battle, but did my part to claim victory! A boy who understood the oppression of your people by a Viking tyrant who knew nothing of tolerance, but of war!"

Turning slowly from her daughter to him, she narrowed her eyes before spitting upon his feet. "You will pay for this, Prince."

"And what shall *you* pay, witch woman? Think I know not of the magic you've wielded against my father? Of how you've no doubt seduced him with poison milk flowing from your tits?"

"Go!" Raising her long arms, the wide sleeves of her silver-spun gown glinting by the light of a nearby fire, she said, "Go now, or I will cast spells of poverty and famine upon the land."

Wolfe laughed. "You but wish to be so strong."

"You think my words mere jest?"

"I know them to be," he said, arms crossed upon his mighty chest. This woman did not scare him. Why would the great Prince of Gwyneddor be frightened of mere claims of magic that he could not see. Men on horseback wielding hot oil and great battle axes—that was the stuff to fear. Spies within his midst. The type of treachery of which his very own mother had been capable. Aye, that was stuff of which to fear. But not this witch woman with her hair so blond it was almost white. And eyes that sparked an unnatural green. "If you insist on wielding this awesome power you claim to hold," he jeered. "Why not go one step further? Why not transform me into the loathsome pond creature you evidently believe me to be. . . ."

\*　　\*　　\*

Lucy dragged in a gulp of air.

"That's my tale," the prince said. "I underestimated the strength of Castanea's spells."

"You think?" She pushed herself up from the sofa, head reeling from all she'd just heard.

"You think less of me. I can tell."

"Well . . . it's just that—" How did she admit that, far from the egotistical monster she'd expected him to be, in reality, he'd handled the last few moments of his previous human life as well as could be expected. Granted, in a perfect world he would have married all the women he'd left pregnant, but the sad fact of the matter was that in those times, he would've had a responsibility to his kingdom above himself. If what he'd said was true, the women who'd lain with him had known this up front. Who was to say that, just as in modern times when women tried trapping rock stars and actors into marriage by claiming pregnancy, Desdemona hadn't done the same with an eligible prince?

*And if so, does that make him innocent? Does that make your decision to poof him back into a frog for your own personal gain any less easy to stomach?*

*Speaking of which, does this mean you've decided to unconditionally believe his outrageous story?*

Lucy nibbled her lower lip. Of course, she knew she shouldn't believe one iota of the prince's story, but really, what did she stand to lose by at least sort of believing him? After all, if his story did turn out to be true, just as soon as he once again turned green, her finances would finally be out of the red. Even better, her tarnished reputation would be shiny and new, as would her lackluster relationship with her dad.

And if it turned out he was lying?

Well . . . all she was out was a month's food.

*Along with that pesky little fact that never again will I be so thoroughly, deliciously, wonderfully kissed.*

Shaking her head, Lucy sighed. "I've got to get some sleep."

At that, his expression lightened. "Then you're ready for bed?"

"Aye—I mean, yes. I'm very much ready for bed—alone."

Expression crestfallen, he said, "I only have til the full moon. 'Twould be much simpler for me if you'd commence with the business of declaring your love."

Blasting him with her most sarcastic smile, she said, "I'm sure it *twould,* but since this is my house, tonight, we're going to do what's easiest for me. Which means setting you up in my guest bedroom, then retiring to our *separate* beds."

After settling the prince into her guest room—no easy feat considering the fact that he claimed to be stricken ill at the sight of all the flowers and womanly colors that decorated the room. Luckily, once he got his first feel of modern-day sheets, pillows and blankets, all complaining stopped. If she hadn't known better, she'd have sworn the big man actually purred with pleasure!

Finally easing into her own bed, Lucy clicked off the bedside table lamp.

She closed her eyes, but nothing happened.

Or maybe something did happen that explained the reason why she couldn't sleep!

Namely, the slow-burning realization that if that story the prince had told her was true, then maybe he wasn't such a bad guy.

On the other hand, duh?

Wouldn't he stand to gain far more sympathy from her by making himself look good and poor, and knocked-up and husbandless Desdemona look bad?

And if that were the case, who was Lucy to say that the sorceress who'd zapped him into a frog hadn't been right? And who was Lucy to say that he didn't deserve to go right back into that little green body from whence he'd come?

After all, he hadn't just gotten Desdemona pregnant, but other women as well. How many, he hadn't admitted, but if his current horn-dog ways were a gauge, who knew? Maybe they were talking two? Four? A dozen? All who might have bore witness were long since dead, and unfortunately, poor little bastard children of noblemen were rarely recorded in the annals of history.

That being the case . . .

She drew her lower lip into her mouth for a quick nibble. Heart racing, mind swimming, she dared finish her thought. That being the case, why shouldn't she make it her mission to see that he carried out the rest of his sentence?

Maybe the prince had been horrid in other ways, as well. Kind of like that bad guy shipped off to outer space in *Superman.* Or was it *Superman II?* Maybe he should be *locked* up for all eternity. And what about Khan in *Star Trek?* And shoot, for that matter, what about historical bad guys like Hitler or Saddam Hussein? Not only Hollywood, but history had proven that bad guys were better off quarantined from civilized society.

Granted, Hitler killed himself, but—

Good grief, she thought, plowing her fingers through her hair. Focus, Luce. Focus.

Like on the fact that Wolfe could have just as easily been telling the truth. And what if in a thousand years of having nothing to do but hop around and dwell on his past transgressions, he'd changed?

Changed?

Lucy choked on her own spit. Right, the guy who less than an hour earlier told her women would be much better off strolling the earth barefoot, bare-breasted and pregnant!

Punching her down pillow into a more comfy shape, she vowed to finally get some rest. Why? Because not only did she have a busy day at school ahead of her in the morning, but a busy day of planning.

In just four weeks, the next World Biological Conference would be held in London. Mere coincidence that that coincided with the next full moon? Could it be another positive sign from Lady Fate?

Again, who knew?

At this point, pretty much the only thing Lucy for sure knew was that this time when she presented her own unique species of frog, there would be no reaction other than wild applause and cheers.

The next morning, ringing interrupted Lucy's deep sleep.

Rolling over, rubbing her eyes, Lucy sat up in her bed, reaching for the phone on her bedside table, but it didn't dawn on her that it was no longer ringing until she picked it up and heard two masculine voices on the other end.

"If you don't tell me what've you've done with Luce, I will call the police!"

Lucy cringed. William was wearing his grouchy voice.

As if put out by this early morning disturbance, the prince sighed heavily. "I've already told you, I don't know a Lady Luce. There's only one wench under my roof, and I know not her name. Now, if you should wish to further rob me of my rest, I suggest you present your person upon my doorstep, so I might instruct you in the ways of courtesy by planting my foot upon your arse!"

Click.

After hanging up her phone, Lucy leaped from her bed, and ran to the guest room.

"Nooo!" she cried when the ringing sounded again and the prince reached for the phone, mumbling something about how the instrument should never have been invented, and how he'd have been better off had he not learned by watching the castle occupants how to use the damnedable thing. Tossing herself across the bed, in the process, landing across sheet-covered muscular male thighs, she said, "Let me get it," before picking up. "Hello?"

"Luce? Thank goodness. I must have rung up the wrong number, because I've just had the strangest conversation."

Trying to sound as if she knew nothing about that conversation, she yawned, then said, "Really?"

"I would have thought in this day and age, people would be more civilized, but—"

"Quit!" Lucy hissed, slapping the prince's roving hand off of her pajama-covered behind.

"I say, Luce, what was that?"

"Nothing," she said in her most chipper morning tone. "Must've just been static on the line."

"Right. Well, in any case, I wanted to wish you luck with Grumsworth."

"Thank you," she said, warm all over that William thought highly enough of her to have remembered yesterday's battle. "Quit!" The prince, on the other hand, she felt nothing but cold contempt for as he slid his hand down the backside of her thigh.

"Bloody foul connection we have," the duke muttered. "Anyway, love, I wish you the best of days, and know that no matter how rough a time the old chap gives you, that there's only one reason for his abhorrent behavior."

"What's that?" she asked, swatting the prince's roving hand out from beneath her pajama top.

"Why, I should think that'd be obvious." In that dear, gentle way of his, William laughed. "Because he's set his fancy on you, and now that he knows we're an item, he's quite jealous."

"You called him?" Swat!

"Well, yes. As a member of the board. I felt it only proper that I let the man know we don't condone this sort of behavior."

"William?" Swat, swat. "Thank you, but I'm capable of handling this on my own. I don't need you rescuing me from every little scrape." Smack!

"Is it wrong of me to want to rescue you? After all, as we established last night, I do feel more than just a fondness for you. And if our relationship is to ever progress to more, people like Grumsworth must know they can't treat you in such a despicable manner."

118

Honestly! Smack, smack! Had the prince slipped out in the middle of the night to give her sweet, mild-mannered William lessons in chauvinism? Squaring her shoulders as best she could with her stomach resting on the stomach of a medieval prince, with his hot, strong fingers massaging their way up her back, Lucy said, "Thank you for your call, William, but I should get ready for school."

"Of course. Will I see you tonight?"

"Yes," she said, gazing over her shoulder at the prince. "But let me come to you."

He laughed. "Haven't yet found time to tidy your nest?"

"Nope."

"All right then, I shall expect you for dinner around say, eight?"

"Sure. See you at eight."

Lucy hung up the phone, then scrambled upright to let the prince have it!

"How dare you!" she cried. "That was an important call. What if William figured out he hadn't called a wrong number, but just talked to a naked man who happens to be sleeping at my cottage! A cottage that belongs to him!"

His smile one of vast amusement, the prince, who was by now sitting up in the bed as well, snatched her onto his lap and lightly smacked her behind.

"Ouch! How dare you?"

"How dare I?" He laughed again. "Might I remind you that not only this house, but the castle and surrounding land for as far and farther than the eye can see belong to me?"

Struggling to slide free, she said, "And might I remind you, that if any of what you've said is true, you stopped owning anything round about the time you traded in your castle for a muddy pond!"

Fixing her with a stare of such handsome intensity that she quite literally had trouble finding her next breath, the prince said, "Have you any idea, Miss Lucy Gordon, how infinitely attractive you look to me with your bed-tousled hair and sleep-filled eyes?"

"Y-you, you called me Lucy. But you just told William you didn't know my name."

"Aye," he said with a slow, sexy grin. "I lied."

# Chapter Ten

"Miss Gordon?" Freckle-faced, carrottop, Lord Randolph stood beside her desk, e-pad in hand. "I don't get this stuff. It seems to me that the brown rabbit and the white rabbit would make an ecru rabbit."

Lucy rubbed her forehead, reaching for young Lord Randolph's finger-smudged pad. "What did you have for breakfast, sweetie?"

"Officially," he said, "oatmeal."

"And unofficially?"

Pale cheeks reddening, he glanced over his shoulder. "Promise you won't tell?"

"Promise."

"Fried chicken. One of the upperclassman Yanks made it last night in his room. He gave some of us drumsticks for standing watch in the hall."

"And you saved yours til this morning?"

He nodded.

"Why? Don't you know it could make you sick leaving it out that long? Not to mention the fact that it's dangerous frying anything anywhere—let alone in a four-hundred-year-old dormitory?"

"Oh. You going to write me up?"

"No," she said, his crestfallen expression tugging at her heart. "But I should. Here, give me that," she said, taking his e-pad to give it a good cleaning.

She patiently helped him with his chart, then, while the other students finished theirs, she asked beneath her breath, "Say, Randy? Did you ever hear from your dad?"

Beaming, he pulled out the monogrammed postcard she'd carefully written doing her best to imitate his billionaire father's scrawl. The same father who'd for all practical purposes dumped his son at the school. Sensing how bummed Randy had been, she'd sent the note to a friend of hers in New York City, then had her mail it, so the postmark would be right.

"He said he misses me." After a quick glance at the other kids, he whispered, "He's never said that before. Said he was sorry for not writing more, but that he was busy, and promised to write more soon. He said not to tell my mum about the notes. Just to let them be our man-to-man secrets."

"That's great," she said, wanting to pull him into a hug. Damn deadbeat dads—especially the one residing under her roof! Oh well, at least as long as Randy was one of her students, he'd continue getting notes along with all the sappy teacher affection he could stand.

Randy back in his seat, she returned to recording grades, but instead of seeing the scores to Friday's midterm exam, all she saw was the prince's smile. And all she seemed capable of thinking about was the fact that as rotten as she'd made him out to be, he'd covered for her. He knew how much her relationship with the duke meant, and despite his jumbo-sized ego, he'd actually put her wishes above his own.

Did that mean she forgave him for his hundred and one other offensive comments? No. But at least now there was a glimmer of hope she'd be able to stomach him for the rest of the month.

Elbows on her desk, fingertips massaging her temples, Lucy tried rubbing panic from her brain.

Would her plan to keep the prince in hiding work? Where was she going to find him some clothes? How would she ever get her papers for the conference written in time? It was unheard of for a delegate to apply for presentation time this late, but would her father, who was chairman of the conference board, grant her a special dispensation once he heard that this time, she truly had found her very own species?

*Yeah! Your very own species of naked prince!*

Wishing for a paper bag to put over her mouth, Lucy forced herself back to her work, and within five minutes the bell signaling the end of her day had rung.

She'd just finished posting test grades when a knock demanded her attention.

Festus Grumsworth peered his bug-eyed face through the window in her classroom door, then barged right in without being invited. "Ms. Gordon," he said, hooking his right arm over her lecture podium.

"Mr. Grumsworth."

He cleared his throat.

Lucy swallowed one of those disgusting burps that taste like puke. Honestly, would this day never end?

"I presume you know why I'm here?"

"No," she said, raising her chin.

He tapped his long, spindly index finger on the podium's edge. "I received a call this morning from a highly influential member of our school's board."

"Oh?"

"It seems he's displeased with certain actions I've taken that I deemed appropriate in light of your latest malicious stunt."

"Stunt?" Lucy gulped. Since when had her harmless goof grown in stature to a premeditated act of malice? Lydia Jenson hadn't heard from her parents in a while, either. What had it hurt—aside from adding to Lucy's already bulging credit card balance—to have all of those pink sweetheart roses and one tiny white puffball of a kitten discreetly delivered to her room on her birthday?

"Don't play the wounded innocent with me, Ms. Gordon. I know all about you Yanks, thinking you can change the world one crazy act at a time."

"Listen, Mr. Grumsworth, with all due respect, I find it highly improper for you to not only degrade me personally, but my entire country."

"You listen," he said, leaving the podium to perch on the edge of Lucy's messy desk. His tweed-covered rear touched the pear she'd planned to eat on the drive home. The pear that would now go directly into the trash! "I've had it with you. I've had it with your pranks. Your endless attempts to make our students feel good. They are here to learn—not *feel*. You might have friends in high places, but I have ultimate authority over this institution."

"Yes, sir."

"And since I have ultimate authority, I could have you put out of here just like that." He snapped his fingers. "And lest you go running to your new beau, the duke, keep in mind that I didn't tell him half of the stunts you've pulled. Next time you think about pulling any shenanigans, Miss Gordon, you think about His Grace's reputation, and how much he'd appreciate knowing just what sort of deviant misfit he's aligned himself with. Have I made myself clear?"

"Crystal."

"Excellent. I trust I won't have need to mention this again, but if I do, know it will be your last time. I'm tired of playing nice. It's time for you and your interfering nature to go." Gaze narrowed, he appraised the paper piles on her desk, and colorful bulletin boards crammed with fun, biology-related press clippings and posters. The windowsills brimming with riotous green ivies and mother-in-law's tongue. Peace lilies and a blooming pot of daisies. And then there were the five spider plants dangling from brass hooks she'd screwed into the coffered oak ceiling. The terrariums housing frogs and salamanders, and crickets and a tarantula named Boo, and a python named Sammy.

While most of her menagerie napped off the remainder of their day, Buzzy the hamster ran a squeaky few laps on his exercise wheel. Eyebrows slanted into the fiercest scowl yet, Grumsworth said, "Clear the lot of this rubbish by the end of the week. This is a classroom, Miss Gordon—not a gallery, greenhouse, social services bureau or zoo."

"I hate him," Lucy said on the drive home, tightening her already white-knuckled grip on the wheel. "I hate his dorky black-rimmed glasses, and his always-perfect slicked-back hair. And lately, instead of liverwurst, he's been smelling like BENGAY. Oooooh . . ." she said, for a split second removing her hands from the wheel to twinkle her fingers. "BENGAY. Isn't that a decidedly *Yank* product?"

"Grrr . . ." Like she didn't already have enough on her plate in dealing with the prince and developing some sort of kick-ass presentation to wow her father and all of his associates.

Correction, she thought, sitting straighter in the mini's seat. *Her* associates. For just as soon as she gave them a peek at her prince in frog's clothing, they'd adore her.

A dreamy smile playing across her lips, she imagined how the afternoon would go. . . .

"In conclusion," she said to the crowd of well over five hundred of her enraptured fellow scientists. "I believe all of you will find the new species of frog I've presented, *Prince Wolfe,* to be not only a magnificent specimen in and of itself, but an excellent opportunity to revisit places on our continents we'd previously thought thoroughly explored."

Thunder. Hail. A stampeding herd of elk. No mere comparison came close to the booming reality of her long awaited cheers. "Bravo! Bravo!"

Blushing a delicate, charming shade of pink, Lucy bowed.

"My fabulously clever girl!" Slate Gordon cried, rushing the stage to wrap her in a celebratory hug. Still gripping her shoulders, staring deeply into her eyes, he said, "I do so love you. Thank you for proving me wrong. Thank you for making me the proudest father on earth."

"Oh, Daddy," she said, swallowing back tears. "I love you, too."

"Darling," he said, grasping her hands. "I know this may be premature, but listening to your brilliant speech, I've been struck with the most fabulous idea."

"Yes?" she said with a breathy nod.

Slipping his arm about her shoulders, guiding her offstage to a crush of clamoring reporters and newly made fans, he said with a wink, "For now, I'll let you get back to your adoring crowd, but over dinner, let's talk about the two of us launching a joint exploration of Myanmar, and then—"

Lucy slammed on her brakes.

Hopping pretty as you please smack down the center of the castle lane was a frog.

Tapping her fingers on the wheel, she watched it hop to the other side, and where at first she'd been annoyed to have had her lovely fantasy interrupted, now she just shook her head and grinned.

Funny how life changed.

Just one day earlier, she'd been cursing her poor, beloved frogs, and now her love affair had started anew. Or was it just her love affair with her very own naked frog prince?

And then, as though conjured up by her imagination the man himself leapt over the castle wall, which ran parallel to the road, and confidently strode her way!

*Dear lord.*

Mouth dry, pulse pounding, she licked her lips.

How, in the course of just one day, could she have forgotten the fiercely handsome angle of his stubble-shadowed cheeks, or the determined glint in his dark eyes? The way his long, black hair served as a utilitarian

127

backdrop to make the breadth of his shoulders and chest that much more surreal?

And then there was his, um, rather large lower package—which, out of respect for her dear William, she wasn't about to appraise. Lucy took a nice, deep breath.

Forget anything else she might've had on her agenda. Clothing the naked prince had just jumped to the top of her to-do list!

Helping himself to the passenger seat of her car, he said, "Good afternoon, Miss Lucy Gordon. How was your day?"

*Much better after seeing your smile.*

Lucy swallowed hard.

*Dear lord.*

Did he have to sit so close? Close enough that his usual masculine scents combined with her very best gardenia bath beads, igniting a slow-burning flame. Why couldn't she forget how good his weight had felt crushing her body? Or how he'd rubbed his knee along her inner thigh, insinuating himself into her robe, parting her legs, making the nest between her legs hum.

*Dear lord!*

"Lucy Gordon?" When he cupped his massive hand to her cheek, it took every ounce of her strength not to lean into his touch. "How was your day?"

"S-since you asked. Awful."

"Tell me about it," he said.

And back at her cottage, over a hodgepodge meal of scrambled eggs, toast, and sections of sweet juicy orange that he'd gone wild for, and after she'd taught him to then tuck the sections between his teeth to make goofy orange-rind smiles, she'd told him about far more

than just her day, but also her long-standing gripes with
Grumsworth. And how seeing the loneliness and confusion in her students' eyes over being virtually abandoned by their parents reminded her a lot of her own
childhood. And how in making their lives a little happier, she was child by child easing her own pain. Teaching both them and herself that they had done nothing
wrong.

Leaning back in his chair, resting his legs on the chair
beside him at the small dining room table, the prince
said, "I know you believe otherwise, but I was not one
of those parents. While I never married the mothers of
my babes, I spent much time with my wee ones. They
needed for nothing. Not food, clothing, shelter or affection."

Placing her hand atop his, stupid, irrational tears
welling in her eyes from his surprisingly passion-filled
speech, she said, "That's good, Wolfe. And hearing you
now . . . seeing you. I-I think I do believe."

He bowed his head, then, snatching his hand out
from under hers, squeezed it into a white-knuckled fist.
"Back to this Grumsworth—would you like me to take
him out?"

Lucy wrinkled her nose. "Take him out? I don't—
*oooh.*" Yikes! Might she have been better off keeping
her big mouth shut? "Um, I've heard of psycho cheer-
leader moms doing their enemies in, but not plain old
biology teachers. We've never been known for possessing that kind of passion outside of our specific fields of
study."

Expression lost, he said, "So you do want me to remove this unpleasant man from your world?"

"No. I definitely don't. You might have handled dis-

129

agreements that way in your time, but in mine, things are a little different."

"Meaning, you don't mind letting people run all over you?"

"Where did you hear that expression?"

"From a woman on the picture box. How do you say her name? Ope-rah?"

"Sure. Oprah. She used to just have her own show, but now she has a whole channel. She looks amazing for her age, don't you think? Anyway, if only you'd had her daily therapy sessions back when you were sowing your oats, you might not be in this mess."

"What mess?" he said, taking her hand. "Because from where I sit, life has never looked better." He winked. "I heard that during a particularly entertaining piece on the subject of bean dip."

*Ka-thump. Ka-thump. Ka-thump.*

Could he hear her heart pounding? The prince at his egotistical best was easy enough to resist, but this guy—this prince charming, whoa! The man's smile made her believe in fairy tales. Especially the kind sure to come true once he returned to his realm, and she was declared by her father to be the most brilliant biologist in the world.

Snatching her hand back to the safety of her lap, Lucy licked her lips. "Bean dip, huh? You wanna try some?"

"That, and poo-sham."

"Poo sham?"

"The white foaming substance used to freshen female hair." Reaching across the table to finger strands of her hair, he added, "I saw a man using it in a bathing pool on his woman. Looked like a most agreeable product that I should very much like to try—on you."

Cheeks flaming, Lucy sharply looked away, then gulped.

*Dear lord!*

Reaching for his plate, then hers, she pushed her chair back from the table, aiming for the kitchen, but the prince cut her off at the pass, taking the plates from her hands. "Ope-rah says real men aren't afraid to scrub all manner of household items."

"Oh, she does, does she?" Eyebrows raised, Lucy slipped the butter and eggs back into the fridge.

"Aye." At the sink, over the sounds of running water and the clink of their juice glasses hitting the frying pan she'd used for the eggs, he said, "In my time, 'twas considered beneath a man of my station to do such menial things."

"Oh?" She put the twisty-tie back on the bread.

"According to this most wise Ope-rah, men must adapt and change. Seeing how after you've declared your eternal love for me, I'll once again be leading my people, I felt it wise to conform to this new way of thinking."

Rolling her eyes, Lucy reached around him for the red gingham dishrag hanging from the faucet. He was too much! And speaking of too much—had any man ever had tighter buns?

Scrubbing a plastic cereal bowl to within an inch of its life, he added, "I will soon be king, you know. And I'd like my villagers to see me as not just their ruler, but as a true man of the people."

Lucy's gaze strayed back to his luscious buns. How wrong would it be to roll up her rag and give 'em a swat?

"Lucy Gordon?"

"Mmm-hmm . . ." she said, having sadly decided bun-swatting would be very bad.

"What do you think of my plan?"

"What I think is that I have to run a few errands." She tossed the rag back into the sink, then reached for her keys. "Keep up the good work," she said, automatically starting to pat his back, then stopping when faced with all of that hot, hard, still gloriously naked muscle. "Um, yeah. Keep up the good work."

"You already said that."

"I did?" Before he could answer, she ran for the mudroom door.

"Something like this, ma'am?" The waxy-complexioned clerk of Rinegeld's Men's Clothing Emporium on the corner of Lake Street and Saville raised his eyebrows as if he thought she was buying the stupid sweater for some strange, nefarious reason. Honestly, hadn't he ever seen a woman shop for men's clothes before? Didn't proper wives and girlfriends do this sort of thing all the time?

"Mmm . . ." Fingers to her lips, appraising the fourteenth sweater the clerk had held out for her inspection, she said, "I don't think so."

The nutmeg color was good, but style bad. The vee neck somehow screamed modern times, and out of respect for Wolfe's royal heritage, she saw him in more of a crew neck ribbed look. Something earthy, but not too schlumpy. Something masculine, but not too— hand to her forehead, Lucy sighed.

Listen to her.

Going on and on acting like any of this even mattered.

The whole point of this expedition was to put clothes on the man's gorgeous naked back. Period. It didn't matter if he looked like he'd stepped off of the pages of *Men's Vogue*.

In fact, ew—*MV*. Way too effeminate for such a rough and ready guy. No, Wolfe was definitely more the sports magazine type. But then no, in picturing that, she saw spandex, and that didn't really suit him, either. Maybe something along the lines of *British Outdoorsman Quarterly*. Not that she'd read it—ever—but he was definitely outdoorsy, and—"

"Ma'am? We close in ten minutes." The clerk held out another sweater, this time a nubby, mossy green wool with a crew neck. "Will this do?"

With the prince's dark eyes, the sweater would be—"Perfect," she said, already reaching into her purse for her lowest-balance credit card. "I'll take one of those in every color you've got. All of those boxers we already picked, and the jeans, slacks, shoes, belts, and . . ."

"The silk lounging pajamas?"

Heart racing at the thought of Wolfe wearing the black silk bottoms and nothing else, Lucy managed to nod.

"Very well, then," the clerk said, taking her card. "If you'll give me a moment, I'll ring these up."

"Sure."

Lucy busied herself by sniffing colognes—none of which came close to smelling as good as the prince managed to all on his own—not that she'd noticed, but—

The discreet bell over the shop's door jingled, and

along with a blast of cool night air came a screechy voice asking, "Lucy Gordon? I thought that was you." Ruth Hagenberry stepped inside, pulling the door shut. "I was taking my evening constitutional, and looked through the window, and thought, why, what on earth is our single girl, Lucy, doing in a men's clothing store?"

Lucy opened her mouth to answer, but Ruth didn't give her the chance.

"But then inspiration struck and I knew you must be purchasing a trinket for the duke. But then I thought, no. It isn't his birthday, and even from outside, I could tell the department you were in was for the big and tall sector of male society—neither of which, big or tall," she said with an exaggerated wink, "applies to our fair William. So? Lucy Gordon, tell me, what were you doing in that section of the store?"

"Well, um, actually I was just looking. You know, with the holidays coming, it's never too soon to get a head start."

"Ma'am?" the clerk called from the register. "This card was declined. Do you have another?"

Cringing, Lucy pulled out the one that really had the lowest balance, and handed it to him. The one he handed back had a dolphin on it, and it was the one with the highest balance. Honestly, couldn't she get anything right—most of all, thinking up a fib Ruth Hagenberry would believe?

"Just looking, eh?" Ruth elbowed her ribs. "I haven't stumbled upon a juicy secret, have I?"

"No, No," Lucy said, willing the clerk to hurry. "I, um, was, ah, just picking up a few things for my dad. Guess I forgot."

Ruth's eyebrows shot up. "I've seen your father on the telly, Lucy Gordon. He's not big and tall, either."

"My, ah, brother is."

"Your father mentioned in his last Britney Spears' interview that he only has one child—you."

"Yes, well . . ."

"Ma'am, this card will only accept five hundred of the eight hundred and forty-seven pounds."

"Here," Lucy said, shoving two more cards at him. "Try these."

"Very well," he said with a prissy nod.

Ruth's yapper hung wider than the mouth of a five-pound tub of pickles.

"What?" Lucy said. "Haven't you ever seen a woman buy men's clothes?" Not to mention nearly faint from spending so much money? Still, every bit of that future debt would be made back and then some once her discovery became public. She'd be rich beyond her wildest dreams—not only financially, but emotionally. Her father and William would adore her, as would Mr. Visa and Mr. MasterCard.

Granted, this temporary financial black hole wasn't all that hot for her credit report, but instead of thinking of Wolfe's new wardrobe as scary overspending, she preferred to think of his dashing new duds as an investment in her future. And after having spent less than twenty-four hours sharing her home with the naked prince, she knew unless she clothed him, her future might not involve fame as a biologist but becoming the prince's only all-too-willing sex slave!

"I've certainly seen a woman buying clothes before, thank you very much," Ruth said, flawlessly manicured red tipped claws to her chest. "What I haven't seen is

135

a woman so determined to hide the garments' recipient. As you well know, Miss Gordon, the duke and I are very old acquaintances. There's nothing the two of us haven't shared. How do you think he'd feel if I told him the current object of his affections purchased an obscene amount of clothing for an unidentified man?"

Lucy sighed. "If you must know, all of this is for one of my students, okay? He's on scholarship, and I hate to see the other boys poke fun of him because he hasn't the proper clothes to wear in those social circles."

"Don't you teach ten- and eleven-year-olds?" Ruth asked, eyeing the Big and Tall sign.

"Here you go," the clerk said, handing Lucy four receipts. Just sign these, and we'll all be on our way."

Lucy signed.

Ruth gaped.

The clerk yawned.

After signing, Lucy snatched the five handled sacks the clerk had set to the side of the register, then flashed Ruth a wide smile. "You have a really nice evening, Ruth. It's always a pleasure seeing you."

"Yes, but—"

Leaving the woman still staring, Lucy hightailed it for her car, only to practically run down Father Bart.

"Slow down, young lady."

"Yes, sir. Sorry."

"Yes, you will be when you run right over the troops. See them?" he asked, pointing to the sidewalk where the only things Lucy saw were a couple of crunched dead leaves and a cigarette butt. "You must be more careful. Without our fine troops, this country will go straight down the loo."

"Yes, sir. Thank you. I'll keep that in mind."

"See that you do."

Tossing her purse and packages on the hood of her mini, she looked after the tottering old man and his troops.

Who was to say he wasn't the sane one?

After all, she had just maxed out all of her credit cards clothing a naked medieval frog!

# Chapter Eleven

"Thank you, Ruth," William said, sliding his right hand into his trouser pocket while she rambled on. "Yes, well . . . I certainly appreciate your call, though I'm sure there's a quite logical explanation. All right, then . . . Of course, I completely understand."

But as William hung up the phone, and the clock in his study struck eight-thirty, he wasn't sure he did understand.

Luce wasn't known for her strict adherence to schedules, but even she had never been this late.

Promptness was an oft-underrated thing he must remember to talk with her about. For he'd always found his days running much more smoothly when not in an endless rush to catch up with late appointments.

But in the meantime, William was back to wondering where she could be. Was she merely unavoidably detained? Or was something more afoot?

She'd seemed odd the night before. Standoffish, and distracted beyond what he'd have expected a tiff with the headmaster to have caused. There'd been that call from Ruth Hagenberry alerting him to the fact that Lucy had been seen driving through town with a naked man in her mini—the very idea of which he'd had a good laugh over. But now Ruth was calling again, supposedly with only his best interests at heart to inform him that his future fiancée just spent a considerable amount of money she did not have on an extensive men's large-sizes wardrobe she claimed had been for a student who couldn't possibly be much over five feet tall.

Leaving the shield of his desk, the desk that had served his ancestors since the very dawn of England, William, no longer a noble, but just a man—a highly confused man, stood beside the dark window, staring across the grounds, wishing he could see all the way to Rose Cottage.

Would he find Lucy there? In the arms of another man?

Or had Ruth finally succumbed to the certain madness so many about town claimed her already to possess?

Sighing, he reached back to his desk and picked up the phone. What was mad was the way he was letting that woman's ravings consume him. Understandably Lucy had been upset with Grumsworth. And tonight, she'd probably just lost track of time.

Normally, he would have just trotted down to her cottage, but after last night's curious behavior, he chose to instead grant her her privacy—at least for the moment.

After punching her number, by the second ring, he'd convinced himself that maybe even her power could have gone out, and she wasn't aware of the time. In a matter of minutes, they'd both laugh about not only her tardiness, but this matter with Ruth.

But when she hadn't answered by the fourth ring, and then on the sixth, her jaunty answerphone message claimed her to not be home, he said upon hearing the beep, "Yes, ah, hallo, Luce. William, here. Cook needs to know whether to keep holding dinner, but I'll tell her to go ahead and serve." Voice softer, he finished with, "Ring me when you get home, Luce. I'm worried."

"Turn that down!" Lucy said to the prince on her way from the kitchen to the living room.

After escaping Ruth, she'd stopped by the grocer for bean dip, chips, apples, poo-sham, dark beer and a few medieval film disc classics she thought he might enjoy. *Excalibur* blaring, she'd thought she heard the phone, but figured it must've just been some knight's pealing scream.

The prince leaned forward, elbows resting on his knees. The classic King Arthur tale had him all but hypnotized—with the exception of the occasional historical inaccuracy he felt honor bound to point out.

Sipping at her light beer, feeling warm and lazy beside the crackling fire, it occurred to Lucy that she was having far more fun watching Wolfe's reaction to the movie than actually watching the movie. Not to mention the fact that as she'd imagined, he looked amazing in just the black silk bottoms of the pajamas she'd bought him.

"Mmm—most agreeable," he grunted while chewing

his latest bite of the dip she'd doctored with sour cream, cheddar cheese and salsa.

"Glad you like it," she said, surprised to find that she actually was. She should be upstairs working on her World Biological Conference report, but for the moment anyway, this was much more fun.

And then he blasted her with a slow, sexy grin that stole her next breath, and the moment was no longer just fun, but erotic when on TV she noticed Uther and Egrain getting busy.

"See that?" Wolfe, said, pointing toward the writhing onscreen couple.

Lucy searched for air. "Y-yes."

"He has not the skill that I do."

"Oh?"

"Were you to declare your eternal love for me this moment, fair Miss Lucy Gordon, I would push back this pillowed seat you recline on and set you before the fire."

"It's called a sofa," she said, wishing for the strength to break his stare.

"As you wish," he acquiesced with a gentle nod. "I would shove the so-faa back, and then free your breasts of their unattractive binding, and—"

"I-I like this blouse," Lucy said, glancing down at the utilitarian white blouse she'd owned for years.

He opened the top button, and like a deer caught in headlights, she sat there frozen and let him. Pushing apart the two halves of her collar, exposing her chest, he splayed his great hand across her fire-warmed skin, the tip of his middle finger searing the pulsing hollow at the base of her throat. Could he feel her heart race? Did he hear her erratic breaths?

141

Onscreen, the heat had ended, but here, in her stupid living room, there was no such relief.

"This garment you profess to like," he said, inching his hand lower on her chest, sliding it boldly into the cup of her simple cotton bra. "I can no longer abide. Take it off."

"T-take it off?" She gulped.

"Yes. I'm no longer amused by watching life on the picture box. After a millennium of virtual death, I'm ready to live. To suckle sweet nectar from your breasts. To mount you and ride you, and spill my seed deep within your womb."

"Whoa. Time out there, big fella." Finally coming round to her senses, Lucy removed his hand from her breast, then straightened and rebuttoned her shirt. "Haven't you learned anything from the last disastrous time you spilled your seed?"

"That is in the past," he said, waving his hand in royal dismissal. "Now—tonight—you must declare your eternal love. Then, once I have granted your much-deserved bedding, I shall strike out across the land in search of my destiny."

"And I'm supposed to declare my eternal love for you, be thrilled for your mercy lay while you fill me with your bionic seed, then wish you on your merry way?"

Expression blank, he said, "I do not understand this bi-on-ic seed?"

"Never mind," she said, pushing herself up from the sofa, and storming for the stairs. She'd had it. Had it with his constant innuendoes, and sexual banter, and even worse, she'd had it with her own stupid longing for the man. She'd had it with the way her pulse raced, and stomach fluttered upon catching just a hint of his wickedly handsome smile.

Honestly, she couldn't blame the women of his time for falling for him. He was undeniably the hottest guy she'd ever seen, but seeing as he was also in one heck of a bind, and very much needing her pledge of eternal love, she also wouldn't put it past him to be highly conniving. More than capable of telling her anything she wished to hear if it furthered his cause—namely, keeping his human form!

She'd halfway expected him to follow her upstairs, but when he didn't, far from relief, she felt a damning twinge of regret. And that, more than anything else that had just transpired, made her loathe her foolish gullibility.

Face it, they both wanted something.

He wanted to remain human.

She wanted him transformed back into a frog.

By her cowardly dash up the stairs to the privacy of her room to indulge herself in a stupid round of tears, she'd just been outclassed in this latest battle. But with weeks to go until the next full moon, the real matter at hand wasn't about winning small erotic battles, but the overall war.

Still reclining in front of the picture box, Wolfe glanced at the living room ceiling, imagining the wench's supple movements with each of the floorboards' creaks and groans.

She was in the bathroom.

Turning on water.

Filling the bathing pool? At this very moment, perfuming her hair with the foamy white poo-sham she'd purchased from the store?

As the current focus of the movie he watched was the type of bloody battle he'd prefer to forget, and the warriors weren't even using weapons that looked anything like the ones he'd once wielded, he rested his head against the pillowed seat—*so-faa*—and closed his eyes, dreaming of *her*.

Her body was much the same as other women he'd known, but at the same time different. Compact. Beneath the ridiculous garment the wench made him wear, his manhood swelled, and he shifted to allow himself room.

Women wore such soft garments—not warriors.

If anyone he knew saw him garbed in such an outrageous manner, he'd become more maligned than the village idiot.

Ahh, but therein lay the rub.

They were all dead.

Not just his much-missed brother, Rufus, but his father, friends, even people like Cook who'd been old with only one good eye even back when his life had been taken. This wench was now the only person in the whole of the kingdom that he knew. If he'd been on a mission to spy, this might not have been a bad thing, but somehow in this particular case, the notion of having only one friend in all the land didn't strike him as good.

Watching with the rage and adrenaline-pumping brutality unfolding on what the wench had called a tee-vee, Wolfe realized he'd been going about this all wrong.

Until the wench made her love vow, she was no

friend, but his enemy. Why, when he but breathed her name across her lips did the colors of her eyes darken, and breasts swell as she leaned into him? An act for which in the past he'd taken as a sure sign of wanting.

Why this constant denial of her body's desires? To mate was inevitable. Why did she fight it so?

Why indeed?

But then he viewed a traitor on the tee-vee, and Wolfe narrowed his eyes. Could the wench not be as simple-minded as he'd first believed? While he couldn't fathom why, could she have reason to want him transformed back into a loathsome frog?

The very thought turned his blood to ice.

No. He was done with living in water, constantly on the look out for predators—even more so than when he'd lived in fear of his enemies trying to oust him from his throne.

Was he forever destined to live in fear?

Glancing down at his missing toe, he recalled the day he'd allowed a four-legged assassin too close. Wolfe had been happily dozing upon a lily pad, soaking in hot summer sun, when—snap! He'd never even seen the jaws that had nearly bitten him in two. Only smelled putrid breath and heard gnashing teeth.

Losing a mere toe had been lucky indeed! Not only had it signaled his survival of the attack, but it jolted him from his lackadaisical existence. For it was that most current brush with death that had led him to notice the wench, her apparent love of pond creatures, and maybe even perhaps her love of him.

To accomplish such a feat of making her love him had seemed easy then, but that had been before making her acquaintance. Before having been formally introduced to that most infuriating stubborn set of her jaw. Or the rising storm clouds forever darkening her eyes.

For alas, he now knew she did not love him.

But, that, as the seasons, would inevitably change.

And come morning, when he once again took up the armaments of war, he'd be fighting for not honor, riches or even land, but the ownership of but one woman's heart, and one man's life—his own.

Lying in bed, staring at the ceiling, Lucy listened to the sounds of Wolfe settling in for the night. The creak of his closing door. Then the opening of his door, and the repeated creak and click of the bathroom lock. He was fascinated by the mechanics of so many of the things she took for granted.

Once he'd apparently had his fill of inspecting the lock, there came a series of flushes, then the sink taps being turned on and off, on and off.

Sometimes, as odd as it seemed, she saw the prince not as a man, but a little boy, exploring his world.

Finally, came the bouncing creak of his bedsprings, and then purely imagined sounds of his clicking off his bedside lamp, then emitting a final sigh before shutting his dark eyes for the night.

Only then did she release her own rush of air, for it was only then that, at least for tonight, her angst where he was concerned had come to an end.

Theoretically, that alone should have been enough to allow her access to the gates of sleep, but no. While her shoulders and back ached with exhaustion, her mind reeled.

*Grumsworth.*

*Ruth.*

*Wolfe.*

*William.* She bolted upright in her bed.

How could she? They'd had plans for dinner that night. Eight o'clock. Because even though he'd said eightish, the duke expected himself and others to always be prompt.

Creeping from her bed, poking her toes into fluffy blue terry cloth slippers, then slipping on her freshly laundered robe, she crept from her room and padded down the stairs. Wolfe, as she'd taught him, had carefully turned out all of the lights, and even turned off the TV. Eyeing the blinking message light on the answering machine that lived on the table in the corner beside the back door, she instead headed for the disc player, curious to see if he'd also been listening when she'd taught him to always remove the disc, and pop it back into the box.

Guided by the few glowing embers radiating heat from the fire, and the soft golden glow of the cottage's exterior lights, Lucy pressed eject, but nothing happened.

Nose wrinkled, she tried again with the same results.

Then looked to the top of the TV where she found the disc back in its box.

Wow, she thought, shaking her head with a smile. If only her students at school did such a great job of applying her lessons!

The answering machine, she approached with trepidation.

Judging by the accusing on/off glow, that time during the movie when she'd been in the kitchen and thought she heard the phone ring, she'd been right.

Finally deciding to get her punishment over with, she

pressed the button fast, then crossed her arms, raising her left hand to her mouth to gnaw the tip of her pinky finger.

Her heart lurched when William's voice flooded the room. At first, he sounded predictably—and understandably put out—but by the end of the recording, he sounded concerned. And the fact that she'd caused him even a moment of needless fret filled her with shame.

*Ring me when you get home, Luce. I'm worried.*

"And I'm sorry," she said, pressing her hand to the machine holding his voice.

# Chapter Twelve

"Wench!" The prince bellowed. "Bring more of this curious colored nectar."

"That would be strawberry-banana-orange juice," Lucy said, refilling his glass. "And in the future, please feel free to help yourself."

Bacon strip to his lips, he said, "Yes, but I prefer having my dishes brought to me."

"Yes," she said, sitting beside him at the dining room table, then snapping open the morning paper. "But I prefer to not be at your constant beck and call."

"Tell me of this," he said, tapping the sheets.

"What? The newspaper?"

"Yes. It looks quite hard to decipher, yet yesterday morning as well, it seemed to hold you in its spell."

Lowering it, Lucy said, "Please don't take this the wrong way, but . . . don't you know how to read?"

"Aye. I signed my name when needed."

"Well, sure, signing your name is good, but I mean reading, as in looking at this headline and telling me what it says." Folding the paper to the front page, she folded it again in half, then handed it to him. When he had it in hand, she tapped the headline, *Local Bakery Burgled for Bread!* "I know our written language must be completely changed from what you remember, but see if you can sound this out."

"Take that away," he said after a good long stare. Attention back on his bacon, he added, "And talk of something else. I find this entire subject upsetting to my digestive efforts."

Lucy shook her head.

Amazing.

If the guy had lived the rest of his life in the ninth century, he'd have ruled quite a sizable chunk of real estate, yet he didn't know how to read. Not that such a thing had been all that uncommon back in his day. And sad but true, it wasn't even all that uncommon in current times, but while all that might be true, it didn't have to be. Not knowing how to read could be easily enough fixed through time and a genuine willingness to learn.

Pushing aside her own bacon and eggs that she had yet to touch, she said, "Wolfe?"

"Aye."

"Would you like to learn to read?"

" 'Tis unnecessary when spoken words speak ever so much more eloquently than those on the page."

"True," she said, sipping at still-steaming orange spice tea. "But these days, reading is important."

Skeptical smile hardly looking convinced, he said, "Name an instance in which it may be beneficial."

"Okay . . . well, take for instance if you wished to go somewhere on an airplane or train. If you couldn't read, how would you know what times were available or how much your ticket cost?"

Eyebrows furrowed, his dark gaze turned menacing. Had she even heard a growl? "I know not of which you speak. Make it plain, wench, or be off with you."

Blaming his gruff demeanor on pride, rather than ill will, Lucy forged ahead, ignoring his comment about her being gone from her very own home—something which if she ever hoped to arrive at school on time, she actually very much needed to do! "Okay," she said, "let's try this a different way. If you ever had need to, say, travel to Scotland, then—"

"Death to all Scots! 'Twould never happen, woman."

"Then you'll have to just take my word for it. Reading's important. Everyone should know how."

He laughed. "Certainly not children?"

"Especially children. That's what I do—teach children."

"To read?"

"No. I teach them about science—about trees and animals and insects and flowers—that sort of thing, but I could teach you to read. That is, assuming you wanted to learn."

"Aye." he said, pushing back his plate. "Make it so. You shall teach me today, right after you bring me more *juuse.*"

"Nay," she said, forking a bite of scrambled egg. "I shall maybe teach you tonight, after I get home from school. And as for your juice, feel free to help yourself."

"But I've already told you I prefer being served."

"And I already told you, I don't mind delivering food if you're sick, or if I happen to be getting something for myself, but face it, Prince, your days of ruling me are over. Capiche?"

"I know not your meaning," he said, the ferocity of his scowl alerting her to an impending royal snit. "But be warned, Lucy Gordon, your flippant tone is tantamount to treason."

Swallowing a bite of bacon, Lucy was again shaking her head. "You don't know capiche, but you know words like flippant and tantamount?"

He shrugged. "Already this morn I have found the Ope-rah Channel quite educational."

When the wench finally took her leave, Wolfe tidied the kitchen just as he'd learned from the tee-vee, then sat down hard at the table, eyeing the empty chair usually occupied by her.

Her offer to teach him to read warmed him.

For far from what he'd claimed—that reading was of no importance—he knew from painful personal experience that it was. . . .

"What are we to do, Your Highness? We appear to be surrounded." Günter, a brave and tireless soul who had fought beside not only Wolfe, but also his brother and father, held his hand over the gushing wound at his side. Even as blood trickled from the corner of his mouth, he sat straight on his mount, sword at the ready.

"We must go forward," Wolfe called to his meager few. There were fifteen total. All mounted, mud-splattered and bloodied on this bitterly cold day when clouds rose from their very breath.

The horses stood skittish. Eyes wide, nostrils flared in this muddied bowl in the land.

On the bowl's rim, stood forty—nay, fifty—of his

father's most despised enemy, ringing them in certain death. But on this day, as any other, Wolfe was in no mood to die. When he died, it would be as an old man, held in a maiden's arms. Dying here, now, in this cold hell was not an option. Chin raised, he said to the men who'd long since circled, backs to each other, swords raised to impending doom, "My father's missive said there are reinforcements ahead. Once we reach those, these fools who only think they have us beat, will soon enough know the errors of their ways."

"Nay, are ye daft?" young Halyard said, new to the King's army, and fresh from the battle for Gaul. "The missive plainly reads for us to retreat. Your father had no time to raise more men. This mission you send us on is suicide."

Wolfe raised his sword. "You dare contradict me?"

" 'Tis not contradiction, but self-preservation."

" 'Tis treason!" Wolfe roared. "You are new amongst us, but these men by your sides, they are brothers to me. And you dare accuse me of leading them to their deaths?"

Günter met Wolfe's stare, only to bow his head. They'd ridden together long enough to know each other's minds with mere looks, and the look he'd just conveyed said wherever Wolfe led, he would follow.

"What say you?" Wolfe asked Godric, the next rider in the circle.

He bowed his head.

As did the next man in line, and the next, and the next until all present with the exception of young Halyard had silently sworn allegiance to their prince.

"Then we ride," Wolfe said, raising his sword to the heavens now crying biting white tears. "We ride! We kill! We succeed in this battle as we have all others!"

All repeated the vow that had been repeated by the mighty Gwyneddor warriors since Wolfe had been but a boy, and still longer. All repeated the vow save for one. One who had dangerously slit his eyes.

Oh, young Halyard bowed his head, but then his words were not merely tantamount to treason, but the actual thing. "I will do this, Your Highness, but know ye if what I said to be true, not just my blood, but the blood of all present will forever rest upon your shoulders. I swear on my mother's grave. Your father's missive said *retreat*. Were you to but read it again for yourself, you'd see that—"

"Enough!" Günter roared, silencing the young man with but his murderous look. "You ride, or we'll kill you ourselves. For when you speak ill of my prince, you speak ill of my king . . . an act punishable by death."

Sensing danger, the horses grew ever more restless, hoofing the mud.

"Aye, the young prince be naught a wolf, but a lamb, Roth! Just as ye said!" Wolfe heard the enemy, up on the rim, shouting and sharing a laugh at his expense.

His nostrils flared with rage. "There. It is there that we shall break through the enemy line. And there that we shall inflict the bloodiest wounds. Ride, warriors of Gwyneddor! Ride!"

With mighty roars, the men did ride, and just as young Halyard had foretold, many of them died. . . .

Wolfe looked up, sharply inhaling while wiping tears from his eyes with the backs of his hands. Günter, young Halyard, Godric, Maurin—four brave souls dead. At his hands. For while he might not have wielded the swords that dealt their deaths, he'd wielded the far more dangerous order. An order based on the fact that had he but known how to read, he'd have known young Halyard's words to be true.

"Luce, hello," William said. "I'm so glad you rang."

Hot relief shimmered through Lucy, weakening her knees. At least William was still speaking to her! Maybe her thoughtless actions hadn't caused damage that couldn't be repaired. Sinking into the chair beside the teacher's lounge phone, she said, "I'm sorry. I—"

"Let me guess," he said. "Lost track of time?"

"Something like that," she said. "When I realized what I'd done, I felt awful, William. Just awful. Can I have a rain check?"

"Tonight?"

"Of course. Eight again?"

"Eight again."

As William hung up his phone, he gazed at his austere, oak-lined office with its uncomfortable brown leather chairs and sofas, and rows and rows of books, and pools of incandescent lamplight and burgundy velvet drapes pulled against the sun, and found himself smiling.

Pushing his heavy desk chair back, he crossed the room, jerking the drapes open, inviting inside brilliant streams of autumn sun.

His secretary entered, and for the first time, he really looked at her. Dark hair pulled into a severe chignon. A severe black suit. Severely pointed heels, the toes of which appeared more accommodating to pizza wedges than feet! "Here are the files you requested, sir."

"Thank you, Ms. Roberts."

She nodded, then, "Would you like me to shut the drapes, sir?"

"Come again?" He looked toward the Thames, at the view that when he'd been but a child, he'd always found enchanting, to once again find it so. The fall colors were glorious. Russets and reds that reminded him of Luce's eternally-mussed curls.

"Your drapes, sir. You prefer them to be closed. I'm so sorry," she said, efficiently heading that way. "The cleaning service must've left them open."

"Leave them," he said.

Mouth gaping, hand on the draw cord, she said, "Did I hear you right?"

"Yes. I said leave them—please."

Fidgeting with her hands at her waist, she said, "Certainly, sir. Will there be anything else?"

"No, thank you." She was almost to the door when he called, "Ms. Roberts?"

"Yes?"

"Am I terribly difficult to work for?"

"Sir?"

Sighing, he looked to the floor. "Come in," he said, "and please, shut the door, and make yourself comfortable. . . . If such a thing is even possible in this lifeless tomb."

"Am I to be dismissed, sir? Have I done something to displease you? If it's your drapes, sir, I promise, that—"

What about his manner inspired this sort of fear? Appalled, he said, "Please, Ms. Roberts, no. No, I promise you I'm quite pleased with your services. You're efficient, prompt, thorough, neat in your personal appearance. All qualities, I assure you, that I hold in very high regard."

"Thank heavens," she said, hand to her chest. "You gave me quite a fright."

"Sorry," he said. "That was the last of my intentions." He'd planned to say more, but was taken on a mental detour. *Neat.* Of course. Was that why Lucy had stood him up? Was that what had led her to be shopping for clothes for another man? A tall, apparently more *hip* man. Because she feared he didn't approve of her not keeping her cottage properly straightened—which he didn't. But what was wrong with him that such a thing even mattered?

Bloody hell, he thought, slashing his fingers through his usually neat hair.

"Your Grace?"

He looked up. "Oh, Ms. Roberts. For a minute there, I'd quite forgotten you were here. Terribly sorry."

"Yes, sir. You already admitted as such," she said with a surprisingly pretty blush. Who'd have thought that his own Ms. Roberts, whom he'd seen every weekday for months upon years without ever having truly seen, actually possessed a charming blush.

"All right, then," he said, "I suppose I should start at the beginning. You see, I have a rather unorthodox question for you, Ms. Roberts. One I hope you won't be offended by, but seeing how you're the only woman of my acquaintance I feel comfortable chatting up who is under the age of sixty, I fear you're the only one who can help."

Smiling now, she leaned forward in her chair. "Sir, I'd be delighted to help in any way I can."

"All right, then," perching on the edge of his desk,

he said, "Hmm, this is rather more awkward than I'd expected, but here is the gist of it. Ms. Roberts, I fancy myself in love with an American hottie, and I fear she finds me dull as an old troll. Do you have any suggestions as to the manner of making myself more attractive?"

Still sniffling and shook up from her latest run-in with Grumsworth, Lucy tried wedging the key in the cottage's lock while holding Buzzy's heavy cage under her left arm, but just as she'd failed her first attempt, and begun her second, the door burst open, and the prince took the cage from her arms.

"Lucy Gordon," he said, flip-flopping her heart with a slow, sexy grin. "You are late."

"I know," she said, brushing past him and into the mudroom. "What is that heavenly smell?"

"Beef stroganoff," he said, setting Buzzy's home on the mudroom's wooden bench. "I learned to prepare it from a young man calling himself *The Naked Chef*. He appears daily on the *Cooking Classics Channel*."

Eyebrows raised, Lucy lifted the lid on the concoction simmering on the stove. "Wow," she said, stomach growling from just the awesome smell. "Not that I've heard of him, but I'm impressed."

He bowed.

"And look at you," she said, so stunned with dinner that she hadn't noticed his duds. Dressed in khakis and a caramel-colored sweater, he'd then gathered his long hair into a pony tail tied with a highly suspicious strip of leather. Was that one of the shoelaces from her best pair of loafers?

Who cared? He looked even more delicious than the food he'd prepared! "Hot stuff."

"Judging by your most pleasing facial expression, I assume this is a good thing?"

"A very good thing," she said, forcing her gaze off of his mouthwatering features and back to dinner, suddenly at a loss as to what to do with her hands. "Well, um, did you happen to notice what was inside the cage you so graciously grabbed from me?"

"You mean the squarish thing?"

"Yes," she said, bumbling past him to the mudroom. An exquisite awareness of him wiped clean the lousy slate of her day. How could she have forgotten his size? The sheer muscular mass that made her feel for the first time in her life, not plump, but petite. Even better—or worse—if the hunger for something far different from food raging in his dark eyes could be taken as an indication, she was wanted. Desired. And the very idea curled her toes with stupid, irrational pleasure. If the past five minutes had been this enjoyable, what did an entire evening hold in store?

Trying hard to focus on the matter at hand, she lifted the cage's metal lid, fishing Buzzy out from his pile of fragrant cedar shavings. Hands cupped round his furry, chubby-cheeked belly, she held him up to the prince. "Wolfe, meet Buzzy."

"Put it down!" the prince said, lurching back. "It no doubt bites."

Laughing, she said, "Sure, he bites, but never too hard, and only if you interrupt his beauty sleep." Offering the tiny creature to Wolfe, she said, "Wanna hold him?"

Shaking his head, he took another step back, and if

she hadn't known better, she'd have sworn he was . . .
No. Impossible. There wasn't a chance in hell that the
big, strapping prince was afraid of furry little Buzzy.

"Set it down," he said, "and I'll off it, then roast it
on a stick for dinner."

"No! He's my classroom pet—or, rather, was our
pet," she said, shocked to see the big, strapping man
not only still backing away, but gripping the edge of
the counter. Holding Buzzy to her cheek for a cuddle,
she said, "You're afraid of this cutie, aren't you?"

"Of course not," he said, leaning back as she approached. "But the rodent is unfamiliar to me, and
looks more suitable to roasting on a spit than keeping
as a pet."

"Shame on you," she said, brushing past him on her
way to put Buzzy back in his house. "And you'd better
get used to him, because thanks to Grumsworth, this
little guy is the newest member of our happy home."

"The rodent is to remain here? Inside?" He actually
looked terrified at the thought.

Why?

"Sure," she said, heading upstairs to change. "But
don't worry. He doesn't do much besides eat and sleep.
I'll take care of feeding him, and cleaning his cage."

"Good," the prince said, following her up the stairs.

In her room, Lucy found another surprise. Clothes.
Three piles of neatly folded T-shirts and jeans, bras and
panties. She reddened, feeling Wolfe's firm, warm
hands on those intimate garments just as surely as if
he'd massaged them over the intimate places they'd
been designed to cover. "Um, thank you," she said. You
didn't have to do laundry."

"No," he said, leaning on the open door. "I didn't have to. I wanted to."

"How did you learn to work the washer and dryer, and use the right amount of detergent?"

He shrugged. "A woman on tee-vee was quite helpful. Little of the process was complex, and as for the detergent, that was easily enough distributed from watching a product report upon it during the many brief breaks between my shows."

"Your shows, huh?" Lucy grinned. What? He'd been a housewife for a whole two days and already he was afraid of mice and had shows? What had she done to this once virile man? Tucking her hands in her jacket pockets, her left hand fingers touched cool foil. "Oh, hey," she said, taking out a candy bar. "I almost forgot. Here," she handed it to him. "I got this for you."

"For me? You brought me a gift?" Though he'd have no way of knowing, the size of his smile was a gift for her.

"It's no big deal," she said, surprised such a small gesture was all it took to make him so happy. "It's just a candy bar. Here," she said, helping him with the wrapper. "You eat it."

"But the silver!" he said, staring in horror as she crumpled it before tossing it in the trash. "That alone must be worth a king's ransom."

"Nah, it's called aluminum foil, and the color is all it has in common with silver."

His eyes still wide, she broke the bar in half, then held it to his lips, wishing she'd let him hold it himself when along with the candy, his warm lips and breath grazed her fingers.

When his taste buds finally kicked in, a shiver tremored through him, and he gripped her wrist. "Wench?" he asked.

"Yes?" Well? Did shivers mean he liked it or hated it?

His strong lips parted in a huge smile, and then he was grabbing the other half of the bar, holding it out to her. "But this is magnificent. Food fit for God Himself. Have you tried it? Here," he said, forcing it to her lips. "You must have the remains. I insist. Even a mere woman should not be without such a supremely divine taste."

"A mere woman, huh?" To show him she could eat every bit as well as any man twice her height, she bit off a good-sized chunk of the remaining half and chewed.

" 'Tis good, eh?"

He'd placed his fingertips to her lips, tracing the curve of her grin. "Yes. *'Tis* good."

The chocolate was good, but even better was the feel of his fingers, easing their way around the sensitive skin. Barely touching, yet filling her with the most vibrantly erotic longings, to—to do absolutely nothing.

No, no, no.

She wasn't playing this game of his ever again. The two of them could have fun together, but not that kind of fun—not that she thought doing those sorts of things with him was fun, because . . .

Aw, hell. Who was she trying to kid?

Face it, she wanted him, and she wanted him bad. But like the good scientist she was attempting to be, from now on, she vowed to always maintain a professional distance from her subject—no matter what outrageous move he next pulled!

# Chapter Thirteen

Wolfe wanted her.

Sitting at her disgracefully small table, he watched Lucy Gordon turn her fork upside down, darting her tongue out to lick creamy white sauce from the tines, eyes half shut with hazy pleasure. Pleasure he'd created, only with pots and pans and cream sauce as opposed to trailing his fingers along her sweet inner thighs.

"Thank you," she said, putting down her fork as if she were done.

Wolfe eyed her half-empty trencher. "For a wench who normally eats her fill, you ate little enough tonight. Though your satisfied smile says other-wise, I'm now left wondering if you found the taste of my meal disagreeable?"

"Hardly. It was delicious." Dabbing her lips with a white cloth, she said, "I still can't believe you whipped that up from what little's in my pantry."

He shrugged. All afternoon, during the assembling

of the feast, he'd desired the wench's smiling praise, but now that he had it, it felt somehow incomplete. What he truly desired was far more complex.

A declaration of love. To be given—now.

Upstairs, in her cozy bed.

The very thought of her not wanting him angered him as surely as if he'd just kneed his mount to charge into a losing battle. For this had become a battle—the toughest battle he'd ever fought, and for the first time in his thousand-plus years of life, he found himself uncertain of his course.

All women loved him.

That was the way it had always been with him.

They'd loved sheltering him and cooing over him when he'd been but a wee boy. And after his mother's death, the women about the house insured he never lacked for a gentle touch. And then when he'd grown older, old enough to want more from a woman than soft hugs, they'd grown to love his strength and size, and legendary bedroom prowess.

Yet with this woman, this woman who held his very life in her delicate hands, who seemed to thirst for him much in the same manner as had all others, the trouble was in her refusal to act upon that thirst.

It made no sense. Why thirst, yet not drink? 'Twas against the very laws of nature.

"You're awfully quiet," she said, reaching for his plate even as she pushed back her chair. "What's on your mind?"

"You."

Carrying both of their plates to the kitchen sink, she said, "That sounds dull."

"To the contrary," he said, following her with the

empty bowl of pas-ta. He set it to the counter, then swept fiery curls from her neck, kissing the tender spot he'd bared. "I find you to be a most intriguing guileless mystery."

"Oh?" He'd pinned her to the counter, but she ducked beneath his arm, skittering to the other side of the room.

"I especially find that interesting."

"What?" she said, wrapping a stick of butter before popping it into the fridge.

"Your habit of denying yourself the pleasure of being in my arms."

"Habit?" She coughed.

"See?" he asked, slipping his hands about her waist. "Your body knows you need me. Why doesn't your heart?"

Chin raised, palms against his steely chest, no doubt itching to explore, she said, "Last time I checked, Your Highness, my body and heart were connected. And both of us have to go."

"Go?"

"Yes, you know what that means, don't you?" Pushing herself free, she said, "Thanks for dinner. Since you cooked, leave the cleanup for me. I'll tackle it when I get home. Oh, and I made you some reading flash cards during lunch—you know, with the alphabet and some sounds. I meant to bring them home, but Grumsworth showed up, and well, you can probably guess the rest. Anyway, I forgot them, and I'm sorry. But we'll get to them tomorrow."

He nodded his acceptance of her apology, pleased that she hadn't forgotten his need. "Where are you going?" he asked. "Because if it's to purchase me more clothes, or—"

"Nothing like that," she said. "I hurt someone, and tonight, I need to make things up to him."

"*Him?*" Eyebrows raised, he said, "You wouldn't be off to visit that insipid duke, would you?"

"Okay, yes." Turning away from him to snatch her quilted purse off a peg on the mudroom wall, she said, "Not that it's any of your concern."

"Not my concern?" he raged, curving his fingers round her shoulders, digging them into her soft flesh. "Nothing has ever been more my concern. Don't you understand, Lucy Gordon? You hold my life in your hands. If you don't soon declare your love, I will cease to exist. What could possibly be more important, or more worthy of my concern than the matter of my own self-preservation?"

"N-nothing," she said with a light shake of her head. "Everything. I don't know. You're confusing me."

"Confusing you?" He laughed. "And what do you think your increasingly passionate nature does to me? The darkening of your eyes. Hitches in your breath. The hardening of buds that have nothing to do with roses and everything to do with your very breasts reaching out for my touch."

A desperate giggle escaped her throat. "You think too highly of yourself, Your Highness."

"Ahh, shall I take that as your challenge to prove me wrong?"

"Take it however you want, just know that it's William I love."

"For now," he said, his voice a low growl. "Just keep in mind, Lucy Gordon, that when he kisses you, you

166

shall never cleave to him as you do to me."

"Let me go." Cold fire flashing in her eyes of pale blue, she squirmed against him. "I hate you. You've brought nothing but havoc to my life."

"Because you know I'm right," he said, her accusations increasing not only the intensity of his hold, but his will to win. "Stop fighting me, and allow yourself the shelter to be found in my arms. As king, I can protect you, I can—"

"No," she said. "The only thing I want you to do is let me go."

"As you wish," he said, abiding by her request so swiftly that she momentarily lost balance. Instinctively, he reached out to steady her, but held back, not wishing to further invoke her anger. "Just know, Lucy Gordon, that tonight, if you should find yourself cold or wanting, it is due to neither climate nor company, but the absence of me."

Lucy stepped calmly outside of her cottage, strolled down the crushed stone path winding toward the castle garden, then, once she knew herself free of the prince's line of sight, she ran. Ran so hard that her lungs ached, but still she ran, on and on until her hair and clothes hung limp with sweat, and tears smudged her already weary makeup.

"Why?" she sobbed, crumbling onto a wood bench. Why did the man affect her so? All she had to do was survive his presence for one month—not even a full month now—and if what he'd said was true, her every dream would magically appear.

All her life, she'd been a scientist first, woman second. Why couldn't she seem to remember that now?

If she somehow managed to keep her wits about her, in less than a month's time, her father would love and adore her. Professionally, she'd be lauded and cheered. The duke would finally propose. Grumsworth would be off of her case, because there was no way he'd hassle a real live duchess!

All she had to do to achieve all of that and more was keep her distance, and keep her cool. She'd be polite to the prince. She'd even help him learn to read and rave over his cooking, but one thing she could not—would not—do was let him get to her.

She had to once and for all get it through her head that nothing the prince said was real. He was a self-professed brilliant warrior and, she assumed, strategist. Meaning he full well knew how to yank her emotional chains!

The man was brilliant. Easily proven by the nifty range of skills he'd picked up just by watching a little TV.

Great. So where did that leave her? Smack dab in the middle of a battle over something she wasn't prepared to give. Something she didn't even have to give! The prince wanted her to love him, but that was going to be kind of hard, seeing how she already loved William!

Ha! Try telling that to her racing heart.

The whole damned time she'd stood there hurling oh-so-brave insults at Wolfe, her lips had actually tingled for his. Had he placed her under some sort of ancient spell?

She wouldn't put it past him, and lord knew the physical signs were there, seeing how all day long, she couldn't wait to get home.

Which was stupid.

She didn't even like him, so why had she wondered what he was watching on TV? And what he'd think of her latest installment with Grumsworth? And if he'd like chocolate? Or amusement parks? Or one of those pricey moon cruises? Or even if he'd noticed the new way she'd styled her hair?

Stupid!

Storming to her feet, arms crossed, lips pressed tight, she paced.

It wouldn't matter if she'd sheared her head and painted it purple!

She loved William!

She would one day marry William!

And then—

"Luce?"

She jumped. "William. I didn't hear you."

"Little wonder, with all of this fuming. May I?" he asked, awkwardly holding out his arms as if he'd like to give her a hug. Did he even have to ask?

"Oh, William," she cried, stepping into his embrace, crying messy tears all over his soft cotton sweatshirt. Sweatshirt? William never wore sweatshirts. Still, that oddity could be pondered later. Right now, she had much bigger issues to contend with. For while she rued the very day the prince hopped into her life, he'd also brought with him the possibility of her every dream coming true. Dreams that came at a price, her nosy conscience reminded her. Wolfe's life. Oh, sure, he'd still be technically alive, but could living the life of a frog be anywhere near as satisfying as life as a man? And would his actual transformation be painful? Did he at least have frog friends out there to keep him company beside the pond?

"Hey," William said, tenderly pulling back to squeeze her hand. "What's Grumsworth done now?"

She shook her head before rummaging through her purse for a tissue.

William took one from his pocket and handed it to her.

"How are you always so prepared?" she asked after a good, hard blow. "How do you always do and say the right thing, and never seem to have a moment's angst?"

"Never any angst, huh?" He laughed. "If only you could have seen me fifteen minutes ago, dashing about the place in preparation for you."

"What do you mean?" Lit by a pale sliver of rising moon, worry knitted his eyebrows and he'd pressed his lips into a concerned frown.

"This is what I love about you," he said, leading her back to the wooden bench she'd originally started out on before giving her hand another tender squeeze. "You have no idea of the mayhem you wreak upon my heart."

Oh! Lucy drew her free hand to her mouth. Was this it? Was he about to propose?

He looked to the stone walk, and kicked a pebble with the right toe of gleaming new Reeboks. Reeboks? Wow, he really had gone all out to impress! Before looking back to her, he sighed. "Ruth Hagenberry called last night."

Argh! How could she be so stupid? William wasn't proposing. He was breaking up.

"And, while you know I don't usually set store by her

outrageous tales, her latest caught me rather unprepared."

"Oh?"

"She said she spotted you out purchasing a rather vast assortment of men's clothes. Large men's clothes—not large in a stout way, but tall, and—bloody hell." Releasing her hand, he stood only to shove his hands into his pockets. "I fear I've quite taken you for granted, Luce, and if I have, I must confess to being terribly sorry in not having made my intentions toward you more clear. While my practical side is not quite ready for a more formal announcement, I should very much like for the two of us to at the very least . . . How do you Yanks say this? Date seriously?"

Tears filled Lucy's eyes.

While this wasn't the marriage proposal she'd hoped for, nevertheless, dating the handsome duke was a good thing.

"Well? Am I to assume tears indicate a negative response?"

She shook her head.

"That's a bloody relief. I've had my secretary counsel me in all ways American, thinking I'd be launching a fight for you. But—"

"Is that why you're wearing a Crimson Tide sweatshirt and sneakers and jeans?" Jeans! William never wore jeans, claiming the casual garments to be the downfall of civilized society.

"You noticed," he said, hands outstretched, heading back her way. "My secretary said I must loosen up. And in that spirit, we're grilling hamburgers for dinner. She suggested hot dogs, but—"

"Hamburgers sound great," she said squeezing her

wonderful man. *Her* man! Eek! They were officially dating. She hadn't felt so romantically giddy since Zane Lundstrom asked her to go with him back in eighth grade.

"So?" the duke said, his arm looped about her waist as they walked to the castle. "Care to tell me who was the lucky recipient of all of those clothes?"

"Relax," Lucy said, crossing her fingers. "They were just for a friend of a friend back home who complains that he can never find high-quality sweaters."

"But Ruth indicated to you also having purchased undergarments and shoes."

"What can I say?" Lucy shrugged. "He loves all things British."

"Can't say as I blame the chap," William said with a grin. "Sounds as if he has bloody good taste—like me."

"Like you, huh?" She poked his ribs. "Might I be so bold, Your Grace, as to include myself in that assessment?"

"You may," he said, pausing beneath an ivy-covered trellis, "under one condition."

"What's that?" she asked, heart aflutter.

"You give me a kiss."

"Mmm, you didn't even have to ask." Surrendering herself to his tender hold, Lucy knew the meaning of bliss. In her dear William was no smoldering passion, but a good, warm and wonderful kiss that when he'd released her to continue their walk left her—

Wanting.

Rats.

*Just know, Lucy Gordon, that tonight, if you should find yourself cold or wanting, it is due to neither climate nor company, but the absence of me.*

No, Lucy resolutely vowed. That wanting had been nothing more than her anticipation for the night to come. Time spent grilling burgers, and talking, and—

*Finally getting back to the cottage to be taken into his arms.*

"Grrr!"

"What was that?" the duke asked on the castle's north terrace.

"Nothing," she said, meaning the word from the very bottom of her heart. "Absolutely nothing."

Cloaked in a veil of shadows, Wolfe smiled.

# Chapter Fourteen

"Have a nice time?"

For the second time that night, Lucy jumped. "Wolfe. Geez. Turn on a lamp, would ya?"

"Why? When I prefer firelight?"

"Because electric lights are civilized." And because lounging on the sofa in just those damned pajama bottoms, the whisker-stubbled angles of his face accentuated by the fire's glow, she could almost believe they'd been transported back to his time. Back to when if he'd tried, he might have made positive changes in his life. This whole frog thing wouldn't even be an issue.

"Weren't you the one who pronounced me wholly uncivilized?"

Ignoring him, Lucy crossed the living room to turn on a light. But the incandescent pool didn't steal near as much of his magnetism as she'd have liked.

Yes, Wolfe, with his battle scars, and long, dark hair and fierce expressions, was the very embodiment of uncivilized. But now that William had declared his intentions, she somehow felt better fortified against the prince's wily charms.

Again, she reminded herself that none of what he portrayed was real, but a carefully calculated act designed not to make her happy, as William's sweatshirt-and-burger night had been, but to make her declare her love. And not because he loved her, but because he wanted to save his own behind!

"I've grown weary of your circular logic." Raking his fingers through his hair, the prince sighed. On his feet, heading toward the stairs, he said, "I bid you good night."

"Just like that?" she said, "You're leaving me, and going to bed?"

"Just like that."

"Dad, hi! It's me, Lucy!" Thursday afternoon on her lunch hour, she'd finally tracked him down in Mongolia, and her cell phone combined with his satellite phone made for a connection crackling with static.

"Lucy? You in trouble? Strapped for cash?"

"Nope. Just, um, needing a small favor." She wrapped the drawstring from her dress's collar round her pinkie, squeezing until the tip of her finger turned red.

"A favor, huh? And it doesn't involve cash?" He laughed.

Swallowing an irritated sigh, Lucy said, "I've made an exciting discovery. A new frog. I can't wait for you to see him, Dad. He's a real beauty." *Especially in his current form.*

"Oh, Luce. Please don't tell me you're back to this search? I thought we'd been over this. You haven't quit your job, have you? I had to pull quite a few strings to—"

"No. That's the best part. I found my new species on the castle lane." Eyes squeezed shut, picturing the unique-to-all-the-world amphibian she'd soon have, she described Wolfe in his frog form. His blazing purple and black diamond ventral, and the deep-set, dark-lashed eyes.

The great Slate Gordon laughed again. "Eyelashes? Oh, Luce. Isn't that a tad over the edge of responsible science, even for you?"

"Dad, please, I'm serious. Believe me, I know how nuts this must sound, which is why I'm calling. I need you to get me on the speaker's list at the World Biological Conference."

"No."

"Please, Dad."

"Absolutely out of the question. Don't you think you caused enough trouble the last time you appeared?"

"Yes, but this time, I really do have a unique species."

While her pulse pounded in her ears, for endless seconds, the only sound on the line was static, then finally, a deep sigh. "Can you e-mail me a picture?"

"I don't have one."

"If you're talking about a formal presentation, Luce, a picture is a pretty basic requirement. Not to mention a physical sample of the specimen itself—either alive or dead."

Crossing her fingers, Lucy said, "I know, I know. Look, I'll take pictures tonight." *Surely, I can doctor one on a photo program at school so that it resembles the frog prince in all of his spotted glory.* "It's just that with all the excitement over my find, I haven't yet had a chance. But if you give me your latest address, I'll get those right out to you."

"All right." Another heavy sigh told her just what a farce he thought her story to be.

"Great, Dad. Oh, and please schedule me by tomorrow. That's the deadline for speakers to be registered. I've already filed the paperwork, all you have to do is give it your okay."

"But, Luce, without seeing the pictures, how can I—"

"Gotta go, Dad. Our connection's breaking up." Reaching for the foil Wolfe had wrapped her ham sandwich in for lunch, she said, "Bye. See you soon."

"But, Luce, I—"

"Sorry, Dad," she said to herself, pressing the end button on her phone. "But I'm afraid your call has been disconnected."

Leaning back in the musty old arm chair, putting her feet up on an equally weary footstool, Lucy gave herself a mental pat on the back, and smiled.

Mission accomplished.


Usually on a Friday afternoon, Lucy was thrilled to park her mini in the cottage's carriage house garage, but on this afternoon, she warily eyed her once cozy home, wondering what to expect. With William in Edinburgh on business, she felt very much alone. She needed his pleasant company reminding her of the light at the end of what now felt like an endless tunnel—a tunnel that however long, would result in amazing gains for not only herself, but the worldwide scientific community.

True, watching Wolfe being transformed wouldn't

be pleasant, but beyond her own impending fame for discovering him, the implications for study were endless.

The U.S. military might even be interested in giving him a closer look. If they unlocked the sorceress's secrets, they'd hold the world's most awesome weapon. Imagine having the power to turn an entire enemy army into frogs!

While that thought should have been a comfort, as she climbed out of the mini, reaching for just one of the six sacks of groceries her houseguest had ordered, plus the mostly picture cookbook she hadn't been able to resist buying him, she felt more saddened by such potential studies than gladdened.

Still, she counseled herself on her way up the curving stone path to the mudroom door, she had to keep in mind that Wolfe had brought all of this onto himself. He'd been the one spreading his seed far and wide. Who was she to say his punishment should be ended?

*Like a thousand years suffering isn't enough?*

Ignoring this latest slap from her conscience, she opened the door to bedlam.

"Come here, you little bugger. I command you to come to me, or I'll roast you on a spit!"

"Wolfe?" she cried, tossing the groceries to the mudroom floor, then running to the sound of his voice. "What are you doing?"

She found him in the living room, corralling a trembling Buzzy who'd sought shelter behind the spindly legs of her buffet. Wolfe had blocked off one side of the tall, narrow piece of furniture with an oversized coffee table book, and the other with the ironing board. He knelt at the head of the impromptu cage, barefoot, dressed in jeans, a mossy green sweater, and oven mitts over his hands. His hair was tied back with the strap of leather she'd confirmed as having been pilfered from the left shoe of her favorite pair of loafers. Something about this new, frazzled side of him squeezed her heart.

"What does it look like I'm doing?" he growled.

"Terrorizing my sweet defenseless pet." Poor Buzzy sat on his haunches, whiskers twitching, nibbling a morsel he'd stashed in his cheeks.

"Ha! I'm rescuing the damned rodent."

"From what?" she asked, scrambling to her knees on the opposite end of the pen from the prince. "It's not as if a marauding tribe was attacking his cage."

Wolfe's expression turned dark. "You don't consider certain death to be an attack?"

"Again," she said, fishing out her pet. "What around this boring old cottage could have been so dangerous?"

"Is the coming of demons danger enough for you? I was preparing the evening meal when smoke rolled from the baking machine. Shortly thereafter came the keening cry of an underworld shrew. So I turned off the baking machine, then ran for your rodent pet."

"But you can't stand Buzzy."

"Correct."

"But you saved him anyway?"

"Attempted to." The prince held out his hand, displaying three nasty red welts on his index finger. "The beast bit me before jumping from my hold. He then scrambled behind this cupboard from whence I have been trying to take him ever since."

Holding Buzzy's chubby fuzz to her cheek, Lucy glanced at Wolfe. At the softening of his gaze.

"I can't claim to understand the affection you hold

for the rodent beast. But I am pleased he is safe."

"Me, too." she said. "Thank you." From the sounds of it, the life of her smoke-damaged oven had been in more danger than her hamster, but seeing how Wolfe couldn't have known that, and that for whatever reason, he seemed downright terrified of Buzzy, the fact that he'd swallowed his fears to save the life of a pet she loved, put a major chink in the wall she'd built around her heart.

Still on her knees, Lucy scooted to the prince, planning to give him a hug, but he held out his arms, motioning for her to stay away.

On his feet, the prince grabbed the ironing board, presumably carrying it to the mudroom closet that housed the washer and dryer.

After putting Buzzy back in his cage, Lucy searched for Wolfe, finding him with his hands braced against the washer, eyes closed.

"Wolfe?"

He jumped.

"Sorry," she said, tentatively reaching for him, then curving her hand to the warm contours of his sweater-covered back. "I really do appreciate what you did."

" 'Twas nothing."

"You conquered your fears to save something that meant a lot to me, Wolfe. That's not nothing." That wasn't something he could have contrived just to get into her good graces.

"I said it 'twas nothing. And I'm not afraid—of anything—especially that rodent beast."

Was he trembling? "Wolfe?" she asked, one hand on his back, and the other covering his right hand. "What's wrong?"

"What's wrong?" A sharp laugh escaped his lips. "Look at me. I am a warrior. I've killed countless of my father's enemies. Faced foes so fierce lesser men ran screaming at the mere sight of such invincible forces. But not me. I fought. I won. Always. Never falling victim myself to exhaustion or pain—especially not to fear. Never have I given in to fear."

"And you didn't today."

He shook his head. Swallowed hard. "You weren't here, Lucy Gordon. The keening. I thought it was the sorceress come to claim me."

"Oh, Wolfe . . ."

"The sound. I-it, it pierced my mind, leaving me unable to form the simplest thought."

"And yet you managed to turn off the oven, and save a rodent-pet you despise. Hmm, I know I may not be an expert in such things, but it sounds to me as if you acted very bravely indeed."

"Aye," he said with another sullen nod. "But that is not the worst of it. Do you know why I cannot abide your pet?"

She shook her head.

"When I was a man of ten and two, I was taken. Ransomed for my father's head. They held me in a black pit along with countless others. But the blackness, that was not the worst of it. Nor the agonized moans or stenches so foul one would believe them summoned from the very bowels of hell. No—the worst of it was the rats. Hundreds of 'em came each night. Crawling over each exposed strip of flesh, their sharp nails scratching, still sharper teeth gnawing, beady black eyes reflecting the glow of oily-smelling torches far above."

"My God," she said, arms automatically slipping around him for a hug.

He brushed her aside, steeling his shoulders and jaw. "I am ashamed to have feared them. I was a man. A man trained to conquer any foe—no matter how large or, in this case, how small."

"Wolfe?" Going to him again, voice soft, she said, "Come on, give yourself a break. You were twelve. Nowadays, twelve is nowhere close to being a man. And what you went through . . ." she shuddered. "No one, not even your great father, could have blamed you for being afraid."

"Aye," he said, far-off expression eerily cold. "Especially not after I scaled the walls of that pit to slash the throats of each and every one of those cowards while they slept."

Though Wolfe seemed sullen much of the rest of the night, Lucy did her best to distract him, starting the first of their reading lessons at which he did remarkably well. After learning not only the alphabet, but a majority of both vowel and consonant sounds, she said, "All right, brainiac, let's call it quits for tonight."

Eyebrows furrowed, he said, "Is this an insult?"

"No. A compliment. To be a brainiac is a good thing. That means you're very smart and wise."

"Oh." Sitting taller he said, "Yes, I would say that is true."

Grinning at his utter lack of humility, wishing for just a smidgeon of his self-esteem, she said, "Well, now that we know who's got the big head in the family, wanna make some popcorn and watch TV?"

"What is pop-corn?"

"Come on," she said, standing, then taking him by the hand. "Let me show you a little kernel of heaven."

Twenty minutes later, they sat side by side on the sofa, a fire crackling in the hearth, waiting for *Survivor Moon* to start. *Survivor Antarctica* had been awesome, but this one was gonna top 'em all.

"Tasty," the prince said, his face wreathed in a popcorn-induced smile. "Very tasty. Do other people know of this delicacy? Or is it your own private creation designed to bend a man to your will?"

Lucy laughed. "Everyone knows about this. No man-bending going on round here."

Mouth too full to speak, popcorn spilling onto his lap, he nodded.

Rolling her eyes, she snatched one of the fallen pieces and pitched it at him.

"What was that for?" he asked when he finished chewing.

"To remind you to keep it in your mouth, and not on my Oriental rug."

Grinning, he lobbed a piece at her.

"What was that for? I got all of mine in my mouth."

"To remind you, Lucy Gordon, that I give good as I get. Should you wish to launch a full battle, be warned, you're in for a terror-filled fight."

"Terror, huh? With popcorn?"

"You doubt my battle skills?"

"Oh, it's not your battle skills I doubt, Your Majesty, just your choice of weapons."

"Ahh," he said, popping another buttery piece into his mouth. "What food might you find more menacing? Cookies crumpled into your hair? Milk spilt upon your clothes? Chocolate melted upon your lips?"

Eyeing him eyeing her lips, she licked them, cursing his innate ability to mentally transfer heat. "Mmm," she said, "chocolate. Definitely the chocolate."

"Shall I take that as your official surrender?" he asked, nailing her left boob with one more piece.

Reddening, she flew two pieces back at him.

He threw two more.

She threw three more.

He threw four.

She threw five.

Laughing, wrestling on the sofa, hurling outrageous battle cries, Lucy threw and threw until, sensing that by Wolfe's sheer size he'd soon have her defeated, she finally just dumped the whole stupid bowl on his stupid, handsome head.

Roaring, he landed her in a playful tackle to the rug where they tickled more until they were both breathing hard from their fight.

"I win," she said with a big smile.

"I win," he said with an even bigger smile, brushing strands of hair from her eyes, then giving one, lonesome curl a tug.

"But I already said I win," she said, tucking her hair safely behind her ears and out of his grasp.

"How about if we both win?" he said softly, rolling onto his side to press a butterfly soft kiss to her lips.

"Prince Wolfe . . ." Now needing to catch her breath for a whole other reason besides a measly popcorn battle, one that centered around mesmerizing dark eyes and a face so handsome he should have been a Greek god instead of a mere medieval prince, she said, "You've got a deal."

After cleaning their mess, popping a new batch of

buttered corn, then flipping on the TV, they watched in companionable silence for a few minutes before Wolfe pushed himself to his feet, and switched off the TV right at the start of the reward challenge where the prize was a night on Hilton's most posh moon cruise.

"What'd you do that for?" she complained.

" 'Tis nonsense. This tale of men playing a game upon the very surface of the moon I find to be an insult to my sensibilities." Back turned on the TV, he crossed his arms.

Tugging on the hem of his shirt, she said, "*Please*, turn the TV back on and sit down."

"No."

"Why?"

"Because I find myself in a rage and know not how to contain myself. I need to ride, gallop across my land with the wind in my hair, and powerful horseflesh pounding between my legs. I need to feel like a man, instead of some kept pet. I need to . . ." He fell backwards onto the sofa, shoulders sagging. "I need to go home. I don't like this time, with its talk of men on the moon, and boxes containing people romping on heavenly objects gracing the sky."

"You like our food," she said, smoothing hair back from his brow. "And chocolate—don't forget how much you enjoy that."

"Aye."

"The rest I can teach you from books. What history you didn't learn watching the unfolding of years beside the pond, we'll study together. Until then, relax. It's understandable that all of this might feel strange. But I promise," she said, smoothing his hair, "all will feel better in time."

He snorted. "Time, milady, is the one thing that without your help, I will never have."

As much as Lucy wanted to reassure him his last statement wasn't anymore true than his belief that he'd never understand the current world, this time even she was stumped.

Even if she wanted to save him, she couldn't.

Because sure, she was forming a certain affection for the guy, but that was a far cry from love, and to break his curse, he had to be loved. And just going out on a limb here, but if the sorceress who'd placed the curse had been strong enough to do that, chances were she was also strong enough to make it so that one woman happening along couldn't be bribed with a quick roll in the hay or even gold coins to declare her love. She'd have to feel it. And love wasn't something easily faked. Even worse, as Wolfe had just painfully pointed out, love took time—the one luxury the sorceress had insured he'd never have.

That sorceress must've been one bad-ass chick. Because from where Lucy was sitting, it looked like Wolfe's curse might never be broken.

While Lucy was still irked at that sorceress for not even giving Wolfe a fighting chance, he shook his head at the TV she'd coaxed him into turning back on. The two-hour premier was winding down. The immunity challenge had just been won by Team Jupiter who'd only barely managed to swallow the foomentary dung considered a delicacy by the Pingjari tribes of Jupiter—recently visited, along with many other planets, due to the advent of nuclear-propelled engines.

"Assuming any of this is real," he said, "those people are the worst of cowards."

"Why?"

"Allowing themselves to lose. In my time, defeat was not an option."

"Somebody has to lose," she said with a shrug.

"True. But not me. If I don't win, I'd just as soon die."

Why did she get the feeling he wasn't just talking about the game playing out on TV?

All the more reason she could never drop her guard around him. Who knew what he might do or say to win her heart? But then, geesh, like that was even possible seeing how she was nearly married to the duke!

Exhausted from just looking at the filthy *Survivor* cast trek through dusty wormhole caverns to get water, Lucy rubbed her neck.

"Did I hurt you during our battle?"

"If I said yes, would you give me the win?"

"Never," he said with a rakish wink.

"In that case, I'll have to confess the truth."

"Excellent. Truth is good."

*Unless you happen to be me, fighting an over-whelming attraction to your charm!* Licking her lips, she said, "I was, um, carrying a plant from my classroom to a coworker's car, and when I slipped it onto her backseat, I think I twisted something."

The prince took the popcorn bowl from his lap, and set it on the cushions between them. "Come," he said, spreading his legs, then patting his inner thighs.

Lucy reddened. "I, ah . . ."

"Am I so virile, that a mere peek in the direction of

187

my manhood turns your cheeks this most charming pink?" His slow smile raced her pulse.

"That is what you're suggesting, isn't it? That sleeping with you might be the magic cure for my aching neck?"

Smile fading, he asked "Do you really think so poorly of me, Lucy Gordon? That I know no ways of making a woman feel good beyond the bed?"

"Well . . ."

"Come," he said with another slap to his thighs. "Trust me."

*Trust him? Ha!*

She cautiously slipped off of the sofa, and onto the rug, scooting to a ramrod straight position between his legs, being extra careful not to touch.

But then he was pulling her back, into the vee of his muscular thighs, until her head rested against his—

*Dear lord.*

Swallowing hard, she fought to get hold of her racing pulse, just as she fought to ignore the warm, soft denim brushing her right cheek, and the faint baked-in scent of a delicious smelling cream-based sauce he must've worked on that afternoon.

"Relax, Lucy Gordon," he said, strong hands on either side of her neck, rubbing, kneading, drowning her in languorous heat. "I promise this won't hurt."

Eyes closed, she'd have liked to have pointed out just how wrong about that he was.

Granted, his masterful strokes were sheer bliss, flooding her stress-wracked body with pinpricks of well-being, but as for them not hurting, he couldn't have been more wrong. They hurt from the standpoint of her relationship with William, and the fact that if she loved him like she claimed, she wouldn't have wanted another man's hands on her body. Even worse, they hurt because here the prince was, for the second time that day, doing something solely for her pleasure, when she knew full well she had no intention of helping him keep his human form.

"Thank you," she said, hands on his. "But that's enough." Slipping out from between his legs, she added, "My neck feels much better."

On her feet, she turned to the kitchen, needing a moment alone, but the prince caught her hand, drawing her back. "Where are you going? I thought we were going to watch a movie."

"Sure," she said, fighting a swell of irrational tears. "I, um, just need something to drink."

"Could you fetch me an ale—please?"

*Please? The high and mighty highness had actually said please?*

"Sure . . ." she mumbled.

*Just as soon as I recover from pleasant shock!*

# Chapter Fifteen

Whipping eggs the next morning, listening to music called op-era on the kitchen radio, his cooking tools spread before him on the hard tile counter, Wolfe decided that with the exception of the stubborn wench he currently resided with, maybe he liked this time very much indeed. In his time, kitchen toil had not been a suitable amusement for someone of his stature.

He'd spent any free time training for battle, or tending to the many duties involved with running the castle. Little had he known kitchen work could be almost as satisfying as leading his people.

Soon enough, he would reclaim both his riches and throne. Just as soon as the wench declared her eternal love, thus releasing him from another wench's curse. Freeing him for the first time in over a thousand years to pursue a life of his own choosing.

He poured the eggs into a pan already simmering with butter, and shortly after added chopped ham, peppers and onion and cheese, still amazed by the apparent bounty of such ingredients. He very much wanted to go to the market where Lucy Gordon purchased his daily list of supplies, but she steadfastly refused on the grounds that he might be hurt or lost. In his time, lesser men would have her gutted for even suggesting such a thing. Yet he stayed, cloistered in her home.

Why?

Was he frightened by the prospect of the greater world beyond? Of the ferocious mechanical growls of moving vehicles and flying machines? And of no longer understanding the politics and people?

Angered yet again at the circumstances that had led him to this point of such cowardice, he brought his knife down hard on the melon he planned to serve with breakfast only to slice cleanly into his thumb.

While the sight of his own blood was not new, in this setting, not knowing where to find proper herbs or healing poultices or even wrappings, he went in search of his wench—home because she said it was Sat-ur-day. And she did not toil outside of the home on this day or the next.

"Lucy Gordon!" he shouted, mounting the stairs, having wrapped his offended appendage in a blue-flowered kitchen cloth after turning off the stove. "I have need of your assistance."

Her bedroom door was closed, and as she'd taught him all too many times with her wicked tongue, he knocked before entering, but when she failed to acknowledge his presence, he tried the knob, only to find it locked.

Using his shoulder as a battering ram, he easily enough found passage through, only to be faced with yet another obstacle in the form of her closed bathroom door. It had been days since he'd been in her quarters, and her unmade bed had been strewn with papers. Clothes littered her floor.

"Lucy Gordon?" he asked, landing a brief rap of his knuckles against the bathroom door before letting himself into the steam-filled chamber.

"Wolfe!" She'd evidently just stepped from the rain cabinet as around her breasts strained two halves of a towel that didn't quite reach. For the first time since the night he'd made her acquaintance, he caught a glimpse of the red thatch between her shapely legs, and beneath his jean breeches, his manhood sprung to life. "I thought I told you to knock?"

"I did, but when you didn't answer, I let myself in."

"I see that," she said, sodden red ringlets streaming sexy rivers down her chest and arms. *Sexy*—he'd learned that word on a program called, *Baywatch— The Next Wave.*

"You look fetching," he said with a wink.

"And you look—Wolfe! Oh my God," she said, rushing toward him. "You're bleeding."

"Yes." The blood had seeped through the kitchen cloth. "I wonder if you might direct me to your healing herbs. Are they in the garden, or have you an assortment in your bathroom such as the men and women portrayed on the tee-vee?"

"Herbs?" Lucy asked. She'd just unwrapped his dishtowel and felt hot and woozy just looking at his thumb. "Okay, um, you might need stitches. Um . . ." Hands trembling, she reached into the linen cabinet for a white hand towel, trading it for his bloodied one. "Okay, um, hold that tight. Do you know about applying direct pressure?"

192

"If you mean pressing the halves of the wound, yes."

"Okay, um, wow, um, I'm going to need to get dressed, and you'll need a shirt, and—"

"Lucy Gordon, why are you so distressed?"

"Look at you," she screeched, clutching the two halves of her towel on her way to her closet. "You could be bleeding to death. Maybe I should call an ambulance?"

An am-bu-lance. Ah, he'd seen one of those flashing conveyances on a program called *Hospital Heat*. The wenches in white showed more teat than the women of *Baywatch*, making an ambulance ride seem on the surface an attractive proposition. But then he recalled the not-so-pleasant ministrations they performed on the sick and wounded left in their care. Having his innards manipulated by a woman was not his idea of a good time!

Planting his healthy hand on her shoulder he said, "While I'm touched by your apparent worry for my well-being, you must calm yourself. You've seen my battle scars. Do you think a mere cut to my thumb will bring me to my knees?" He laughed. "If nothing else, I'll slice it clean off, then stop the seepage with a hot coal."

"No!" Just the thought of such barbaric medical care turned Lucy's legs to Jell-O. "You're going to a doctor."

"Look," he said, unwrapping his wound. "It's stopped bleeding."

Sure enough, it had, shimmering relief through her. Dropping to the edge of her bed, she said, "Whew. I'm not sure how I'd have explained you at the hospital.

You're not even registered with the National Health System, and—"

"If I didn't know better, Lucy Gordon," he said, sitting beside her, nudging her with his shoulder. "I'd say you actually care what becomes of me."

"Of course I do."

"Then why such reluctance to declare your eternal love?"

"You say that as if love is something I can just slip into, like a robe or sweater. We hardly know each other, Wolfe. If you think about it, aside from the fact that we temporarily live together, we might as well be strangers."

"Strangers who do this," he said, lowering his lips to hers, parting them with a crazy-sweet pressure that all at the same time managed to be urgent, yet soft. It seemed like years since they'd last kissed. Had it really only been days during which she'd focused on writing her papers, and on her kids at school? *And . . . wow. Oh, wow . . . How much I'm* not *affected by the hard/ soft molding of your lips to mine?*

Moist heat purred between her legs, contrasting with the cool air in the room, reminding her how little she had on, and how easy it would be to give in to temptation.

"I must apologize," the prince said, backing away. " 'Twas not my intent to ravish you, simply to inquire as to the location of your medicinal herbs."

"Sure," Lucy said, lightly shaking her head to clear the sex-charged fog. Dear lord, what the man did to her body with one simple kiss! "Um, it was no big deal."

Yeah, right!

So not a big deal that her heart still hadn't stopped

hammering! To heck with his thumb, she needed CPR!

After directing him to a drawer in the bathroom where she kept a hodgepodge of first aid supplies, she cleaned his cut with peroxide, then squeezed on salve and topped that with a large bandage.

Eyes wide, he said, "In my time, we had no such techniques. Merely herb poultices and rags. Thank you, Lucy Gordon."

"You're welcome," she said, blushing from the heat of his stare. Was he once again going to kiss her? The mere thought raced her pulse, and stopped her breathing.

*Kiss me! Kiss me!*

"You get dressed," he said, crushing her ego. "And then we'll eat."

"Um, okay," she said, wiping sweating palms on her towel, trying to act as if kissing him had been the last thing on her mind. "You, ah, cooked? Already?"

"But of course." His handsome smile stole the last of her breath. "I am but a lowly prince, while you are a princess, and you know what everyone says about them, don't you?"

"What?"

"While princes spend their days hard at toil, princesses spend their days lolling about on their beds, greedily consuming sweets, and counting gold."

"Hmm, guilty on that first count," she said, not even trying to hide her sheepish grin at having been caught sleeping late. "But as you can plainly see, I have no sweets or gold."

He tweaked her nose. "Ah, two tragedies we must change."

\* \* \*

Lucy Gordon held a strawberry to her plump lips, sucking with such enraptured pleasure that Wolfe reached beneath the wholly inadequate dining room table to adjust his blue jean trousers.

What had the woman done to him?

In choosing her to woo, had he not encountered a woman, but another sorceress? For surely she must have placed him under her spell for him to constantly be fighting an engorged manhood?

"These are sooo sweet," she said, eyes half closed. "Did you happen to read on the package where they—" She popped the remainder of the juicy red morsel into her mouth and chewed.

"Go on," he said, his previous predicament all but forgotten in the sting of that one little word. *Read.* "You forgot the second half of your statement. The part where you call me an imbecile child for not being able to read the side of a berry parcel."

"That's so not true," she said, reaching for his hand, which he drew away. "You've come a long way with your flashcards and sounds. The rest is just stringing the sounds and letters together."

"Teach me now," he said, taking her plate with its half-eaten omelet and pile of berries, "and I'll feed you more later."

"Wow," Lucy said with an easy grin. "Too bad my kids at school aren't this motivated. Your Highness, you've got a deal."

They spent the rest of the morning on his lessons, and by that afternoon, he was reading short sentences. Talk about a shocker! He'd admitted to having some rudimentary schooling back in his time, though, so she assumed his will to succeed combined with what had to be an off-the-charts IQ were the causes for his meteoric rise to the top of her reading class.

While she made a simple lunch of chicken noodle soup and at his request, peanut butter and strawberry jam sandwiches, he cleared the table of papers, and set it with spoons and napkins and glasses of milk.

And while they ate, Lucy found herself once again spilling her guts about Grumsworth, and once again being surprised when the prince not only listened, but hung on her every word as if her dull life was as exciting as one of his dozens of shows.

After cleaning up, the prince stood at the living room windows, staring at the late afternoon gloom.

A merry fire crackled in the hearth, its orange glow dancing upon the walls. Buzzy, after having stuffed his cheeks with peanut butter and jelly crusts, had curled himself into a ball in the cozy hamster condo at the top of his cage.

Hands in his jeans pockets, the prince sighed, then turned to her where she sat on the sofa grading papers, and said, "I think I should very much like to take a walk."

Lucy snapped her red grading pencil.

"Lucy Gordon? Did you hear me."

Staring at Lyle Orvitz Dickenson IV's genetics exam so hard that her eyes hurt, she said, "We've been over this. The reasons why I don't think it's a good idea for you to leave the cottage."

"Ah, yes . . . your reasons. How dangerous it may be, were I to venture off on my own—as if I were some small child not yet trusted to leave my mother's skirts."

"That's not what I meant, and you know it, it's just that—"

"What? Are we back to you not wanting your insipid lover to learn of my existence? A ludicrous proposition seeing how in but a short while, once you come to your senses and declare your eternal love, that he will learn of me soon enough when I resume my rightful place in the home where he currently resides—*my* castle!"

"Okay," Lucy said, trying to ignore her latest hot wave of confusion. "First off, the duke isn't even home at the moment, so why would I be trying to hide you? And second—"

"Good. Then come with me." He held out his hand. "I shall entrust you with my safekeeping."

Gazing up at his massive form, at the stony challenge in his dark eyes, she realized that the very thought of her protecting him was about as likely as Buzzy protecting her classroom's python—currently living with her friend Bonnie who had a thing for snakes. "That's ridiculous," she said, "And anyway, it looks like it's going to rain."

"It already is raining."

"There you go. Then why are you even suggesting we take a walk?"

He held out his hand. "Come with me, Lucy Gordon. Walk with me, and share the remainder of the day."

"You, um . . ." The black on Lyle's test paper swirled. "Don't have a raincoat or boots."

Still holding out his hand, he laughed. "You think I wore a coat for rain the night we stormed Drogo's camp? Sleet fell so hard it raised welts on my forehead and cheeks."

"See? Weather like that, you'd have been better off at home, curled up in front of the fire."

"Come with me. Take my hand . . ."

Fresh out of excuses, heart beating its own storm at the thought of sharing something so intimate with him as a walk in the rain, Lucy took a deep breath and surrendered her hand to his.

" 'Twas here, I had a close call with a wild dog." Standing beside the pond he once called home, Wolfe resisted the all-too-familiar urge to flee, reminding himself he was no longer a loathsome frog, but a man on the dawn of regaining all he'd once held dear.

"Is that what happened to your toe?"

"My toe? Oh—yes, but how did you know?"

Her cheeks blazed a pretty pink blush.

"Lucy Gordon?"

"The pond's pretty, isn't it? The way steam's rising from the surface, and the rain sprinkles are—"

Grasping her shoulders, he turned her to face him. "I've seen enough of this pond to last me a thousand years more. The dank smell of mud. Chirping insects. Weeds, hiding predators. It's you I'm taken with the sight of, and your blush intrigues me. Makes me think you have a secret you're trying to hide."

"Me?" Her smile reached all the way to her eyes of sky blue. If only for a moment in his head, gone was the rain, making way for hot sun. "What about you? I feel like the more I know you, the less I know."

"In what sense?"

"Well . . ." she said, licking her lips. "For instance, why you seem so eager to learn to read. It's almost as if you were driven."

Wolfe stiffened. "Maybe I am." By thousand-year-old guilt. But she would care not for his crisis of conscience. He doubted she'd care to hear of him leading his men to slaughter, but out of loyalty to them, and out of a perverse need to have their tale finally outside of himself, he told her of the massacre in detail that roiled his stomach, and made her pale eyes of blue streak with silvery grays.

"My God." Hand covering her mouth, she said, "I've read about this kind of stuff. Seen it in movies, but I always thought, no way could it have been all that bad. When here it was worse." Even though her hand touched only the damp wool of his sweater's sleeve, the warmth of her gentle touch and sad smile spread all the way up his arm, and deep into his chest. "I'm so sorry."

"Nay, do not be sorry for me. Be sorry for the poor souls whose deaths I carry upon my shoulders entirely because of my damnedable pride."

Lucy was without words.

Knowing Wolfe even marginally as she did was more than enough to have acquainted her with his inflated ego, but still . . . Interlocking his fingers with hers, she said, "You didn't lead those men to their deaths on purpose, Wolfe. You only did what you thought best. No one can blame you for that."

"Aye," he said with a bitter laugh. "I can blame me for that, and have most every day of the past thousand years. Along with an assortment of so many other grievous acts that my head oft times swims with grief."

"Maybe it's time you stopped thinking about any of those things? Maybe a thousand years of regrets are enough?"

He shrugged, gazing at his feet. "Did you know that

at twilight on a sun-flooded summer day, this pond teems with life? Flying, chirping, jumping, croaking— no noise is more offensive than that of one of my rutting former counterparts."

She laughed, and sensing this was his attempt at changing the subject, she released his hand to nudge his waist—she'd aimed for his ribs, but he stood too tall. "Did you ever have a special lady frog?" Imagine the research to be gleaned from hearing his perspective on everything from mating habits to hibernation!

Hands in his pockets, he shook his head. "Other frogs found me hideous in complexion. I did once have the companionship of a female turtle. Her shell had been disfigured by Gypsies planning to make her into their evening's soup. I lost count of the number of summers we shared, but in her I sensed a true friend."

Amazing! He'd been friends with a turtle! Who knew species communicated amongst themselves, let alone others? Yikes, talk about truth being stranger than fiction—calling Dr. Doolittle! "What sorts of things did you talk about?"

"Nothing you would find interesting."

Was he nuts?

There was nothing about a frog/turtle conversation she wouldn't find interesting!

"She hurt." The light rain had stopped, and turning from her, the prince walked a short distance down the sloped bank, kneeling to pick up a stone he skipped across the pond's glassy surface. "Her shell grew into her flesh, and only with me did she share her pain. I hurt, too, only in a much deeper place, and she listened and understood."

Amazing!

"When she died, I thought surely I would die, as well, but . . ." In that masculine, pride-filled way of his, presumably designed to hide any true depth to his feelings, he shrugged before picking up another stone.

Geez Louise . . . a frog had mourned the death of a turtle friend. Imagine what the scientific community would say to such a thing! Yet here it was. The truth standing right here before her.

*It?*

*Whoa, Luce, if you've learned anything from this conversation, isn't it that the prince as a man is far more complex than he ever was as a frog?*

"I am ready to leave this place," he said. "You were right. It is dangerous."

"Why?" Glancing over her left shoulder, then right, she asked, "Is something with big teeth headed our way? Can you sense predators?"

"Only those deep within." Holding out his hand, dark eyes brimming with complexity she couldn't begin to read, he said, "Come, Lucy Gordon, rescue me from myself."

# Chapter Sixteen

Like the cold rain driving against the windows, Wolfe's multilayered statement drove Lucy to be especially kind to him the rest of the night.

To help with his reading, she walked him through an agonizingly slow game of Scrabble. Slow not because of his still limited written vocabulary, but because of his insistence on sitting side by side at the dining room table. Across from him, she could ignore his sheer breadth. But up close, dwarfed by him, yet at the same time sheltered by his latent strength, so far she'd been lucky to come up with a single word longer than "cat" or "zoo."

Even worse was the nagging memory of why he wanted to learn to read, and her guilt for even bothering to teach him a skill he'd never again have need for.

She tried consoling herself with other memories.

Memories of how often she'd been played in college

by guys pretending an interest in her only to suck up to her father.

Who was to say Wolfe wasn't playing her now? Sensing that his raw sexuality wasn't having the desired effect, he'd switched to preying on her soft heart. Being the warrior that he'd once been, no doubt he inherently recognized an enemy's fatal weakness. Only what he couldn't know was that the one thing that had made her weak in the past, she now depended upon to make her strong—naïveté.

For back in college, she'd been too trusting to see anyone beyond face value. If a guy said he was attracted to her, she'd been flattered—not suspicious.

At the start of her career, she'd never delved beneath the upper crust of research. When the first source she'd searched for documentation on *Helena's Dream* had come up in her favor, she'd run with it, not once pausing to consider the fact that the frog she thought unique might have already been discovered.

While all of those mistakes had been costly in terms of the emotional wounds they'd inflicted, she was now older, wiser, and infinitely stronger. She wasn't falling for any of the prince's heart-wrenching verbal tricks any more than she'd lose sight of her end goals.

Respect.

Riches.

And above all—earning her father's love.

"You win," she was finally able to say about the Scrabble game—as for the more subtle game they played . . .

She'd declare herself the victor on the day of her World Biological Conference presentation.

"Thank you," he said. "That was fun, even though you did most of the work."

"Hey, don't sell yourself short," she said, sliding the letters off of the game board and back into the Crown Royal bag she stored them in. "You've learned an amazing amount since just this morning."

He beamed. "Thank you. It pleases me to know you think of me as a good student. In the coming days, perhaps you can teach me even more."

"Reading?" she croaked, or about the most effective ways for frogs to catch insects? A fresh wave of guilt consumed her for the mere thought.

Hmm, him being a warrior, wonder if he knew where she could pick up a sturdy set of emotional armor? Because knowing on an intellectual level that she was doing the right thing in letting Wolfe change back into a frog was one thing, but in her heart? That was a whole other story.

"Maybe we could also add mathematics to my lessons? And even more current events?" Pushing back his chair, he stood, walked to the window to moodily stare outside. "At the pond, I saw things. Changes in fashion styles and the like. I oft heard the ramblings of lovers and fishermen and small children frolicking by water's edge, but I should like to know more." Turning to her, stealing her breath with the intensity on his handsome face, he said, "I know not even the name of the person currently wearing the country's crown."

"Well, sure, I can help with all of that," Lucy said, avoiding his gaze. "We'll start with reading the newspaper together. That way you'll learn a little about reading *and* current events."

"Yes." Slipping his hands into his pockets, he gave

her a succinct nod before curving his lips into a generous, white-toothed smile that flip-flopped her heart. "Yes, that would be good. Let us start on your first day back to work."

"Okay, then. I'll pencil you in for Monday afternoon."

"But Monday is hours from now. Can you teach me anything this moment?" In one of the myriad of changes she'd grown to recognize in his expressions, just then his smile transformed from happy, to hungry. Only that hunger had nothing to do with peanut butter, unless he planned to spread it all over her—she gulped for air, imagining the scent of peanuts on his hot breath.

"Y-you want to, um, learn something now?"

"Why are you answering my every question with a question, Lucy Gordon?"

"I-I'm not," she said, snatching the Scrabble box from the table.

He followed her to the living room where she knelt to slide the game onto a low cabinet shelf. And when she closed the door and stood, he was there, strong hands on her shoulders, gaze locking with hers.

"You're bothered by something. Is it my request? Do you not wish to teach me?"

She licked her lips.

*What I don't wish is to be so near you, having your body remind me that while you may have been a frog in the past, and will be again in the future, for the moment, you are nothing but one hundred percent man.*

"Perhaps you're tired? If you've no wish to teach, we could do something else? Watch a movie? Eat more popcorn you could make and then deliver to me—please."

"Um, sure. That sounds great." And for a moment during her short trek to the kitchen, hearing another of his demands made her once again sure in her conviction to trade him for her career . . . at least until she remembered he'd said "Please!"

Ruth Hagenberry, binoculars still to her eyes, ducked behind a rhododendron and uttered the kind of soul-deep happy sigh the likes of which only accompanied someone else's impending grief.

"Buying those clothes for one of your Yank friends my lily-white behind," she said with a huff. "Lucy Gordon, you've taken a live-in lover. And when the duke finds out, you'll be out on your tail. Making plenty of room for my sweet-tempered Abigail to move right in."

"Did you say something, Mum?" Twenty-two-year-old Abigail flicked off her torch and set it in her lap, along with the movie magazine she'd just finished. Gum cracking in time to the song playing in her head, she sat in the car's front seat, feet propped on the dash. Was now the right time to make her big announcement?

"Nothing, doll," Ruth said with her brightest smile, scooting out from the bushes while brushing leaves from her shoulders and hair before she got into the car. "Mummy's got everything under control."

Abigail cringed.

When _Mummy_ found out just how little she actually controlled of her daughter's life, she'd throw a bloody wobbler. Until then, though, Abigail figured she might as well try to relax.

\* \* \*

"You're crazy!" Lucy shrieked Sunday afternoon, dodging behind the sofa to escape Wolfe and his feather duster.

"Ahh . . ." he said with a wink and one of his sexy-slow smiles. "Crazy for you."

"That thing is for cleaning, not playing."

"But just think how much more fun it could be teased across the tips of your teats."

"Look," she said, furiously blushing at his not-all-that-bad idea. "You don't have to do any chores around here. I mean, I appreciate your cooking and doing dishes and laundry, but . . ."

Edging around the left side of the sofa, he said, "But you prefer to service yourself in the pleasure department?"

"No!" She ducked to the right, but with one step, he'd cut off her escape.

"No, you don't prefer servicing yourself? Or no, you've changed your mind on allowing me the pleasure?" The wicked spark in his dark eyes spoke volumes as to the sincerity of his question. He knew full well what she meant, only he didn't care!

Tossing a pillow right, then darting left, she'd thought she could get a head start on him, but he must've called on some of those old frog leaping skills, because he'd jumped her way in seconds, launching an all new tickle attack on the strip of exposed belly between her T-shirt and jeans.

Breathless and laughing, she squirmed away from him again, then raced upstairs. But before she could shut and lock her bedroom door, he launched a fresh attack, this time simultaneously tackling her to the bed.

He landed on her only to slip his arms beneath her, rolling her on top of him.

"Ahh . . ." he said, still breathing hard from laughter. "Now I am yours for you to do with as you please."

"Bonk you on your head is what I'd like to do."

"I'm not familiar with this word, bonk," he said, skimming hair back from her eyes with his open palm, "I'm assuming it is much the same as kiss?"

Despite her best efforts not to, she grinned. "Has anyone ever told you you're incorrigible?"

Matching her grin, melting her resolve to keep her distance and cool, he said, "I know not—"

"Wait. Let me guess, you don't know what that means, either."

"Right. But you could teach me . . ." He slid his hands under her shirt and up her back, cinching her close. "I'm assuming it's good?"

"No," she said, wrestling away. "It's bad, but then to your warped logic, probably bad is good."

"Now I'm really confused," he said, sliding her up the long, hard length of him, pressing a steamy kiss to the base of her throat. "Let's go with the bad part of that speech . . . although how a wench who tastes so good could be bad for me is beyond my comprehension." He slid more kisses perilously up the curve of her neck, where surely he'd gotten a taste of her frenzied pulse.

Talk about bad—no way it could be good for him to know the effect he had on her senses!

She wanted to stay strong. To think about her victorious round of applause and father's crushing hug, and the duke's proud smile, but at the moment, all she could think of were those strong warm hands kneading their way beneath the cotton back of her bra, and how now that his kisses had reached her chin, surely her mouth couldn't be far behind?

Ahh . . . the indent at the base of her chin.

Ooh . . . the tip of her nose.

*The tip of my nose? What about my lips?*

*Come back!* every stupid, needy, lonely nerve ending in her mouth screamed.

Even worse, he was rolling her off of him, then sitting up, leaving her beached like a big old horny whale!

"I'm so sorry," he said, his smile not the least bit apologetic.

His long, dark hair hung loose, framing his face with an innate raw sex appeal guys from her time couldn't come close to replicating. The kind of raw sex appeal she knew far better than to ever even think of messing with. So what was she doing lying belly-up, staring at him from her cold bed?

"As you've told me many, many times," he said, "we are not to partake of such things, so how about you make pop-corn instead?"

Easing onto her elbows, Lucy shook her head. How had they gone from kissing to popcorn? Looking away, then back to him, she said, "Are you immune to what just happened here, because, I—"

"Wait, let me guess. You want me?"

"No. Not at all, I just—"

"Are sorry for not being able to keep your hands off of me?"

"You were the one kissing me!"

"Ah, but you were the one crushing yourself to me, releasing those soft mews with my every touch. I was only doing what I thought you wanted."

"Argh!" Pushing herself off the bed, she stormed past him and down the stairs.

As usual, he followed. "Where are you going?"

"To make popcorn."

"Good. After servicing you in the bedroom, I'm hungry."


Monday morning, Lucy slammed her curling iron to the white tile bathroom counter and scowled at her reflection. Her stupid red curls stuck out at a gazillion stupid angles, and if she wouldn't have had to trek downstairs to find a pair of scissors, she'd have hacked every stupid inch of them off!

"What's the matter?" the prince asked, strolling through the bathroom's open hall door to slip a pile of fresh-washed towels into the linen cupboard.

*Besides the fact that you're a better housekeeper than I've ever been?*

"This," she said grabbing a chunk of her spastic hair. "Grumsworth suggested I adopt a more professional look. And I thought I said you don't have to do my laundry."

"I want to," he said, closing the cupboard, then meeting her in front of the mirror. Grabbing the curling iron, he said, "This is much like the rod Desdemona taught me to use? May I?"

He'd used a curling iron on the woman whose mother turned him into a frog? Trying to politely hide her shock, she said, "Please. At this point, I doubt anything could make it worse."

"Desdemona was a most vain creature," he said, wielding the iron like a salon pro. "Oft after we made love, she'd insist I repair the damage I'd done to her

211

hair, fisting it as I thrust ever deeper within her womanly folds."

Lucy gulped.

*Dear lord.*

"Seeing as she was shy about our union, she refused me to grant entrance to a servant. So she taught me to fashion her hair." He shrugged. "I know, 'tis not a manly pursuit, but in exchange for the pleasure she gave me, I figured 'twas not too large of a price to pay."

"What kind of hair did she have?" Eyes closed, Lucy relished the curling iron's heat combined with his hands' competent strokes.

"Long. Pale as the sand along the sea. I'd never known any other woman to use such an object to bring life to her hair, but then Desdemona was unique in many ways—not just in her appearance. There," he said, setting the iron on the counter. "What do you think?"

She opened her eyes to a bona fide miracle.

Gone was her normal riot of curls, replaced by smooth waves, tucked just so about her forehead and cheeks. "Wow. I can't believe you did this."

"All I have done is enhance what God has already given." Running his palm down the back of her head, he said, "You're quite lovely, Lucy Gordon."

"No I'm not, but thanks for saying so."

"Why do you not think of yourself as a beauty?" Hands on her shoulders, he turned her to face him instead of the mirror. "Surely even your insipid duke has told you of your many charms?"

"Well, yes, but he was just saying nice things. He didn't really mean them."

Grasping her chin, he said in his fiercest growl,

"Never again will such heresy pass your lips."

"E-excuse me?"

"Among women, I am renowned for my bedroom skills, yet among men, I am known for not only my prowess on the battle field, but for always securing the loveliest of wenches within the circle of my arms. And you, Lucy Gordon, with your fiery hair and eyes the intoxicating shade of a clear summer sky, are the most ravishing of them all."

Swallowing hard, Lucy jerked her chin free.

Funny, but in a different time and different words, her freshman year at Vanderbilt, Chad Bartholomew had said virtually the same thing. Right before she'd told him her father would be out of the country for the next six months. Two days after that, he'd dumped her for Gretta Larson. "I should finish getting ready."

"Not before admitting your beauty."

"I'm beautiful. There. Are you happy?"

He released her. "I won't be happy until I've made you writhe with such mindless womanly pleasure that when you next repeat this to me, you'll know it to be true."

"You will not put that on me!" Lucy cried Wednesday morning in the bathroom, clutching the halves of her robe at her throat.

The prince rolled his eyes. "I merely need see if the garment fits. I hand-washed it, but the wench on tee-vee says sometimes these delicates shrink." As if wagging her bra were supposed to bend her to his will, he gave it a light shake.

Lately, he'd been taking his laundry duties more and more seriously. Pretreating the stains she always managed to come home with, adding the fabric softener at just the right cycle of the wash, and now, he'd taken to hand-washing her lingerie!

"Look," she said, "I appreciate the work you do around here. Really, I do, but I don't see why you're holding my bra hostage to check the size. It looks fine to me. And if you'd just hand it over, I'd be happy to try it on, finish dressing, then report back later."

"You make a mockery of my work, Lucy Gordon." Shaking his head, he tossed the garment her way, and she caught it midair. "Most wenches I know would be thrilled to have a personal maid help them dress each morning. And here, you not only have that in me, but a housekeeper and cook." Parking himself on the edge of the tub, he pouted.

"Oh, for heaven's sake," she said, "Like you know all that many women around here. And even if you did, they wouldn't let you put their bras on them, either." Unless they happened to be single. In which case, all bets were off considering how hot he looked in his khaki pants and mossy green sweater. Good thing she had her upcoming engagement to the duke to keep her mind otherwise occupied!

Still pouting, he said, "You would let me try the garment on you if you loved me."

"True, but since I don't love you, that's kind of a moot point."

"In light of the fact that I'm running out of time," he asked, chin raised. "What would it take for you to love me, Lucy Gordon? Gold and silver coins? Jewels? Land? Horseflesh?" Snagging her by the belt of her robe, he reeled her in, resting his hands on her behind, and his cheek against her breasts.

Sucking in a breath, leaning back far as she comfortably could, she said, "My love can't be bought. Love is something you have to earn. Take the duke for instance. On our last date, he wore a sweatshirt, just to prove how much he cares for me."

"What is a sweat-shirt?"

"A not exactly regal form of attire that he ordinarily wouldn't be caught dead in."

"Oh."

"My point being, that it's not money a woman loves, but the small gestures."

"Example?" he said, resting his cheek against her breasts where her stupid traitorous nipples grew toward his hot breath like sprouts reaching for the sun.

"You'll have to let me go first. I can't think like this."

"With your buds so close to my mouth?"

Grrr. "Yes, if you must know."

He held her tighter. "One example, and I'll let you go."

"I already told you, I can't think."

"Then we'll be here a while."

"I'll be late for work."

"Want me to phone Grumsworth?"

"What I want you to do is—"

He seared her lips with a mind-blowing, heart-galloping, soul-melding kiss that rendered her incapable of all but the faintest mew.

"Was that more what you had in mind?" he asked, eyebrows raised, his breath warming her swollen lips with the lingering taste of peanut butter and strawberry jam.

"Um . . ." Still dazed, she shook her head. "You wanted an example?"

He nodded.

"That," she said, touching her fingers to her still tingling lips. "Definitely lots more of that—hypothetically speaking, because as you know, I'm practically engaged to the duke."

"Of course. The duke. Who I'm sure kisses you just as satisfactorily each time you meet."

"Y-yes. He does."

*Liar, liar, pants on fire!*

"Then despite my profound wish for you to declare your eternal love, even I must admit the honorable thing to do would be for you to go ahead with your plans to wed him. At least then you'll be happy."

"And you'd be satisfied with that? Living all eternity as a frog to insure my happiness?"

His only reply was a formal bow before releasing her, then asking, "Which would you prefer for your morning meal? French toast or omelets?"

# Chapter Seventeen

"You're thirty minutes late," Grumsworth said, arms crossed, bespectacled eyes beady when she stepped into her classroom just as the first period bell rang.

As students rustled about, scrambling for their chairs and gossiping about the upcoming dance and what was that muck supposed to be that they'd been served for breakfast, Grumsworth continued to stare.

"Is there something in particular you'd like to talk about?" Lucy innocently inquired. "Because if not, I should get on with my day."

Without saying a word, he pointed his arrow-straight index finger toward the few ivies still lining the classroom's sill. "I thought those were to be gone by the end of last week, along with the posters and animals."

"I took the hamster home," she said, "and Bonnie graciously invited Sammy to live with her."

"Sammy?"

"Our classroom snake."

Her students had quieted save for the low-level

paper-rustling and shifting about of preteen limbs that never fell totally silent.

"My patience is wearing this thin, Ms. Gordon." He held his thumb and forefinger a sliver apart. "I want the remainder of this sentimental rubbish out of this classroom by the end of the day or—"

"Or what?" Lucy said, incensed at this oaf's intrusion upon her happy glow. A cheese omelet breakfast, complete with cottage fries and a bouquet of silky fall leaves and mums that she preferred not to think about Wolfe's having ventured outside for, tended to make a girl happy. Throw in the great hair Wolfe had styled for her, and there was no telling how much she'd accomplish! Speaking of which, if there was one thing Wolfe had taught her during their time together, it was to stand up for herself! Hands fisted on her hips, she asked, "Even though my students regularly have the highest science grades for their level, are you going to release me from my contract?"

From the back row came a cough, then a mumbled, "Way to go, Miss Gee."

A healthy round of laughs followed Grumsworth right out the door, and followed by that came a rush of acid indigestion that left Lucy reaching for her purse.

Rolaids. Must have Rolaids.

"Okay, gang," she said to the class. "Get your e-readers fired up and onto screen 132."

While they grumbled, she sat behind her desk, and unzipped the quilted azalea pink floral purse that, Bonnie teased her, looked more like a carpetbagger's suitcase. Only at the top, she didn't find a shiny roll of antacids, but a miniature bouquet of the mums and leaves that just that morning graced the dining room table. A scrolled sheet of paper had been slipped into the red ribbon tying the stems.

Lucy glanced at the kids to find them still messing with their e-readers, then, fingers trembling, unrolled the note.

In painstakingly perfect letters, Wolfe had written, *hav a happee daae luucee goordon.*

Swallowing past the lump in her throat, she rolled the paper back up, held it to her chest for the few seconds it took to regain her composure, then set the bouquet on her desk, and opened her purse, easing the note into the zippered side pocket she reserved for treasures like theater ticket stubs and her favorite lipstick and lucky Petoskey stone.

Thanks to the prince and his talent with hair, eggs, and note writing, she *would* have a happy day—whether Grumsworth liked it or not!

In the elegantly appointed boardroom of William's Edinburgh office, he sat at the head of an endless oak table that his father had sat at the head of and his father before him. This latest batch of negotiations with the Labour Party had been exhausting, but by the end of the week, he hoped to have reached an agreement equitable for all.

"Your Grace?" Ms. Roberts asked, pausing just inside the room.

"Yes?"

"I have a Missus Hagenberry on line two who claims to have rather urgent business. She says she's your neighbor, and has tried reaching you at two of your other stops. Shall I tell her you'll ring later?"

Elbow on the table, William put his hand to his forehead and rubbed. Bloody hell. What did the woman want now? "While your offer of shelter is most welcome, Ms. Roberts, I fear she may march north to hunt me down in person."

His secretary cast him a most sympathetic smile.

Feeling strangely fortified, he picked up the phone, and punched line two. "Yes, Ruth? This is William."

After gushing at length about what a time she'd had locating him, she said, "I hate to have to tell you this, but . . ."

William's heart sank. What dreadfully scandalous tale would she report about Luce? And when would she get around to declaring her ultimate goal, no doubt wedding him to her daughter Abigail? It was no secret that the woman had long since had eyes on him in that regard. But even while his holding affections for the most plain of British girls would make his dear old mum infinitely happier than his relationship with Luce, such a match would not please him. Women of his own heritage lacked Luce's *joie de vivre*.

"Since I was already headed that way," Ruth said, strangely out of breath, "I'd volunteered to the posty to carry a rather large parcel of yours to the castle. Well, you can't imagine what I saw upon my arrival."

Crop circles? Aliens?

"Well?" she said, "Can you? Can you imagine?"

"I'm quite sure I can't."

"Well, then I'll tell you. It was that Lucy Gordon of yours with a *man!* A *big* man, standing at her dining room window. And then again I've seen him at the kitchen window, and at the back win—"

"Thank you, Mrs. Hagenberry. That is some bit of news. Unfortunately, there's no real story there, as I believe she has family visiting from the states."

"Oh?" Judging by the keen-edged disappointment in her tone, he'd smushed the poor woman's heart like a bug. "I hadn't heard."

"Yes, well, sometimes news is slow to spread." Waving frantically for Ms. Roberts who'd returned to her own stack of paperwork, he pointed to the sign he'd written: H-E-L-P!

Smiling, she loudly called, "Urgent call for you on line one, Your Grace!"

Giving her a thumbs up, he said, "Ruth, so sorry, but I really do have to go."

"B-but—"

"Hope to see you soon." Click.

Ms. Roberts lauded him with a round of applause. "Very well done, sir."

"Thank you," he said with a dapper bow.

Clearing her throat, she set her pen on the table, "Not that I meant to intrude, but—"

"It's hard not to when sitting five feet from me?"

Reddening, she nodded.

"Go on," he said. "We've been together for years—" Now, he reddened. "What I meant to say is that we've worked together for years. You should feel free to speak your mind."

"Thank you, Your Grace."

"And while we're at it, don't you think you should call me William?"

"Thank you," she said, blushing again. "You may call me Penelope."

"Penelope." Hmm, he'd always taken her for more of an uptight Elizabeth or Catherine. "Yes, well, with that out of the way, go ahead. Give me your worst."

"I don't mean to criticize, but your Ruth is a rather loud speaker, and having plainly heard both sides of the conversation while having the added benefit of seeing the changes in your expression, I have to ask, does your Lucy indeed have guests from the States?"

Hardening his lips, he said, "No."

After a long silence, she gently asked, "Why cover for her?"

"Because I love her. And I have to believe that whatever's transpiring in that cottage, she loves me, too. And that she'll tell me the whole story as soon as I get home."

"Would you like me to ring her? I have her number at the school."

He thought a moment on that, then said, "No . . . I think not. I'd rather just see her." *Hold her.* Bowing his head at almost having shared such an intimate thought, he said, "I'm sorry, Ms. Roberts—Penelope. It was never my intent to burden you with such personal concerns."

Her warm, brown gaze holding his, she said, "It's no burden, Your Grace, but an honor to be held in such high regard that you'd trust me with such matters. Know that I will hold them in the strictest confidence, and that my only desire is for you to find the happiness you deserve."

Bathed in dazzling morning sun on an autumn day so sweet-smelling with the scent of burning leaves and resting earth that if Wolfe had closed his eyes he could almost be home, he pressed open palms to the castle's stone-capped wall walk, soaking in not just that morning's, but centuries' radiant heat.

So much had changed within the castle that was rightfully his. Yet up here, surveying the vast rolling hills of his kingdom, he was relieved to find the view much the same.

Beyond formal castle gardens growing nothing the least bit useful lay sheep-dotted pastures of green stretching far as the eye could see, kissed by skies of the palest blue, and beyond that, the great sea.

Closer at hand was his pond with its wind-tossed reeds and grassy banks. And at the castle's rear, a forest rich with game.

Gone was the village, and all of its mayhem. Chickens and geese squawking. Old women chasing after their flocks of fowl and children while the younger women worked in either the fields or castle.

He'd known them. His fine children.

Blinking away the moisture blurring the view, he saw them now. Fine, tall, Lambert, with his brown eyes and eager mind, always solving problems. He alone had devised a fix for the mill. Sweet Nesta with her purity of spirit and halo of her mother's sable curls. Colin, who, even at four years of age had looked most like him.

Argh, God, how his chest ached at the thought of them. His babes. Loved one and all.

Throat tight, Wolfe tried tamping his rage.

Rage at the sorceress who'd done this to him. Rage at her daughter whom he'd seen at the pond not a week after his transformation, rutting with Greylond, his cousin! Even worse was witnessing the end of Desdemona's sad life so many long years later when, even then, she had not been with child. And there he'd sat in the pond, paying for all eternity for a sin he did not even commit—at least not with Desdemona.

But, aye, he admitted guilt in bastarding his other wee ones. Would but he could, he'd have changed the course of his life. Seen that perhaps there was more to life than the conquering of foes.

Rubbing his forehead, he squeezed his eyes closed tight.

Everything had been so different then—and he wasn't just talking the advances in invention. It was everything. The thoughts. The angle of the sun—the very air. He remembered none of this self-awareness. He'd been what he'd been. And that was all. Nothing more, nothing less, just himself.

Wolfe.

Prince of Gwyneddor.

Son to the king. Father to Lambert, Nesta and Colin.

Hands on his hips, chin raised high, hair streaming behind him in the sweet-scented breeze, he was once again master of his kingdom. Lord of all he surveyed. And while he remembered well his father once telling him that to be king was a solitary existence, Wolfe found himself wishing for others with whom he might share this bucolic scene. Not just his children, but a woman with laughing eyes the same fathomless blue as the sky, and hair of burnished copper like leaves on the forest trees.

Alas, if Lucy Gordon were with him, though, he'd most likely know not her pleasant companionship, but fiery wrath. She would no more understand his need to be up here anymore than his need to earn her love.

Earn?

Ha. In his time, he would have been entitled to that love.

But then the glint of sun on a far-off car windshield

caught his eye, reminding him he might never again know such absolute power. Mere days earlier, he would not have conceived such a thing. But he now knew from his long talks with Lucy Gordon that while this new Eng-land indeed had a king, the man held no power.

The absurdity of this never failed to stir him, and alas, in his more truthful moments, scare him.

For if he wasna king, he was but a man residing in a stolen home and country. For without reclaiming his title, even if he were to regain his life, what was he to do? Where was he to go?

Even more unsettling, how much longer was he to be in the most unfamiliar—indeed most unwanted— position of being at Lucy Gordon's mercy?

She not only met his most basic needs of food and shelter, but according to the curse's damnedable rules, she, and only she, held the power to save him.

Always, up to now, he'd controlled his destiny.

*Aye, which is why you've spent the past thousand years as a frog?*

He clenched his hands into fists.

If not for the one rule stating that he only had one shot at finding a woman to save him, and that only that woman's vow of eternal love mattered, the conditions binding him to that damnedable green skin would have been so simple to meet.

In his time, women had said they loved him after the briefest tumble upon soft pond grasses. Of course, those women had known him to be a man of power, and now, he was but a man.

But without firsthand knowledge of the respect he once commanded, how was Lucy Gordon to know she was supposed to love him? Everyone had loved him, from the serving wenches, to his hound, to his father the king.

*What of your mother? She loved you so little she took her own life.*

"Arrrgggh!" he shouted to the heavens, clenching his mighty fists.

Lucy Gordon was not his insane mother. And even his mother had once loved him, but she loved herself and her lover more. Perhaps he'd chosen the wrong path in deciding to woo comely Lucy? Perhaps he should offer more. Coin and jewels? In and around this castle was the whole of his father's fortune. An unimaginable hidden treasure any woman would find suitable in exchange for love.

"Aye," he said with renewed hope and conviction. "Jewels. All women lust for jewels." He'd give her a fistful of trinkets, then demand she love him, or take the whole lot of loot back from whence it came.

*My love can't be bought. Love is something you have to earn.*

With a disgusted grunt, Wolfe turned away from the rolling green hills and sky of remarkable blue. For green reminded him of the last woman from his past, and blue of the woman who might very well be the last woman in his future.

"Thank you," Lucy said to the prince that night at the dining room table.

"For what?"

"Listening." Gazing down at the bowl that had an hour earlier been filled with a hearty beef stew that would've put even the duke's cook to shame, Lucy said, "I haven't had many people in my life who'd listen to me. My dad was always too busy. And even at my high school—the place I lived since my father traveled all the time—I never had a lot of friends. I guess I always had my head off somewhere in the future, dreaming of becoming a famous biologist like my dad. Senior year, there was this guy I really liked, Brad Fulman. He was tall and blond—the classic jock."

"What is a jock?"

"A guy really good at tournaments."

The prince nodded.

"Anyway, my roommate Wendy convinced me that he liked me—you know, in a romantic way, and said I should ask him to our Sadie Hawkins dance—"

"Help again. I know of dance, but . . ."

"The Sadie part means that instead of the usual boys asking the girls, girls ask the boys."

"Continue."

"Well, I wasn't at all sure about this, but Wendy said Brad had told everyone he liked me a lot, and that this would just finalize everything."

The prince leaned forward, that warrior-heading-to-battle expression steeling his dark eyes and strong jaw. "Your mere tone tells me this boy/man must be off'd."

Lucy laughed. "Am I that easy to read?"

"Only to me." Clasping her fingers in his, he skimmed his thumbs along the tops of her hands. "When a matter angers you, your blue eyes harden to gray, and you get lines here, and here," he said, softly tracing twin paths on her forehead between her eyes. "And when you're pleased, your eyes transport me to the sky, granting the gift of flight, and those same eyes crinkle at the corners, giving me the urge to kiss them, like this." Leaning forward he placed a whisper of a kiss to the outside corners of her eyes. "But when you're sad, Lucy Gordon, it shows not just in your eyes, but in your soul." Hands curving over her shoulders, he said, "Your posture becomes defeated, and your lips turn down. Your eyes dull like pewter, and I feel somehow lacking for not knowing the right path to once again make you smile."

Swallowing hard, Lucy did smile, only it was a smile mixed with goofy sentimental tears for the girl Brad Fulman had called a fat loser. And for the girl whose own roommate had set her up only to laugh behind her back. And for this wondrous man who with a simple yet eloquent speech had brought her both laughter and tears.

When the phone rang, intruding upon this sense of wonder, it took her a moment to regain her composure.

"Want me to off the damnedable nuisance?

Shaking her head, wiping another tear, she was already standing when she said, "Sorry, that's probably my friend, Bonnie. I'll be right back."

He nodded.

Only when she picked up the phone, it wasn't Bonnie on the other end, calling as planned to chat about their chaperoning duties for the upcoming school dance, but her father.

"Luce!" he said over crackling static. "Can you hear me?"

"Yes, Dad. Loud and—" Well, he might not have been clear, but at least he was loud. "What's up?"

"I got the e-mail photo of your frog—spectacular. And I added you to the closing night's agenda, but I really do need a clearer picture. That one's slightly blurred, and we don't want any screw-ups this time. My reputation's on the line."

Tracing the grout line in the countertop tile, she eyed the prince who was clearing the table. His blown kiss lurched her heart.

"Luce? Are you hearing me?"

"Um, yes, Dad. I'll get you that new picture right away."

After that, they chatted about the weather, and the poor quality of food at his mountain camp. He made a barb about her weight, how even she might've lost some if she'd been there, and she in turn, silently internalized it, biding her time until when she presented her frog, no one would ever again put the size of her body before the size of her mind.

"I never thought I'd say this, Luce, but no one will be more impressed with you on the day of the WBC than me."

"Thank you, Dad," she managed to say past the instant lump in her throat. Coming from him, that didn't just mean a lot, but the world.

"You're welcome, polliwog. Now, do me proud."

*Polliwog.*

He hadn't called her that since she'd been a little girl, and even more than his direct words of praise had touched her, this implied show of love moved her beyond words, and gave her the support needed to see her through. The connection fell dead, and cradling the phone between her breasts, Lucy leaned hard against the wall, squeezing her eyes shut tight.

This just had to work. It had to.

She jumped upon feeling warmth pressed to her cheek. Warmth in the form of Wolfe's fingers cupping her face. The rough pads of his thumbs wiping silly tears. Eyes open wider than maybe they'd ever been, she said simply, "Wolfe. You're here."

"Aye. Where else would I be?"

She shrugged.

"You're crying."

She shrugged again.

"What kind of father is this who makes you openly weep?"

"I'm not weeping," she said, putting the phone back on its charge pad while wishing it were possible to crawl inside herself. "And he's an okay guy."

Gently grasping her chin, forcing her to meet his gaze, he said, "Anyone who makes you cry is not o-kay. Shall I off him, too?"

That caused her to smile. "No," she said, pushing his hand away. "You can't solve all of my problems by offing those who wrong me—and for the record, I'm not crying because my dad made me sad, but happy."

Looking dazed, the prince said, "You cry happy and sad tears?"

She nodded.

He shook his head before pulling her into a hug.

"Quit!" Lucy screeched later that night when the prince pelted her with a cotton ball. It was the tenth in a row, and for at least the last ten minutes she'd been trying to remove her makeup. "What happened to that big stud who used to live here? Remember him? The guy who scoffed at all things woman?"

"Ahh," he said, catching her off guard with the potency of his rakish grin, "That was before I discovered my flair for womanly pursuits." Taking her latest cotton ball from her hand, he tossed it across the room where it landed beside the trash basket.

"Hey!" Lucy complained. "I was using that."

"Aye, but I have a much better method."

"Right," Lucy said, rolling her eyes and crossing her arms while he turned on the sink's hot water. "Don't mind me, I'll just be standing here, waiting to witness your glory."

"Excellent," he said, grabbing a washcloth from the linen cupboard. "But first, we must do this." Planting his hands on her hips, as if she weighed no more than a cotton ball, he lifted her onto the bathroom counter.

"W-what are you doing?"

"I should think that would be obvious by now, wee one," he slipped the cloth under the water. "I'm washing your face."

"I have special stuff for that."

"So do I. It's called water. And for centuries, it's worked amazingly well. Close your eyes."

# Chapter Eighteen

"No," Lucy said.

"Please?"

"Well . . ." Heart raging, she licked her lips. "I suppose since you said please . . ." She did his bidding, and when he touched the steaming cloth to her face, first came pleasurable chills, then sinful heat as he stroked the cloth over her eyes and cheeks. When the cloth cooled, she opened her eyes, but he barked at her to keep them closed, so she did, bracing her hands behind her on the counter while awaiting his next order.

Only there was no ordering, but sharing of his bold strokes and luxurious heat. He moved on to her chin, and then throat, and then he was again sweeping the cloth higher and higher, while his free hand moved lower, curving lightly round her throat, thumb planted at the base of her chin.

*Are you going to kiss me?*

No—and she didn't want him to. She loved the duke.

"Mmm . . ." she groaned as Wolfe, and only Wolfe,

dowsed the cloth in liquid heat once more, easing it across her eyelids and down the sides of her nose.

*Kiss me,* her lips silently begged, aching for the same attention as Wolfe lavished upon the rest of her face.

Dressed in an oversized pale pink T-shirt, her bra long gone, her nipples swelled and hardened from just the memory of his touch. And then that memory swept lower. And with her legs already spread for balance, she couldn't help but spread them wider still in anticipation of whatever next to come.

*Nothing,* one part of her screamed.

*Everything,* yet another railed.

He wet the cloth once more, stroking it behind her ears, and back down her throat, smoothing lazy strokes across the exposed strip of her collarbone peeking out from beneath the shoulder of her shirt.

*Are you going to kiss me now?*

The waiting was the worst.

No. This mounting hunger was the worst, knowing that she could deny it all she wanted, but the fact remained that she very much wanted Wolfe's kisses. And that was wrong. Not only because it betrayed her feelings for William, but because kissing Wolfe would make it that much harder to let him go.

Still, the future was in the future, and now he was—turning off the water?

Okay, so she'd peeked.

"All done," he said. "You can open your eyes."

*But I don't want to!*

*What happened to my kiss?*

"Tell me," he said, draping the cloth over the faucet. "Do you feel clean?"

*No! I feel like a dirty, dirty girl wanting to get dirtier!*

*I feel like I've been abandoned at the moment of my greatest need! Abandoned at the doors of—*

"Because if not, I'd be happy to draw you a bath, and continue the process on a much larger scale."

*Yes!*

No.

"Was that larger scale thing a crack at my weight?"

Wearing that confused look he got whenever their languages didn't quite translate, he said, "What does cleanliness have to do with weights?"

"Nothing," she said, forcing herself to hop down from the counter and once and for all forget about that girl who'd been dissed by Brad. "Nothing at all. And no, thank you, a full bath won't be necessary."

"You sure?" His wicked grin turned her a thousand shades of hot and bothered red.

He knew how frustrated she was! He knew, and he didn't care! Which only frustrated her all the more because she shouldn't care! She wasn't even supposed to like him!

"Yes, I'm sure," she said, elbowing him out of her way so she could brush her teeth. "Now, could I please have some privacy?"

Still ginning, he bowed before backing out of the room.

"You did not," Lucy said the next afternoon, a home-made sugar cookie to her mouth as she sat cross-legged on the end of the couch, listening to Wolfe tell his latest outrageous tale.

"You dare doubt I could perform such a fearless feat?"

Shaking her head, chewing the last of the delicious

cookie he'd baked, she said, "What I doubt is the fact that for one, any horse would be stupid enough to charge with you standing on his back. And two, that even you would be stupid enough to try such a thing."

A smile tugging at his lips, he shrugged. "Believe what you will, Lucy Gordon. But—"

The phone rang.

"Want me to get it?" he asked. "Might be Grumsworth, and I could off him with just my rapier-edged tongue."

"Thanks for the offer," she said, already across the room, "but I think I can handle it—whoever this may be. Hello?"

"Luce? How are you, darling? I'm home."

"William," she said, turning as much as possible away from the prince's prying eyes. "Um, how are you? How was the trip?"

"I'm quite well, and while the trip was oftentimes tedious, I did manage to accomplish all that I'd had in mind."

"Good. I'm, ah, glad."

The prince stretched himself across the sofa, his feet jauntily propped onto one end, then yawned.

"I want to see you," William said.

"Yes. Me, too. I mean, I do want to see you."

The prince made a few obnoxious kissy noises.

Covering the phone, she mouthed, "Quit!"

"What was that?" the duke asked.

"Nothing."

"All right, then," he said with a heavy sigh. "Would you mind, ah, preparing dinner for me tonight? Cook's under the weather, and I'm afraid it's been quite some time since I've wielded a pot."

"Tonight? Um . . ." Lucy chomped so hard on her lower lip, she winced, turning her back on the smiling prince. "Um, that's bad. Couldn't we meet somewhere in town? The Hoof and Toe maybe?"

"Luce, I didn't want to get into this over the phone, but—"

The prince rolled off of the sofa and crashed onto the Oriental rug, filling the room with gagging noises.

"Oh my gosh! I've, um, got to go."

Hanging up on William, she ran to the sofa, only to have strong fingers clasp about her ankle. Strong arms tackled her the rest of the way to the floor, landing her square atop the prince's dirty rotten, trick-playing chest!

"Damn you!" she raged. "That call was important, and you knew it."

"Aye. Just as you know the importance of you declaring your eternal love to me, and not that insipid duke. What? You feel I should have remained here silent on the so-faa? Doing your bidding like a good little boy?"

"I didn't say that."

"No, but you meant it," he said, giving her a squeeze. "When will you learn, Lucy Gordon, that I am not a boy, but a man, trying everything in my power to win your affections?"

A knock sounded at the mudroom door, and Lucy's heart lurched. "That's him. He must've been on his cell phone already on his way over. Oh my gosh—hide."

Wolfe laughed, squeezing his wench tighter still.

"Please," she said, tears springing to her eyes. "You don't know what this means. The duke is a powerful man. He doesn't like to be kept waiting."

"Oh, like I do?" he said, ignoring the fear flooding her eyes. "Like I'm not powerful?" And then it hit him, at the moment, he was anything but powerful. He was but a single man at the mercy of a single woman. She alone controlled his destiny. She alone held all the power. And the knowledge hit him as surely as a battle axe ramming his gut. Releasing her, he said, "Go to him, Lucy Gordon. Just know, that I will also go."

"Where?" she asked, still fisting his white lawn shirt.

"Why do you care?"

Another knock sounded at the mudroom door, and having had all he could stand of her looks of pity, Wolfe removed her himself. Hand on the back door, watching her run trembling hands through her hair, he said, "I wish you well."

Frozen in front of the cold fireplace, only her gaze roving from the mudroom door to the back, Lucy's head reeled. Which door to choose?

Through the back door just walked her every hope and dream. If Wolfe didn't safely return, she'd once again be the laughing stock of the biological world. Only rarely did her father give second chances, and if she failed this time, she feared it a real possibility he might never speak to her again.

Already, she'd had those few wondrous inquiries from *The London Times* and *Science Review,* asking her to confirm rumors that she'd found a remarkable new species right there in Wales. And while she'd politely declined to comment, she couldn't even try denying the thrill.

At the mudroom door stood William. Her kind, gentle benfactor who made her feel safe like no one else ever had. Dare she take a chance at explaining Wolfe to him? No. The very idea was ludicrous. William was the one person on the globe who hadn't even enjoyed *Star Wars Episode Ten*. No way was he going to grasp the concept of a thousand-year-old frog having to live with her in the form of a strapping medieval prince!

She was all set to wrestle Wolfe back into the house and lock him in her bedroom closet until she saw William cupping his hands to the paned mudroom window.

"Luce?" he called out. "Whatever are you doing?"

"Um, just heading for the mudroom door," she called back, already on her way to let him in. "I was in the bathroom."

Shaking his head once she led him inside, he said, "Shall I have you a loo installed on the ground floor?"

"No," she said, pulling him into a hug. "Don't be ridiculous. For just one person, one bathroom is fine."

"If you're sure then . . ."

"Yes. Promise. My life here is perfect."

Hands grasping her shoulders, he inched her back, staring into her eyes. "Do you mean that, Luce? Do you really, really mean to tell me you're quite content with this quiet life?"

"S-sure. Why?"

"It's nothing." Leading her to the sofa with his arm about her waist, he said, "Just more tomfoolery on the part of Ruth Hagenberry."

Good grief. Now what?

"Oh?" She sat beside him on the sofa, pretending to be comfortable in resting her head on his shoulder with her palm on his smooth, navy cotton sweater. His heart pounded, and she peered up at his face. "You're nervous."

"It shows?"

"Your chest feels like you've just finished a marathon. What's the matter? What did she tell you?"

He took a breath, then, "She says you've had a man living with you."

"A man?" Lucy coughed. Dear lord, how did that woman come by her intel? Had she lived a previous life as a Navy SEAL? "That's crazy."

"That's what I essentially told her," he said, shoulders sagging. "The woman's plainly off her rocker, and should be taken straight to the nearest asylum."

"Do they still have those in England?"

He laughed. "Why, I rather suppose I don't know."

She laughed, too, and for that moment at least, their easy friendship slipped back into place.

Lucy did cook him a simple meal of pork chops, instant scalloped potatoes and frozen peas, but the whole time he stood chatting beside her at the stove, fear lived within her.

When would Wolfe appear? Demanding she love him? How would the duke react? When he undoubtedly called the police on the both of them, how would she ever live with the shame? How would she last the remaining weeks until the full moon to prove to not just William that she was trustworthy, but to her father and the rest of her small world that she was a legitimate scientist, as well.

*Are you?* a quiet voice asked.

*How can you claim to be trustworthy when only one night past, you sat on your bathroom counter, eyes closed, practically begging Wolfe to kiss you full on your quivering lips?*

*And how can you claim to be a legitimate scientist when you didn't play any part in finding Wolfe. How could you have, when in actuality, he found you?*

Pushing aside the voices in her head, Lucy forced herself to finish preparing dinner and set the table. One task at a time, she'd somehow get through this night. And if Wolfe did burst through the door, she'd handle that, too.

One task at a time.

One second at a time.

And so the minutes wore on. . . .

"This is good," the duke said, occupying the prince's usual place at the dining room table. A pea rolled off of his fork and onto the white linen tablecloth she'd taken out for the occasion.

Eyeing the pea, longing for a moment of levity to ease the knot in her gut, she picked it up and lobbed it at him, quipping, "Good thing you're not dining with the queen."

The pea hit him on his chest, then plopped with a single bounce onto the hardwoord floor. William looked from the pea, to her, then back to the pea before asking, "What was that about?"

"What?"

"Hitting me with a vegetable."

"I'm sorry," she said. "I was just goofing around."

Lips pressed tight, he said, "Yes, well, in the future, perhaps I should strive harder to keep my peas on my plate."

*La dee da. Perhaps you should. Wolfe would've gotten my joke.*

240

Though the words never left her mouth, Lucy put her hands to her lips just the same. What was wrong with her? Wolfe wasn't even a real person, but a frog man! And William was a genuine flesh-and-blood duke. They don't come much better than that for fairy-tale endings.

*Uh-hmm, might I remind you that most fairy tales end up with the lucky pauper girl landing the prince and not a duke?*

"Can I get you anything else?" Lucy asked. "Coffee, tea, or me?"

With his napkin pressed to his lips, she thought William smiled, but couldn't really be sure. "I'd take a spot of brandy if you have some."

"Sorry," she said, standing, then reaching for his empty plate. "I've got dark beer." Wolfe's favorite.

"That's all right. How about we retire to the living room and talk?"

"Sure. Let's just clean up these dishes first."

"Leave them," he said, hand on her arm.

"Ordinarily, I would, but . . ." *Once Wolfe gets home, I'd hate for him to clean our mess.*

She sucked her lower lip. *If* he gets home.

Had he taken a jacket? No. He didn't even have one, but he had at least been wearing that mossy green sweater that looks so yummy with his dark eyes.

Was he hungry? He was a big guy and, judging by her latest grocery bill, he ate a lot. What was he doing for snacks?

William sighed. "Is there something on your mind, Luce?"

Beneath the accusing yellow stare of the library's one lamp, directly in Lucy's line of sight on the library table, the prince had left his reading flash cards, along with his tablet of wide-ruled paper and three *Star Wars Episode Ten* pencils, because contrary to what the duke had thought of the film, Wolfe had liked it very much!

"Huh? What?"

"Where were you just now?" he asked, giving her arm a light squeeze. "You seemed a million miles away."

"I'm sorry," she said. "Guess it's been a long day."

"Would you like me to go?"

*Yes!*

"No. Come on," she said, gazing over her shoulder out the dark window, before taking his hand. "Let's go sit down."

This was not good.

Glancing one last time at Lucy Gordon, Wolfe saw her take the insipid duke's hand, leading him toward the so-faa. The so-faa where the two of them watched movies and shared pop-corn and conversation and kisses. By all rights, that so-faa belonged to him—that woman belonged to him—and the thought of seeing another man lean her against those soft cushions filled the back of his throat with bile.

The cottage window glass was not thick enough that he hadn't heard snippets of their conversation. All polite conversation and no meat.

If the man intended to declare his intentions toward her, why hadn't he already done so?

Ad nauseam, Lucy had reminded Wolfe of how she and the duke were almost betrothed, and while granted Wolfe was no expert on current-day courting rituals, in his time, he'd been considered quite the stud. And to his way of thinking, Lucy's heart was fair game up until the point the duke slipped his ring on her finger.

Ruth Hagenberry put down her binoculars and tssked tssked.

Unbelievable!

Now, Lucy Gordon had one man waiting for her outside, while she held court with the duke inside!

The woman's escapades were scandalous, and it was high time the duke found out just what sort of soiled woman she truly was. The duke's family came from a long, noble line of Englishmen, and the last thing he needed was to be mucking the family bloodline by marrying this wholly unsuitable Yank.

Her hair was unsuitable.

Her taste in clothes deplorable.

Everything about the woman screamed poor taste.

Now, her Abigail, on the other hand . . . She was the very definition of well-bred decorum.

"Yo, Mum!" her angel called from the front seat of the car. "You about done? I'm missing me shows!"

"Hush!" Ruth fired back. "Do you want us caught?"

"I'd say it's rather late for worrying about that, wouldn't you?" Was it just the shadows making the deep masculine voice so ominous?

"Who's there?" Ruth asked, pulse hammering as she switched on her high-beamed torch and aimed it toward thick rhododendrons. "You'd better show yourself, or I'll summon the law."

A rustling came from the brambles at forest's edge.

"Who's there?" Ruth repeated, gaze and torch darting about.

"Who's there?" the deep-throated voice ever so politely inquired, stepping out of the shadows not two feet behind Ruth to tap her on her left shoulder. "Your worst nightmare."

Ruth tried to scream, but from behind her, the killer clamped his hand over her mouth.

Her torch clattered to the ground, and the light went out.

"If you know what's good for you," he said, "you'll leave my land never to return. Understand?"

Eyes frantic and wide, nostrils flared, heart hammering, Ruth nodded, and when the man released her, she ran straight to her car and jumped behind the wheel, gunning the engine so hard it coughed and nearly died out before she fishtailed onto the dirt lane.

"It's about time," Abigail said. "And step on it. You know how I hate missing me shows."

# Chapter Nineteen

"You're back," Lucy said, standing on the threshold of Wolfe's room wearing her oversized pink T-shirt, her bare feet cold on the hardwood floor.

"Aye," he said with a grunt, sweeping first his sweater, then a white T-shirt over his head. Save for the faint light eking from the hall, the room was dark, but not dark enough for Lucy to miss his stormy expression.

He'd already removed his shoes and socks, and standing before her magnificently bare-chested, noble chin raised, eyes unbearably dark and formal, angular cheeks shadowed with stubble, long black hair wild as if he'd become one with the night, she'd never seen him look more like a true prince. She'd never felt more apprehension about being with him alone—not because of what he might do to her, but because seeing him like this, chest bared in all his primal glory, she feared it would be all too easy to forget her true goal.

This man was a frog, for heaven's sake! *Her* frog.

The frog that if she just held her course for a couple of weeks, would make her every dream come true.

"You're staring," he said.

"I'm sorry."

"What do you want?"

*You.*

She cleared her throat. "Um, nothing. I'm just glad to see you back safely."

His only answer was a grunt.

"You don't believe me?"

"I saw you with him on the sofa, Lucy Gordon. I saw his hands on you, and his lips on you, and I didn't like it."

*Me, neither.*

Lucy squeezed her eyes shut.

While the duke had been kissing her, she'd traitorously done nothing but compare him to Wolfe and found him lacking.

What kind of woman was she? Comparing her future husband to a man only found in her imagination. For essentially Wolfe was a ghost, here on earth for but a short time.

"I'm sorry." Choking back frustrated tears, she added, "I don't know what else to say."

"How about that you love me?" he said. "How about that I'm the only man possessing the power to drive you senseless with desire."

*Dear lord, it was true.*

Just standing there in the dark, feet away from him, she felt him cupping her cheek, her breasts, her belly. If she but closed her eyes, she'd once again know the heated graze of his fingertips working her nipples to pleasure-cored aches. And his lips. His torturous, bruising lips that left her mouth swollen and wanting. Always wanting, yearning for the forbidden.

But all of that was lust, not love.

It was wrong. William. She had to remember William.

Raising her chin, she dared ask, "Who are you to demand love from me, when you yourself don't give it?"

"I have neither the time nor patience for fairy stuff such as love."

"Yet you expect a declaration of it from me?"

"Women are different. Such things come easily to you."

"You think?"

"I know."

All right. That was it. She had just about enough of his self-righteous egotism.

"Let me tell you what I know, mister." Marching a few feet forward, she planted her index finger against his chest. "I know every single thing you've said and done has been nothing more than a cleverly designed campaign to win me over to your affections. I know that guys like you only care about one thing—your own agenda. How do I know? Because all my life, I've had to deal with the likes of you ingratiating yourselves to me, only to gain access to my father until I finally got so sick of being lied to that I eventually gave up dating all together. That's when I met the duke. Who's kind, caring, and since he's already wealthy and a smidgeon famous—at least in his social circle—he couldn't give two figs about my father."

"And you suppose I do?" he said with a royal snort. "Unless he's a border king come to exchange your hand for land, I don't care about him, either. What I do care about is you, Lucy Gordon." Softening his tone, he slipped his hands beneath her heavy fall of hair, cupping the back of her head. "I care about your happiness, and even if I were out of the picture as you seemingly claim to desire, you would not be happy with the insipid duke."

"H-how could you possibly know?"

"Because even now, when I but hold you, you tremble. Even in the dark, I feel your lips quiver with fear. But is it my kissing you, you fear? Or the notion that I might not kiss you? Thus leaving you alone and wanting in your cold bed."

To stablize herself, Lucy pressed her palms to his chest, but when they met with smooth, hot muscle dotted with coarse hair, her mouth went dry, and her fingertips longed to wander. Up, she'd find an inconceivably broad set of shoulders attached to arms that found even a weight such as hers no burden. Down, she'd find an abdomen so honed as to make her fingertips rise and fall with the waving ripples. And down lower still, was a steel shaft she knew by sight and feel, but not yet by touch.

Not yet?

What was she thinking?

"I-I've got to go." Pushing away from this insanity that just being near him brought on, she said, "I-I can't do this anymore. What I share with William means too much."

"Your William is a fool."

At the door, steadying herself with a white-knuckled grip on the knob, she said, "Then consider me a fool, too, because he's the man I love. He's the man I'll one day marry."

Ms. Roberts—Penelope—popped her head through the crack in William's London office door and said with grinning wink, "Your Missus Hagenberry's on the phone. Line three."

"Bloody hell," William said, slamming his pen atop the Morganstern file. "What does that nut cake want from me now?"

"Do you mean fruitcake?" she asked with another wink.

"Fruitcake." William couldn't help but smile. "Yes, that about sums her up to perfection. Thank you, Penelope. Whatever would I do without you?"

"Let's hope you never have need to know."

When he stared at her, she said, "Line three?"

"Oh, yes. Right." After putting the nasty woman on speaker phone, he pressed line three's blinking button. "Hallo, Ruth. Having a pleasant day?"

"I most certainly am not."

"Oh?" he said, making a note on a copy of that morning's meeting minutes. "What seems to be the problem?"

"The problem is that only just last night, I was viciously attacked—and on your land!"

"Attacked, you say. On my land?" He put down his pen, and sat straighter in his chair.

"Yes. By a deranged killer claiming the land to be his. And while I didn't get a good look at him, I feel quite certain that this man and the man your Lucy has been living with are one and the same. And what's worse, is that—"

"Dear Ruth," he said, praying for patience where she was concerned. "If you must know, I had dinner with Lucy at Rose Cottage just last night, and I assure you, everything seemed quite in order, with no signs of additional occupants, be they male or female."

Harrumph.

"Ruth? Did you hear me? You've got to put this obsession with Lucy Gordon out of your mind, or I fear you'll be needing professional help."

"Need help?" Lucy asked the prince Sunday in the cottage's cozy library. Hard rain pelted the windows, and after they'd shared a silent afternoon snack, silent dinner, and now still more silence, while she'd managed to get a lot done on her conference papers, all of this quiet, save for the relentless rain, was starting to be disquieting. He hadn't even eaten the candy bar she'd brought him Friday afternoon from one of the school vending machines.

"No, thank you."

"Wolfe, please . . ."

"What?" He looked up from the children's world history book she'd checked out for him in her school library.

"Can't we talk? This silence is—"

"Hurting you?"

"Y-yes."

"Good. Then maybe you'll know a mere fraction of what my pain will soon be." Easing his book shut, slowly setting it on the mahogany side table, he leaned forward in his chair. "Maybe you'll think about what it will be like for me spending not an afternoon in silence, but hundreds upon thousands of years."

250

"Y-you'll make friends."

"More turtle friends?" Pushing himself to his feet, he laughed. "That gives me something to look forward to."

Heart tight with sympathy, Lucy brought her hands to her mouth.

Granted, his being turned back into a frog would be sad, but it was the way things were supposed to be, right? He'd long ago been imprisoned within himself for orphaning all of his children. Shoot, he was no better than the deadbeat dads who abandoned their kids at her school.

*Oh yeah? Do those dads ever play games with their children like Wolfe reported he'd done? Do they talk to their kids, and care for them in every way but giving them proper last names?*

Sighing, Wolfe headed for the back door. "I'm going for a walk."

"But it's raining," she said, feet frozen to that spot.

"I wouldn't trouble yourself with worry for my health. After all," he said with a cold smile. "I've been wet before, and if you have your way, will soon be again."

After he'd gone, Lucy stood there in the middle of the library for a long time, eyes closed, hugging herself, gently rocking while wishing for some way to grant Wolfe his dreams while keeping hers. If only she could find some other new species of frog to present—but considering the fact that the conference loomed closer every day, the likelihood of finding a replacement was less than zero percent.

The phone rang, and she jumped.

"Geez," she mumbled under her breath on her way to the kitchen.

Heart still racing, fearing with her luck it could be no one but her father, she was relieved to hear Bonnie's chirpy hallo, then, "Say, Luce, do you remember telling Luke he could borrow one of the duke's dinner jackets for the dance?"

"Sure," Lucy said. "Does he still need one?"

"Yup. I thought I could squeeze him into my brother's, but I'd somehow forgotten it was baby blue."

"Ugh. Say no more, I'll call the duke right now, then call you back."

"Thanks, Luce, you're a doll. Anyway, gotta run. I'm babysitting my nephew, Bryant, tonight, so I've got to baby-proof the house, and make sure Sammy's secure."

After saying good-bye to her friend, Lucy hung up the phone and frowned. Bonnie sounded so happy and bustling and busy and in love. And here she sat, almost a household name—at least in scientific circles—but not quite yet. Almost at peace with her father, but not quite yet. Almost happily engaged, but not quite yet.

Impatience stormed through her, along with the frustration of not just this wait, but seemingly having waited her whole life for the elusive happiness always just around the corner.

Consoling herself with the certainty that in just less than two week's time, at least part, if not all of her waiting would finally be over, Lucy called the duke, and arranged to meet him in the gardens to get what was just one of his dozens of dinner jackets.

The rain had mercifully let up, and shrugging on a light red and blue polka-dot jacket over her jeans and Mickey Mouse sweatshirt, she headed into the cold, damp night.

Though the crushed stone path was well-lit with discreetly placed electric lanterns, she still carried a queasy batch of nerves. What had she been thinking? Agreeing to meet William in the garden when she had no idea where Wolfe might've gone?

She assumed he'd be at the pond, but as she was quickly learning, where he was concerned assumptions could be dangerous. Just like her assuming he'd quietly revert to his life as a frog without giving her a moment's trouble.

But then were she in his place, could she blame him? Would she willingly spend eternity as a frog?

*Sure. If he were a frog with me!*

Cheeks blazing with heat, she scowled while rounding the final corner leading to the wooden bench where she and William had agreed to meet.

"Hallo, gorgeous!" William called out with a jaunty wave. He'd folded a dark garment bag over the back of the bench.

"Hey, handsome." His flirtatious mood was a welcome diversion. "I see you brought the goods?"

"One dinner jacket, as requested. Though to get it, you'll have to pay the toll."

"Mmm," she said with a grin. "I don't know, I'm feeling awfully broke at the moment." Especially since her credit card bill carrying the majority of the prince's clothes had arrived.

"Really?" he said once she sat beside him. "Because if you find yourself in need of a spot of cash, you know all you need do is—"

"Shh . . ." she said, fingers to his lips. "Thank you. You're sweet to offer, but I'll be fine. Just need to pinch pennies until my next check."

"There's no need to do that, either, you know. Because—"

"Could we please talk of something other than dry old money," she said, hoping her tone came off as light, instead of desperate. She had a feeling whatever he'd been about to say was serious, and she didn't want to be serious. Not tonight, or ever again. In a matter of days, her every dream would come true, and that was cause to celebrate.

*Even if in achieving your dreams, you'll be selfishly taking a man's life?*

Commanding her conscience to hush, she leaned forward to give her future husband a kiss, and thankfully he responded by slipping one arm about her shoulders, and his other inside her coat to rest upon her waist. The kiss was by no means soul-stirring. But it was sweet and wholesome and good. And for now, that was enough.

"Dear, Luce," he said once they'd pulled apart. "I've missed you."

"But I haven't been anywhere."

"Yes, you have," he said, even in the pale moonlight confusion, and maybe even pain visible in the smooth planes of his aristocratic face. "I'm not blind. I know something beyond this silly feud with Grumsworth has been causing you concern. Now," his breath hitched, "if you feel comfortable enough with me for us to talk it over. Please know that I'm always available to you. And if not, that's okay, too. Granted you promise that whatever's on your mind, it's not second thoughts concerning your future with me."

"Oh, William, no," she said on a gush of relief for his being so understanding and kind and gentle and all-around wonderful in every sense of the word. Cupping her hands to his smooth cheeks, she said, "Yes. I have had a work project consuming me, but I can promise you two things. One, that it has nothing to do with you."

*Unless you consider my living with an incredibly virile, hunky medieval stud to be personal.*

*Shut up, conscience!*

"And two, that you'll know all about it very soon."

A long while later, still in a happy daze, Lucy shut and locked the mudroom door, then leaned against it with a contented thud. Even though her hands and toes were freezing, the time spent with William had been well worth the price of a little chill.

She'd spent so much time with Wolfe lately that she'd forgotten just how well she and the duke got along. In ways, he reminded her of her father. He was older than her, miles more responsible, planned his days down to the minute, and had a genuine knack for being dull as the hills.

*What?*

William, dull? Ha! If one called wealthy and respected and gentle and caring dull.

After washing her face with her hands, she looked up only to gasp. "Wolfe! Geez, you've gotta stop sneaking up on me like that."

"I would apologize" he said, voice lethally low. "But I'm not in the least bit sorry."

"O-okay," she said, angling toward the kitchen, but he pinned her right where she stood by planting his hands on either side of her against the door. Licking her lips, she said, "What do you want? I'm tired, and was going to bed."

"I want you to look at me. Really look at me and tell me you prefer the duke's lukewarm kisses to this."

He ground his lips to hers with such force that at first she fought him, clawing at his chest, but then he softened, probing her lips apart, boldly stroking the tender flesh of her tongue and, try though she might, she couldn't deny that every word he'd said had been true. Compared to this, this carnal bliss, the duke's kisses might as well have been saltine crackers competing with filet mignon.

Be that as it may, she wasn't doing this. She wasn't falling for the prince's seduction routine again. She wasn't going to yearn for the laughter they'd once shared. She wasn't, she wasn't, she—

"I can't breathe without you, Lucy Gordon."

"W-what?" she said on a gasp.

"I need you," he said, burying his face in the curve of her neck hidden by her hair. Sliding his hands down the door and onto her butt, he lifted her up, up, crushing her midsection to him, leaving no doubt as to the urgency of his need. Rock didn't begin to describe the exquisite hardness of his package, as still holding her with one hand, he urged one of her knees round his hips, then the other.

Lucy knew this to be sheer lunacy, yet she felt powerless to stop. The moist throb between her legs had taken control and the sensation was all at once terrifying, yet exhilarating.

Yes, she would soon be marrying William, but if she had this one wild night with the prince, who was to know? After all, she'd already established the fact that he didn't even really exist. Who did it hurt if she were to get it on with a man who might as well be a ghost?

*Who did it hurt?*

*Lucy Gordon, are you freakin' out of your mind?*

Arms wrapped round Wolfe's neck, fingers buried in his hair, Lucy indulged in one last kiss before resting her head on his shoulder and shaking her head. "No," she said. "I'm sorry. Believe me, I'm sorry, but this just isn't me. I can't do this to William."

After abandoning her on the mudroom counter, Wolfe slammed his fist into the centuries-old plaster wall, cracking off a huge chunk. "I can no longer do this. These games you insist upon playing—" Looking away from her, then back, he said, "I'm losing all sense of control."

"How do you think I feel?" she said, tears in her eyes. "Never have I been more attracted to any man. Geez, half the time, I can't even watch TV or do dishes or read without thinking of you. Of your fingers in my hair each morning, and the taste of your meals on my tongue each night. But the fact remains that technically, you're living on borrowed time. Who am I to say the sorceress was wrong in putting you under this spell? Yes, you've given me your version of what went down, but I know what it feels like to be trashed by a guy. It hurts, Wolfe. Bad. By your own countless admissions, you've told me how smooth you've always been with the ladies. How do I know you're not playing me right now? How do I know this isn't the same kind of crap you pulled back in the ninth century? How do I know that once I give you what you want, you won't soon be long gone?"

Eyes narrowed, hands fisted on his slim hips, face excruciatingly handsome and fierce, he said, "You don't."

# Chapter Twenty

"So?" Bonnie said in the school lunch line Monday afternoon. Her voice barely carried above the chatter of sixty-three nine-, ten- and eleven-year-olds. "You excited about Saturday night?"

Grabbing a tuna sandwich and plastic-wrapped green blob of Jell-O, Lucy said, "I guess."

"What do you mean, you guess? What if this is the big night?" Grabbing a brownie and a baggie of peanut butter cookies, Bonnie said, "What if the duke finally proposes? You'll be a real live duchess, and then I have to start bowing and stuff whenever you come around."

"Right," Lucy said, heading to a table in an especially gloomy corner of the room. Outside, as usual, rain pelted the windows. "And next they'll make me queen."

"Stranger things could happen."

"Give me one," Lucy said, collapsing onto her seat. Though her conference papers were nearly done, Wolfe's black cloud loomed over her every waking and sleeping thought. She'd started having vivid dreams of him, howling with pain at the moment of his change. What would it be like? It had to hurt changing from such a big guy into a tiny frog.

And it was a pain so easily avoided with just three small words. *I love you.*

The trouble was, she didn't love him.

Oh sure, he was great fun to hang out with. Have popcorn fights with while watching movies and talking and laughing and she'd certainly loved his cooking for her and cleaning and washing her face and fixing her hair, but none of that equaled love, did it? None of that began to rival the all-out jubilation she'd feel upon hearing that deafening roar of applause.

*Applause gained from his pain.*

Squeezing her eyes shut, Lucy pressed her fingers to her temples.

This was madness.

All day, all night, this constant circular logic. When would it end? Sure, she'd told herself it would end just as soon as she made her WBC presentation, but what then? She knew better than anyone the hours of poking and prodding Wolfe would then be subjected to. It wasn't as if she could just release him back to his pond with a final bittersweet kiss. And what happened when other scientists found out he wouldn't die? What happened when he'd outlived them all? Would they treat him like some sort of freak frog and set him up in a nice terrarium suite at the Smithsonian?

"Lucy?" Bonnie put her hand on her arm. "Need me to get you some aspirin?"

"No, thanks." Blinking back tears, Lucy looked up. "I'm fine."

"No, you're not fine. Maybe you should go home? Get some sleep?"

"I can't just leave my class."

"Me and the rest of the crew'll cover for you. Go on. Go up to the office and clock out."

Nodding, Lucy put her hand over Bonnie's. "I guess you're right. Maybe I should nap off this funk."

"Either that, or go have yourself a good half-dozen green apple martinis. Whatever your pleasure." When Lucy laughed, Bonnie said, "Ah, there's our girl. I thought we'd lost you."

Lucy shook her head. "Just have a lot on my mind."

After taking a quick glance at her watch, Bonnie said, "I've still got fifteen minutes if you want to talk."

"No . . ." If only she could talk all of this out with someone. Not that anyone would believe such a fantastic tale. But what could it hurt to get a little female perspective on at least the broader points of this multilayered dilemma? "Well . . . okay. Let's say you'd been looking for this fancy goldfish that you wanted more than anything in the world. But when you found him, you were so excited that you kissed him, and then he turned into a dog."

Frowning, Bonnie said, "Go on, I'm sort of following."

"Okay, so say you already had a dog that you loved a whole lot, but the apartment you were staying in only allowed one dog, and so you had to choose between them."

"What happened to the fish?"

"Oh—if you don't tell him you love him by the next full moon, he turns back into a fish, at which point, you could have your fish and your old dog, but you wouldn't have your new dog, who you really started to like a whole lot—like more than you ever thought it was possible to like a dog, and—"

"Lucy?"

"Yeah?"

"I really do think you should go home. You might even be running a fever."

"You think?"

Bonnie answered with a solemn nod.

Oh, Lucy knew she had a fever all right—frog fever. But as she entered the cottage that afternoon, it was to the heavenly smell of Wolfe's beef stroganoff and the lilting strains of *Aida* playing on the kitchen radio.

"You're home early," he said, rounding the kitchen corner to land an all-too-brief kiss to her cheek. "I missed you."

Eyebrows raised, alarm bells ringing, she said, "I, ah, missed you, too." Easing her school bag and purse onto the mudroom bench, she said, "Not that I'm complaining, but what's up with your good mood? You've hardly talked to me in days."

Stirring his sauce, he shrugged. "I don't want to spend my last days of life scowling."

"These aren't your last days," she said, somehow talking past the sob lying in wait to make a mockery of her words. "Have you forgotten the fact that you have a whole new life ahead of you? Lounging around in the warm sun all day . . ." *Ha! More like the cold fluorescent glare of a lab.* "You know, just hanging around. No work, and all play." *Yeah right, playing around with electrodes and test tubes.* Turning away from him, she swiped at a few stupid, sentimental tears.

261

Dammit. For a so-called scientist, she had the intestinal fortitude of pond scum!

Removing the sauce from the stove and setting it on a stainless steel trivet, Wolfe said in a remarkably calm tone, "If you believe my life as a frog was a mere frolic, Lucy Gordon, either you're daft or intentionally blind. And since I know you to not be the former, it must be the latter that has you afflicted. For you see," he said, dark eyes menacing slits, "I neither had fun, nor eternal life. Aye, I'd live forever, assuming I steered clear of those who would eat me." Creeping closer, he said, "Have you ever found true sleep knowing a predator with glowing eyes lurked just inches away—so close that you smelled the putrid rot of his last meal on his breath? And have you ever spent the entirety of your seasons in the out-of-doors? Cold? Always cold, no matter the heat of the sun. Aye, Lucy Gordon. What I have to look forward to is a grand time, indeed."

Mouth dry, pulse at its usual gallop whenever he was around, she said, "E-even if I said right now that I loved you, Wolfe, since it wouldn't be true, what makes you think your curse would be broken? You look at me as if I have a choice in the matter, but I don't."

*Liar!*

Falling for this man would be embarrassingly easy—which only proved the sorceress's point. He was no good for women—especially formerly gullible women such as herself.

"Look," she said, pressing her hands to the wall of his chest, unwittingly making herself one with the powerful beat of his heart. "You'll never know how sorry I am about all of this." Evidently just not sorry enough to put her own selfish wants ahead of his life.

But then why didn't she deserve a little happiness? All her life, compared to her high and mighty father, she'd been a second-class citizen. Now, was her time to shine.

*Yeah, but at Wolfe's expense?*

Ugh—she'd said it herself, even if she said she loved him—which she didn't, there was nothing she could do to help him.

*What about trying to see if the two of you could share a real future?*

Right.

Even if she fell for him, the second he discovered himself hundred percent mortal, he'd dump her for a supermodel, then—

"Are you sorry?"

"Huh?" She jerked her gaze up, up, up to his.

"Are you truly sorry about not being able to love me?"

Swallowing hard, gazing into features so handsome she'd have had to have been a poet rather than a scientist to adequately describe him, she somehow found the courage to nod. Oh, she was sorry all right. Sorry that she wasn't the kind of woman he would truly find attractive. Sorry that they couldn't have met under different circumstances. Sorry that she'd ever kissed him at all.

"Want to play Scrabble or eat?"

"Just like that?"

"What do you mean?"

"Don't you want to talk more?"

Expression unfathomably sad, he shook his head. "I'd much rather live."

\* \* \*

And live they did. Starting with eating dinner and playing Scrabble. Far from the first time they'd played, Wolfe had become amazingly competent. When she asked him about it, he admitted to having practiced. From Scrabble, they moved on to popcorn and TV, and a spirited debate on the Monday night bonus episode of *Survivor Moon*—he was cheering on Team North Star, while she was for Team Jupiter—and from there to companionably washing the dishes, their movements in the kitchen orchestrated like those of an old married couple.

Swishing a hot rag about a glass while Wolfe picked up the remnants of their latest popcorn battle, Lucy thought of what it might be like married to a man like Wolfe compared to a man like William.

Well, for one, she probably wouldn't be doing much more housework. A good thing. But then at times like these, when you worked together, it wasn't all bad. Caring for the fork Wolfe had put to his tongue, curving her fingers round the glass he'd held to his lips.

Her lips tingling from the mere thought of Wolfe's, she switched her mental topics to other differences, like Wolfe's love of games and TV.

William rarely watched TV, and when he did, it was either one of the government channels or something hoity-toity like an economic lecture or a documentary on the collapse of the Roman Empire. As for games, she wasn't even sure he had any. He was so busy all day, probably when he got home, he preferred to chill. With him, she'd no doubt spend quiet nights in front of a crackling fire reading, or just talking about their days.

When they one day had children, what kind of father

would he make? Like his own father, would he insist their children be shipped off to proper boarding schools like the one where she taught? Would he demand the kind of perfect mini-adult children who were to be seen and not heard?

Surely not. William was no monster. So, he preferred living his life on the quiet side? So had she before meeting the prince. Shoot, a little over three weeks earlier, her idea of a wild night was starting a new needlepoint project.

And now she was laughing, and having tickle and popcorn fights.

She didn't have to even think about what kind of husband Wolfe would make because she already knew. Living with him even this short time had proven him beyond fun. Everything about him was bold, brash, larger than life and energizing. Just look at the courage he'd instilled in her to deal with Grumsworth.

"You've gotta stop accosting me with popcorn," Wolfe said, kneeling beside the cabinet beneath the sink to dump popcorn kernels into the trash.

"Me?" She flicked soap bubbles at him. "You're the one who kept cheering for the wrong team."

"The smart team. Notice they didn't have to vote anyone off? It's a loooong walk from their camp to the tribal crater."

"Listen to you," she said. "A guy from the ninth century chatting about moon lingo. Does it ever just blow your mind?"

"What?"

"What's happened to you? I mean, there are times I still can't quite buy your story. But then I'd have an even tougher time figuring out why a guy like you would make something like this up just to hang out with me."

"Like the pleasure of your company isn't enough?" he said with a potent grin, slowly rising to his full height, using her hips for balance.

"Oooh, you're a charmer," she said, pulse pleasantly racing despite her seemingly eternal vow to stay cool. But when he stood close like this, close enough for his wholly masculine scents of earth and sweat to blend with the creamy sauce they'd shared for dinner, she just wanted to throw her arms around him and gobble him up for dessert.

"Wanna play a game?" he asked, nuzzling her neck.

Half-heartedly pushing him away, she teased, "What kind of game?"

"Mmm, a naughty one," he teased right back. "Definitely a nau—"

A knock sounded on the mudroom door, then William shouted, "Luce? It's me! Let me in! It's raining!"

"Oh my God," she whispered to Wolfe. "Hide. Please, hide." With her palms on his magnificent chest, she felt his muscles tighten beneath her fingers.

"Granted, only a moment earlier, it was I who suggested we play a game," he said, voice lethally low. "But I now find myself tiring of games. Especially yours, Lucy Gordon. With the full moon nearly upon us, can't you see that you need a man in your life? Not this boy? Were it I standing outside your door, and I knew you to be inside, I would storm it down, not stand there politely knocking whilst I suspected you carried on with another."

"Luce? Are you in there? Can you hear me above your telly? Bloody bother her love of shows," he grumbled, his footfalls crunching on fallen leaves the groundskeepers hadn't yet gotten around to raking as he walked around the side of the cottage. What would he think when he reached the back door only to peer inside and find the TV off?

"Please, Wolfe. William wouldn't understand. He—"

"You dare talk of understanding when my very life is at stake?"

"But you—"

"Silence!" he roared. Gripping her roughly by her shoulders, he gave her a shake. "Now! This instant! Declare your love for me and demand that insipid creature to be on his way!"

Torn—not to mention terrified of what Wolfe might do, Lucy peered around his massive shoulders to where knocking could now be heard at the back door.

"Go to him then," he said, casting her off with a disdain-filled sneer. "For I should rather spend eternity as a loathsome frog, then taste one more morsel of swallowed pride. I have lowered myself to the level of a common house servant for you, Lucy Gordon, brushing your hair, washing your clothes, preparing your meals and all for naught. It has become increasingly apparent that you value nothing in me but my strong arms and back."

"That's not true," she said. "I mean, yes, I love what you do for me, but I'm not in love with you. There's a huge difference. And I wish I had more time to explain, but—" Standing on her tiptoes, she kissed his cheek, then snatched her rain slicker off the wall peg in the mudroom before slipping out the door and into a cold drizzle.

"William!" she called into the shadows. "I'm here."

"Whatever are you doing outside?" he called, meeting her halfway around the cottage beneath the pungent-smelling shelter of a cedar of Lebanon.

"I-I had to get some school things from the car."

"Oh. Well, let's go inside."

"Um, I'd rather stay out."

"In the rain?"

"It's not really a rain. More of a mist. Romantic in a spooky sort of way." Wolfe would love walking in this kind of weather.

"Romantic? Are you daft?"

Odd, that in one night, two men who might as well be a thousand years of time and miles apart when it came to their differences had both called her the very same thing. And yes, she was starting to think she might very well be daft for ever daring to hope she could pull all of this off. Chin raised, she asked, "What's wrong with the occasional eccentricity like walking in the rain?"

William snorted. "Do you consider catching pneumonia to be an eccentricity, as well?" Taking her hand, he said, "Come on, let's get inside by your fire. I saw through the window that you have a rather nice one lit. It gladdens me to know your fire-making skills seem to have vastly improved."

"Yes, but I still don't have anything good to eat. Let's go to your *cottage* and raid the fridge."

He raised his eyebrows.

"You know, eat everything in your refrigerator."

"Oh. Oh yes, of course."

"Well, then?" Tugging his hand, she turned him toward the castle just as Wolfe scowled from the living room window.

268

# Chapter Twenty-one

"And then straightaway after the midday meal, we had to endure another round of negotiations and by the end of . . ."

Lucy's chin touched her chest, and she jerked awake with a start. "Wolfe?"

"Luce? Are you quite all right?"

Crackling fire.

Dark paneling.

Lumpy furniture that'd been in this musty old castle since the dark ages.

William's endless talk of business.

It all came back.

"Sure," she said, pushing unruly hair back from her eyes to tuck it behind her ears. "Sorry. I guess the heat and all must've had me dozing off."

"Would you like me to open a window?" he asked, voice laced with concern.

"No. I just think it's probably a sign for me to head home."

"Probably so," he said with a sigh. "It is well past ten."

*And I do still need to apologize to Wolfe.*

"Let me ring for Freidman to bring our coats, then I'll walk you back."

"No!"

"Why ever not?"

"There's no need for you to go out in this weather."

"But I want to," he said with a wink. "Besides, weren't you the one just saying it was romantic?"

"Well, sure, but that was before I realized I was so tired." She yawned. "See? I'd be terrible company."

Eyes narrowed, he reached for her hand. "It's not company, I crave, Luce, but you. Surely you must feel close enough to me now that you don't feel every second must be filled with conversation? We are allowed our silences, you know."

"Thank you," she said, surprisingly touched by his admission. Or was it the warmth in his eyes? The look that plainly said he loved her, and the knowledge that for the past two weeks she'd been hiding a terrible secret. *I never meant to hurt you,* she longed to explain. *And it'll all be over soon. I'll listen with rapt interest to your every business story, and—*

"Luce?"

"Yes?"

He glanced down, then back up, Adam's apple bobbing. "Before we go, while we're still here by the fire, where *I* find it rather romantic . . ."

"Yes?" Was this it? Was he finally going to propose? And if so, why was there a tight knot of dread fisting her stomach instead of zinging champagne bubbles and happy butterflies?

"As you know, Christmas is approaching, and, well," taking her left hand in his, he raised it to her lips, kissing her bare ring finger. "I was rather curious if there's anything in particular you'd like Father Christmas to bring?"

*I want to keep him.*

*I want to keep Wolfe* and *be a world-renowned biologist. I want my father's love, and my very own species of frog, and my very own frog prince. That's what I want, along with nights filled with crazy, laughing popcorn fights and TV debates and kissing. No—not just kissing, but fevered kissing, the kind that leads to torn clothes and popped buttons and—*

Lucy's cheeks blazed. "I-I guess I haven't much thought about Christmas." But now that she had, the thought of not sharing it with Wolfe felt inconceivable.

"Perhaps you should," he said, grazing her finger with another light kiss before releasing her hand.

"Y-yes," she said, "perhaps I should." Think very hard about the insane notions flitting through her head. Because they were a sure sign that she was losing it!

Keeping Wolfe wasn't an option.

Unless, of course, she'd meant keeping him in his form as a frog, which was already a foregone conclusion. "I-I have to go," she said, already heading for the door. "Thanks for the snacks."

"But I'm coming with you," he said, following her into the hall.

"No," she said, landing a hasty kiss to his cheek. "But thanks for offering."

"Where could he be?"

Slashing her fingers through her hair, Lucy swallowed the coppery taste of panic. She'd searched the cottage from top to bottom, mucked her way over to the pond, and all about the grounds. Where could he have gone? He knew better than to leave the house.

Oh please, she thought with a strangled laugh. He knew better?

And when had the prince ever done what she'd told him? In fact, wasn't it far more the norm for him to do exactly the opposite of her wishes?

Gnawing on her lower lip, snatching her keys from the hook in the mudroom, she ran outside to the car.

By now, rain fell in silvery sheets, and the dirt lane had turned to deeply rutted mud. By some miraculous twist of fate, she finally made it the ten miles to paved road, then turned toward Cotswald. The likelihood of him being in town was about as possible as her meeting up with a lost ship full of Martians, but then hey, two weeks and a day ago, would she have ever believed she'd find herself living with a ninth century frog?

Much like the first night she'd found him, then lost him, Lucy drove round and round, only to park at the town rose garden, then strike out on foot, peering into the High Street's few alleys, and behind parked cars, and in Talbot Havard's leaning gazebo. The spooky graveyard looked extra creepy in the rain, and all of the residents of the duck pond were huddled in a circle on their island, beaks tucked beneath their wings.

Soaked and shivering, Lucy climbed back into her mini, gazing into the darkened chemist and grocery and Rinegeld's Men's Clothing Emporium.

Good grief. She was probably overreacting. Probably at this very minute Wolfe was back home, lounging in his black silk PJ bottoms in front of a cozy fire, snarfing a big buttery bowl of popcorn while she was out here worried sick searching for him.

And wasn't that just like a man? Driving her crazy with worry about him lying somewhere hurt or cold or hungry or lost or—

*Whoa. Don't you mean frog instead of man?*

*And shouldn't your worries be more about what happens to your newfound relationship with your father if Wolfe isn't back at the cottage, politely waiting for you to watch him get poofed back into a frog? And what about the duke? What if Ruth Hagenberry sees you roaming the streets like a madwoman and reports back to William? What's he gonna think?*

"I don't care what he thinks," she ground between her teeth. "I don't care what anyone thinks. I just want him back." Him. Wolfe. Her frog prince who had somehow become so much more.

And then there he was, laughing behind the brightly lit fogged window of the Hoof and Toe. All this time she'd been worried sick, and he was yucking it up at a bar!

Careening the mini into the only vacant spot at the back of the tavern, she forced her wild mane into a purple scrunchie she'd fished from beneath the passenger seat, then marched inside, guns loaded for loud-mouthed medieval type bear!

Inside, though, blessed heat kissed the freezing tip of her drippy nose just as she caught sight of her prince.

Holding court at the bar, with a good twenty adoring subjects at his feet, sat Wolfe, long, lean legs astride a bar stool, dark hair streaming about his shoulders as he tossed his head back in a hearty laugh. Compared to him, other men in the room looked like mere boys, and like the born leader he was, the townsfolk seemed drawn to him.

Raising a frosty mug of dark ale, he said, "To big-bosomed wenches!"

"To big-bosomed wenches!" all gathered shouted—even the grinning bartender and a few women staring at the prince as if he were the masculine answer to their every lusty prayer.

Steeling her shoulders, Lucy marched across the room. When she got her hands on that man, she was going to—

"Aye, my fine friends. Here she is. Me very own big-bosomed wench."

She'd just parted her mouth to tell him to hush, when he snatched her about her waist, hoisting her onto his lap for a claiming kiss.

Lips pliant and warm against hers, when he had her so dazed with relieved longing that she could hardly remember her name, let alone the fact that she was in a very public place kissing who should have been a private man, he deepened the kiss still, brazenly stroking her tongue, tasting of beer and salty pretzels and man—all intriguing, wickedly thrilling man.

By this time, the crowd had gone wild with ribald taunts and laughing applause and cheers.

Lucy knew full well she had to at least put up a struggle, or else William would know for sure that she'd enjoyed being held in the prince's strong arms, but then what was the point anymore in trying to hide what days earlier she must have already known in her heart?

Like it or not, she was falling for Wolfe.

Now, her only problem was, how to remember to breathe when he was gone. For while it was one thing admitting herself infatuated with his conversational flare and kisses, it was quite another admitting herself in love—which she wasn't.

Which meant he was leaving—soon.

Granted, she and William shared no great passion, but what they shared had to be love, for it had grown over time, and didn't have this all-consuming urgency that made her lungs feel near exploding from lack of air whenever she even thought of never seeing Wolfe again, let alone what her fellow scientists would do to him once they happened upon his many secrets—which she must make certain they never do.

Right after the conference, she'd spirit him away, back to the castle pond, where at least if he were a frog, he'd be in familiar territory.

But then all of her thoughts went blissfully blank as to the delight of the cheering crowd, Wolfe deepened their kiss still, crushing her to him as if he'd never let her go.

Finally drawing back, he stared long and hard into her eyes before reaching for his mug, then raising it high. "One last toast, my friends! To my wee one, Miss Lucy Gordon, the finest kisser I've ever known!"

"To Lucy!" they all somberly said, raising their mugs in salute of her.

Happy chills ran through her.

She'd never been toasted even by her father or friends—let alone strangers! And yet here she was, on an ordinary weeknight, seated on the lap of the most extraordinary man, laughing, putting her hand atop his when he held his mug to her lips. And then she was being lifted onto her own bar stool, close enough that their arms still touched. And there was rowdy music and chips and pretzels and even more laughter as Wolfe finished one after another of his outrageous tales.

All present assumed the lot of them to be pure fiction, and while Lucy had doubts as to the authenticity of the entire lot, some of his stories she knew to be true by the scars raging across his chest.

"Aye," he said, finishing a tale about a small boy he'd once known named Colin, whose father had gallantly attempted to save him from a flock of angry geese only to end up getting nipped on his own arse. "The child was grateful enough then, to have been saved by his dear old dad finally hauling the goose off to Cook's pot. But later, when he'd grown into a fine young man, yet his dad had been called off to battle never to return, he had nothing much in the way of kindnesses to say. He blamed his dad for deserting him. But what he didn't know was that the man had been taken prisoner. Held against his will for year upon year, and would, but he could, have seen the boy into adulthood."

"A toast!" one of the men called. "To boys and their fathers."

"To boys and their fathers!"

While everyone else raised their mugs, Lucy studied Wolfe, the sudden wet shimmer in his haunted eyes. *Colin.* Was that the name of one of his sons?

He took a hasty sip of his ale.

"Wolfe?" she said, glad the tavern's other occupants were occupied in a new round of ever increasingly maudlin toasts. "That story was about you, wasn't it?"

"What of it?" he asked, taking another long drink.

"Here you are, punished for all eternity for being some sort of emotionless monster, when you very much loved each and every one of your children, didn't you?"

For a long pause, he stared before taking another drink.

Hand on his wrist, she guided his mug back down to the bar, then took his fingers in hers. "Tell me, Wolfe. Did you love your children?"

"I was a warrior. What could I have known of love?"

"You loved your land, didn't you? And your brother and father."

" 'Twas different."

"How?"

"Because looking at land or my father never once filled me with such quiet pride in what my seed had become."

"Come on." Leaning forward to press a gentle, reassuring kiss to his lips, she said, "Let's go home."

# Chapter Twenty-two

To the cheers of the crowd, Wolfe swooped his wee wench into his arms, then carried her out of the tavern and into the rainy night, kissing her full on her lips just before reaching her carriage. "I want you," he said. "I'm tired of games. I want there to be naught between us but fevered skin."

She nodded against his chest, her soft curls tickling the underside of his chin.

Being the man, he longed to carry her all the way back to the cottage and into his bed. But alas, the past weeks plus a thousand years more had taught him the humility of his own limitations, and just as he'd known to hide from a wild dog rather than trying to outrun it, he knew 'twas infinitely more practical to allow Lucy Gordon to drive them.

Seated beside her, twining her hair betwixt his fingers as she drove, he promised himself to add controlling her carriage to his growing list of skills he must learn.

But then they'd returned to the cottage, and he was shutting the door, pinning her to it while kissing her swift and hard, mounding her breasts to his chest, aching much lower to impale her now, but knowing full well she deserved a far better show. For the love she would soon declare, for the remainder of his life her declaration would save, she deserved to be taken leisurely, at a pace allowing for exploration and grace.

Having lain her across her bed, he parted her red coat, and then her blouse, and unlatched the protective garment she wore over her breasts. And through it all, he expected her to cry out, to slide her fingers into his hair, shrieking for him to stop, but she did not.

Eyes closed, she arched into him when he stole her bud into his mouth for a swift hearty suckle. Soft mews of longing parted her ripe lips and when he'd had his fill of her breasts, he moved upward for more lingering kisses and sweeps of his tongue.

On himself, he tasted ale. But on her, the most potent of all liquors—desire. Aye, he might have been a thousand years without bedding a woman, but a man did not forget the nectar-sweet smells a woman in need of a man unwittingly produced. He hadn't forgotten the faint taste of salt between her breasts, or honey between her legs . . .

But that would come later, much later, when she'd all but cried out her need.

For now, he unfastened the top closure of her denim trousers, then lowered the zipper with nary a sound, splaying his fingers to the curve of her belly, imagining it ripe with his seed.

Even pale moonlight couldn't hide the intensity on his wee one's beautiful face. Rising, pinning his hands on either side of her, he asked, "What's wrong? You wish me to stop?"

She fiercely shook her head.

"Then what?" he asked, skimming the backs of his fingers along her jaw. "I've never seen your expression so burdened—as if you carry the weight of the world upon your shoulders, when 'tis only the weight of me upon your chest." He smiled, pleased with his joke.

Her lips, however, did not budge.

Lucy swallowed back tears.

She wanted this. Lord, how she wanted this, but she wanted other things, too.

She wanted her father's love, the respect of her peers. Maybe even to become William's wife. But surely she didn't want all of those things badly enough for them to be bought for the asking price of Wolfe's life?

But seeing how she supposedly loved the duke, what could even this one night of pleasure bring beyond pain?

Love took time, time that she and Wolfe would never have. Given time, seeing how many qualities she'd already come to love in him, she felt sure she could come to love all of him. Any doubt of that had been banished by the look he'd had in his eyes while speaking of his son. No man as vile as the sorceress had claimed could carry such a look of tenderness for his offspring. It was the kind of look that could come from only one place—his heart.

"You're crying," he said, brushing away a single tear.

"I'm sorry," she said, hands to his magnificent chest, running them up and over his shoulders and down his arms. His scars, those all-too-painful reminders of just what a treacherous life he'd once led, were savage enough that she could still feel them even beneath the cool white cotton lawn of his shirt. Oh, how she ached for him. For what he'd been though.

"Take off your shirt," she demanded, and sitting back on his haunches he did. Seeing him risen above her, scars and all, only worsened her pain, and increased her want. And she rose to her knees, pressing butterfly-soft salty-teared kisses to each badge of courage he so proudly wore. Which had been gained in battle? Which as a mere boy? Trapped in a filthy, rat-infested pit? "Wolfe . . . My poor Wolfe."

At that, he stopped her, hands on her shoulders, dark gaze locking with hers. "Tell me what troubles you. For I assure you, at the moment, the only thing poor on me is my neglected manhood."

"But your scars. All you've been through."

"All well in the past," he said, sweeping her hair behind her ears. "Now the emotional scar I'll have if ye don't bed me soon . . . That'll be another matter."

"How can you joke at a time like this?"

Dropping onto his side, he pulled her against him.

"Shh," he murmured into her hair. "Now that you are ready to declare your love, there is nothing to fear."

"But that's just it," she said. "What I feel for you—it's so strange. Overwhelming. Even scary in the way I'm incapable of thinking of anything or anyone but you. But that's wrong, because I don't even know you. You're like some intoxicating myth come to life. And the duke, he's real. My work is real. But then I look at you, and I can't think beyond our next kiss. And I want so much more. I want to taste you and breathe you and feel you buried so deep inside that this hunger for you will finally be fed. But then I think of dear, William, and all the times he's stood by me, and I . . ."

Wolfe released her, then pushed himself off of the bed.

"W-where are you going?"

"Anywhere."

"But I thought this was it? I thought we were about to make love?"

His answer was a sharp laugh. "You just admitted what we share is not love, so how can we make it?"

"But . . ."

Savagely drawing on his shirt, he said, "Go to him if you've need to be bedded."

"But it's you I want. Think about it, Wolfe. According to your own rules, only true love can save you. But the two of us will never have enough time to find true love. All we have is tonight, and the precious few nights yet to come."

"Unlike my own mother," he said, a muscle twitching in his hardened jaw, "I'll not be party to adultery. Any woman I am with will want me and only me. My name will spill through her trembling lips, and when we have both had our fill, we shall sleep. And then we shall sup of each other—and *only* each other—again and again."

"Yes," she said, scrambling onto her knees, mindless of her gaping clothes, only caring for him, that she somehow make him understand. "What I feel for you is night and day different from what I share with the duke. Please," she said, clutching his shirt. "Please understand. Share what time we have left with me. Give us both something to cherish and remember."

"You are but a child, Lucy Gordon, desiring two

treats when only one is what you may have. Choose. Choose between us right now."

"Don't you see? I can't."

"Excellent. I'll take that as your answer." Eyes impossibly dark, mouth an angry slash, he said, "Good night, Lucy Gordon. I know not—if ever—we will meet again."

Alone in her cold bed, the quiet of the cottage crushing, Lucy swiped away still more tears.

What had she done?

Her speech had been meant to justify the wrongful act she longed to commit, but in explaining herself to Wolfe, she'd only made herself look the part of a traitorous fool. Traitorous for wholly loving Wolfe before breaking things off with the duke, and a fool for believing she could ever have it both ways. Even worse, she was a fool for believing she'd ever be able to willingly trade Wolfe for scientific glory. And she was even more of a fool for believing that while she might very well love him heart and soul, he might very well be using her for no other reason than to stay alive—reason enough in any sane person's eyes!

Washing her face with her hands, she drew her knees to her chest, asking herself over and again, why?

How could she have let things come to this? She was a scientist. She'd been trained to look at things objectively. But when it came to her study of Wolfe, she should've known she'd been doomed from the start.

From that first look at him in his full naked splendor that forever-ago day on the castle lane. To the way they talked for hours about nothing, and played games and read. And when she'd had problems at school, he'd listened to her—truly listened.

For the first time in her life, in him, she'd felt as if she'd found someone who truly cared what she had to say, and hadn't just felt obligated to listen. Her father had always been patronizing—and that was on his good days. And while the duke was unfailingly polite, seeming to hang on her every word, she felt the hum of his brain, always moving one step forward, as if even in the midst of her latest sentence, he were formulating the profits-and-loss ledgers of his latest account.

And who was to say? Maybe she was wrong about all of it? Maybe like Wolfe had pointed out, she *was* a child, and not even thinking in her right mind. But like children didn't think about anything, but instead followed their hearts, maybe that was the course best taken? And the one thing her heart was currently telling her—no, screaming at her—was to see where things with Wolfe might lead.

If they only had this time together, so be it.

If come to the next full moon, and he was still living and breathing, only not alongside her, but some other woman who could give him whatever it was he would next desire, so be it, too.

Like him, she had to adopt a conquering warrior's spirit, only the war she now battled raged within herself.

"You don't look so hot," Bonnie said Wednesday morning in the teacher's lounge. "Rough night?"

"Rough life," Lucy said, nursing her coffee.

"Chin up," Bonnie said, toasting her with a butter cookie. "At least the dance is just three more nights away. I'll bet once the duke slips a great big jewel on your finger, you'll feel super."

Doubtful.

How was it Wednesday already? What'd happened to Tuesday? Not to mention her every hope and dream beyond a magnificent man named Wolfe? Monday night, after their argument, he'd left. She hadn't seen him since. She hadn't cared about anything since.

Staring out the window at the day's drizzling gloom, at skeletons of trees and tall brown weeds, she asked her friend, "What if the duke asks me and I don't want to marry him?"

Bonnie gaped. "Why would you even say such a thing? You've been mad over William for years. The only possible thing I can think of that—" She put her hand over her mouth, and shook her head. "Please tell me it isn't true? Luke came in from the hospital this morning and said one of the orderlies told him he'd seen you mugging on a strapping bloke at the Hoof and Toe. Luke told him no way. You were as good as engaged to the duke, but—"

"Can't a girl have any privacy around here?"

"So it's true? You've got another man on the side?"

Lucy pressed her lips tight.

Bonnie lurched forward in her brown armchair. "To be virtually throwing away a scrummy catch like the duke, I can't even imagine what your other guy must be like."

"Nonexistent, okay?" Lucy slammed her coffee mug onto a side table, then stood, straightening her somber blue skirt and jacket. "A few nights ago . . . he, he—"

The bell rang.

"He what?" Bonnie asked, glancing toward the hall

already swarming with chattering students.

"He left me, all right? I offered myself to him like a trussed-up Christmas ham, and then he stormed out of the cottage."

"The cottage? You've been seeing him right under the duke's nose?"

"It's not as bad as it sounds. It's complicated. I—"

"Ladies?" Grumsworth stepped into the room. Eyebrows furrowed, he tapped his watch before saying, "Don't you think it's high time you got to your classes?"

Lucy snatched her purse and dashed past him, Bonnie hot on her heels.

In the crowded hall, Bonnie elbowed her. "Don't think just because Grumsworth mucked up the juiciest part, that I'm letting you off the hook. I want details—now."

"I have to go," Lucy said, wishing she'd never even said anything. What was the point? It wasn't as if all the talking about him in the world would ever change her situation. She was in love with a thousand-year-old frog prince who couldn't care less about her beyond the fact that he'd somehow managed to finagle that love right out of her supposedly already taken heart!

"Miss Gordon?" Lady Regina Cowlings wildly waved her hand.

"Yes?" Lucy said from behind her lecture podium, highlighting wand in hand.

"Could you please go back over species competition?"

"Sure." On autopilot, glad she finally had a few years of teaching behind her to let experience carry her through, Lucy patiently explained the lesson again, the whole time, aching for her next break so she could call home.

She'd tried an hour earlier, but Wolfe either still wasn't home, or wouldn't pick up. Not that it mattered. What was she going to say?

*Um, look, I'll tell you I love you, but only if you promise you're not playing me for a fool. 'Cause if you are, I'll personally zap you straight back to the pond.*

Even worse, she'd had a message from her father, commanding her to e-mail him a clearer picture of her frog. And while he'd been gritty as sand in her eyes through the first part of the message, he'd ended it with a simple, heartbreaking, "Love you, Polliwog."

"Miss Gordon?" Now Randy waved his hand.

"Y-yes?" Lucy swallowed hard, trying to dislodge the terror of indecision from her throat.

"If a sea turtle lays eighteen hundred eggs, I fail to see how only four hundred hatch, and only two or three ultimately live. Somewhere along the line, someone messed up, and should be fired."

She grinned. Randy's parents probably had highly paid consultants tasked with rating other consultants! "Okay, here's the deal. The eggs are actually a food source for—"

"Miss Gordon?" Timothy Gerardo Beamoneaux V joined the hand-raising club.

"Just a sec, Tim. Let me make sure I've answered Randy's question, then I'll get to you."

"Yeah, but—"

"I promise, Tim. I won't forget—"

The class laughed.

"What's so funny?" she asked.

Tim pointed toward the door where a glorious bouquet of at least three dozen red roses bobbed up and down.

Lucy's heart lurched.

Wolfe was smiling behind them.

"Oh," she said, licking her lips with a tongue that'd suddenly gone dry. "Um, you all go back over this on your e-readers. I'll be right back."

In the hall, classroom door closed behind her, she said, "What are you doing here?"

He winked. "What kind of greeting is that for a man bearing roses?" Holding them out to her, he said, "I'm sorry for Monday night."

Taking the tissue-wrapped bundle, breathing deeply of the sinfully rich aroma, she shook her head. "I was the one in the wrong. I should never have assumed we could . . . Well, you know, change things between us in the bedroom, then go back to the way things were. I'm pretty confused at the moment about a lot of things, but—wait a minute. Where have you been? How did you even get here?"

Gracing her with a broad, white-toothed smile that toppled her heart, he said, "I took the liberty of borrowing one of the duke's stallions, and have been riding cross country getting the cobwebs out, so to speak."

"You've slept outside?"

He shrugged.

"And the roses? Did you borrow those, too?"

"Nay. A village antique dealer was only too happy to trade me an obscene amount of your paper money for but a few of my coins."

"What coins?"

He sighed. "Wench, must you know my every secret?"

"Yes—and don't call me wench."

"Very well, then . . ." He politely bowed his head before blasting her with another wickedly handsome smile. "If you must know, there are caches of coins and jewels all over the castle grounds, and inside the castle itself. Sadly, my mother taught my father to trust no one but himself, and me. Consequently, all that he or I ever won in battle was hidden from those whose loyalty may have been less than golden."

"Wow." Head spinning, Lucy leaned hard against the door. If she confessed her love, and he was playing her, with his own fortune at his disposal, he needed her for nothing beyond her eternal vow. Shoot, for all she knew, she might not even get that much-touted bedding he'd promised!

But then what was she thinking?

Was she really prepared to give up her every professional hope and dream—not to mention her future relationship with her father—on this pipe dream? There was no way Wolfe would want a woman like her.

How many times had he told her that unless a woman possessed great wealth or land, he had no need for her?

Even knowing all of that, though, at that very moment, she realized she had to give up all of her dreams because they were just that—dreams. Dreams that without taking his very life, she had no right to obtain. She'd done nothing to deserve them . . .

Nothing except stopping one rainy afternoon to allow passage to a hopping frog.

"Lucy Gordon," he said, taking her roses and setting them to the polished hardwood floor. With her hands in his, he dropped to one knee, raising her pulse. "I didn't mean to be gruff when last we spoke. It's just that, woman, you're making me quite mad. I want you, but up until that night, you had yet to declare your want for me. But by your own admission, want isn't enough. I must have no less than love. Love I fear you feel for some insipid duke not nearly worthy of your many charms. And so that leaves me in a netherworld. For until you decide which of us you will ultimately choose, I know not even of my own future."

A fresh batch of tears welling Lucy's eyes, she drew this proud man to his feet.

"Never," she said. "Never again do I want to see you on your knees." Taking a deep breath, taking a plunge from the highest professional summit she might ever have imagined, let alone achieved, she blew her last shot at scientific fame by saying, "God help me, but I do love you, Wolfe, and I'm afraid I always will."

"That's it then?" he asked, eyes wide, expression incredulous. "You love me? I'm saved?"

Smiling through happy tears, relieved she'd made the right decision—the *only* decision, no matter what he felt for her—she nodded while he took her into his great arms, lifting her off of her feet, twirling her round and round.

"She loves me!" he bellowed to the curious few peeking their heads through cracked open doors—her own classroom included. When he kissed her, a round of preteen ooohs sounded. And when she kissed him, she didn't even care that Grumsworth was scowling his way down the hall.

# Chapter Twenty-three

Squatting behind a leafless azalea just outside the ground floor study of Sinclaire Castle, Ruth slowly lowered her binoculars, shaking her head. Never in all of her days had she seen such perversion. It was bad enough that Lucy Gordon had been carrying on, but now the duke was stepping out on her, as well? Sick. "Both of them are just plain sick."

"What'd you say, Mum?"

"Nothing," she spat back to her daughter who she full well knew to be pure as a babe straight from the womb! "And turn off that torch. You want we should get caught?"

"What I want," Abigail said with a put-upon sigh, "is to go home and watch my shows. It's cold out here," she added, rubbing sweater-clad upper arms. "And I don't know what you're trying to prove, always skulking about, meddling in other people's private affairs."

"Do you want a husband of noble birth, or not?"

"What I want is to watch my shows—not to mention find my own man."

"What do you know about men?" Ruth said, back behind her binoculars. "You're just a child."

Abigail slapped her movie magazine onto her lap. "A twenty-two-year-old child who has a right to choose who I marry."

"Nonsense."

"Would you think it nonsense if I told you I've been indulging in a bit of rumpy pumpy with Bobby from the market? And not only that, but I'm preggers with his baby? And he's asked me to marry him straightaway and seeing as I'm deliriously happy save for what to do about you, I've agreed?"

"I'm dying." Eyes closed, Ruth plopped her rump onto the cold, damp ground. "No—I'm already dead, and gone straightaway to hell."

"You're not dead, Mum. Just finally letting go of this crazy notion you've always had of me marrying the duke."

Ruth's chin shot up. "But—"

"No buts. You're going to be a grandmother. I'm going to be Bobby's wife. I need you to show me how to run a proper house and change nappies. You're done nosing into other people's private affairs, and you're going to start following mine, okay?"

Tears glistening in her eyes, realizing it was probably for the best that she shield her poor, pregnant daughter from the likes of the philandering duke, Ruth said, "Okay."

"Luce," William said, standing at his study door. "I wasn't expecting you."

"Sorry to just drop in like this," she said, Freidman, the butler, clearing his throat behind her, "but we really need to talk."

"Sure," the duke said, clearing his throat, too.

She frowned.

He forced his lips into a smile while hedging out of his study, then firmly shutting the door. How had he landed himself in such a precarious spot? "Shall we, ah, retire to the white sitting room?"

A few minutes later, both of them took seats on an endless white brocade sofa that seemed far more suited to someone of Penelope's dignified stature than his dear Lucy's fun-loving American style. Quite at a loss as to what he should say—for in light of current circumstances, he was quite obligated by conscience to surely say something—he cleared his throat again.

"Is everything okay?" she asked.

Bloody hell.

Everything couldn't be further from okay.

And just think, he had her to thank for the whole bloody affair! For before meeting her, he'd never given two figs for what he found attractive in a woman, but now, it was as if in just knowing her, he'd opened new facets of himself that he felt quite certain she'd not like.

Clearing his throat once more for good measure, he took a deep breath, then said, "Luce, I fear I have troubling news."

"Me, too," she said in a gush.

"You do?"

She nodded.

"All right, then, which of us should give it a go?"

"Go ahead," she said. "Mine's a real humdinger."

"Yes, well . . ." Clapping his hands together, he gave

them a good rub. "It's like this, I've quite by accident found myself smitten with another woman. Known her for years actually. Ms. Roberts—Penelope—you've met her on several occasions, and—"

"Oh, William!" she said, tossing her arms about his neck in a downright jubilant hug. "But this is wonderful! Congratulations! Yes, I remember her, and she's perfect for you. Always dressed to the nines, hair nice and neat. Never late. Reads nothing but the classics and only watches the government channels on TV. You two will make a fabulous couple."

"But . . . What of you and me? I thought . . ."

"That's what I came to tell you, and I felt horrible about it, but now that I know you'll be better off, we can both be happy." She glanced at her lap, toying with the fuzzy-frayed ends of her orange wool scarf. "You see, I found someone else, too."

"Then all of those reports Mrs. Hagenberry delivered were true?"

Averting her gaze, cheeks adorably, happily red, she nodded.

And had Penelope not been lounging before a crackling fire back in his study, dressed in nothing but a lacy black teddy and stockings and garters, he'd have been furious to have been taken for a fool. But in the end, he realized that while he and Luce had been great friends, they'd never come close to being lovers. And far from being upset with her, he wished her the same passion he'd only so recently found.

"It is done?" the prince asked upon Lucy's return to the cottage.

Closing the mudroom door, then turning the lock, she nodded.

"And how do you feel? Still at peace with your decision?"

"Ask me after you've finally made good on your promise," she said, slipping her arms round his neck, then boldly raising her lips to his for their first official kiss as a couple.

Sure, that afternoon, she'd made her feelings known, but before officially breaking things off with William, a small part of her had been holding back. Now, she was one hundred percent his. One hundred percent tremulously hoping he'd still have her.

She wished at that moment to be more secure in her own feminine wiles, but she'd never been much good at portraying anyone other than herself—a chubby, not particularly successful biologist with a love of her students and popcorn and sci-fi flicks and sinfully handsome medieval princes who with just a single look held the power to launch her to the stars.

"Does that mean you're ready?"

Swallowing hard, she nodded.

Cupping his massive hand to the back of her head, he drew her to him for a spellbinding kiss. Lips closed, yet yielding the most exquisite pleasure before he was urging her mouth open and stroking her tongue, she found him tasting familiar. Of peanut butter and strawberry jam, and that earthy flavor she'd long since recognized as being uniquely his.

Her hands crept to his chest, pressing against him, then fisting the cool white cotton lawn of his shirt. "I've dreamt of this since you first kissed me," she confessed. "I've pictured you taking me everywhere from the bathtub to the bed and all places in between."

"How 'bout the kitchen counter," he said, nuzzling her neck, the heat of his breath delivering torturous hot/cold chills.

Unable to speak, she nodded.

And then he was ripping at her rain slicker, forcing it over her shoulders while kissing her throat.

She pulled at his shirt, in a frenzy to undo buttons.

"No," he said, brushing her hands aside. "Like this." In seconds to what for her would have been minutes of fumbling, he'd swept his shirt over his head, and was then gliding his hands under her soft pink sweater, up her rib cage and under her bra, taking it along for the ride.

The cool night air instantly pebbled her nipples, but then he was there to comfort—or would that be to increase her aching hunger as he fervently sucked and laved one hardened bud, then the other with his nimble tongue.

Fingers at the waistband of her jeans, he made quick work of unfastening the buttons, then hefted her onto the counter to cinch them the rest of the way down, tossing her red rubber mules landing with a double thud somewhere across the room.

Naked save for woefully inadequate panties, she folded her arms over her breasts. Fixing her with one of his sinfully handsome, white-toothed smiles, he shook his head. "No covering up for you, wee one. I've waited as long for this joining as you, and I want to see every glorious inch of you."

"But I'm not—"

"Shh," he said, fingers to her lips, then tracing a torturous path from her chin to her throat, down her chest and the valley between aching breasts, all the way up and over her belly, in and out of her navel to rest on the chaste elastic band where she wished there were silk lace. "These are all wrong for you," he said. "From now on, you shall wear no underclothes."

"E-excuse me?" she said on a strangled laugh.

"They are in my way."

"T-then what should we do?"

"About your unfortunate remaining garment?"

Swallowing hard, she nodded.

"I could launch a search for a dagger and cut it off." He hooked his index fingers on the white cotton sides, burning a dagger's planned path. "But that would be far too crude for the modern man I hope I have become."

Releasing the breath she hadn't realized she'd been holding, she said, "Mmm-hmm . . ."

"But then maybe that's part of my charm, eh? The notion that even knowing me as well as you do, you don't always know what I might do."

"True," she said with a wavering nod.

"And that being the case, I could just rip into them with my teeth? Or go the more modern-day route and slash them with scissors?" Right hand index finger dangerously on the prowl, he slid it over the soft shadow of strawberry blond just visible through the utilitarian panties, then down between her legs. Scooting the offensive fabric aside, he pressed that roving finger of his into the damp folds between her barely closed thighs.

"U-um, sure," she said on a pleasure-filled gasp. "Either of those methods would work."

"Yes, all of the aforementioned would work, but

297

which do you prefer?" The intensity behind his dark gaze flooded her with heat.

What was she doing?

Sitting nearly naked on her kitchen counter with this medieval warrior asking her how she'd best like her panties removed? The whole scenario was nuts! Yet her pounding heart told her loud and clear which scandalous option she'd most prefer.

"I'm waiting." he said, causing her to suck in air when he dowsed his finger ever deeper within her now not just damp, but wet core.

"I-I can't say."

"Why?"

She blushed furiously.

"Why, Lucy Gordon?"

"Because nice girls don't do things like this."

"Things like what?"

"Have sex on kitchen counters, okay?"

"And . . ." He crept another of his fingers inside the slit between her panties and sweat-dampened inner thigh, and out of her mouth came another shocked gasp.

Easing her legs farther apart, hoping he'd get the hint, she said, "I don't care, okay? Just do something—*anything*—now."

"Ahh, but where's the fun in that? This is after all, your special night. I owe you my life, Lucy Gordon, and your gift is not one I take lightly."

"T-that's nice."

"Nice? Oh—that's the last thing what we're about to share should be. I want it to devastate you," he said, leaning forward, his breath warm on her lips, his bare finger plunging deep inside her hot, wet slit. "I want you to wake in the morning knowing you'll die were you to ever leave my side."

"That's, um, awfully egotistical of you, isn't it?"

He plunged deeper still, and she arched her head back on the throes of another gasp.

"Nay." Brandishing his sexiest slow grin, when she next looked up, he said, " 'Tis not ego, but honesty. Now, tell me, Lucy Gordon, what shall it be? Scissors? My teeth? Or dagger? And don't even think of lying, for you'll only be taking the coward's way out of cheating yourself of pleasure."

Closing her eyes, praying no one ever found out, praying still more for the reckless devil-may-care attitude to not care if anyone did find out, she said, "T-the dagger has a wicked ring to it—not that I even own a dagger, but—"

"Shh . . ."

One finger still deep inside her, with his free hand, he reached to the counter knife stand, drawing out a suitable blade. Cold steel to her fevered skin, he made a clean slice in first the left side, then right, then slid the knife back into the holder to survey what he'd done. Grunting at the remaining flap of fabric, he reached for the blade once more, then cleanly cut through that as well, baring the whole of the vee between her legs. "Much better, don't you think?"

Grasping the edge of the counter so hard her knuckles showed white, she nodded.

And then he covered her hands with his, leaning in again close, stealing her very breath with the soul-rocking intensity of his kiss. Hands fumbling at his waistband, he continued kissing her even while she heard a metallic zip.

Eyes already tightly closed, she saw him again as she had the first time, standing before her in all his naked glory on the castle lane, only she now knew the glory yet to come. She was no virgin, but never had she been with a man even remotely as *gifted* as him.

Fingertips gliding over the jagged scars on his chest, she said, "Later, when we're lounging in the tub, tell me how you got every one of these."

" 'Tis not of importance."

"Yes—it is," she said, crown of her head tucked beneath his chin, cheek and ear pressed to the wild pounding of his heart. "It's very important to me."

"Then tonight—your night, I shall tell you whatever you wish to know."

Nodding against him, her mouth formed a puffing "o" when he gripped her knees and pushed them apart to open her to him. Hands now on her outer thighs and buttocks, he slid her off of the counter, lifting her, impaling her with a single, breathtaking thrust of such tightly reined power she could but cling to him, mouthing his name against the cruel, salty-tasting scars on his chest.

*Wolfe . . . Wolfe . . .*

Over and over he thrust, easily bearing her weight, one hand on her buttocks, the other in her hair, fisting it tighter with each excruciatingly pleasurable thrust.

Deep, so deep.

Over and over.

Building and building pressure.

When would it end?

Please, God, let it never end.

Over and over. In and out. Crushing his lips to hers,

300

twining their tongues. Nipples grazing the coarse hairs of his magnificent chest.

"I love you," she said.

"Aye," he gave her in return.

For any other man, she'd have been crushed, but knowing him as she did, knowing what he'd lived through, she took his simple statement as equal to her own. She'd chosen so wisely. Who needed fame, when for the rest of her life, she'd have him. Wolfe. Her frog prince.

Over and over. In and out.

Panting, grunting, raw, elemental joining of bodies and souls.

While they'd both just admitted to sharing love, what now transpired between them was borne of weeks' desperation.

Tenderness could come later. Now, here, passion must be won.

"Wee one . . . I can't hold out much longer."

"Me, neither," she said tossing her head to and fro, alternately kissing and nipping his shoulders and chest.

Rising, building, spreading insane frustrating pleasure the likes of which she'd never known mushroomed inside. When would it end?

*Never!*

Now.

*Never!*

Now!

Behind her eyes strobed white hot light, and then finally, finally, release, sweet release.

Wolfe stiffened, then groaned, spilling within her his

age-old seed. Clutching her close, he whispered into her ear, "Thank you."

Lips curving into a womanly smile, while she whispered, "You're welcome" in return, what her heart said was, *Thank you, too, my darling. Thank you.*

# Chapter Twenty-four

"Be good," Lucy said Friday morning on her way out the mudroom door.

"Have you ever known me to be bad?" he asked with a dashing wink.

"All the time."

"Ahh, then I'll presume you like this bad behavior and carry on in my usual way."

She stuck out her tongue, reminding him of all the wickedly clever tricks she'd recently played with that moist, pink appendage!

Wolfe had never known such contentment as he had during this past day and night spent in Lucy Gordon's arms. Before meeting her, he'd thought the very notion of men and women pairing for all time for no other reason than love was but a silly notion straight from children's fables. But now, handing her the sack lunch he'd prepared especially for her, patting her fondly on her pleasingly plump behind, he fought a surge of anger for the fact that she was leaving him at all—even for a few hours of their day. Just as quickly as his anger swelled, it passed. For he knew how much she enjoyed spending time with her children. And one thing he would now never do is deny her any pleasure—no matter how large or small.

She was his woman, and as such, she deserved the best of all he had to give.

"I love you," she said, standing on her tiptoes to give him a teasing kiss.

"Aye," he said on a dissatisfied grunt. "If you truly loved me, you'd quit this teaching and stay home to properly satisfy your man."

They teased round and round on the matter until she was late, and running, laughing to her carriage, waving her goodbye in the dazzling morning sun. And then he was back inside, shutting the mudroom door, hoping to find enough diversions so as not to miss her too badly until the time she returned home.

He tidied the kitchen and dining room.

Went upstairs to retrieve soiled sheets from their bed. Went downstairs to load those sheets into the washer.

He dusted her many fine figurines.

Cleared the rugs of any stray pop-corn kernels.

Watched an hour of *Baywatch—The Next Wave*.

Ate a newfound delicacy called the ice cream sandwich while loading the sheets into the dryer, then retired to the library to study his reading.

Lucy Gordon had brought him a fascinating stack of books from her school library, and he had a hard time choosing which to read first. She'd taught him the difference between fiction and nonfiction, and he saw that she'd included three of each type. The fiction, he had difficulty deciphering, but the nonfiction—books with many pictures dealing with history and science and recipes—those he very much enjoyed.

A book entitled *The Amazon,* with its spellbinding images of places so green he doubted their existence, held him enraptured until the buzzer on the dryer startled him from a passage on a most fiercesome flesh-eating fish called a piranha.

Rufus had been right, Wolfe thought, smiling all the way to the mudroom. To be compared to a fish was perhaps not such a bad thing!

Upstairs, Wolfe carefully fitted the bottom sheet to the mattress, then smoothed the top sheet over that. He lovingly nestled into their cases the pillows upon which Lucy Gordon rested her fiery hair. And then he arranged them just so upon floral blankets he'd once found offensive but now, because she held them in such high regard, found them pleasing enough to behold.

Stepping back to assess his work, his gaze landed on a corner of white peeking above one of the nightstand's drawers. He opened the drawer to tuck the paper in, only to find a whole pile of messy papers very much in need of his cleaning assistance.

"Ah, my fair, Lucy," he said with an indulgent grin. "You are certainly a disorganized wench." Not that he cared, especially not when he was charged with the wholly pleasant task of looking after her many messes!

Grasping the ungainly wad, he set it on the bed, intending to square up but a few sheets at a time, when from out of the sea of words, he recognized his name. *Prince of Gwyneddor.*

It took a moment to even realize that was his name,

but by the time he had, tears pricked the backs of his eyes.

What an amazing moment this was!

Yes, he'd known for days how to read, but to recognize his own name in print was a truly heady thing.

More—he had to read more. And sure enough, there his name was again and again, and quite a bit of rubbish about an . . . *as yet undiscovered species of frog.* And . . . *the scientific merits of such a discovery to the world biological community is heretofore unparalleled,* and how Lucy Gordon hoped that her discovery . . . *might one day open the door for further such discoveries in lands thought to be previously explored.*

Wolfe read on and on, his expression growing increasingly more dark.

He wanted to pretend he knew not what these papers meant, but he did know. Oh, did he know.

The wench did not love him as a man—she loved him as a frog!

The whole of this blissful time while he'd made a fool of himself by revealing the true depth of his attachment to her, she'd been but biding her time til the full moon.

At which point, she'd no doubt trap him in a cage, then parade him about for all the world to see while she basked in applause.

Blinded by fury, Wolfe flung the papers across the room, burying in a sea of white the rug he'd just swept clean.

It seemed he was not to be saved after all.

"Damn you!" he thundered. Damn what the conniving wench had done in making him actually believe himself in love. He'd known better. Love was for but women and small children. Men knew war. And on this night, he thought, fists clenched tight, Lucy Gordon would know war. She'd know war that started as a dream only to end in her own personal nightmare.

"Mmm, that feels good," Lucy said Friday night, seated in the tub between Wolfe's legs, back resting against his chest while he *poo-shammed* her hair.

Slowing down the raw pace he'd set when she'd first come home, they'd made love again on the rug in front of the fire, and again in her bed—each time more poignant than the last. Even though now, every muscle in her body ached—some muscles she hadn't even known she'd had—she felt deliciously content. Whole. And it hadn't taken finding a frog, or even her father's respect. All it had taken was this magnificent man's love.

"Close your eyes," he said, rinsing the soap from her hair, using a bowl that had once housed a floating candle as a ladle.

The sultry water streamed down her shoulders and breasts and back on its return trickle to the tub. And then there were his strong fingers in her hair, massaging away not just physical aches, but years of emotional pain.

On the surface, love seemed such a simple thing, but here she was, deep into her twenties, and only just now barely understanding what the word meant. Yes, concerning her growing affections for Wolfe, it had been a gradual thing, but where had it come from, and why?

It was like a rare surprise gift, neither expected nor deserved, but wholly welcome all the same.

Hair rinsed, she leaned back against his chest, twining her fingers in the coarse hair on his arms, stretching her legs languorously. "This is one time when it's good to be short," she teased, eyeing Wolfe's bent knees.

"Aye," he said with a throaty chuckle, kissing the top of her head. "In my day, bathing was more of a chore than a pleasure. Mostly I took my baths in the pond."

"Even when you were a man?"

"Aye. 'Twas much simpler to wrap a woman's legs about my waist in chest-deep water than in a wooden tub."

When he laughed, she reached behind her to land a playful swat to the side of his head.

"What do you mean by hitting me after I spent the whole of my evening servicing you?"

"That's funny, because," though she'd heard the smile in his tone, she scrunched round to give him a mean stare. "I seem to recall a certain guy having a good time, too."

"Who, me?"

That earned him another swat!

"So tell me," he said, arms wrapped back around her, cuddling her close. "What finally made you fall for me? Was it the roses that won you? Or my charming smile?"

"The smile. Definitely, the smile."

"Hmm, and here I'd thought studying all of those man-and-woman movies you love would have done the trick."

*Done the trick?*

Though the water around her still steamed, something about his tone scurried goose bumps up her arms and legs. "Um," she licked her lips. "What do you mean by that?"

"By what?"

"You know, that you *studied* movies?"

308

"What else could I have done? I'd already tried cooking my way into your heart to no avail. I'd tried sharing your love of tee-vee and Scrabble. I'd tried those little things *you* yourself suggested. Fixing your hair. Washing your face. None of it worked. Not a damnedable thing. What else was I to do? Make no mistake, Lucy Gordon, these past weeks, I've waged the fiercest battle of my life—a battle about nothing *but* my life. There is nothing I wouldn't have done to make you see your love for me. Nothing. And now the deed is done. And before being on my way, I wish to thank you from the bottommost level of my heart."

Pushing herself out of the tub, she mumbled, "Yeah, right."

"What was that?"

"I said, yeah right you loved me from the bottom of your heart! Kinda hard to do when you don't even have one!" Afraid she might be sick, she ignored the swoosh of hot water trailing her onto the white tile floor.

"Where are you going?" he asked.

"I-I have to think."

"No. What you have to do, is get back in this water. I still have thanks to show you."

Swallowing unfathomable pain, she reached for a fluffy white towel, wrapping it sarong-style around her, only it didn't quite reach all the way.

Grrr. Why now, was the only clean towel, the evil, ill-fitting rogue towel?

"Where is it?" she asked, launching a frantic search for her robe. "Did you wash it?"

"Where is what?"

"My robe. The blue one with the clouds."

"I disposed of it."

"You what?"

"I found it unsuitable for your frame. I prefer you naked."

"What have I done?" she asked on a strangled laugh.

All of her fears had been true. All along, he had just been playing her. "None of this was real. What did I do to deserve this?"

"Wee one, climb back into the tub, and I'll make you glad I've disposed of your robe."

"I'm not talking about my robe anymore, you egotistical creep! I'm talking about my heart!" Tears streamed down her face as pride and the stupid rogue towel she should've long since torched turned her away from his stare. But then she turned back. What she needed to say, had to be said to his face. She had to at least have the satisfaction of knowing he'd heard her—even if he would never truly listen. "Everything we did tonight. I thought it was about *our* love. *Our* commitment. But all it meant to you was the end of your game. You got what you wanted, and so making love to me meant nothing more to you than a silly bonus prize."

Out of the tub, he wrapped his arms around her.

She struggled to escape, but was no match for his strength. When she'd gone limp in his arms, and her pitiful excuse for a towel had tumbled to the floor, he smoothed her hair. "Whether you believe me, or not, I have grown to admire your cunning, Lucy Gordon. This is a first. My having been bested by a woman. Still, you taught me to read, and had you not, I'd now be oblivious to your duplicity yet to come. For that, I owed you a debt. But now that I have felt your trembling release, and in that release, your pleasure, my debt is paid, and I must go. For I'll be damned if not only do

I spend all of eternity as a loathsome frog, but allow you to prosper from my pain."

"P-prosper from your pain? What are you—"

She brought her trembling hands to her mouth. *Did he know of her former plan? Could he possibly know?*

Heart pounding with the terrifying implications of his words, she asked, "Wolfe? I don't know what you mean. I-I love you."

"You love me?" He laughed.

"O-of course I love you. You know that."

"How dare you speak to me of love?" Storming naked into her bedroom, he tore out the upper drawer on her nightstand, raining dozens of loose pages from her WBC report down upon her, burying her in cold shame. "Most especially when after claiming nothing matters more than love, you were only too willing to turn me back into a frog for all eternity just to satisfy your whim to be as famous as your father."

Staring at him in stunned silence, Lucy's formerly oh-so-righteous heart whispered, *he did know.*

Everything.

But then why had she expected different? He'd been alone in her house for weeks. She'd blabbed on and on about her miserable relationship with her father, but how she hoped that one day soon, he'd see her as the special someone she'd always wanted to be. Hell, she herself had taught Wolfe to read, then left her notes all over the house, only to finally stash them away in a forgotten drawer. What had made her think for one second that he wouldn't have read the most damning irrefutable evidence proving that she'd been far more conniving than him.

Head still bowed, she said, "I'm sorry. I wrote all of

that before. Before we made love. Before I told you how much I love you. Other than that, I don't know what to say."

"Nor do I," he said, "other than that perhaps it's time for me to bid you farewell. For since your vow of love was anything but true, I wish to be alone when the deed of my transformation is done."

"But, Wolfe, haven't you heard a word I've said? I *do* love you. Your curse is broken. Trust me on this. Please stay."

"Stay? The cunningly beautiful Lucy Gordon wishes me to stay?" Shooting her a cruel smile, he said, "Ah yes, but why wouldn't you? For if I leave, you lose our little game when your one-of-a-kind frog is forever lost. And who should know better than I how much you hate to lose?"

"Nooo . . ." Openly weeping now, sinking onto her knees on the cold white tile floor, she sobbed, "No. Please believe me, Wolfe. I love you. I never meant to cause you harm. Please don't go. Please."

"Even knowing the treachery living in your soul, your tears move me, Lucy Gordon. But alas, I declare myself victor of this game—at least until I'm changed once more into a frog. And on that day, when I am far, far from you and this place, we shall both be defeated."

While she sat alone and naked and shivering, desperately searching for something—anything—to say to make him believe her, he stormed to his bedroom where she heard much slamming of drawers. A few minutes later, he strode by dressed in jeans and the mossy green sweater she so loved.

"I've left more than adequate amounts of coin and jewels to compensate you for your inconvenience, Lucy

Gordon. Thank you for your hospitality."

"Just like that?" she said, heart breaking in a thousand shimmering hopes. "You're leaving? You won't even try listening to reason?"

Lips pressed tight, eyes dark, unreadable stone, he shook his head.

"But it's the middle of the night. At least let me drive you somewhere. To a train station or airport or inn."

"Don't you see? I'm onto you? No matter what you say, I know the truth to be opposite, which is why I must go."

"You're lying. You do believe me, but since I'm not your perfect princess—rich with a whole continent just waiting to be joined with your precious Gwyneddor, you don't want me. Is that it? You don't want me? But are too cowardly to admit it, so you designed this whole elaborate ruse to make me look like the bad guy?"

Sadly smiling, he said, "Believe what you will. My honesty will be proven by the light of the next full moon."

"Lucy?" Bonnie shouted into her cell phone above the noise of a tinny teenaged rock band. "What's going on? Where are you? You're not going to believe this, but the duke showed up at the dance with another woman."

"I know." Lucy said, hand to her forehead, watching Buzzy spin round and round on his exercise wheel.

"What do you mean, you know? Does this have something to do with that rumor about you making out with some long-haired giant in the school hall?"

Eyes tearing, Lucy said, "Can we talk about this some other time, Bonnie? I'm really beat."

"Sure, but—"

Before her friend launched into a whole new set of questions, Lucy pressed the disconnect button on her phone, then cradled it to her chest, staring into the cold fireplace, and then into the black beyond paned windows.

The dance.

How could she have forgotten about something that she'd once been looking forward to? She'd hoped the duke would propose. But now, that dream, along with so many others was gone, and she had only her stupid, gullible self to blame.

Oh sure, Wolfe might've claimed he was leaving because he believed she planned to sit by gleefully watching his transformation, but no man could be that blind. Surely he'd recognized the true depth of her love? Maybe he'd even been embarrassed by it? Maybe he'd realized that once again, in a whole new millennium, he was up to his old tricks of loving women only to leave them? And so no matter what she told him, he'd been ready to fire off his own arguments.

Excellent arguments, that had she not shown him in a hundred ways how much she truly did love him, that she could've readily accepted.

Yes, the fact that she'd ever written her WBC papers was wrong, but she'd apologized. She'd begged his forgiveness. Wasn't that enough?

Ha! Not for a man who'd already made up his mind to go. All she'd done was hand him the perfect heroic excuse for carrying out his original plan. Get her to declare her eternal love, then start his new life without her.

How could she have done it? Fallen for Wolfe so completely, even after repeatedly telling herself every word out of his stupid, handsome, charming mouth had been nothing but carefully calculated lies?

How could she have given up her professional hopes, and her future with her dad, and certain stardom all for one man?

Maybe because he was no ordinary man?

*And maybe because noble as all of your perceived goals seemed to be, they weren't. For how can something wonderful come out of something so tragic as taking a man's life—even if that man is the same man who just broke your heart?*

*Now it's time to take the high road, Luce.*

*Suck it up.*

*'Cause you've got much bigger problems noosing your neck than a few crushed feelings. Starting with how do you plan on telling dear old Dad you've made another mistake?*

"Okay, gang," Lucy said Monday morning, voice raised to compete with the driving rain. "It's been a rough weekend, so work with me. With a minimum of groaning, please turn your e-readers to screen 242."

"But that's a quiz!" Lady Regina complained.

"Yes, but since you've had a lovely two days to study, you should be bursting with knowledge."

Groans rounded the room.

Olivia asked, "How come you weren't at the dance?"

"Bet she was with that giant bloke she was muggin' on out in the hall!" Tim turned to his best friend Philip for a high five.

"E-readers? Quiz? Any of this ringing bells?"

Randy politely raised his hand.

"Yes?"

315

"I read in yesterday's *London Times* that you're to be the star of this year's WBC. Is this true? And if so, will you be leaving the school after your presentation and wedding?"

Wow. Count on kids to ask the really tough questions. While she stood at her lecture podium, debating just how much of her personal life to share, whispers rounded the room. The temptation to ignore both of Randy's questions was strong, but her affection for these young lords and ladies stronger. They deserved the truth—at least the abridged version.

"Randy, you're partially right." Clearing her throat, she said above still-pounding rain, "While I won't be leaving you little darlings, I will be making a presentation at the WBC. But just in the form of a brief apology."

"Why?" Olivia asked. "Have you done something wrong?"

*Besides offering my heart to a frog prince?*

"No." Lucy fought a fresh round of tears. "Just made an error in judgment, that's all. I thought I'd found something special. A quite extraordinary new species of frog." *Not to mention, love.* "But I was wrong. He was just like all the others." *Only pretending his attraction, then using me to get exactly what he wanted.* Only this time, this man, she couldn't really blame.

After all, Wolfe's very life had been at stake.

All she'd stood to lose was her heart, reputation, credit rating and father's respect. No biggees in the overall grand scheme of things!

"Sorry," Randy said. "I thought it smashing to see you achieve such success."

"Thanks." *Coming from you, sweetie, that means the*

*world.* To keep from bursting into tears, Lucy took a deep breath. "Okay, then. Enough about me, let's start those quizzes."

"But what about your wedding?" Regina inquired. "Is it to be soon? Are we to be invited? If you'd like, I'll ring my mum's event planner and he'll give you the names of all the acceptable wedding planners."

"Thank you, Regina. That's a lovely offer." Hand over her aching heart, Lucy said, "Unfortunately, there isn't going to be a wedding, either."

"You mean, you're not to be wed this term?" Olivia asked.

"No, I mean—" *Not ever.* Unable to hold back tears a second longer, Lucy snatched a wad of tissue from the box on her desk, then bolted for the door. "B-be good," she said over her shoulder. "I'll be right back."

"Bugger me," Tim said. "Guess Miss Gee got dumped."

"Belt up!" Randy said. "Can't you see she's hurt?"

Olivia turned in her desk, glaring at Tim. "Anyone ever tell you, you're a royal arse?"

Regina slipped from her desk, and walked to the front of the room. "All of you get your e-readers to the quiz screen."

"Who died and left you queen?" Tim asked.

Randy gave Tim a hard thump to the back of his head. "Me."

Somehow, Lucy managed to live through the week, due in large part to the fact that she'd turned off her home phone, and at school her kids were kind, considerate angels—even usually cocky Tim. Even better, Wednesday morning, Randy had shyly told her that he'd started replying to his dad's postcards, and that his dad answered back—without Lucy's help!

Ironic, how she spent so much time trying to reunite her kids with their parents, yet she'd turned the game of avoiding her own father into an art! Oh, she knew she couldn't avoid her dad much longer, but at least until she thought up a plausible reason for why she'd been so convinced she'd found a new species of frog, only to now have lost him.

Late Friday afternoon, she was curled up on the sofa, watching *Star Wars Episode Ten*, when a knock sounded on her door. Figuring it was Bonnie and Luke, self-appointed broken-heart menders with more buttery oyster stew, she padded in her thick white socks and new pink poodle bathrobe to the mudroom door.

Jerking it open, she said, "You guys don't have to keep popping up like this, I'll—Dad."

"How ya doing, Polliwog?" he asked, pulling her into a bear hug. "Mmm mm, you feel good. Lost a few pounds?"

"Um, no," she said, clinging to him out of old childhood habits.

It'd been three years since she'd seen him. Sure, they talked on the phone, but he was always far too busy to waste his valuable free time visiting her.

God, listen to her, she thought, swiping a rogue tear. She sounded like some spoiled bratty kid. He was an important man. A man who did indeed have far more important things to do than standing around listening to his misfit daughter.

"Why aren't you in London?" he asked, pushing past her to shut the door on blustery rain.

Fussing with the tie to her robe, she said, "I, um, haven't packed."

"I'm sure you've been busy with documentation," he said, helping himself to her fridge, "but you've gotta get a move on. Come on, darlin'," he said, unscrewing the lid on a jar of green olives. "Time's a wastin'. That last photo you sent was sweet—sheer frog perfection."

*Ha! Amazing what a great picture-doctoring program could do.*

Through the three olives stored in his right cheek, he added, "There's a lot of important people psyched to meet you, Polliwog. The fact that you've made such an incredible discovery on land long thought to be a virtual biological desert when it comes to new discoveries, opens up possibilities for new finds right under our noses all over the world." Eyes narrowed, he said, "What do you have planned for your hair?"

Lucy fought back tears. Without Wolfe here to tame it, there wasn't much she'd ever been able to do.

"Doesn't matter," he said with a grand wave. "I've got a publicist waiting for us back at the Ritz. She'll put us in touch with a hair guy." Rummaging through the bottles and jars in the fridge's side door, he asked, "Got any brie?"

"No."

"Damn. How about an Asian pear?"

"Sorry. Fresh out of those, too."

"Well, what do you eat? Blech. What's this?" he asked, holding out a half-eaten can of beef stew for her inspection. "Oh, Luce. No wonder you're looking a little hippy."

"You just said you thought I'd lost weight."

"Yeah, well, that was before I got a good look at you.

319

Anyway, we'll get a personal trainer to whip you into shape. And why are you just standing there, diddling the belt to that hideous robe? Get upstairs and get dressed."

"I'm not going, Daddy." She'd been planning to. She'd even told her kids she'd make a public apology, but now that the time was at hand, she just couldn't put herself through that kind of public humiliation all over again.

"What do you mean you're not going?" he asked. "Aw, don't tell me you've got a case of nerves?" Slamming the fridge door, he settled his arm about her shoulders. "I'm sorry. It's been a while since I've been in the company of a girly girl. I'd forgotten how sensitive you can be."

"I'm not sensitive, Dad." She shrugged out from under him. "I'm just not going."

"But what about your new species? Everyone's waiting. You're mere hours from being a global star."

Mouth dry, palms sickeningly damp, she shook her head. "Like you told me a long time ago, there's only one star in this family, and that's you."

"Oh, now, I'm a big boy. I can take a little competition from a girl pretty as you."

*He'd called her pretty.*

How much would she have given to hear that back when she'd been a teen? But she wasn't a teen anymore, and at the moment, the only person whose opinion mattered on what she looked like was Wolfe. And he was long gone.

*Suck it up, Luce.*

Time to tell Daddy the truth—that *you* screwed up again. Big time.

Cinching the belt to her robe, she squared her shoulders, took a deep breath, then said, "I'm not going to the conference, Dad, because there's no reason for me to go. The frog's gone."

"What do you mean, gone?"

"Poof," she said, fairying her fingers. "I don't know what I was thinking. I left the lid off of his terrarium, and the next thing I knew, he was just gone."

"Well, find him!"

"I can't. He's been gone for a week." *If he ever really existed at all.*

Grasping her roughly by her elbow, her father marched her to the stairs. "Get up to your room, and get dressed. You *will* be ready within fifteen minutes, or I'm coming up after you. Do I make myself clear?"

"No," she said, defiantly raising her chin.

"Oh, so you were just planning on being a no-show at the conference? Do you have any idea how many strings I've pulled to get you on the schedule? How many personal jabs about your last fiasco I've had to endure?"

"I'm sorry," she said. "I was sure this time. Truly, he was unique, but he just . . ."

"Hopped away?" her father asked with a cruel-lipped sneer.

"Yeah."

"Well, you do me a favor and hop on up those stairs. You're going to that conference tomorrow, and you're going to apologize for wasting all of my colleagues' valuable time."

"Why? Because the great and powerful Slate Gordon told me to?"

"No." Her father bowed his head and sighed. "Because this time, I'm afraid there might be enough back-lash that even your teaching position may be on the line. But mostly, because not Slate Gordon, but your dad, is asking you to."

# Chapter Twenty-five

"Get the hell out of my way, you freakin' wooly mammoth!"

Wolfe leaped to the edge of what he'd only recently learned was called a sidewalk, and flattened his back to the nearest stone wall. Damned cyclists. He'd have hurled an insult right back, but the bugger'd gotten away too bloody fast!

In his own time, a man had either to listen for the clip-clop of a lone horse, or the creak of a horse-drawn cart to alert him to being crushed. But here, in this London that save for the cold rain bore no resemblance to the place he'd once known, all was strange . . . and at the same time, he thought, staring across the river at the creation called the Tower of London, strangely wonderful.

Had Lucy Gordon seen this magnificent fortress?

He laughed at his own ignorance.

Of course, she'd seen this, and countless more sights he had yet to imagine.

After taking a wary glance over his shoulder to check for another silent yet deadly bicycle predator, he resumed his walk, wondering what the devil to do with his life.

In his time, all had seemed so simple.

Conquer his enemies. Celebrate his victories with his friends.

But where were those friends now? Dead and gone, and here he was, alone in this wondrous city with its limitless possibilities whirring like invisible bicycle wheels through his head, and yet in spite of all the infinite paths at hand, he was lost.

The day Lucy Gordon had first kissed him, he'd believed it possible to conquer the world and regain his throne, but now reality, like a cold, insidious fog, was slowly eking in. Showing him in a thousand different ways just how inconsequential he was to this new world. And just how alone he was forever destined to feel.

Even if he had his life, here in this bustling city where he was but one face among *millions,* what did his life even mean?

Tired of thinking, Wolfe stopped in the dead center of the sidewalk. While men and women in all manner of odd garb pushed their way around him, he reached into his coat pocket for a candy bar.

Unwrapping the foil on his new favorite, the most agreeable Cadbury Flake Bar, he raised the chocolate to his mouth, and took a big bite, closing his eyes as the sweet, gooey goodness kissed his tongue.

Gazing upon the rain-tossed river, he recalled how one time Lucy Gordon had returned from her teaching only to eat and eat. She'd called it stress eating, and he'd laughed at her, but considering the fact that the only time since leaving her that he'd managed to feel even somewhat capable of taking his next step was when he held a bar of chocolate to his lips, remembering the times she had done the same, perhaps he was no longer in the position to point fingers.

Stress.

The *Ope-rah Channel* had taught him much about the word that in his day had been nonexistent.

Oh sure, people had had worries. Fears of not having enough food. Or lack of warm shelter for cold winters. But this stress was different. It was knowing you had much to accomplish, but not knowing how to start. It was knowing you had somewhere to be, but not knowing why you should be there. Most of all, it was knowing you seek, but not knowing how to find.

Still transfixed by the great tower, Wolfe walked again. Toward it. Toward the feat of its very existence. He'd once planned to be part of such greatness.

But then he'd planned on finishing his life as well. He'd planned to marry, and have still more children. Legitimate heirs he would care for every bit as much as the rest of his motley brood.

Argh, where had he gone wrong? he thought, slicing his fingers through his hair? Aye, it was a given he ought not ever have bedded the daughter of a sorceress, but even before that things hadn't been right. He'd been master of his domain, but he hadn't truly been at peace. Not like he'd been those few idyllic weeks with Lucy Gordon.

Her deceit still crushed his chest with unspeakable pain. That afternoon he'd uncovered her plot, he'd planned to crush her, but upon once again seeing her sweet smile, all of his plans for war crumbled.

In leaving, he'd presumably inflicted enough pain to even them in score.

But then what did that matter? As he himself had said, in the end, they'd both lose.

Wasn't his own mother's death proof enough of that, seeing how his father had never been the same after she'd gone.

Wolfe gazed upon the great bridge leading to the fortress. Pausing alongside a rock wall, he rested his hands upon the cold, wet stone. How many men before him had stood at this very spot, pondering their sad state of grace with a particularly comely wench? And how ironic was it that after being cursed for supposedly being unable to love women, a woman had been his final downfall. He wasn't talking about the sorceress' curse, either, for that he could bear, but losing Lucy Gordon— the pain of that was turning out to be indescribable.

Strolling farther, deep in thought, the fact that he'd barreled into another pedestrian hardly registered—at least until he'd heard a decidedly feminine ouch, then gazed down to see a purple-haired woman dressed in black leather as a man, gathering strewn newspapers at his feet.

"Let me help," he said, kneeling beside her, gathering three papers to her every one.

"All right?"

"Aye," he said, "And you?"

She shrugged before tapping the headline. "Some excitement, huh?"

"What?"

"The conference."

Upon gazing at the picture to which the wench

pointed, Wolfe promptly felt far more than mere excitement seize his system.

'Twas *her*—Lucy Gordon's image graced the paper's front page! Her sky blue eyes, and curls of fiery red. Only where her most comely smile should have been, lived a most unflattering frown.

"She looks so serious, huh?"

"Lucy Gordon?"

"Yeah. She's the bee's knees. If you haven't heard of the conference, it's good you've at least heard of her."

"Aye," he said, stacking the last of the strewn papers.

"Then you also have to have heard about the new species of frog, found right here at home. You'd think she'd be smilin' what with all the splashing out she'll soon be doing."

"What do you mean?"

"You don't smell sloshed on ale," she said, "but to not know something so blatant." She shook her head. "Once she presents that new species of frog, she'll be bloody well set."

"But she doesn't have the frog."

"Belt up!" The purple-haired wench glared. " 'Course she has the frog. Why else would she be speakin' at the conference? If she didn't have the wee bugger after making such a fuss, we'd all laugh her arse right out of the country."

Wolfe growled, and evidently knowing what was good for her, the purple-haired wench gathered her papers, then scurried off.

Mission now clear, Wolfe turned to the direction from whence he'd came. The time for feeling sorry for himself had ended. Lucy Gordon needed help, and it was high time he stop acting the part of a petulant child and start acting the part of a true and noble prince.

Whether Lucy loved him or not, he loved her.

And she would have her frog.

"Um, hello," Lucy said, reaching for the sweating glass of ice water beside her on the podium, wishing she were anywhere in the world besides standing in front of these five hundred beady-eyed scientists who were probably much like her father in not giving a damn about anything but their careers. Everything about the evening was the same as the last conference she'd ruined, only instead of tofu lasagna, dinner had been eggplant parmigiana and the flowers on the dais birds of paradise rather than gardenias. Other than that, the rustling papers were the same, the smattering of discreet coughs. The terror lodged in her throat and the pounding of her heart.

Well, this time, there was one slight difference.

Somewhere in the middle of the night, reaching out for the man who would never be there, she had finally realized one thing—and that was that for her, there was a lot more from life she hoped to gain than professional glory. Or even her father's respect.

Who knew? If Wolfe hadn't seen her report, detailing plans for locking him in an antiseptic-smelling lab for further study, maybe she'd be with him now? Maybe they'd be lounging beside the fire back in her cozy cottage, sharing a popcorn fight or game of Scrabble or just each other. How long had he known about her plans for him? And had it made a difference in the way he'd felt? Before knowing, could he have imagined the remainder of his life spent with penniless her? Or had what they'd shared never been more than a game?

Straightening the stack of papers before her, she said, "As many of you may already know, the presentation I'd planned to be making on a new species of frog I discovered named the *Prince of Gwyneddor*, won't be going as smoothly as I'd hoped. I thought right about now I would be wowing you with his glory, but instead, here I am," she said with a tight giggle, "on the verge of apologizing yet again for yet another scientific blunder. But—"

A wave of furtive whispers and outright rude laughter further twisted the dagger of embarrassment in her gut.

Still, she raised her chin high.

So, she'd made a little mistake? Big deal. For just that one night in Wolfe's arms, she'd oh-so-willingly make a thousand mistakes more.

"Some of you may think me not fit to be in your lofty club," she said, voice raised above the still buzzing crowd. "But you're wrong. This time, I truly did have a unique species, but I lost him. True," she said with a wry grin, "he was brash, crude, egotistical, and utterly clueless when it comes to women, but given time, I could've changed him. But no. Because of stupid things like pride, and wanting to impress all of you, and my dad, I let him get away. Because of all of you, and your stupid, snotty elitism, I even looked down on myself for being a teacher. But you know what?" She laughed. "No matter what you say about me behind my back, to my face, my kids tell me in a hundred different ways that what I do makes a difference. Maybe not to the entire world, but to them. And since to me, they are my entire world, then—"

"Stop, Lucy Gordon! Stop!" A man bolted through

the ballroom doors, starting the whispers anew.

*Wolfe?*

Hand to her forehead, shading her eyes from the stage lights' glare, Lucy didn't dare hope her eyes confirmed what her heart already knew. The command had come from Wolfe. Wolfe, who was storming his way down the side aisle looking better than he had even in her many dreams.

His hair looked freshly cut. Short and spiked and rakishly sexy. His impeccably tailored black suit making him look every bit the part of a modern-day royal. Never had she seen him look more handsome, and her chest ached with the crushing realization that no matter what egotistical outrage he next spouted, she loved him.

She might not like him, but God help her, she loved him.

He vaulted onto the stage, straightening his suit coat before growling at the gasping crowd. Upon reaching her, he raised her left hand to his lips, never dropping her gaze. "Hello."

"Hello." His touch, his achingly familiar dark gaze toppled her heart—her still-broken heart! "What are you doing here?"

Gracing her with a formal bow, he said, "Like a true prince, I've come to rescue a lady in distress."

"But—"

Fingers to her quivering lips, he said, "Stop your conciliatory speech. I am yours."

"What do you mean?"

"I mean, I surrender. I saw your face on the newspaper, and to wash away the sadness in your eyes, I would gladly give ten thousand of my lives were they mine to give. Alas, all I have to offer is one. And so it is with swallowed pride, I offer myself unto you, Lucy Gordon. In but a day's time, I will again be a frog. And all you've wished for will be yours."

When he fell to one knee before her, she was crying so hard that she could barely see him when she drew him back to his full height. "I-I told you I never again wanted to see you on your knees, Wolfe. And you're not going to be a frog, because just like I told you, I love you. The curse is broken."

"Are you sure?" Dawning hope laced with understanding brightened his dark gaze. "Because if you aren't . . . all of this," he said, sweeping his arm to take in the blinding stage lights and whispering crowd and her glaring father. "All of this can still be yours."

She shook her head. "Without you, it wouldn't mean a thing. But the fact that you were willing to trade your very life for my happiness . . ." Her throat was too full of her love for him to go on.

Crushing her in a hug, he said, "I've missed you, Lucy Gordon. The smell of your hair and breath. The sound of your laughter and happy tears. For over a millennium, I believed women subservient to men, but seeing how empty I felt in just one week not by your side, I finally see what the sorceress must have been trying to teach me. That men and women are not only equal, but necessary to each other. You fill me in such ways as I've never been filled before."

"Lucy?" her father said. "While this latest fiasco of yours is entertaining, you do still have an apology to deliver."

"Okay." Her gaze still locked with Wolfe's, she said, "Here goes . . . I'm sorry, Dad, but something better than a stuffy old career in biology just hopped along."

A week earlier, Lucy wouldn't have dreamed of offending her father or this prestigious crowd, but that had been before realizing the true source of her dreams—not finding fame, but love.

Later, Lucy fell onto a posh hotel bed, dragging Wolfe by his tie along with her.

Roses. The room smelled of dozens and dozens of roses. Red, yellow, white, lavender. All for her. All reminding her fairy tales do come true.

The elegant suite with its gilded furniture, and soft ivory everything else. The priceless penthouse view of glorious nighttime London. And most especially of all, her very own Prince Charming, who just happened to go by the name of Wolfe.

"Happy?" he asked, lying on his side, hand stroking her hair.

Snuggling closer, she nodded. "All in one day, you've made my every dream come true. Thank you."

Tugging one of her curls, he shrugged. "You gave me life. And in doing so, you sacrificed your professional dreams."

"You're wrong. Those were old dreams. Shallow dreams."

"What of earning your father's respect?"

Now it was her turn to shrug. "Right now, I'm so high on our future, I could give a flip what he thinks. I don't know, maybe in forty or fifty years, when the newness of us wears off, I'll sometimes think of him and wish for more, but I figure if I ever need anyone to talk to about him, you'll always be there."

"Aye."

"I love you, Wolfe. And even if I could have my father's unconditional respect or professional fame, I'd trade both for just one more night with you."

"Mmm," he teased, his smile sexy-slow. "Let's make it a long one. Here. In this bed. You—naked in my arms."

"Okay. Any other requests?"

"Popcorn—strung in a chain across your breasts."

"Anything else?" she said, a hitch in her breath when he unfastened the top two buttons of her white blouse.

"Peanut butter. Lots and lots of peanut butter smeared across your belly for me to lick off."

"Hungry, are you?"

"Starving . . ." Rolling atop her, bracing his elbows on the bed while smoothing mischievous hair back from her eyes, he said, "You're so lovely. Sometimes, just looking at you, I get a pang in my chest."

"And this is supposed to be a good thing?" she teased.

"Aye," he said, kissing the tip of her nose. "For it reminds me how much you mean to me, and how much I still have to learn."

"About what?"

"You. Me. This new world."

"Pace yourself," she said. "We have the rest of our lives to figure all of it out."

"In that case," he said in a sexy growl, nuzzling the side of her neck. "We'll surely have time for this."

When she giggled, he parted the collar of her blouse, baring her throat to his hot, open-mouthed kisses that turned her quivery with anticipation.

One by one, he unfastened her all-too-many buttons, easing himself off of her, then parting the halves of her blouse, skimming his rough hand over her smooth abdomen and up to her breasts. Pausing over the lacy cups of her bra, he said, "I thought I told you no more undergarments?"

"Ever?"

"Aye."

"So even during a formal event like tonight, I'm supposed to let it all hang free just in case some sex-starved medieval warrior strolls onstage?"

"There'd better not be any man you'd even think of lying with besides me, Lucy Gordon."

"Oh, of course," she said with a grinning nod. "That's what I meant."

He'd long ago removed his suit coat, and now loosened, then yanked off his tie. "Damned nuisance these things."

"But you sure looked handsome wearing it. I like your hair, too." She skimmed her fingers over his shorn mane, torn as to which of his looks she'd most preferred. Rock solid on the notion that she wholly and completely loved all of him no matter how he wore his hair or clothes.

"As much as you like this?" he asked, dark gaze locked with hers as he swept his hand up, up, up her skirt.

"Mmm-hmm," she said, closing her eyes when his fingers found her wicked surprise. The one she'd never dared dream he'd ever discover.

"Ah, I see you've learned to follow at least some of my orders."

"O-only some," she said with a gasping pant when he slipped those roving fingers of his deep inside her already slick core.

" 'Tis only some that are of importance . . ." he said,

334

pressing a claiming kiss to her lips. "And at the moment, you, never again wearing undergarments, ranks at the top of my list."

"Fabulous," she said, wriggling on top of him, crushing her breasts to his chest, loving the way that much lower—while the great prince claimed to be in such total control—her touch had him once again rock hard. "Tell me more about your list."

Hand at the back of her head, he pressed her to him for a fierce claiming kiss.

When they'd both had their fill of kissing, she slid back, sitting up. Knees bent, feet firmly on the bed, skirt scrunched high, she spread her legs wide, pushing herself up only to swallow him whole.

He dug his fingers into her thighs, and she rode him, showing him who was truly issuing orders—their passion.

He tried rising up to take control, but she just arched her head back, easing her lips into the confident smile of a woman well on her way to staging a sexual coup!

"Bloody hell, wench," he said on a groan. "What have you done?"

"Claimed you."

"But I'd already claimed you."

"Wrong," she said, frissons rocking her when he thrust particularly deep. Eyes closed, she tossed back her head, nipples rock hard and swollen, aching for her love's touch. "T-this latest battle is fascinating," she said, "b-but do you think you could concentrate on the matter at hand?" To insure there was no confusion as to her request, she took off her blouse and bra, then delivered his hands to her breasts, planting his palms square across the hungry buds. "They need you."

"Aye, milady. And I need them." He stole her breath by teasing the tips of her nipples with the pads of his thumbs.

Riding faster, deeper, harder, she lost all track of time and place. The only thing she knew was that for the first time in her life she felt wholly cherished. And beautiful. And if she wasn't soon granted release, she'd surely melt of anticipated pleasure!

Hands on her hips, as the prince rose up, he pressed her down, filling her mind, body and soul with his magnificent thrusts.

"Yes," she mewed, hands on his, touching her own hands to her aching breasts. "Oh, please, yes."

Tearing from the intensity of the arduous climb, she rode on, pounding him into her, granting him access to not just her body, but soul. Starving, desperate, quivering for all he had to give and more, she cried out when white-hot light momentarily struck her blind, and then white-hot pleasure struck her speechless as well, as his hot seed filled her womb.

She had so much to say to this amazing man, but at the moment, all she could do was sit perilously still, fingers laced with his, feeling him, loving him still deep inside. Hoping, praying he was still every bit as virile as he'd been a thousand years before. For though he hadn't even asked her to marry him, she knew he soon would. And one other thing she knew, was that she wanted to be heavy with his child. She wanted to feel blood of his blood growing deep within her. She wanted her breasts full with nourishing milk from which her son would draw strength.

She wanted to then see her sons and daughters grow strong together under the loving gaze of their father, whom she knew from his many kindly changes toward her, and especially from his story that night at the Hoof and Toe, that he had finally, awesomely changed for the better.

"I love you," she said while he eased himself upright, wrapping his great arms around her in a hug.

"Aye," he said, brushing fallen hair back from her eyes. "I love you, too."

Late that night, Lucy stood at their suite's window, staring at the full moon's sparkle on the winding Thames. Hand to her womb, she wondered what were the odds of her already carrying the prince's child?

Probably slim, seeing how she was no longer a high school virgin, and actually wanting a baby, but still, she thought with a secret smile—it never hurt to hope.

After all, wasn't it hope that had brought him to her in the first place?

Turning back to the bed, to the sight of her beloved, sound asleep, his newly cropped hair dark against the white pillow, she went to him, pressing a kiss to his cheek before easing between the cool sheets beside him.

Judging by the liquid heat already pooling between her legs at just grazing her naked backside to his groin, she doubted they'd find sleep for long, but until then, she needed to rest up for the delicious night ahead.

Wolfe stirred, tossing his arm over his wee one's ripe hips. Hand curved over her belly, he cinched her close. After a millennium of escaping nighttime predators, it took but a breath to wake him. But here, nesting beside the woman he'd searched a thousand years to find, he wasn't awake out of a need to defend, but to love.

\*     \*     \*

After a nighttime of more loving, Lucy woke to bright sun streaming through open drapes. In the mood for being pampered and lazy, she stretched, wondering if Wolfe preferred waffles or eggs from room service? Deciding the simplest course would be asking him, she turned to her beloved, and screamed.

Where Wolfe had once lain beside her, now sat a frog.

# Chapter Twenty-six

"No," Lucy calmly said through a wall of impending tears. She shook her head for extra vehemence. "No. It's *not* him. Could never be him. This must be some kind of sick joke."

Ever-so-gently, she scooped the frog into her palm, vision blurred as agonizing pain mixed with stubborn refusal to see the black diamonds on his purple ventral, and those long, long lashes that had prompted that long ago first kiss.

*Try again*, her conscience pleaded.
*Kiss him again.*
*It'll work.*
*It has to work.*

But she did kiss him again—and again and again, but it didn't work.

Trembling all over, knees too weak to stand, she crumpled onto the bed, cradling him to her chest, rocking while crying, while begging the answer.

Why? A thousand times why?

"I love you, Wolfe. I swear to God, I love you." Yet obviously, she hadn't loved him enough, or this wouldn't have happened. Her love would have been strong enough to save him.

As it was, he'd put his trust in her for nothing, and there wasn't a damned thing she could do.

"We've done everything you wanted!" she cried to the sorceress who'd reneged on her deal. "Are you slow on the uptake? What don't you get about the fact that I love Wolfe, and he loves me? He's learned from his mistakes. He's a changed man. A better man. A *perfect* man! How dare you destroy our future before it's even begun?"

"How dare I?" Where once blinding sun streamed through the window, now swirled choking fog. Thunder rolled, followed by a high-pitched female laugh that turned Lucy's blood cold.

When the thunder and keening laughter had reached such a fevered pitch that Lucy wanted to cover her ears, yet couldn't because her hands cradled Wolfe, the fog thickened still more, and the swirling took on the shape of a willowy blonde.

Mouth gaping, Lucy clamped it shut.

No. This wasn't real.

None of it was real.

She was having a bad dream, that's all.

She'd wake up and everything would be blissfully normal.

The way it had been the last time they'd made love.

The woman laughed again and glided across the room, reducing Lucy's tortured hope to a cowering tremble.

"Want normal, do you? Then I suggest you find another man. For this one is now damned to forever be the warted diminutive creature I knew him to be."

Instinct told Lucy to crawl under the covers and hide. To run screaming from the room, but how could she do any of that when her mouth had gone dry with terror and her chest ached from the out-of-control racing of her heart?

Even worse, if she didn't for once in her life find the courage to fight, then who would?

Wolfe had been prepared to give his very life for her at that conference. Was she now prepared to sit here cowering? Or from somewhere deep within was she going to find the courage to do battle?

"Please, my pet, give him to me," the sorceress said in a hypnotic tone. She held out smooth, long-fingered hands, beckoning Lucy into her realm. Palms flat, index fingers curving invitation, she smiled. "Closer, my pet. That's it. Closer, closer . . ."

As if no longer controlling her body, Lucy rose from the bed, gliding across the now vast chamber to where the sorceress stood, long silvery gown fluttering in a sickeningly sweet lilac-scented breeze.

"Come to me, my pet . . . Surrender him to me . . . That's it . . . Bring him to me . . . I know you must be frightened, but you needn't be. I am your friend. And while you are but a mere mortal, I am a god. Bring him to me, bring him to me . . ."

Lucy wanted to block the hypnotic voice by putting her hands to her ears, but her fingers instinctively wouldn't budge from where they'd long since frozen in protective cover over Wolfe.

"That's it, my sweet pet. Closer . . . Closer. All you need do is surrender him to me, then be free . . . Free to live that blissful life you so desire. Free to find a wonderful man, and have babies. Lots and lots of babies. Your father will be so proud. No more work for you. Just years and years of domestic bliss . . ."

Deeper, deeper, Lucy glided into the seductive fog. *Yes. Bliss. That was what she wanted. All she'd ever wanted.*

"You've known all along your father was right. You don't have what it takes to ever be more than the most mundane field mouse. Just like your own silly pet, Buzzy, runs on his wheel, you run through life, aimlessly adrift. But that's okay, dear one. None of that will matter if you'll just give Wolfe to me."

"Why?" Lucy dared ask.

The sorceress's gentle laugh rose above the fog. "Surely even you can't be so pathetic as to not know the answer to that? I want him because he's *mine.* He rejected my daughter, and if it takes an eternity more, I intend to see that he suffers the same cruel fate as she."

"But he's changed," Lucy said, her voice flat and unfamiliar even to her own ears. The closer she glided to the sorceress, the stronger the scent of lilacs grew, and as best she could, she tried holding her breath. "I've changed. I'm not a mouse anymore than Wolfe's a frog."

Again came the laugh, and Lucy trembled anew from lack of air.

"Breathe, my child. Breathe. Being weak is not a crime. It's delicious relief. Surrender to me, give me control, and I promise . . . All you've ever desired will come to pass."

"But all I've ever desired is Wolfe. Will you return him to me?"

"Enough!" the sorceress raged, lightning bolts striking on her either side. "Give him to me, you pathetic mouse! *GIVE . . . HIM . . . TO . . . MEEEEEEE!*"

Though Lucy's nostrils flared from fear, just as Wolfe would have done in the face of battle, she held her shoulders straight, and thrust her chin high.

"He's mine!" Lucy warred. "And by your very own curse, you vowed that if he found love, he'd live the rest of his life as a man."

"Oh, he might've found love," the sorceress said with a cruel laugh. "But even as his seed now grows within you, he still hasn't learned his lesson. For he still hasn't made even you, his so-called beloved, his wife."

"But he soon will!" Lucy cried. "You just haven't given us a chance."

"A chance? You want another chance?" The sorceress laughed. "Very well, I'll give you until the moon rises tonight to find a priest willing to marry you to a loathsome frog. But be warned, should you fail, you'll spend eternity together all right. Wolfe as a frog, and you—as a mouse!"

Sunshine once again flooding the room. As if her show of bravado had been nothing more than a puppet being held in battle by strings, Lucy crumpled onto the floor.

See?

It *had* been just a dream. And if she but dared look over her shoulder, she'd find Wolfe sleeping soundly, his dark hair a stark contrast to the white pillow, his own battle-scarred features finally at peace.

*Ribbet. Ribbet.*

Her heart thundered.

Palms sweat.

Stomach roiled in pain.

Body trembling anew, she found the courage to look down. Lifting her top hand, she looked at the frog she'd once thought the answer to her every prayer, and cursed herself rather than him.

Gazing at him now, her previous day's success at the conference seemed stupid. If only they'd known about this addendum to the curse, they could have been out getting married instead of wasting time on those pompous scientists!

Scrambling to her feet, she said to Wolfe, "Hang on, sweetie. I might be a mouse—but I'm a mighty one. Shoot, even a big strong warrior type like you is afraid of mice. So can you even imagine what your typical everyday mild-mannered priest is gonna think?" Tenderly placing him on his pillow, she kissed the top of his green head. "Just like you didn't let me down, Wolfe, I promise, *promise,* to do the same for you."

But several hours later, Lucy—padded train case in hand with its air holes she'd cut with cuticle scissors—stormed into her eighth church in two hours. Though she wasn't for a second thinking of backing down, for all of her earlier bravado, she was now just plain scared.

After getting directions from a handyman and several industrious, brass-polishing parishioners, she found her latest man of the cloth seated behind a desk. Ordinarily, she'd have found his oak-paneled nook of an office, aglow with late afternoon sun, enchanting. But for now, all that sun represented was impending doom.

And the air smelled stale—a little like dirty socks.

"Excuse me," she said, knocking on the open door.

"Yes?" The kindly-faced priest glanced up from his paperwork. "May I help you?"

Licking her lips, Lucy raised her chin a notch higher and entered the room. "Do you do fast weddings?"

"Um, certainly." Eyes wide, the man cleared his throat, then gracefully returned his expression to its former calm. "We're rather booked over the coming Christmas season, but if you're willing to settle for a time other than Friday night or Saturday, I'm sure we can fit you in."

"No," Lucy said. "I'm afraid you don't understand. I need to get married now—today. This instant."

"Oh dear," he said, bushy eyebrows furrowed. "That might be a problem. You see, marriage being the life-long commitment that it is, I insist on at least six weeks' premarital counseling for any couple I agree to marry. I'm sorry."

"That's good. I mean, yes. I appreciate your diligence on that kind of thing. But I'm not talking about any ordinary marriage." She laughed to cover impending tears. "You see," she said, awkwardly unzipping the train case, then scooping out her betrothed. "This is who I want to marry. So if you could just get on with the til deaths do us part, and all that jazz, I'd—"

"Miss, it is not my place to judge, but perhaps instead of seeking marriage, you might be better off seeking a good drug counseling center." Pulling open a squeaky desk drawer, he retrieved a well-worn pamphlet, then stood, holding it out to her with a kindly smile. "In here are the names of several highly respected hospitals that have far more experience than I in such matters."

"Let me start over." Lucy shook her head in the hopes of clearing it. "You seem to have misunderstood my request. I don't have a problem with drugs, but with getting married. I have to marry this frog by tonight, or he'll stay a frog for all eternity and I'll turn into a mouse. Get it?"

Judging by the speed with which he summoned police, Lucy soon found herself out on yet another sidewalk, assuming that no, this priest, just like all the others she'd seen, hadn't *gotten* her plight even a little bit.

And so she climbed into her tired mini, set Wolfe's case on the passenger seat, then dropped her head with a thump against the wheel.

What was she going to do?

Where would she ever find a priest willing to go along with her oddball request?

*Ribbet, ribbet.*

"I know," Lucy said. "No doubt you're hungry, and tired, and frustrated with me for not being able to get you out of this mess. Can't you see, I'm trying?" she said, a fresh batch of tears streaming her cheeks.

*Ribbet, ribbet.*

"Oh, right. Just sit there ribbeting like you'd know what to do."

*Ribbet, ribbet. Ribbet, ribbet.*

"Hush. You sound just like you did the first day I found you on the castle lane—all talk and no action. If I had any sense at all, I'd march right down to the river, and—"

*The castle lane.*

Cotswald!

Crazy old, dear Father Bart!

Heart thundering, Lucy unzipped Wolfe's case, scooped him out and planted a big ole kiss right between his beady little eyes. "You're a genius! Father Bart. If anyone'll perform a nutso quickie marriage, it'll be a nutcase like him. Now, if only I can get to him in time . . ."

A couple of hours later, Lucy turned her mini onto Cotswald's main street, then seconds after that, careened into the church lot.

The sun had already set, bathing the always spooky cemetery in an especially morose glow. Orange and red laughed in malicious glints off of the polished marble of new gravestones, and merely smirked off the dull stone of the centuries-old markers.

High in the branches of a gnarled oak, a lone raven cawed.

The stench of lilacs left Lucy yet again holding her breath.

Snatching Wolfe from his case, she cradled him between her breasts, then leaped out of her car and ran up the few church steps. But once she reached the door and gave it a hard tug, tears loomed anew, for it was locked.

"Nooo!" she raged, jiggling the handle.

But it was no use. The place was locked up tighter than the guest list at a World Biological Conference.

Ironic—since before meeting Wolfe, that had been her life's sole purpose—once again regaining entry to that snooty bunch of boring scientists.

But now, with Wolfe, she could've have had so much more.

She could have had life, and love, and laughter, and

babies, and the joy she'd felt in not just teaching him to read, but in teaching students like Randy and Regina and so many others to share her love of science.

With Wolfe's help, she'd have hauled all of her pets and plants and posters back into her classroom where they belonged. With Wolfe's help, she'd have raised their son into a fine, strong man they'd both be proud of.

"Did you know I'm already carrying your child?" she asked him on a fresh batch of tears.

*Ribbet.*

"And did you also know I'm scared to death of having this child without you—and as for the thought of me being a mouse when I do it . . ." She laughed hysterically, then once again started to cry.

*Ribbet, ribbet.*

"Oh sure," she said with an ugly sniffle. "I put on a brave show back there for the sorceress and all those priests, but I really am the mouse that Castanea claimed me to be. I really am—"

"I say? Is that you, Lucy Gordon? Carrying on talking to a frog?"

She looked up. "Father Bart?"

"Of course, it's me. Did you think I was your Yank Tooth Fairy?" he said, jangling his keys.

"No." With the back of her free hand, she swiped away her tears.

"Well, then? What're you doing here? Blubbering all over my just-swept stairs? And just when Napoleon's finest regiments are preparing to march."

"I, um," she bit the inside of her lower lip. What was the use? Just like all the others, he'd only turn her down.

"Well? Spit it out, girl. I don't have all night. Got a fish fry to attend over in Farthingdayle—that is if our lovely Princess Di doesn't stop to shop on the way over."

"Yes, well, you see, it's like this. I need you to marry me to this frog."

He rolled his eyes. "I've got no time for a wedding."

"Please, Father Bart."

For the longest time he stood there, jangling his keys, darting his gaze between her and Wolfe. "If I agree to marry you to the frog, will you then be on your way?"

Her heart leapt with joy. "Yes! Yes, yes, yes!" Laughing, crying, crushing him in a one-armed hug, she said, "Marry us fast as you can, and we'll even drive you and Princess Di to that fish fry."

"Come on, then." Frowning, he freed himself from her rather desperate hold, then found the church door key and slipped it into the lock. "Let's get this over with. She doesn't like to be kept waiting—and stay off of Napoleon!"

At the front of the small stone chapel, he lit three candles to ward off night's approaching gloom. "Power's out," he said. "Damnedest thing. Went out early this afternoon, and hasn't been on since."

Did the sorceress's power reach this far?

With all of that lilac in the air, did she even have to ask? Lucy shivered.

Father Bart's stomach growled. "Let's be on with it before me and my princess starve."

He began with the usual singsong vows about love and honor, then cleared his throat before whispering, "What's the groom's name?"

"Wolfe. Prince Wolfe of Gwyneddor."

As if he'd heard it all before, the priest nodded. "Do you, Prince Wolfe of Gwyneddor, take thee, Lucy Gordon, to be your wedded wife? And to be faithful unto her, and only her, until God shall separate you by death?"

*Ribbet, ribbet.*

"And do you, Lucy Gordon, take thee, Prince Wolfe of Gwyneddor, to be your husband? And to be faithful unto him, and only him, until God shall separate you by death?"

"I do."

"Then I now pronounce you, frog and wife. Lucy, you may kiss your frog."

Eyes filling with hot, liquid hope, Lucy closed them and swallowed hard. Heart pounding, cradling Wolfe in her palms, she said, "I love you. Please, God, let this have worked."

Eyes closed, she kissed him square on his lips.

And then—poof!

She fell to the hard stone floor, pinned beneath two hundred pounds of manly muscle—naked manly muscle.

"Jesu," Wolfe said, voice back to its thick Welsh brogue. "That was a damned intolerable nightmare I'm glad to be rid of."

"Wolfe?" she asked, cupping her hand to his whisker-stubbled cheek. "Do you remember me? It's me? Lucy."

"Now I know it's way past time for my evening meal." The priest calmly stepped over them both. Tossing a key clanging to the floor beside Lucy's head, he said, "Be a dear, and lock up when you're done."

"Aye," Wolfe said, brushing mischievous hair back

from his wee one's eyes. "For what we have to say may take a while."

The priest's only answer was to let the heavy church door fall shut.

"Then you do know it's me?" Lucy asked. "You didn't forget?"

He laughed. "Does that knocking at your lower door tell you anything?"

"Yeah, but practically the first thing out of your mouth when I met you a month ago was all of that egotistical bravado about you wanting to bed me."

"Aye, and I still do. Have a problem with that, wench?"

Face wondrously aching from the size of her smile, she said, "Nope," just before he cupped her cheeks with his one hundred percent mortal hands, crushing his lips to hers for the first of a lifetime's claiming kisses. Nope. At this magnificent moment in time, held in the arms of this magnificent man, for the first time in her life, Lucy Gordon had no problems at all.

Well . . . except for that eternally pesky dilemma of how to get her once-again-naked prince discreetly home!

# Epilogue

"Look, Mommy!"

Lucy looked up from her sketch of the pond. Dark-haired Colin, only three and already rakish as his father, proudly held a frog in his chubby hands. Golden summer sun backlit him, surrounding him in an ethereal twilight glow.

Perfect, the entire scene was perfect.

Not a breath of wind marring the glassy pond. All manner of insects happily humming. That mossy, musky smell she so loved mingling with the scents of wildflowers and ripe earth, still damp from a recent shower. And there was her son, with a frog wriggling to be free.

"He's cute, sweetie. But put him back. He looks like he wants to go swimming with his friends."

"No. He doesn't want to go swimming. He says he wants to come live with me."

"Oh, he does, does he?"

She nudged Wolfe, who was lying beside her on the

blanket, napping after having spent a rare day not fussing with something having to do with his recently earned seat in Parliament. "Huh? What?" He sputtered awake.

"I'm sorry," she said, "I didn't think you were really sleeping."

"What is it then? Are you all right? Is there something wrong with the baby?" He patted her mountainous tummy, ripe with their second child.

"No," she said. "It's Colin."

"He's had an emergency?"

"No! He has a frog he wants to keep."

"Out of the question. None of the frogs round here are fit to converse with a lad of such high moral fiber."

Lucy rolled her eyes. "He's just a frog. Please, Wolfe. I'll help Colin take care of him."

Eyeing his boy, he snorted. "Where have I heard that before? My whole damned Castle looks more like a zoo than the home of royalty."

For Christmas the year before, Wolfe had purchased Sinclaire Castle from William and Penelope for a sum that still made Lucy dizzy. Still, if he demanded his princess live in a castle, who was she to deny him? Especially since he was right, in that the move had given her much more room for pets!

A good thing since she was now chairwoman of the science department at her school. Upon her appointment, Grumsworth promptly quit. The sight of him driving away, never to be seen again, still brought a smile to her lips!

"Look, Daddy! He has long eyelashes, and purple stripes on his tummy."

"What?!" Lucy shot up. "Bring him here, Colin."

Proudly running her way, Colin held out his prize. "Look! Isn't he cute?"

Lucy's heart pounded as she took the precious creature into her cupped hands. "Oh my God, Wolfe. Look at him. He's amazing. A totally new species."

Wolfe yawned.

"Look at him, Wolfe. I'll be famous after all, and you and Colin can join me on a worldwide speaking tour, and—"

"Wench," Wolfe said as she brought the miraculous specimen toward her lips.

"Yes?"

"Put down the frog."

"Why? He's gorgeous."

"He's also my cousin."

# Single White Vampire
# Lynsay Sands

**SWM** – Successful biographer of family; books recently categorized as "paranormal romances." Doesn't like sunbathing, garlicky dinners or religious symbols. Likes old-fashioned values; spicy Mexican dishes; warm, nice-smelling necks and plump red lips. Currently unaware he's seeking a woman to share eternity.

**SWF** – Newest editor of Romance at Roundhouse Publishing. Has recently discovered a legacy author dying to be broken out. (The tall, dark, handsome writer just needs to go to romance conventions and be introduced to his fans.) Dislikes "difficult, rude, obnoxious pig-headed writers." Currently unaware she's met the man of her wildest dreams.

----------------------------------------

# SUSAN GRANT

# THE STAR PRINCESS

Ilana Hamilton isn't an adventurer like her pilot mother, or a diplomat like her do-right brother; she's a brash, fun-loving filmmaker who'd rather work behind the camera than be a "Star Princess" in front of it. Heiress or not, she's a perfectly normal, single woman . . . until Prince Ché Vedla crashes into her life.

With six months to choose a bride, the sexy royal wants to sow his wild oats. Ilana can't blame him—but fall for the guy herself? Hotshot pilot or no, Ché is too arrogant and too old-fashioned. But when he sweeps her off her feet Ilana sees stars, and the higher he takes her the more she loves to fly. Only her heart asks where she will land.

------------------------------------------------------------

# SPELLBOUND
## IN
## SEATTLE

# GARTHIA ANDERSON

With enchanted blood on her carpet, a house full of Merlin-wannabes unable to clean it up, a petulant cat, and houseguests scheduled to arrive momentarily, Petra Field needs a miracle. She gets a wizard, a whole lot of unwanted sparks, and a man-sized hole in the middle of her living room—a hole into which her feline promptly disappears.

Vorador hasn't felt so incompetent since his days as an untried sorcerer. The girl who leaps after her cat and into his arms causes his simplest spells to backfire—quite literally setting his hair ablaze. And though she claims to be no conjurer, he knows that he's never felt so bewitched, for Petra has a mesmerizing energy of her own: love.

-------------------------------------------------